A MELODY OF DEATH

ISLES OF BRIGHT AND SHADOW
BOOK TWO

C. E. PAGE

First Published in 2024 in Australia by Enchanted Castle Press
Copyright © Cassandra Erin Page 2024

PAPERBACK ISBN: **978-0-6 452 845-3-9**
EPUB ISBN: **978-0-6 452 845-4-6**

 A catalogue record for this work is available from the National Library of Australia

Cover by: Joolz & Jarling – Julie Nicholls & Uwe Jarling
Map by: Fictive Designs
Edited by: Creating Ink – Anna Bishop

All text and images in this book were created by a human with no assistance from any kind of content generating program or generative artificial intelligence.

A MELODY OF DEATH

ISLES OF BRIGHT AND SHADOW
BOOK TWO

C. E. PAGE

ENCHANTED CASTLE
— PRESS —

CONTENT NOTE

Please be aware that this novel is intended for a mature audience; as such, there may be some situations or scenes that readers may find confronting. In particular: mentions of death, violence, and the trauma associated with a past act of sexual violence.

Reader discretion is advised.

FARIDEAN ISLES

ARMADA

DUMURA

(THE ISLE OF SPLENDOUR)

WATCH
TOWER

REEF

WEEPER'S COVE

SPIRE

RUINED
FORT

SPLADE'S WATCH

For those that meet defeat and yet choose to listen to the whispered voice telling them, "Try again tomorrow."

CHAPTER ONE

BRAN

The chill of night still clung to the sand beneath Bran's folded legs and the salt-kissed breeze that ruffled his hair was cool. Not cool enough to soothe his turbulent emotions though. They remained a writhing mess of determination, annoyance, and anxious confusion.

Two days ago, Deana had disappeared. The entire crew of the Azure Queen had scoured the small island for any sign of her or her kidnappers but had found nothing save the persistent ghost of a curious and frustratingly cryptic old woman. If Bran had wanted help in the form of riddles and stories rife with allegory, he would have stayed at Hartswood.

The longer they searched for Deana, the more apparent it became that she meant more to him than he'd realised. That discovery had impacted his ability to think straight. If he could just quiet his mind long enough to focus on it, it was almost as though he could feel her keen calling to his own. Here in the calm of the predawn, it was easier, but it was still like trying to catch the echo of a whisper on the breeze—too indistinct to make any real sense of.

Cold fingers tickled up his spine and thumbed across his nape, announcing the arrival of the spirit. She said nothing, just settled herself on the sand beside him and turned her gaze to the horizon.

But after a while, the chill of her spectral gaze shifted to him again. She didn't change form like the Hartswood spirits, though he suspected she was tied to the island in a similar way to how they were tied to the grove. He also got the sense that, despite being the only spirit to make herself known, she was not alone here.

"You're not in a talking mood this morning, Foundling?"

He let out a huff of breath and raked his fingers through his hair. "Not unless you've decided to shed more light on who took Deana."

Her nostrils flared in a fashion that reminded him of Agatha, the matriarch of the Hartswood spirits. "You already know the answer to that question. The damned have her, and you will not get her back sitting on the beach and feeling sorry for yourself."

"Idir—"

A rush of cold buffeted the back of his head. "Idir is not the only adversary in your game."

"The woman from the re-enactment ..." He glanced sideways at the ghost. She had been tight-lipped about the identity of the woman who—as far as Bran could tell from the re-enactment he performed to see who had taken Deana—was a shrouded one.

"I told you already you should know who she is. If time has taken that knowledge from your mind, then your flesh and bones will remember—when they are good and ready. Flesh can be stubborn and bone even more so."

He bit down on his lip as frustration tightened his throat.

"Did you know the ocean-singer talked to the memory of her brother? Have you tried talking to your people? Perhaps one of them knows a way to find that which has been lost or that which doesn't want to be found."

A finder? They had asked Elijah to draw a map to find Deana and he couldn't. He wasn't a true finder though, and his maps were good for locating lost things but not people. But Bran didn't know any finders. They were one of the rarer types of mage, and even if he could luck out and find one, chances were their gifts would be similar to Elijah's. He studied the ghost beside him, and one of her milky brows arched. What had she said? Perhaps one of them was a finder? No, perhaps one of them knows a way to find lost things or those—

"That don't want to be found!" He leapt to his feet, kicking up a little flurry of sand. "Garret knows a finder. He used one to find Nea when no one else could." Technically, he had happened upon her in the middle of the road, but Garret's finder had given him a way to locate Nea that put him in the right place at the right time.

Bran's fingers edged towards the silver rose in his pocket, but he drew them away again and clenched his fist. Every time he went to Nea and Garret for help, he risked drawing them deeper into the mess he had found himself in. He didn't want that, and hadn't he already insisted that he could do this himself?

"Ah, yes ..." the spirit crooned, and his attention snapped to her. Her face split into an indulgent grin. "The dilemma of youth. So eager to stand on its own feet and prove itself that it foolishly hesitates when it realises that it still needs to rely on others. There is strength in knowing when to ask for help, and needing it is not weakness."

"I'm not afraid to ask for help. But they've already—"

She lifted a hand, cutting him off. "It is their choice how deep they wade into the water. You made the decision to dive in headfirst, not knowing the depth. If they choose to do the same, you have no right to stop them."

He stared at the horizon and dipped his fingers into his pocket to find the silver rose. The dawn light caught the edge of it as he lifted it into view and ran his index finger along one of the smooth petals.

The chill of the spirit beside him intensified as she drew closer. Her fingers ghosted over his forearm, inching towards the enchanted silver only to stop and draw back again leaving a wave of gooseflesh in their wake.

Her tongue darted over her lips as she met his eye. "The pull of the Shadow is as intoxicating as the richest wine. But it is not for us ..." Something shimmered in her pale eyes as she studied the metal bloom in Bran's fingers. After a moment, a shudder ran through her, and she backed away a handful of steps. "We have made peace with that."

"Thinking about contacting Nea?" Varlan's voice preceded the scuff of his boots on the sand.

The spirit's gaze flicked from the rose to the mind mage then she disappeared in a shimmer of silver and violet.

"I don't necessarily want to, but I think I need to," Bran said as he turned to face Varlan.

"The old woman tell you that?"

Bran arched an eyebrow at him, and Varlan shrugged. "You're standing in a patch of winter air. Either she's present or she's been here recently."

"She just left, actually, and no, she didn't tell me in so many words but she heavily implied it." He turned his gaze to the horizon where the peach-toned sunrise was melding into the mint-green dawn. "Garret knows a finder," he said after a while. "One who specialises in finding people."

"And you didn't think of that earlier?"

"I had forgotten. But I doubt Garret even knows where Marcus is these days."

"He'll know."

"Shadow's teeth, Gendry. Where the fuck did you come from?" Varlan spun to face the man who had spoken.

Gendry could go completely unnoticed when he wanted, which was surprising given he was a barrel-chested bear of a man. The lower half of his face was obscured by a thick black beard, and he sported a wicked scar that ran from the corner of his left eyebrow across the bridge of his nose to the middle of his right cheek. To anyone who didn't know him, he looked mean, like *cross the street to avoid encountering him* mean.

"You should pay better attention to your surroundings," he said, his beard splitting into a wide, teeth-baring grin.

Varlan rolled his eyes and opened his mouth to retort, but Bran cut him off with, "What makes you think Garret will know where Marcus is? He hasn't needed the services of a finder since he was warden commander."

"He might be living the quiet life at Hartswood these days, but he will still know exactly where that old mage sniffer is hiding — I can assure you of that."

Bran thumbed the silver petals again, the icy bite of shadow-tainted necromancy stinging the tips of his fingers and sending a jolt across his palm to the indigo crescent that marked the inside of his wrist. His keen stirred in response, thickening behind his navel and frosting through his hair until Gendry's hand landed heavily on his shoulder.

"Wren wants to set out for Weeper's Cove this morning—"

"But, Deana—"

"She's not on this island anymore and it's not safe for us to linger here much longer. But we aren't going to abandon her; we'll find her. I promise." He gave Bran's shoulder a squeeze.

"You told Wren that you don't make promises you know you can't keep," Bran said.

"True. But as long as Garret can put you in touch with Marcus then I am certain we can find her."

"And if he can't?"

Gendry shrugged. "We'll cross that ocean when we reach it."

"You've been quiet, Varlan. What do you think?" Bran asked Varlan, who had his attention trained on the rolling whitewash.

The mind mage licked his lip and turned his gaze to Bran. "I think we need to find Deana as quickly as possible, so our focus is not divided. Kent still has Agnes' golem. If he gets his hands on a suitable heartstone then Idir won't be our only problem."

"I thought Agnes was going to include a flaw in the machine that would make it less of a threat," Bran said.

Varlan gave a heavy sigh. "She was. But that was before Savita's *involvement*." The word was a steel-edged growl.

"Right." Bran dropped his gaze to his feet. After a few moments, he pulled the rose from his pocket once more and gave a nod. "I'll go ask Garret about Marcus."

Gendry echoed Bran's nod with one of his own. "I'll let Wren know what's happening," he said then turned and hurried away.

"Would you mind asking Nea if she knows where we might find a heartstone capable of animating the golem? Elijah is still having trouble locating one but that doesn't mean it doesn't exist, and I would rather we found it before Kent."

"I don't know that she will be much help, but I will ask her."

"I appreciate it." Varlan turned towards the camp then glanced at Bran over his shoulder. "Good luck with the finder. If it's the same Marcus I've heard of then you're going to need it." He grinned then followed Gendry.

Bran studied the silver rose before closing his fingers around it. The edges of the petals pressed into his palm and its cold magic zinged up his spine. Keeping level-headed enough to stop Nea from being suspicious was going to be a challenge, but maybe he could distract her with Varlan's question about the heartstone.

He let his magic run over the rose and then the cool fingers of Nea's keen fluttered through his hair before the source pulled tight and the glittering violet-coloured miasma of a portal opened in front of him. A warm breeze carried the familiar scent of the

Hartswood grove to him: ripe apples, lush grass, and the rich sweetness of the mother hawthorn.

"What is it this time?" Nea asked, the hint of a smile evident in her voice.

"I have a question about heartstones and I need to ask Garret for a favour," he answered as he stepped through the portal.

"I thought you didn't want to involve us in everything that is happening in the isles." She was sitting at the base of the hawthorn at the centre of the Hartswood grove, her bare toes in the grass and her hands resting on the swell of her stomach.

"I don't," he said once the discomfort of travelling through the pocket between realms had passed. "But I need help locating a heartstone suitable to animate a colossal serpent golem."

She opened her mouth and then snapped it shut again, one corner tucking in as she regarded him with a soul-scouring look. "You realise what animating a golem requires?"

"I don't want to animate it. I just want to prevent someone else from doing so. I thought if we could prevent him from finding a suitable heartstone then ..."

There was something flickering in the depths of her violet stare, and he licked his lip.

"Heartstones are extremely rare and the type that would be required to animate something as large as you are implying ... I doubt there would be one this side of the barrier." She shook her head and her features softened as she let out a sigh. "The only place I can think of that you might find such a stone is in the repository beneath the Arcanarium, though it is still highly unlikely. But I can get word to Mateus and see if he knows something. Now tell me about this favour you need to ask Garret, because I doubt that has anything to do with your hunt for a heartstone."

"I just need him to put me in touch with one of his contacts from his warden-commander days," he said in what he hoped was a nonchalant tone.

Her eyes narrowed and the right corner of her mouth tucked in again.

"The less you know the better."

"That has never been the case, but everyone, from Father to Leith, has told me I need to keep my nose out of it. So, I won't hound you for answers." She held her hands out.

He took hold of them and helped her to her feet. "I appreciate that."

She stretched and then started across the grove towards the manor. "It doesn't mean I won't get those answers eventually, you know. You're all just lucky I am in no fit state to be traipsing across the isles hunting down tyrants."

"Right ..."

When they reached the edge of the field, a girl with silver hair and vivid hazel eyes came running over. "Bran!" She threw her arms around his waist and squeezed. "What are you doing here? I thought you were in the isles."

"I am. I just needed to see Garret."

"Would you mind fetching him for us, Nora?" Nea asked.

"Of course," she said as she raced away.

"Has Deana gotten better control of her keen?"

Bran ran his fingers along his lip. "She is starting to."

Nea studied him. Her violet eyes seemed to see straight through him, but he was spared the lecture he was sure she was about to give by the arrival of Garret.

"I wasn't expecting to see you back here for a while. Is everything alright?" the warden asked as his grey gaze flicked from Bran to Nea and back again.

"We're on top of it but we need a finder."

"A finder?" Nea asked.

"I'm guessing you were hoping I would put you in touch with

Marcus," Garret said.

Bran nodded.

"Why Marcus? Who do you need to find?" Nea folded her arms.

"It's complicated and I don't want you to ..."

"Worry? I've been worried since you told us about Idir. You should—"

"Nea," Garret said softly, and her sharp gaze snapped to him. "You promised you would stay out of it."

"I know I did but you can't expect me—"

Garret's eyebrows arched, and Nea pressed her lips together.

"Fine. Just make sure you stay safe," she said to Bran before she gave Garret a look that said 'We aren't done discussing this' and started towards the manor again.

"I love you," Garret called after her, and she waved over her shoulder at him. "She gave up far easier than I was expecting her to," he said to Bran with a half laugh. "Now I'll take you to Marcus, but I want to know what happened and who you are asking him to find."

Bran retrieved Deana's pendant from his pocket and held it out. "Deana is missing, and it appears she was taken by shrouded ones."

Garret's hand landed heavily on his shoulder. "Don't worry. Marcus will find her." His keen brushed against Bran's in a hot rush then the source prickled and a portal opened.

"And if he can't?"

"He has never failed me before, even when it came to finding Nea and she really didn't want to be found." He gave Bran's shoulder a squeeze and then stepped through the portal.

The air on the other side was thick with the scent of stale ale and sweat. The gloom didn't tell Bran much, so he summoned a mage light and immediately wished he hadn't. The lilac light dipped low over the bed at the far side of the room, revealing the two naked people who were sitting there staring at them. The woman had pulled the tattered sheet up to cover herself, but the man was just leaning back and letting everything hang out. His red-rimmed watery gaze was pinned on Garret as a wide smile split the beard that covered the lower half of his face.

"Well, well, well. This day just got a whole lot more exciting." He gave the sheet a tug, freeing it from the woman's grasp. "Out," he barked, and she scooped up her clothes and used them to cover herself as she ran from the room. "Right. What can I do for you, Commander?"

"You know that's not my title anymore," Garret tossed a set of clothes at the man. "Get dressed and meet us out in the bar." He ushered Bran towards the door.

"My rate's gone up."

"Just put your Bright-damned clothes on and get out here," Garret said as he snapped the door shut.

Bran extinguished his mage light and followed Garret down the corridor into an open bar space. "Where exactly are we?"

"The Vengeful Duck."

"The Vengeful ... *Duck*? Who comes up with these names? And where exactly is this charming establishment located?"

"I don't know about the names, but we are currently on the outskirts of Port Agatha." Garret indicated an empty table at the side of the room. "Wait here while I sort out payment for Marcus." He headed for the door just as the finder appeared from the corridor that led to the back rooms.

"You one of those Hartswood spooks then?" Marcus asked as he settled across from Bran and waved three fingers at the woman behind the bar.

"Yes, I'm from Hartswood."

Marcus inhaled slowly and pushed his dirty blond hair out of his eyes. "Did the commander tell you how many mages he executed with my help?"

"Garret didn't execute them—Evard did."

"Evard might have done the killing, but he wasn't the one who dragged them to the slaughter." He sat back as the barmaid delivered three mugs of—ale; if the smell was anything to go by.

"I'm not here to discuss Garret's past. I need you to find someone for me."

"Well, no shit." Marcus took a long gulp from his cup before smacking his lips together. "But I won't discuss business until the commander returns with my payment. That is what he's gone to sort out, isn't it?"

Bran nodded and studied the pale amber liquid in his own cup before taking a sip. It was bitter enough to suck all the moisture from his mouth. He swallowed and placed the mug back down.

They sat in silence until Garret returned and dropped a purse of coins on the table in front of Marcus.

"Feels a little light," the finder said as he hefted it in the palm of his hand.

"That's because it's only half. You'll get the rest once you've set the enchantment."

"You have something that belongs to the mage you want found then?" He pocketed the purse and held his hand out.

"Give him the stone," Garret said to Bran then took a mouthful from his cup and winced. "It's worse than last time."

Marcus just grinned at him. "It's an acquired taste and you've gone soft."

Bran pulled Deana's protection charm out of his pocket and placed it on Marcus's open palm.

"Well now, this is a very special trinket, isn't it?" He closed his eyes and inhaled slowly, his mouth working back and forth as his fingers caressed the edges of the stone. "Why yes ... Now where are you hiding ...?" His keen plied against the edges of Bran's with inquisitive fingers but then shifted away again. "Come on now. Don't be shy."

Bran glanced at Garret. Did it normally take this long for

11

Marcus's keen to work? What if something was blocking him from finding Deana?

"There you are." Marcus suddenly opened his eyes. "You like the challenging ones, don't you?" He said to Bran, "I found her though. She's in the isles."

"I know that much—"

"Can you enchant that stone like you did Nea's bracelet?" Garret asked.

Marcus studied the stone then his keen flared and a shimmer of light ran over its surface. "Done."

Bran reached for the pendant, but Marcus snatched it back towards himself and held out his other hand.

"Aren't we forgetting something?"

Garret fished another pouch out and held it towards Marcus. "Give him the stone."

"Of course." Marcus tossed it across the table, and Bran barely caught it as it plummeted towards the floor.

Garret tilted the pouch of coins just out of Marcus's reach. "Does it work? You should feel it pulling you in a certain direction."

Bran rubbed his thumb over the hole in the centre of the stone. The feeling was faint, but it dragged just at the edge of his keen-sense, telling him to go south. "It works."

"Good." Garret dropped the purse into Marcus's hand.

"Pleasure as always, Commander," Marcus said and pocketed the payment with one hand as he lifted his cup with the other.

"Alright, let's go." Garret ushered Bran out onto the street.

Once they were a short distance away from the tavern, Bran slowed his pace. He pulled the spirit anchor that connected him to Nea from under his shirt and studied it. As long as he had it in his possession, it was too easy to just run to Nea for help. And even though he would never have found Marcus without Nea and Garret, he kept saying he didn't want to drag them into the mess that was happening in the isles. But he was doing the opposite.

Every time he went to them, he pulled them in a little deeper.

"Garret, wait."

The warden stopped and turned to face him.

"Here." He held the rose pendant out. "Don't tell her I gave it to you. But I need to stop coming to you both for help and as long as I have it, it's just too easy to skip away and get you to solve my problems."

Garret traced his finger over the scar on his lip as he studied the pendant. "She'll be absolutely livid when she finds out, you know?"

"I know, but let's hope she doesn't find out before I put an end to Idir's plans." He dropped the necklace into Garret's hand.

"Are you sure?"

Bran nodded. "I have to do this alone now."

"You're not alone."

"You know what I mean."

Garret clapped him on the shoulder. "Just be careful."

"I can't make any promises, but I'll try."

The source tightened and a lilac seam of light appeared beside them before springing open into a portal.

"Don't worry about Nea—I'll get Declan to distract her." He gave Bran's shoulder a nudge.

"Thanks." Bran stepped into the glowing doorway, the source dragging over his skin and plucking against the edges of his keen in a way that turned the contents of his stomach to water.

As he stepped back onto the deck of the Queen, he drew in a lungful of briny air and then let it out with a groan while he waited for the world to stop swooping away from him.

"Did the finder locate Deana?" Varlan asked. He was leaning on the rail a short distance from where Bran had emerged.

"Not exactly, but he enchanted her protection charm so it will lead us to her," Bran replied, lifting the stone in question from his pocket.

Now that he was back in the isles, the pull against the edges of his keen-sense was stronger and it was guiding him south, towards Weeper's Cove.

CHAPTER TWO

DEANA

"De-ah-na," her mother's voice called in a singsong tone.

Deana watched her younger self burrow farther under the table and press her chubby hand over her mouth to stifle a cascade of giggles.

"Oh, where could that girl be?" her mother asked as she entered the kitchen, a playful smile on her face and a basket of herbs tucked against her hip.

The Deana under the table bit down on the side of her hand as her shoulders shook in an effort to contain her laughter. But the older Deana drank in the sight of her mother, who she had last seen in a dream—a nightmare. Looking at the woman before her now was like viewing her own reflection, though her mother's eyes were the same warm brown that both Kai and her father shared.

Her mother placed the basket on the table, the gold bangles around her wrists jingling against each other as she turned on the ball of her foot and placed her hands on her hips. "I guess she's not here. Oh well ..." Her mother's grin deepened, and she moved as though she was going to leave. Then, at the last moment she spun back around and dragged the girl out from under the table.

The younger Deana let out a squeal of laughter and kicked her legs.

"Found you, my sweet," her mother said as she pressed a kiss to the tip of her nose.

Thunder shook the foundations of the house and the adult Deana bit back a gasp as the door slammed open. Neither her mother nor her younger self seemed to notice the sudden chill wind that drove into the room, bringing the scents of salt water and death. A shadow loomed in the doorway; a large hand reaching towards the girl. The warm brown skin that covered the fingers peeled back to reveal coral-studded bone.

"No!" Deana sat up and the remnants of the dream scattered. Her mouth was dry, her hair stuck to her neck under an itchy layer of sweat. She shuffled to the edge of the bed and let her toes meet the boards of the floor as she drew a series of deep breaths to shift the band of pressure that had closed around her chest.

A voice carried from the other room. Astrid. The woman who was keeping Deana captive. It wasn't a cage as such. She could walk freely around the small island with its ruined fort, but the moment she stepped outside Rami started dogging her footsteps. If she tried to run, he would capture her again and drag her back to Astrid.

She stood and walked to the small window. The sky outside was still dark, a watery circle of silver betraying the position of the moon through the sheet of inky clouds that hid the stars from view.

Something moved below her; a hulking shadow that edged towards the pool of golden light spilling from the lower floor window. He lifted his gaze. Orbs of yellow-green mage light shone where his eyes should have been. One hand rested on the hilt of the wicked sword at his hip and the other was hidden in the depths of the tattered cloak that covered his body. Rami. She drew back from the window and ran her hand through her hair, wincing as her fingers tugged through the knots.

"You're up early," Astrid said behind her.

Deana turned.

The other woman was leaning against the doorframe, her pale hair glowing like a halo of gold around one side of her face. The other half of her skull was hairless, branches of green and purple coral growing out of her skin like a morbid crown. She traced her finger along her chin as her dark blue gaze studied Deana. "Are you hungry?"

Deana shook her head.

A tight frown crossed Astrid's lips and her nostrils flared as she let out a long breath. "When will you realise that I am not your enemy? That you and I want the same thing?"

"When you let me leave?"

Astrid released another huff. "I can't do that. Like it or not, this is the safest place for you."

They stared at each other for a few moments, and after a while Astrid pushed away from the doorframe and pointed at the pile of clothes on the small table by the window. "Get dressed then come and have something to eat."

"I told you I'm not—"

"It wasn't a request." Astrid's song pressed against Deana's, laying a heavy melancholy over her. "If you are not downstairs before I have a pot of tea prepared, I will have Rami drag you to the kitchen" She left but the bittersweet notes of her song lingered, and Deana swallowed as she moved to get dressed.

There was a comb beside the pile of clothes, and she used it to tease the knots from her hair before securing it in a thick plait. The wheaten coloured shirt and brown pants were an ill fit but at least they were clean. She was just tying the laces at the front of the pants when the oppressive silence that accompanied Rami rolled over her. He ducked through the door and reached for her, but she dodged away from him.

"I'm coming. There's no need to drag me down there."

He grunted and lunged for her again, thick fingers closing vice-tight around her upper arm and propelling her towards the door. The thick cloud of silence radiating off him smothered Deana's song and brought a heart-thumping panic to her core. It wasn't like the effect of the silencers. When they silenced someone's song it simply cut off the magic. Rami's silence stripped all sound from the world—nothing seemed to penetrate the bubble of power that surrounded him. Not even the static hiss of white noise.

Bile edged up Deana's throat as he shunted her down the stairs and into the kitchen where Astrid was placing a steaming cup on the table in front of a vacant chair. Rami dragged Deana to the chair and pressed on the top of her shoulder until she sat.

"Thank you, Rami," Astrid crooned and patted his large cheek before waving him away.

Deana's head swam as Rami released her and all the sound returned to the world at once. She pressed her face into her hands and rubbed her temples as she drew several gulps of air to force the lump that had risen in her throat back down.

"I did warn you not to dawdle," Astrid said as she placed a plate next to the cup in front of Deana.

The plate contained a whole cooked fish with charred herbs and spices clinging to its flesh. Deana nudged the plate away and Astrid frowned.

"Eat. You will need your strength if I am to teach you how to embrace your song."

"I'm not hungry." She was ravenous. The smell of the fish ignited a painful rumble in her stomach and made her mouth water, but she didn't want to give Astrid the satisfaction of the victory.

"Do I need Rami to restrain you while I force-feed you?"

Deana glanced at the doorway the huge man had left through and shook her head. She pulled the plate towards her and took up the fork.

Astrid's smile was wide as she plated another fish and then sat across from Deana.

The sweet, white flesh flaked easily away from the bone, and she had to bite back her groan of delight as it all but melted on her tongue.

They ate in silence, the dark of predawn out the window slowly lightening to a deep grey as a misting rain started to drizzle.

"I don't enjoy threatening you," Astrid swirled the tea in her cup, "and see how much nicer it is when you cooperate?"

Deana picked up her own cup of tea and gave it a sniff; a cloying sweetness tickled her nose.

"Liquorice and mallow," Astrid said.

The liquid tasted as sweet as it smelled but had an odd earthy note that settled at the back of her throat. She took a second sip and then placed the cup down with a frown as she swallowed to try and clear the aftertaste.

"You don't like the tea? I can make you something else."

She looked up to find Astrid watching her with an almost doting smile. The other woman's midnight blue eyes reminded her of Bran's, and she tore her gaze away to study the far wall. "The tea is fine."

"The truth won't offend me; Rami could never stand the taste of it either."

Deana flicked another glance at the door that led outside. She'd never seen Rami eat or drink anything.

"I can make you some smoky black or peppermint, but I don't have much else on hand." Astrid had moved to the bench and was sorting through the jars on the shelf.

"I'm fine. I don't want any more tea." Deana shifted in her seat.

Astrid let out one of those long breaths then a sweet smile worked its way across her mouth. "Very well then. Shall we make our way down to the beach?"

By the time the sun had lightened the clouds from moody charcoal to a soft smoke grey, Deana was exhausted. Her knees quivered beneath her, and a trickle of sweat ran down her back as she focused on maintaining the bubble of air around her and Astrid.

Fish twisted through the wall of water in front of them and then darted up and over their heads as the rippling water threatened to collapse and drown them.

"Very good. Now give us a path back to the shore."

Deana licked her lip and lifted her hands. She parted them slowly and focused on her song as it twisted with the melody of the tides. The bubble above her opened as a seam of teal light shot towards the beach and the water parted to reveal a path of damp sand to the shore where Rami stood waiting for them with Samir at his side. Astrid started forward but Deana's hands shook, and the water splashed as it fought to break her hold.

"Concentrate," Astrid warned.

A glimmer at the corner of Deana's vision snagged her attention and she tilted her head to examine the pearlescent white fish that was drifting beside her. It flipped to show its black underbelly before darting away again. She'd seen that fish before, at Weeper's Cove and in her dreams—the ones where Grandmother Ocean spoke to her.

Cold water plunged over her, knocking her from her feet and dragging her swiftly towards the reef that edged the far side of the beach. Something solid slammed against the back of her skull and her gasp of pain dragged salt water into her lungs.

Silence stole through the roar of the waves as a tight band encircled Deana's chest, and she collided with a solid form. Bright spots of pain flashed across the insides of her eyelids as the current dragged over her and her lungs began to ache for air.

Sand rubbed against her skin as she was pulled through the whitewash. She opened her eyes to the moody sky above and closed them almost immediately as the grey clouds dimmed in and out of focus. Heavy hands lifted her, thrusting her forward over what felt like a thick log as the oppressive silence tightened around her. She wheezed and spluttered as a meaty palm pounded against her back. Not once, but twice and then again.

Salt water and bile erupted from her with a grating cough, but the hand pounded several times more as though not satisfied.

"That's enough, Rami. Lay her on her side," Astrid's voice said from somewhere behind her.

"Dee?" A blurry Samir crouched in front of her as she was rolled sideways. "Astrid, she's bleeding."

"A knock on the back of the head doesn't worry me as much as losing her to drowning."

The rocks beneath her bare toes were slick with clumps of vibrant green algae. She slipped and caught herself on her hands. A graze on her knee stung as sand and salt water clung to it. She ignored the pain as small rainbow coloured fish darted away from the shadow her body threw across their rockpool. The fish weren't the only residents; a small black and white eel peeked from under the overhang of rock on the opposite side of the pool and several beige crabs burrowed into the sand leaving little clouds in the water.

"Deana," her brother called from the beach, his voice nearly lost in the crash of the waves along the rocks.

White froth ate the rockpool and washed over her toes. It was almost achingly cold against her sun-warmed skin. A song caught in the back of her mind, and she lifted her gaze to the woman sitting on the edge of the rocks. Her skin shone with the iridescence of mother-of-pearl, and her dark hair was threaded with brightly coloured shells and ribbons of seaweed. She flicked the large glittering tail that took the place of her legs. The long, delicate fins were almost transparent and shimmered as though they were woven from pure magic.

She tilted her head as she studied Deana and a note of curiosity fluttered through her song.

"Dee!" her brother called again, and she turned to face him.

He was standing on the beach with his hand held out towards her. "It's not safe. Come back before the tide washes you away," he urged.

Cold water splashed up her legs, biting her grazed knees and eliciting a gasp from her throat. She glanced back at the woman, but she was gone.

Another wave hit her as she turned to move to her brother. It knocked her off balance and she teetered a few steps before she fell. The water seemed to grab hold of her and drag her over the rocks towards the open ocean. It roared in her ears and stole into her mouth as she opened it to cry out.

Cool hands gripped her and turned her to face their owner. The woman from the rockpools. Her dark hair fanned out in an inky cloud around her, and her silver-green eyes met Deana's before an eerie song coiled through the water and the woman glanced wildly towards the deep. Her grip on Deana tightened and her powerful tail began to beat, propelling them towards the shore.

She pulled Deana clear of the rolling waves. Her cool fingers brushed Deana's hair from her forehead as her worried green gaze studied her face. She opened her mouth to speak—

"There!" Deana's brother shouted.

The woman gave a panicked look in the direction the shout had come from and then she was gone.

"Dee?" Her brother skidded to a stop beside her, kicking up a small spray of sand that peppered her stinging legs. His fingers pressed against her neck as the sky above her dimmed. "Hurry!" he called to someone over his shoulder, but whatever was said next was lost as darkness ate the world.

She awoke with a grating cough in her own bed. The scent of her mother swirled around her as she sat up.

"Easy, my girl." Her mother came into view and touched her fingertips to Deana's forehead. "I think the danger has passed but you took on a lot of water so I can't be sure."

Deana blinked at her mother as she pressed a warm cup into her hands.

"Drink every last drop. It will help you heal." She moved away again, and a soft thump sounded as she set something on the table. "What were you thinking? Exploring the rockpools with the tide turning?"

The sharpness of her mother's tone startled Deana and several drops of liquid splashed from the cup onto the bed. "It was—"

"You're just lucky your father and Kai were there. If they had been any slower ..."

Deana glanced at her mother as she shook her head.

"You need to be more careful. Now drink that tisane before it gets too cold."

She did as she was told, wincing at the bitter taste. "What happened to the woman who saved me?"

"Woman? What woman?"

"She was really pretty, with glowing skin and a long tail like a fish."

Something smashed against the floor and her mother swore under her breath. "Did she say or do anything to you?" Deana's mother was suddenly in front of her again, gripping her shoulders and searching her face as her soothing song brushed against Deana's.

Deana shook her head. "She saved me when I fell off the rocks."

Her mother licked her lip and stared at the open window, a crease of worry forming between her brows. When she turned back, a strange calm had smoothed her features but her song was tight, fraught with the erratic notes of fear. "Forget the woman, Deana," she said in a tone that Deana had never heard before. "Don't ever mention her again. And, if you ever see her ... run."

CHAPTER THREE

AGNES

"Why won't you work!" The metal parts strewn across the table rattled as Agnes slammed her hands down amongst them.

The broken body of her mechanical cat shuddered as though it were trying to move but the magic that powered it was nearly gone. She ran her finger over its forehead to the tip of its nose and then shut her eyes to steady her focus. The tingling that accompanied her magic remained elusive; the world-consuming hum of the trance completely silent. A dull throb stirred at her temples, and Savita's dark-eyed stare flashed across the back of her eyelids, forcing her to open her eyes again.

Her magic hadn't worked since she had left Armada. Luca, Varlan's healer, had told her it was a combination of exhaustion and the after-effects of the mage bane, that once her body had time to heal from what Savita had put her through it would come back. She wasn't so sure. It was like a shroud had been lowered over her, dulling the world and leaving a layer of itchy fibres against her skin.

She raked her fingers over her face and drew a deep breath before picking up her pen again. The thin twist of mahogany had always felt unusually heavy in her fingers, but now it was a dead weight—a loaded promise that would never come to fruition. Her teeth sunk into her lip as she closed her eyes once more.

"Come on," she whispered as she pulled her focus back to the broken cat and her desire to fix it.

The magic-heralding tingle stirred softly. So softly she wasn't certain if she had imagined it. She took a breath in and then released it again, and the feeling grew stronger. Her fingers shook with relief, and she nearly dropped her pen. The magic was still there, building slower than it ever had before, but it hadn't abandoned her. Cautiously, she turned her attention to the cat once more and the tingle deepened as the hiss of the trance crept into the edges of her consciousness—until an itchy burn replaced the tingle and her elation fled as she forced her eyes open and dropped the pen. The itching tore up her arm, and Savita's sickly-sweet laughter echoed in her ears.

Agnes let out a yell of frustration and grabbed the closest object: a delicate orb of dark metal. It made a satisfying clang against the wall beside the door before thudding onto the floor.

"I'd ask if you're alright, but you're clearly not," Wes said as he bent to pick up the metal sphere.

"Did Varlan send you to check on me?" She sniffed and busied herself, reorganising the things in front of her.

He passed her the sphere and then leant on the edge of the table; concern swam in his hazel gaze as he studied her face. "Varlan didn't send me. I was passing by and heard you yell. Do you want to talk about it?"

She shook her head and pushed away from the table to pace the small hut she had been sharing with Dara and the twins since they had arrived at Weeper's Cove.

Wes folded his arms as he watched her. "Would you like me to get Luca?" he asked after she turned to complete her fourth lap across the room.

"No." The word came out harsher than she had intended, and she released a sigh. "He's already told me there is nothing more he can do. That I just have to *give it time.*"

"He's right you—"

"I don't have time! *We* don't have time! Deana is out there somewhere with Bright knows who and we're just all sitting on our hands *waiting.* Waiting for what exactly? For Idir to sort out his shit and make his move? Or for Kent to get his hands on a heartstone for his war golem and come find us?" Agnes had been throwing her things into her bag as she spoke, and she stopped when she reached for the body of her cat and met Wes's gaze.

"I am done waiting, Wes. I did enough of that on Armada." She scooped the cat into her bag.

He chewed his lip as though looking for the right words. Everything he did was rehearsed—an act to keep his cover. She had rarely seen him drop that composed façade, those carefully chosen words and choreographed actions.

"Agnes—"

"No, I don't want to hear—"

"Bright damn it, Agnes! Would you shut up and let me speak?"

She blinked at him.

"What is this really about? Is it your absent magic or your concern for Deana? Or is it about something else entirely?" He had that look in his eyes that her father often got when she was being unreasonable.

She wasn't being unreasonable now, was she? She twisted the strap of her bag around in her fingers.

His brow arched as though he was waiting for her to answer the question, and she glanced at the door.

"It's ... well ... I ... I honestly don't know." She shut her eyes as the wet heat of tears threatened. She had never felt as fragile as she had in the last few weeks. It was as though she was a ship with no keel which could capsize at any moment. She collapsed onto the edge of her bed and let her satchel *thunk* onto the floor.

"I'm scared, Wes," she murmured.

The bed dipped beside her. "It's alright to be scared," he said as his arm slid around her shoulders and he folded her against his chest.

"What if my magic never comes back?" A slight pressure rolled down her spine, but it was gone so quickly she might have imagined it.

"Your magic isn't broken, but the strain it went through under Savita's compulsion and the unpredictable side effects of using mage bane on a mage like you ... Luca is right. It will take time and you can't force it, but eventually it will come back. I promise."

Wes and Luca and Varlan and everyone else could make all the promises about her keen that they wanted, but what if they were wrong? None of them knew for sure that Savita hadn't caused permanent damage to her magic. The way Idir had. He was responsible for her broken keen-sense. Keen-sense was as integral to mages as the ability to create mage lights. It was one of the traits that all mages shared regardless of the nature of their magic and without it she wasn't only abnormal, she was vulnerable. Especially to mind mages like Savita.

"Varlan might be able to help your magic return faster you know," he said carefully, as though he expected another outburst. "Mind mages are able to—"

"I can't. Not after Savita ... and everything." The everything being the fact that somewhere in her past she and Varlan had been intimately close, and he had erased those memories to protect her. Not that it mattered. Idir and Kent seemed to be several steps ahead regardless.

Wes made a noise, but she felt the vibration through his chest rather than heard it.

"You can't avoid him forever."

"I know. I'm just ... not ready."

Wes chuckled. "That is completely understandable. Is it just your missing keen that is bothering you? You mentioned Deana during your tirade."

She pushed away from him. "Bran saw a shrouded one in the re-enactment. What if they took her straight to Idir?"

"If that were the case, he would have had her raise Dumura by now. And given that the world hasn't begun to fall into complete chaos just yet, I would say Idir doesn't have her. We will find her before he does—Bran made sure of that when he sought out Marcus's help."

"But what if she's being tortured or they kill her?"

"They won't kill her. Her magic is too valuable for that, and I doubt they will torture her—"

"Torture isn't always obvious ... or deliberate." Her mouth grew suddenly dry as Savita's dark gaze swam across the back of her mind.

"If that happens, we will help her through it." He stood and offered her a hand. "Are you still considering running off and taking matters into your own hands?"

She let him pull her to her feet. "If I were, would you give me a head start before you told the others?"

He gave her a lopsided grin. "I would, but I'd also insist on coming. I promised Varlan I would take care of you, and I owe him too much to ever break that promise."

She studied his face; he was an attractive man with his bright hazel eyes and golden blond hair. The freckles across his nose softened his features and made him look younger than he was. But she had seen that soft, light-hearted look drop in an instant to be replaced with an almost frightening coldness.

"Thank you, and I'm sorry for yelling at you earlier."

"After what you've been through the last few weeks, I think you're entitled to a little yelling." There was a hint of a smile beneath his words, but it was tempered by the deep concern that swam across his gaze. "I can't promise it will all turn out alright in the end, but none of us are going to just roll over and let Idir or Kent have their way." He started for the door and stopped to run his finger down the edge of the frame before tapping it a couple of times and turning back to face her. "I really think you should talk to Varlan about your keen." Then, with a small nod, he was gone.

Agnes bent and scooped up her satchel. It was heavy with the weight of the mechanical cat. She dumped it onto the bed and dug the cat and a small grey wrapped bundle out. She took both to the table where she gently placed the mutilated body of the cat down on the scarred surface before opening the parcel. The shards of purple crystal that had been wrapped in the grey cloth rolled out. They seemed to glimmer from within, the edges of several of them glistening with the oily sheen of magic. Magic she couldn't feel, even before Savita's abuse had brought her keen to the brink of exhaustion and left it in seemingly irreparable tatters.

She moved back to the bed and retrieved her tool roll from the satchel, untying the laces and letting it fall open across her palm as she returned to the table. She selected a small set of pliers from the folds and placed the roll down next to the cat.

Carefully, she gripped the fractured plate at the centre of the cat's chest and attempted to pry it up farther. It shifted slightly but not enough for her to access the cavity beneath. She took hold of it again and pulled up as she put her full body weight on the rest of the cat. One of the robrillium rivets holding the plate cracked, and when she yanked upwards again it went flying across the room as the plate shifted.

The shard of purple crystal at the cat's core caught the light. Agnes reached for it but then drew her fingers back. If she removed it now, the magic animating the cat would dissipate and it would become nothing more than a pile of scrap. Did it matter though? The magic was fading anyway and there was nothing she could do to stop that. Especially without access to her keen. But would the shard itself survive if she removed it now?

She glanced at the door and chewed her lip. Would she be able to fuse the stone back together without her magic?

"Bright damn—Ouch!" In her frustration, her finger had slipped and sliced open on the raw edge of the metal plate. She pressed her thumb against the stinging cut to stem the flow of blood while she fossicked for a cloth to wrap it.

A gentle knock sounded against the door.

"Come back later," she ground out through her teeth.

"Wes said I should check on you," Nari said from the other side of the door. "He thought you might prefer my bedside manner to Luca's," she added, a slight note of humour in her tone.

Agnes studied the cut as fresh blood beaded along its length. Thankfully, Wes had gone for the healer and not Varlan. "You can come in."

The second Nari entered, her gaze zeroed in on Agnes's bleeding finger and she made a tutting noise. She crossed the room and swept her grey dreadlocks over her shoulder before holding her hand out. Agnes placed her hand palm up on Nari's.

The healer's fingers were always warm, almost uncomfortably so at times. The heat intensified for a moment and the skin along the edges of the cut itched before pulling back together and leaving a neat pale line in the cut's place.

Nari ran her fingertip along the scar and nodded. "Now. Wes didn't mention a cut, but he did mention your exhausted keen. Unfortunately, there is no easy fix for that, as I am sure Luca has told you. There are tonics but given the trauma your body has been put through, both by Savita and the mage bane, it would be far better to just wait it out." As she studied Agnes's face, something akin to remorse ghosted across her features. "The exhaustion isn't permanent. Both Wes and Luca informed me that they have already told you that, but Wes believed you may find it more comforting to hear from a healer you *trust*."

"We don't have the luxury of time. If there is a tonic that will fix it—"

Nari held up a hand, stopping Agnes. "Your keen is volatile. More so than any other mage I have met. It is unpredictable and that was the case even before Idir altered it. Luca was not aware of the true nature of your magic, and he did what he thought necessary to thwart Kent's plans, but he is extremely lucky that it did not send you insane or kill you outright." She released a sigh and frowned. "The mage bane tonic he drugged you with is dangerous, even for a mage whose keen presents in a typical fashion, and both your father and Varlan are justifiably angry that he took that risk. But I cannot say for certain that *I* would not have done the same thing were I in his shoes. Still, it over-complicates an already complicated and delicate situation, which means that we must be careful how we approach fixing the damage that was caused."

"You're certain my keen will come back on its own?"

Nari nodded. "Wes assures me that he felt no lasting damage beyond the exhaustion and even if I hadn't assessed you myself, I would trust his judgement on that. He also told me that he advised you to speak with Varlan about it. If you want a *quick fix* then I have to agree with him. Employing the services of a mind mage, particularly one as skilled as Varlan, is your best course of action. Though do I realise that Savita may have tarnished your opinion of mind mages and it is understandable that you would be wary of them."

It wasn't just his mind magic that made her want to avoid Varlan, but perhaps both Wes and Nari were right. Of course, Wes could just be using Agnes's relationship with Nari to get her to follow his advice.

"Do you know where Varlan is now?"

A small, almost smug smile curved the corners of Nari's mouth. "I believe he was with Bran and Gendry, discussing the next course of action in the search for Deana."

CHAPTER FOUR

VARLAN

Varlan studied the map that spanned the table between him and Gendry. "South-west you say?" He shifted his gaze to Bran.

The necromancer rolled a grey seer stone between his fingers and his thumb, tracing the hole at the stone's centre. His keen stirred the air in a cold pool around him as he gave a nod.

"They could have her at Splade's Watch?" Gendry said, his index finger tapping the thin depiction of the shattered island on the map.

"Isn't that where we thought Idir might be holed up?" Bran asked.

"It's possible that he has chosen the watch as his bolthole," Varlan replied. "If that is the case though, I doubt Deana is there. Once Idir gets his hands on her, he won't hesitate to raise Dumura."

"He had ample opportunity over the last two decades to exploit Deana's keen and raise the island, but he didn't. How can you be sure he isn't just biding his time now?" There was an edge to Bran's tone, a bead of concern that echoed across his keen as his dark blue gaze met Varlan's.

"Bran does have a point," Elijah said from his seat across the room as he laid his pen beside the map he had been working on.

Gendry made a soft noise and traced his finger around the midpoint of the empty expanse of water at the centre of the map. "Raising an island can't be a simple matter. And even if he manages to dredge it up, he still has to figure out how to open the tomb or temple or reservoir of untold power or whatever the fuck it is he is expecting to find down there. Are we certain Deana is the key to that as well?"

Varlan rubbed a hand over his face. "No," he replied after a while, "I don't think Deana is the key. Or if she is she's only part of it."

Bran let out a small huff of breath and ran his fingers through his hair, making the snowy waves stand on end. "So, it's highly likely that Idir has her and he has hidden himself away in the labyrinthine husk of an island that is going to make it near impossible to rescue her."

"It's not like you to be so defeatist," Gendry said with a hint of a chuckle. "Whilst I believe that we should investigate Splade's Watch, I don't think that Idir is holed up there. I think he's still back on Lethata acting as though nothing is amiss. He might be the mastermind behind this plan to raise Dumura, but he's never struck me as the type to actually get his hands dirty."

It was an astute observation. Gendry might look like nothing more than a sailor, but he had been a bounty hunter for the merchants' guild before he encountered Wren and her obsession with procuring the Azure Queen. Beneath the simple, sometimes thuggish exterior, Gendry's mind was sharp and his ability to judge character uncanny to the point that, if Varlan didn't know better, he'd think magic was somehow involved.

"What about this run of islands here?" Elijah asked, his arm brushing Varlan's as he indicated a small band of islands between Weeper's Cove and Splade's Watch.

All bar one looked too small to be inhabited.

"Why would Idir be there?" Bran asked.

"I'm not talking about Idir," Elijah replied. "There's plenty of islands small enough to be overlooked but big enough to hide on all across the isles, but particularly between us and Mintura. For all we know, south-west could mean Mintura itself. It's big enough to get lost on and that south-most end is practically nothing but ruins and dense jungle. A perfect landscape for hiding in if you're of the mind."

"That enchanted stone will let us know if we are on the right track once we leave Weeper's Cove, and I still think we should head for Splade's Watch," Gendry said as he pushed back from the table. "As I said, I don't believe Idir is there, but the settlement went quiet for some reason."

"It is likely whatever has happened at the watch has nothing to do with our fight. We aren't responsible for taking care of every degenerate hiding in every bolthole in the isles," Varlan said.

Gendry levelled a dark stare on him. "I know you're smarter than that."

"You just said yourself that you don't think Idir is there."

"That doesn't mean he's not the reason the watch went silent."

"What could he possibly have to gain from attacking a colony of Armada's rejects?"

"They were standing between him and a treasure trove of dark magic, or have you forgotten what lies at the centre of that destroyed island?"

Varlan hadn't forgotten. But it was extremely likely that whatever secrets that mage's tower held had been destroyed when the volcano it was sitting on erupted and dragged not only the tower but half the island down with it. "I doubt there would be any secrets left to find, and any that might have survived the destruction are unlikely to be of use to Idir."

Gendry opened his mouth to object so Varlan ploughed on. "We cannot afford to spread ourselves too thin. Finding Deana should be our priority and following that—getting her and Agnes somewhere beyond Idir's reach until we can kill the bastard and put an end to his plans permanently."

"We don't even know if he can be killed," Elijah muttered.

"Everything can be killed," Bran tilted his head ran his finger along his jaw. "Or, at least in the case of gods and spirits, have its power stripped and be imprisoned," he added with a shrug. "I agree with Varlan. We need to find Deana and get her to safety, then we can figure out how to stop Idir."

"If we're heading that way anyway, I don't see how taking a detour to Splade's Watch will harm us." Gendry looked like he might have been about to say more when a small knock against the doorframe drew his attention.

"I hope I am not interrupting," Agnes said as she stepped into the room. Her face seemed paler than normal, making the freckles that covered her skin stand out. Her dark mahogany gaze swept past Gendry and flicked from Bran to her father before settling on Varlan.

Elijah took a step towards her. "Is everything alright?"

Her attention pulled away from Varlan and fell on her father as she let out a tired-sounding breath. "I'm fine. Nari told me I might find Varlan here." She glanced back his way. "I'd like to talk when you have a moment."

"I have time now; I doubt matters here are going to resolve themselves any time soon." He shot a look in Gendry's direction.

"No, it's probably wise for us all to have a break. We've started talking in circles and tempers are likely to get heated if we continue," he said and headed towards the door, herding Bran and Elijah ahead of him.

"Oh, alright. It's about my keen," Agnes said, stepping farther into the room.

Elijah crashed into Bran's back as the necromancer stopped dead in front of him.

"You know—oof." Bran's words were cut off as Gendry gave him a not-too-gentle nudge past Agnes.

"If she wanted your help, she would have asked. Now off you go. We'll chat with Wren about getting the Queen ready to depart." He gave Varlan a nod and then disappeared after the other two.

The air in the room grew quiet, but it was that thrumming quiet like the world around them was waiting for something to happen.

Agnes studied the map on the table as though it held her full attention, but she was coiling the end of one her plaits around her fingertips the way she did when she was preoccupied. "Is this one of Dad's?" She asked as Varlan said "I owe you an apology."

Her head snapped up, her eyes widening as they met his. "What for?"

"For my actions during the escape from Armada. I should have never—I thought I might—you nearly—I was acting on instinct." He cleared his throat and rubbed a hand over his face.

"It's alright. It was a bit strange, but it didn't bother me." She made a small sound that could have been a laugh.

"It won't happen again." He wasn't sure if he could keep his word on that, but he would certainly try. No matter how he felt, Agnes had no memories of their time together and it was likely that she would never feel the same as him again. He had to come to terms with that. He thought he had already, but then seeing her, hearing her voice, feeling the bright zing of her keen—he clenched his fists and let out a long, slow breath.

She was watching him, the starbursts of copper at the centre of those dark mahogany eyes threatening to be his undoing all over again.

He cleared his throat. "You wanted help with your keen?"

"Wes said if I wanted it to mend faster, you may be able to help me and Nari agreed."

"Agnes." He bit the inside of his cheek and let his keen-sense roll over her. There were hollow patches in her keen that hadn't been there before. Remnants of the trauma Savita's magic had wreaked on it. "Under normal circumstances, I would agree with Wes. I could help your keen mend faster, but I don't think it is a good idea given the damage Savita caused."

A tremor ran through her, and her gaze dropped to her feet. "What about what I want?" Her tone was harsh, and she clenched her fists. When she lifted her gaze to meet his once more, fire burned behind her eyes. "All of you keep telling me you need to do what's best for me. Wes and Luca and Nari say to just wait, give it time, it will heal when it's ready. But what if it never heals? None of you know what it's like to have to exist without a part of you that is as essential as breathing!" She had moved around the table as she spoke until she was standing almost toe-to-toe with him.

"I do understand, Agnes." Perhaps more than he could ever admit out loud. "But the damage that we could cause if we forced your keen before it was ready—" He shook his head. "It would make us no better than Savita and Kent." He tucked his hands into his pockets to fight the urge to reach out and touch her.

"But you can't know that unless you try."

He sighed. "I know your keen, Agnes. Intimately." The last word came out in an almost heated whisper, and he cleared his throat before continuing. "From when we tried to undo the blocks that Idir had put on your keen-sense. So trust me when I say it will endanger you. And I can't risk … Your magic *will* return on its own. You used it to finish the golem, didn't you?"

She chewed the side of her thumb and stared past his shoulder, her eyes glassy. "That doesn't mean anything. For all I know that was Savita's doing as well."

"Agnes …" he shook his head and held his hand out, "to examine your keen more closely I will need to touch you. May I?"

She nodded.

He placed his fingers delicately against her temple and reached for his keen. It stirred across the top of his shoulders before rolling up the back of his neck and over his skull. The room faded to white. Agnes was still standing in front of him, her eyes closed and her body tense. He turned slowly to get his bearings. The world was a colourless bubble around them but there were shadows moving just at the edges of his vision. A whisper of fabric over stone sounded to his left and he turned, catching a glimpse of a tall woman with long starlight-hued hair. She winked at him then disappeared in a cloud of glittering, golden flower petals. The petals rolled gently across the ground as though stirred by a soft breeze.

"You can open your eyes," he said softly.

Agnes let out a soft gasp as she turned slowly, taking in the pale void around them. "Where are we?"

"Our bodies are still at Weeper's Cove, but we are currently somewhere inside your mind."

"I've been here before." She knelt and brushed the petals away from the white stone at her feet. Crystalline freckles mottled the smooth surface, catching the light and glowing as though they held tiny droplets of imprisoned magic.

Agnes fanned her fingers out over the only patch of dark stone. It was stained, as though someone had spilled ink on the floor.

Varlan bit back a smile. Spilled ink was a common occurrence around Agnes, so it was fitting that even her mind bore the stains.

"This is where—" She vaulted to her feet and spun in a circle, scattering the golden petals into a wild flurry. "There was a woman and a panther."

"I believe I saw the woman, though I didn't recognise her, but I haven't seen any signs of a panther."

"She ..." Agnes touched her fingers to her brow, and it furrowed. "She saved me from Savita."

Varlan rubbed his fingers along his lower lip. "She saved you? Do you know who she was?"

Agnes frowned. "I *think* she saved me, but I don't know who she was. Whenever she spoke, I couldn't hear what she was saying."

A chime rang through the expanse of white, and the miasmic shadows at the edges of Varlan's vision deepened. They twisted fully into view, materialising into a colossal metal serpent before shattering into a pile of black sand. A sweet, sinister laughter echoed across the void and Agnes gasped, once more turning about to try and find the source of the sound.

"Agnes." A singsong voice followed the laughter. "You can't hide from me. My father made sure of that." Whatever was said next was stolen by a roar of wind that scattered dark sand and golden petals alike.

"Get out." Agnes dropped into a foetal position, her head tucked under her arms.

"Savita," Varlan growled, and a shade appeared through the white mist.

It certainly looked like Savita, but her colours were all washed out. Her normally glossy jet hair appeared grey, and her warm brown skin was ashen with a pallor akin to death. The sharp coal-dark stare was not muted though, and it glittered in smug triumph.

"You think you're clever," Varlan said, allowing a note of venom to sharpen his tone.

"I outsmarted you," the shade cooed and edged forward. She lifted her hand towards Agnes.

"Don't you dare touch her."

The shade gave an indulgent laugh. "Even if I could touch her, I don't need to. She will serve her purpose soon enough. Now that I control her magic, it is only a matter of time before I breach this fragile defence and claim what is left of her mind." She fanned her fingers across the air between them.

"Kent got what he wanted. Let her go."

"You're in no place to be making demands. However, if you bring Deana and Agnes back to Armada, I promise you can have what is left of them both when Father's business has been concluded."

40

Idir didn't know Deana had been kidnapped then. Whilst that was a relief, it was a hollow one as it meant that someone else had taken her. But who?

"I can't do that."

Her smile deepened. "Then you can watch while I claim your dear Agnes. I'll make it agonisingly slow until she is nothing more than a drooling husk."

Panic crept in icy fingers up his spine. It wasn't an idle threat. If he was correct, then Savita had somehow seeded a piece of her own magic alongside Agnes's. It wasn't impossible but it was extremely difficult to do, and if the invasive magic wasn't extracted carefully then the result would be—death would be kinder. He shook his head.

"Don't like that corner you've been backed into, do you?"

He had to think but he couldn't do it here. "I need time."

"Of course you do, and I can be reasonable. I'll give you until the next full moon to deliver them both to me. How does that sound?"

Varlan drew a deep breath and studied Agnes's curled form. Finally, he nodded to the shade.

A peal of overly sweet laughter rang out and then she was gone.

"I'm sorry, Agnes." He rubbed his hands over his face before raking them through his hair and clenching his fists.

Magic rolled over his shoulders and the white void dematerialised until he was once more standing in the hut at Weeper's Cove. Agnes was swaying on her feet in front of him with her eyes closed. He swallowed the wave of nausea that accompanied exiting the memory and grabbed her shoulders, guiding her back into a chair before her legs could collapse out from under her.

He then turned away from her and stormed to the table, slamming his hands down on the top. "Fuck!" He swept the map from the table with a growl. "Bright damn her. Bright damn the fucking lot of them."

"*Varlan?*" Agnes's fingers squeezed his arm. "What happened?"

"Savita." He tried to keep the rage out of his voice, but the effort made his tone tight. He pulled away from Agnes and strode for the door. "I need to speak with Wes."

"Varlan! Tell me what's going on?" She put herself between him and the door, pressing both her hands against his chest to stop him.

"Savita"—red washed his vision and he paused to temper his tone—"has placed a barb of her magic into yours. Every time you attempt to use your keen, her power over you will grow stronger until she can break through your defences and take control of your mind. I can't drive her out without harming you."

Her shoulders slumped. "That's why I can't access my magic. It's not just exhaustion, is it?"

"I honestly wish it were as simple as exhaustion." He stepped around her, pausing midway across the threshold. "I am truly sorry, Agnes." He drummed his fingers against the doorframe. "She gave me an ultimatum. Deliver you and Deana to her by the next full moon or she will wipe your mind completely. You would become nothing more than a mindless conduit through which she could exploit your keen until it killed you."

Her eyes widened in alarm. "You wouldn't though. You'll work out a way to beat her, won't you?" she asked in a shaky whisper.

He bit down on his lip and shut his eyes.

"Varlan, please." There was a desperate edge to her voice that tore through his insides.

Handing her back over to Kent and Savita was the last thing he wanted to do, but if they couldn't extract Savita's keen from hers ... "I'm sorry." The words came with a rush of breath that nearly stole them. "I need to find Wes."

CHAPTER FIVE

DEANA

Deana stood on the edge of a cliff with nothing between her and a life-ending drop but an arm's length of red stone. Far below, a ship was being tossed about by a violent storm. The woman beside her murmured softly under her breath, her gnarled fingers clutching an equally gnarled stuff. A band of tattered fabric hid her eyes, and the rising wind stirred the beads, shells, and bones that adorned ends of her long, dreadlocked hair.

"You have lingered here too long, little one," the woman said, her many layered voices rolling over each other.

"Why do I keep being drawn here?" Deana asked, as the ship finally lost its fight against the massive waves.

"There is something for you down there." The woman indicated the ocean with a tilt of her chin.

The churning waves had been replaced with an expanse of sodden sand and dying fish, in the centre of which lay the skeleton of the capsized ship. A lone figure walked through the dark shapes of drowned bodies that littered the ground around the wreck. Idir. A note of familiar song rattled through Deana's mind, and Idir clutched his chest as he jolted to a stop. He bent over as though in extreme pain before a chilling trill rang through the song of the world and he straightened again. He turned and marched to one of the bodies before lifting the much smaller figure from the ground. The person fought feebly against him as he snarled something into her face. Then with brutal efficiency, he snapped her neck and let her fall back to the sand with a soft thump. A cry of sorrow-tainted rage drew his attention to another dark shape back towards the busted hull of the ship. He stalked to the dying man with dogged purpose as the cloying notes of his song stirred the air.

All moisture had fled Deana's mouth. She had watched this scene from a dozen different angles—the outcome was always the same. The outcome would never be different. This was how her parents had died. Idir had killed them. But why, when he could have just used his mind magic to force them to give him anything he wanted?

It was a small comfort to know that once her father was dead the dream would release Deana and she would wake. This particular nightmare had a definitive end, one that tarnished her waking life, but an end nonetheless. She drew a deep breath, waiting for that moment, the seed of hatred for Idir growing with every second. At first the blind rage she felt had been foreign and frightening, but now she welcomed it. It would be something to cling to, to dampen her fear when she eventually had to face him again in the waking world.

Idir turned away from her father's corpse. Any minute now she would wake.

But the dream lingered.

A tremor quivered through Deana's fingers, and she clenched them in an attempt to still their shaking. The dream had never held her this long. It usually forced her to watch her parents' last moments and then it spat her out to wake in a cold sweat.

As Idir walked through the bodies, he crouched and touched several of them. His song morphed from cloying allure to a chilling dirge that spoke of icy darkness and death. The bodies he caressed rose on shaking legs and followed him across the wet sand to the edge of the water where they disappeared.

Deana turned to the woman beside her, but she was gone—a small pile of silver scales glittering where she had been standing. The scales stirred into a flurry that twisted around Deana before flying over the edge of the cliff and across the sand to wash over the shipwreck.

She took a step forward. One more and she would be in the open air. Closing her eyes, she sprang into a swan dive. The sand shifted once more into waves that enveloped her in cold as she splashed into them. A light flickered in the dark water; a pearlescent white fish with a dark belly. It darted away from her only to swim back and then away again as though beckoning her to follow. She kicked to the surface, sucking in a deep breath of salty air before diving again and swimming after the fish. It took her past the shipwreck and down deeper into the black depths where a glittering spire came into a view. The drowned husk of an ancient tower. Darkness started to edge her vision as her lungs burned through the last of the air. A woman appeared in the gloom. Ink-coloured hair, mother-of-pearl skin, and a long, pale tail that glittered in the enchanted light of the tower. She gripped Deana's cheeks and pressed her strangely warm lips over Deana's own. Magic zinged along Deana's veins and the alluring notes of the fathoms swirled around her as the cold darkness rose up to claim her.

Seabirds squabbled somewhere at the edge of her hearing. The soft aroma of baking sweetbread drifted across her senses, mingling with the scents of dust and mouldering wood. The bed beside her dipped and the slow, shifting song of necromancy brushed against hers. It wasn't the deep melancholy of Bran's song, but it was as familiar—even with the sorrowful notes of shrouded magic tainting it.

"Dee?" Samir's voice joined the shrieking birds, and his cold fingers gripped her wrist.

She let out a groan and rubbed her other hand over her face to dislodge the grit from her eyes. "Samir?"

"I'm here, Dee," he said as he squeezed her wrist tighter before turning to the door. "Ast—"

"No. Don't call her." Deana sat up, immediately wishing she hadn't as her head swam and the vestiges of her dream scattered leaving her with the feeling that she was on a rocking boat.

"But—"

"I don't want to see her right now." The back of her skull was aching, and she touched her fingers to it, wincing as they found her hair matted over a large lump.

"You hit your head on the rocks," Samir offered as an explanation, "but Rami saved you."

"I drowned."

Samir shook his head violently. "No, Rami saved you."

"No, I ..." She pressed the heel of her palm to her forehead. "It was just a dream."

"I really should get Astrid." Samir let go of her and made for the door. "I'll be right back."

He disappeared into the hall, and Deana swung her legs over the side of the bed. As she went to stand, the room swayed and she took several mincing steps before she fell against the side of the small table by the window. A glance outside told her Rami was standing guard in his usual spot. However, he seemed to be staring towards the beach rather than up at her. As though he could feel her eyes on him, he turned and levelled his unsettling gaze on her.

"You should not be out of bed." Astrid's sharp tone sent a jolt through her.

She tore her gaze away from Rami and shifted her grip on the edge of the table so she could turn to face Astrid without losing her balance.

Astrid's mouth was a tight line, her fingers white-knuckled where they gripped the tray she was carrying. She marched to Deana's side and set the tray down then those same fingers encircled Deana's elbow.

"Back to bed," Astrid ordered as she pulled against Deana's arm.

Deana wobbled on her feet and gripped the edge of the table harder. "No."

"You took on too much water. We can't risk—"

"I am not going back to bed." Deana shrugged her arm out of Astrid's grip. The force caused her to lose her balance, but she caught herself and landed clumsily into the chair beside the table.

Astrid's nostrils flared and she shook her head. She took a cup from the tray and set it heavily in front of Deana. "It's a restorative. Drink every drop."

Deana did as she was told, and Astrid gave a satisfied grunt before taking another cup from the tray and swapping it with the first. This was warmer, a gentle coiling steam rising from the surface and scenting the air with its soft sweetness.

"It's just tea. I thought you'd like something to chase the bitterness of the restorative away," Astrid said.

Deana took a sip. She couldn't place the flavour. It wasn't unpleasant, but the sweetness lingered long after each sip.

Astrid waited until Deana had consumed half the tea before she lifted the cover off the final dish on the tray. Two small hunks of bread sat neatly on a plate. "You should eat and then I want you back in bed. You will need to be fully rested before we can test your magic again."

Deana eyed the bed as she picked up one of the warm rolls. "I will rest but won't go back to bed." She broke off a small piece and set it on her tongue. The sweetness was laced with a gentle spice that brought her brother to mind. Kai had always been fond of Osmarian spices.

The scowl on Astrid's face chased the fond memories away. "Your stubbornness will be the death of you. You need to learn to control your magic and for that you need to be—"

"I can control my magic."

Astrid set her hands on her hips and her midnight-blue gaze bored into Deana's. The depth of colour and the shape were almost identical to Bran's, but Astrid's eyes were sharper and they never held the same softness or light-heartedness that Bran's often did. There were other similarities too—in the line of Astrid's nose and the set of her mouth. They couldn't be related though. Astrid by her own account was several centuries old.

"You have barely scratched the surface of what your magic is capable of, and if Idir gets his hands on you he won't take the time to make sure you can handle the full extent of your power. He will exploit it to get what he wants, even if it destroys you in the process. I am trying to prevent that from happening, to give you a chance against him. So, stop fighting me and start working with me."

Deana dropped what was left of the roll onto the plate. "If you want to help me, why are you keeping me a prisoner? Why did you—"

"I am keeping you *safe* from Idir. You cannot hope to stop him until you learn to control your power. Now, if you want to insist you are a prisoner, I will start treating you as such." Her song trilled through the air and moments later heavy footfalls sounded on the stairs.

Deana stood as Rami appeared at the door, and his aura of silence rolled into the room. "No—" Her words were cut off as Rami marched to her and grabbed hold of her wrist.

"Gently please, Rami," Astrid muttered as she left the room.

Rami gripped both of Deana's wrists and towed her to the bed where he pushed her down. He held her securely with one hand as the other drew a length of rope from the folds of the tattered cloak he wore.

She thrashed against his hold as he shifted his grip to weave the rope around her wrist and secure it to the bed. Her pleading gasps for him to let her go were stolen by the silence around him.

He turned his attention to her other wrist, the rope biting as she struggled and managed to her get her hand free. Her nails raked down his cheek, leaving angry red welts on his sallow skin, but he didn't even finch. He just caught her hand firmly as it came sweeping back again and pinned it as effectively as the first.

With a grunt, he stood and backed away from the bed then settled into the chair Deana had moments ago been sitting in.

She turned to watch him, but he was staring blankly at the door, his hands resting on his knees. The silent bubble that accompanied him brushed the edge of Deana's song and threatened to drown her as effectively as the churning waters of her dreams.

Deana refused to sleep. Even if she was ready to slip back into the heartrending landscape of her dreams, she wasn't sure she could with Rami's oppressive presence at the other side of the room. Sometime after her arms had started to ache and her wrists were stinging from fighting against the ropes that bound them, Astrid arrived with a small cup.

"Something to help you rest," she said as she approached the side of the bed.

Deana thrashed and tried to kick her away, but she stepped neatly back and snapped her fingers at Rami.

He crossed the room and pinned Deana's legs to the bed.

"Oh, don't look at me like that. You wanted this. You kept insisting that you were a prisoner. Now drink this and go to sleep like a good girl." She brought the cup towards Deana's lips.

Deana turned her face away, nearly knocking the cup from Astrid's hand.

Astrid tsked and shook her head. "Rami."

Rami settled his weight down on Deana legs and took hold of her chin, pulling it around so she was staring directly at Astrid once more. Silence washed over her and though Astrid's lips were moving there was no sound. Astrid rolled her eyes and pinched Deana's nose.

Pain burned in her lungs as and she opened her mouth to draw a rasping breath, only for Astrid to dump the contents of the cup down her throat. She coughed, half choking on the wickedly sweet liquid. Her senses dimmed and her lips felt oddly thick, then the room dissolved into a turbulent mass of dark waves and screaming dead.

CHAPTER SIX

BRAN

They stayed two days too long at Weeper's Cove. By the time they set sail everyone was on edge, and the bickering about what their next steps should be had dissolved into a seething tension that left tempers short and Bran's shoulders tense. He leant on the side rail of the Queen. Thin spray misted the air as the ship cut a path through the waves with the assistance of Wren's magic, which had conjured a stiff wind that tossed his hair and bit the skin of his cheeks.

Deana's protection charm was heavy around his neck. The subtle pull to the south-west had grown faint in the early afternoon yesterday. Bran didn't know if that meant the enchantment Marcus had set on it was wearing off or if something had happened to Deana. He hoped it was the former.

An elbow brushed his as Agnes settled in beside him. Her face had been paler than normal since they left Armada. The lively glow that normally smoothed her cheeks was absent, leaving them a stark background for the dark crescents beneath her eyes and constellations of freckles that covered her creamy skin. Her fingers shook as she pulled a thin piece of string through them, twisting it around their tips and then unwinding it again as she let out a sigh.

"Do you think we'll find her before something bad happens to her?" she asked after a while.

"I ..." He touched his fingers to the stone against his chest. "I don't know. I hope we do, but even if it isn't Idir who has her, there is no guarantee whoever took her has her best interests at heart." He shook his head. "More likely it is quite the opposite."

Agnes let out a heavy breath and her fingers tightened around the string.

Bran felt a pang of remorse for confirming her fears, but they had to consider all the realities of what Deana may be going through, even the harsh ones. "Varlan told me about Savita," he said in an effort to change the subject.

She spun to face him, a look of betrayal in her dark russet eyes.

"He just wanted my advice. I was raised by a family of mages who have made it their life's work to study things like this, so he thought I might know something that could help. I don't, unfortunately, but we will make figuring it out our first priority as soon as we know Deana is safe." Varlan had also asked about the possibility of taking both Agnes and Deana to Hartswood to keep them safe until Idir was dealt with. It wasn't the worst idea, but Bran doubted either of them would allow it.

She turned her gaze away from him, and he followed her line of sight to Varlan. The mind mage was farther down the deck with Wes, their heads bent together as they argued in hushed whispers. Luca approached them and Wes shook his head and muttered something, but then Varlan lifted his scowl to the healer and he backed away with his hands raised.

"Still hasn't forgiven him for slipping you mage bane I guess," Bran said.

"Sorry?" Her brow furrowed as she turned back to him.

Bran rubbed the knot at the back of his neck. "I'm talking about Varlan and Luca. It was dangerous and I understand why Varlan is so angry about it, but Luca probably prevented Savita from getting a true hold on your keen which means it should be easier to extract her when the time comes."

She ran her fingers down one of her plaits, weaving the ends through her knuckles before repeating the whole process again. "You said your family have studied unusual magic?"

Studied, devoted their lives and that of several generations to—it was all the same really. "They have. And given that a few of them possess unique keens, magical parasites, or a combination of the two, they are quite well versed on the topic of *weird magic*." He released a small chuckle.

"Magical parasites?" Her eyes widened. "Like what Savita has done to me?"

He shook his head. "No. We're talking pieces of souls that may or may not have been human sharing the body of their host. *Symbiotically*. For the most part at least. What Savita has done to you is set a trap within your own keen that will trigger when you use your magic. I don't know why you *can't* use your magic; the barb of Savita's keen shouldn't be preventing that. If anything, quite the opposite because she can't spring the trip unless you engage your keen. Of course, it could be magical exhaustion, or the trauma caused by the mage bane or some combination of the two." He brushed his keen-sense over her, testing the edges of her keen. Savita's abuse had left it ragged and wounded, but it seemed to be mending itself, so the damage wasn't permanent. At least, not yet. If Savita managed to trigger the trap she had set in Agnes's keen, that might be another story entirely.

Agnes blinked at him, her mouth dropping open slightly.

"I'm sorry. Family of scholars, remember?"

"Pieces of souls? Can souls be broken? If they can, does that also mean they can be put back together again?" She clenched and unclenched her hands.

"It's not easy to break a soul but it's not impossible. Mending a broken soul though? That would be extremely difficult. Not just any necromancer could do it either. Breaking or mending, you'd need to possess a certain kind of keen." He studied her face. "If you're concerned you possess a piece of Savita's soul, don't be."

"I wasn't. I just ..." She pressed her fingers to her forehead and squeezed her eyes shut.

A soft fluttering keen tickled the back of Bran's neck, and he grabbed hold of her shoulder. "Agnes, you can't use your magic now."

She didn't open her eyes. Didn't acknowledge that she'd heard him.

"Agnes." He gave her a small shake and she drew a rasping gasp as her eyes flew open.

The relief that shone in her gaze was quickly consumed by a wide-eyed panic. She lifted her hands and studied them and then clenched them into tight fists that left her knuckles blanched.

"Agnes," he said her name again, and her attention snapped to him. "You can't risk using your keen until we figure out how to extract Savita."

"I can't control it," she said in a panicked whisper and pulled away from him before barrelling backwards into Wes and Varlan.

The warden caught her as she stumbled. He shared a look with Varlan, who drew a long breath and nodded.

Wes released his hold on Agnes and then hurried away.

"Your keen has returned," the mind mage said as his attention settled on Agnes. There was a stiffness to his shoulders and a clipped formalness to his tone.

"So it would seem." Agnes swallowed.

Varlan switched his gaze to Bran as though he couldn't bear witnessing Agnes's reaction to what he was a about to say. "We need more time to figure out how to remove Savita's influence and we can't risk you using your keen. You know I wouldn't ask if it wasn't the only option available to us, but you need to consider letting Luca dose you with mage bane again."

"What?! No! I can learn to control it. You said that yourself."

"We don't have the luxury of time. If your keen activates then Savita will have all the opening she needs to take control of you."

"I can fight her. I can—"

"You don't know that! Without keen-sense you are a slave to your own magic. How can you hope to defend against a mage as skilled as Savita?"

Agnes blinked at him and then turned a glass-eyed stare towards Bran, her throat working as she swallowed.

Varlan's gaze softened as it returned to Agnes, and he lifted a hand as though he would touch her shoulder. "I'm sorry. That was unfair of me. And you're right—I do think you can learn to control it, but we are simply out of—"

"I won't take anything Luca gives me," Agnes said, her fists clenching as she stood on her toes.

"It's the only way to guarantee you are protected from Savita," Varlan snapped.

"There has to be another way." Agnes shifted her watery gaze back to Bran. "Tell him there's another way."

He rubbed the knot at the back of his neck again and flicked a look between them. Varlan was tense, a bowstring ready to let fly, and Agnes was wilting under the threat of another dose of mage bane—one that wouldn't do her any good in the long run, and Bran was sure Varlan knew that. Why then was he insisting that she take it? He didn't seem like the kind prone to panicking, but none of them had gotten much sleep in the past few weeks and the cracks were really starting to show.

"Bran, please, you must know something," Agnes pleaded.

He sighed and glanced at Varlan out of the corner of his eye as he said, "All I know is we can't rush it." If he hadn't insisted that Garret take the spirit anchor, he could have contacted Nea and asked her opinion or even sent Agnes to Hartswood. Between Nea, Declan, and Niall, surely they could figure out how to fix this. "I'm sorry, Agnes, but unless you can learn how to control your keen in the next few hours, then maybe Varlan is right."

Her eyes narrowed and she backed away from both of them.

"Agnes ..." Varlan started, but she shook her head violently then spun on her heel and hurried away to where Pippa and Kiki were playing liar's dice with Dara.

"Surely you wouldn't force her to take the mage bane," Bran said softly.

"Of course not." Varlan leant heavily on the side rail of the ship. "But she needs to see reason. If Savita—" His knuckles paled as he tightened his grip. "Savita will destroy her from the inside out. If she has her way, there will be nothing left that is Agnes."

"Can't you go into her mind and extract Savita?"

Varlan shook his head. "I don't know that I can."

"Luca needs time to prepare a new batch of the mage-bane tonic." Wes's tone was tight as he joined them. "You can't honestly be thinking about putting her through that again."

"We might not have another choice."

"We always have a choice. You weren't there—you didn't see the toll it took on her."

"And what if her magic pulls her into the trance and Savita takes over? What toll will that take?"

Wes frowned, anger burning behind his eyes and giving his usual friendly appearance a dangerous edge. "You're letting your emotions get in the way of your better judgement." The thick weight of Wes's suppression smothered the air around them.

An idea tickled the back of Bran's mind. It wasn't as simple and secure a fix as dosing her with mage bane, but it was far less dangerous. "What if Wes guards Agnes? He would be nearby to use his suppression to block her magic as needed and that way the mage bane would not be necessary," Bran offered.

Varlan studied the warden. "It has its share of flaws, but it is a valid option."

Wes gave a nod. "If it means we don't have to resort to the mage bane then I have no issue with it. But we need to figure out how to fix this fast. Not only for Agnes's sake—we can't afford the distraction." He gave Varlan a pointed look then turned on his heel and wandered over to join Agnes and the twins.

"Nea would know exactly what to do," Bran said with a shake of his head.

Varlan, however, was studying Dara, his eyes narrowed shrewdly, and he turned to Bran. "What do you know about dream-singers?"

They set anchor for the night by one of the smaller islands just north of Splade's Watch. The tracking charm on Deana's protection stone had been silent for hours, leaving a heavy lump in Bran's stomach and a restlessness in his feet. He paced across the deck, the chill breeze stirring the hairs on the back of his neck.

Unrecognisable cold magic itched at the oath mark on the inside of his wrist. It wasn't necromancy but rather something akin to it. His steps faltered and he rolled back his sleeve to inspect the soft violet glow radiating from the indigo crescent. He wrapped his fingers around the mark as the creeping sensation of being watched crawled between his shoulders. Slowly he turned, scanning the waters beside the ship, and a glimmer of light caught his attention. A white fish swimming in lazy circles. It rolled as it completed a loop, showing an ink-black underside before flipping right-way up again.

Bran gripped the side rail and leant forward to get a better look at the fish as it is started to glow brighter. Its body was doubling in size, the front fins elongating into distinctly human arms as a head of dark hair wreathed in seaweed and coral breached the surface. Silver eyes shone in the moonlight as did the bioluminescent markings that swirled across the woman's skin. She tilted her chin as she regarded him, a soft, almost familiar smile playing across her lips.

Words whispered through his mind, too soft to make any real sense of. They were laced with fear and longing, sorrow and urgency.

Footsteps sounded on the deck behind Bran and a heavy hand landed on his shoulder.

"It's a long swim to the watch if that's what you're thinking," Gendry said, his grip on Bran firm.

Bran hadn't realised how far over the side of the ship he was leaning until he looked down. Any further and he would have lost balance and fallen into the ocean. He scanned the water for any sign of the woman, but she was gone. The woman hadn't been a shrouded one—of that he was certain. They were wraiths of some nature. But whilst the shifting magic of the Between had rolled off the woman, she was not a spirit. If she were, she was unlike any he had encountered before. He pushed himself back onto the deck and turned to Gendry. "I thought I saw something."

Gendry studied his face for a few moments. "The ocean will do that to you. Best to ignore it and keep your eyes on deck once the moon gets high. They're ready for you in the captain's quarters."

Bran gave him a nod, and with one last glance at the rippling water he headed along the deck to Wren's cabin.

Varlan was inside with Agnes, Nari, and Dara.

"You're sure this will work?" Agnes asked, her attention fixed on Varlan's face.

He shrugged. "I wish I could say with complete certainty that it will, but ..." His gaze shifted to Bran, his eyebrows lifting in silent question.

"If we can find where Savita placed the seed of her magic then we should be able to extract her easily enough. Hopefully, by going in through your dreams rather than directly into your mind we can sneak up on her," Bran said.

"Are you all ready?" Nari asked as she lifted a vial of greenish liquid.

Agnes nodded.

"Alright, on the bed with you." Nari said to Agnes before turning her attention to Bran and Varlan. "You two will have to take the floor I am afraid."

"You're sure you can pull both of us into Agnes's dreamscape, Dara?" Varlan asked.

"I think so," Dara said, her tone unsure. "I've only ever tried linking two dreamscapes before."

"Link Varlan first then," Bran said.

Dara nodded. "Alright. Ready when you are, Nari."

The healer gestured to the floor and when both Bran and Varlan had lain down, she moved to Agnes and gave her a cup. "Just let it take you. You'll be fine, I promise."

After Agnes had consumed the liquid in the cup, Nari repeated the process with Varlan and then finally Bran. He recognised the bittersweet smell of sleeping tonic. It had a very similar scent to the one Margot made but there was something more earthy and less sweet about Nari's version.

He swallowed the contents of the cup in one go and passed it back to her as he laid his head down. His whole body grew heavy as a numbness started to slink across his mind, dulling his thoughts. At the last moment before sleep, the woman from the ocean flashed across the back of his eyes—her slender, glowing hands dragging him down into the cold, ever-shifting magic of the Between.

CHAPTER SEVEN

AGNES

Agnes could barely hear herself think over the wild roar of wind that sent sand driving against the back of her legs. Shielding her eyes with one hand, she clutched her journal to her chest with the other and squinted at the washed-out landscape in front of her. Sand. Nothing but sand. White and pure, blown into ribbed drifts by the incessant wind. Ahead was a shimmer. Heat pretending to be water, never getting any closer despite the distance she walked.

She glanced around, trying to determine which way she had come, but the drifting sand had stolen her footprints, so it was impossible to tell. Wind snagged the edge of the journal, almost succeeding in tugging it from her fingers before she managed to tighten her grip once more.

A sound drew her attention and she turned. The gleaming coils of a colossal metal serpent confronted her. She staggered backward, falling heavily onto her behind and losing her grip on the journal.

The wind flipped the book head-over-tail until it was just beyond the reach of Agnes's grasping fingers. Another gust snapped the cover open, and the pages took flight.

"No!" She pushed to her feet and scurried after the papers but each one she touched turned to ash.

"Agnes." A deep, achingly familiar voice invaded the landscape. It echoed around the inside of her skull as she chased down another flurry of papers.

"It's okay," the voice said. Memories stirred the darkest recesses of her mind. Warmth and laughter, shadowed by regret and then— nothing, as though the memories had been cut short.

The voice had said it was okay, but it wasn't. Agnes was lost. A host to parasitic magic that would never let her have control. She would never have autonomy as long as she shared her body not only with her own magic but the seed of Savita's keen.

The papers twisted into the shape of a tall man with bronze skin and dark hair. He caught Agnes's shoulders as she dashed past him, to catch the remaining pages.

"It's just a dream," he said, his golden-brown eyes searching hers and setting a churning in her stomach that had nothing to do with her current predicament.

Just a dream. That realisation made the world spin around her. Of course it was a dream, and she was here for a reason. The man was here for a reason, too.

She shook her head to try and clear the fog that was holding her memories trapped. A name fluttered to the surface; a memory or perhaps another dream, one of a different time. Soft lips pressed to the sensitive skin just beneath her ear, warm breath stirring the delicate hairs along her neck. She squeezed her eyes shut, chasing the foreign and yet familiar sensations away before the name found the tip of her tongue and she opened them again. "Varlan?"

Relief softened his features and he nodded.

"Where's Bran?"

"Dara wasn't certain she could link all three of our dreamscapes. If she did manage it, then I'm sure he'll be along soon but we can't wait for him. The longer we are here, the greater the chance Savita will discover what we are attempting."

"How are we going to find her in all this?" Agnes thrust her arm out to indicate the desert that stretched beyond the horizon in all directions. The wind picked up again, twisting the sand into a flurry around their feet.

"Close your eyes."

"I—"

"Just close them." There was the slightest of upticks at one corner of his mouth.

"Alright." She shut them. The wind bit at her back and sent her plaits whipping. After a moment, it seemed to soften, though she could still hear the howling roar all around them. "Now what?"

"Focus." His voice came from behind her, the air between them charged with something more than the turbulence caused by the racing wind. "I'm going to put my hands on your shoulders." He warned her seconds before the weight of his palms settled into place. "Now, focus on the void around you. Savita's magic should stand out."

The heat of his hands was almost comforting. She focused on that sensation first, then let her other senses wander outward. The howling wind was accompanied by the rasp of sand rubbing against sand. Scents reached her: metal, oil, spilled ink, and something softer—cedar wood and spice and smoky black tea. She inhaled deeply. A nagging sense that she was forgetting something important accompanied the softer scents. A headache of memories that had no substance.

"Don't allow yourself to get distracted," Varlan whispered, the husky familiarity of his voice stirring the empty memories into a frenzy. "Focus on your breathing if that helps."

"You need to stop talking," she muttered.

The rumbling chuckle that came from him turned her insides to molten metal. Her mind might not remember the intimacy that had once been between them, but it would seem that her body had not forgotten.

Focus. She pushed the nagging sensation of forgotten moments to the back of her mind and turned her attention to her breathing. *Inhale ... Exhale ... Inhale ... Ex—* Something snagged her. A lump beneath the fabric of her dreamscape. It shifted as she poked at it. She opened her eyes and lifted her hand to point towards the far horizon.

"There is something that way." She turned to study Varlan's face.

He was staring in the direction she had pointed. The ticklish sensation of fingers brushing the back of her neck made her roll her shoulders, but his hands hadn't moved from their perch. A few moments later, he dropped his gaze to hers and gave a nod as he released her and started forward.

After a dozen or so strides, he looked back over his shoulder. "Are you coming?"

She shook off the torpor that had overtaken her and jogged to catch up to him. "Yes. Sorry, I was just caught up in my thoughts."

He glanced at her out of the corner of his eye, and she shifted her gaze to the featureless landscape of sand ahead of them.

"Shall we?" she said after a moment, gesturing towards the horizon.

They marched across the sand in silence. Even the wind had died down to a gentle breeze. As they walked, the landscape around them began to change. The pale sand still shifted beneath their feet, but at intervals that seemed to be getting closer together, struts of metal rose from it in gleaming pillars. Patterns were etched over the surface of the pillars—stars and strange flowers that Agnes didn't recognise interspersed with sharp geometric shapes.

Finally, the sand petered out and the ground became a slab of glittering dark stone. Agnes bent and brushed her fingers over it; the glitter was coming from millions of tiny glass beads that were trapped in the rock. Each bead had a glowing core that was pulsing as though it held a heartbeat. She traced her fingertips over them hesitantly, and they lit up in shades of gold and bronze before fading to black. The black spread like spilled ink, rushing across the ground as a deafening grating sound announced the arrival of an ominous door. It rose from the stone in front of them, golden speckles of light shimmering across its surface. The black splashed up the door, settling into grooves in the stone until it formed an image of two crossed branches of coral.

"Shadow's teeth, I didn't think I was ever going to catch up," Bran said from behind them.

He had one hand pressed to his side as he inhaled deeply, catching his breath. The other hand clutched a mass of papers which he held out to Agnes. She took them from him and tucked them into the tattered covers of her journal.

"Any ideas how to get through the door?" Varlan asked.

As Bran moved to examine the structure a wash of cold air followed him. He lifted a hand and touched the centre of the crossed coral motif and the iciness in the air intensified.

"Is it just me or is it getting cold?" Agnes rubbed her arms.

"You can feel that?" Varlan asked, his brows arching.

"Can't you?"

"I can ... but I never expected you to." He and Bran shared a look. An infuriating look as though they were both in on some private knowledge that she was not privy to.

"Is it something to do with the door?" She nudged Bran out of the way.

"Wait. Don't—"

Bran's warning was cut off as she pressed her palm to the middle of the motif and the bottom dropped out of her stomach as she tumbled forward. There was no floor beneath her—just a dark, twisting staircase which she rolled head-over-tail down until she landed with a boneshaking jolt at the bottom.

A pool of soft, golden light surrounded her. But just beyond its glow, darkness shrouded the rest of the world. Darkness that moved in glossy, serpentine coils. She pressed her hands to the floor and staggered to her feet as the coils began to tighten inwards like the constricting sides of a python. She stumbled forward, chasing the fleeting pool of golden light, just as the coils slammed down on the place where she had been standing moments before. A deafening hiss stung her ears and drowned out her thoughts as she ran only to crash into an ebony wall of rippling, velvet scales. She spun around, looking wildly for an escape, but the coils closed her into their silken folds, constricting until they stole the remaining breath from her lungs and swallowed the last of the golden light.

CHAPTER EIGHT

VARLAN

"No!" Varlan dove forward as Agnes disappeared through the door. His hands slammed against unyielding icy stone and a pulse of foreign magic reverberated up his arms and into his jaw. "Bright damn it!" He spun to face Bran. "You were trying to warn her. Do you know where this door leads?"

The necromancer raked his fingers through his hair and puffed his cheeks out as he released a breath. "Not exactly. All I know is that it doesn't belong in Agnes's dreamscape. Everything else here is completely infused with her keen, but that door ..." He eyed the slab of dark stone. The coral motif was glowing with a seething red that overshadowed the glittering speckles of soft gold and bronze. "That door was charged with the same magic that created the shrouded ones, so if I had to guess I would say it leads to the place where Idir locked up her keen-sense."

Varlan let his magic drift over the door, searching for a way through. Bran was right; the stone was made almost entirely of Idir's keen. The darker twisting version of his keen, well concealed by his mind magic, but that clung to the man in question like rot once you got beneath the surface.

"Now, this is a delicious turn of events," a silky sweet voice said.

Varlan turned his attention to Savita's shade where she stood at the very edge of the sand as though not willing to step onto the magic-studded dark stone that led to the door.

"You came here to drive me out and yet have led Agnes straight to my father. I would have been a kinder fate, I can assure you."

The chill of Bran's necromancy slid over Varlan, and Savita's obsidian gaze found the necromancer, her gloating smile dimming for just a moment before snapping back into place.

"How did *you* get here?"

Bran shrugged as he moved towards her. "I'm just full of secrets I suppose." The indigo tattoo on the inside of his wrist was glowing with a soft lilac hue. Swirling patterns radiated out from it and up his arm as a shifting magic washed over Varlan and left him feeling like he was on uneven footing.

The air behind Savita shimmered and a wall of dense pines appeared, extending as far as the eye could see across the dreamscape. The shade turned to view the wall, backing up a step until her foot met the edge of the dark stone. Shadows leapt from the stone in coiling hands that gripped her ankle and pulled her off-balance.

"Find Agnes," Bran said as he dove towards Savita's shade.

The sound of branches rustling was accompanied by a flash of purple light so bright that Varlan had to shield his eyes. When his vision cleared, the wall of pines, Bran, and Savita had all disappeared.

He turned back to the door. It hadn't responded to either Bran or Varlan, but the second Agnes had touched it she had been sucked through to whatever was on the other side as though her magic was the key. A stiff breeze ruffled his hair, and something fluttered to the ground beside him. It was one of Agnes's journal pages. He picked it up and turned it over. An eight-pointed star was drawn on the centre of the page in crisp and neat lines, and Agnes's keen shifted over the parchment in a warm flurry. Was there enough residual magic on the paper for the door to recognise? He stepped up to the door and pressed the paper to it. Nothing happened. How was going to find her if he couldn't get through the door?

The breeze grew stronger, buffeting against his back and snapping the parchment from his grip. As he made a grab for the page, it twisted away from him again only to settle near the edge of the dark stones where Savita's shade and Bran had disappeared. He took a lunging step towards it, but the wind twirled it out of his reach again.

Another lunge took him off the dark stone and onto the pale sand. A grating sound filled the air as the ground beneath his feet shook. When he turned back to the door it was gone, the dark patch of stone scarring the sand the only sign that it had ever been there.

"No." He ran onto the stone, but nothing happened. "Come on." Crouching, he pressed his palms to the ground and let his magic feed into it, but again nothing happened. After a moment, the journal page fluttered down and landed between his hands. He snatched it up and lifted his head to find himself nose to nose with a panther.

It was constructed of gleaming dark metal riveted together with tiny studs of rose-gold robrillium. Varlan rocked onto his heels and lifted his hands. The panther made a rumbling sound and then pressed its cold forehead into the centre of Varlan's left hand, rolling its neck and rubbing its head along Varlan's skin until his fingers glanced over the smooth curve of its ear.

"Ah, hello to you too, I guess."

Agnes had mentioned a panther when they had been inside the white void.

The panther sat on its haunches and folded its tail over its front paws. The orbs of magic light that took place of its eyes glowed softly as it stared at him.

"Do you know how to find Agnes?"

It tilted its head then lifted its snout to the breeze before getting to its feet and walking away from him. When it had gone several metres, it stopped and looked back over its shoulder as though waiting for him to follow.

He folded the parchment and tucked it into his pocket as he started after the panther.

The beast led him across the dunes at an uncomfortable pace, almost too fast to be considered a walk. When he thought he couldn't go any farther, a glowing dome appeared on the horizon. It was a brilliant white that reflected the light and forced him to shield his eyes. The panther broke into a loping run that quickly ate the ground between them and the dome. Varlan's lungs burned in protest as he sprinted to keep pace with the cat, but he didn't slow until they reached the edge of the shining structure.

Shadowy forms moved on the inside, but Varlan couldn't make sense of either of them. The breeze returned, tickling the hairs on the back of his neck and playing with the front of his jacket as though searching for something within the coat's folds. Varlan retrieved the parchment from his pocket and unfolded it. The wind whipped it from his hand and slammed it against the side of the dome. Swirling lines of golden magic expanded out from the edges of the page. They formed a tall door edged with geometric patterns and with a glowing bronze flower at its centre. The moment Varlan's fingers brushed the centre of the flower, the door swung open, sending a wash of glittering magic over his feet.

When he stepped across the threshold, he met the silver gaze of the tall woman with pale hair. Her golden gown clung to her curves and glittered as though covered with a layer of diamond dust as she moved. She nodded once to Varlan and then disappeared in a cloud of golden petals that formed the lines of an eight-pointed star around the figure curled on the floor.

"Agnes." Varlan rushed forward, sliding to his knees beside her and scattering the petals.

Her eyes were closed, her chest rising and falling softly as though she were in a deep sleep. He gripped her shoulder and gave it a gentle shake, but she didn't stir. His fingers found the pulse point at her neck. Her heartbeat was strong and steady and her skin warm. He bit down on the quiver of worry and tried shaking her shoulder again. "Agnes?"

The movement caused her arm to flop to her side, and her hand fell open to reveal her fingertips which were stained with streaks of black. The marks ran down her fingers like spilled ink and pooled in her palm where they radiated with a soft red glow and the sinister throb of Idir's keen.

Varlan was on his feet the moment his eyes opened. The floor swayed as he staggered to the side of the bed where Dara was sitting watch over Agnes's sleeping form.

The girl turned her crystal green eyes on him as he stopped beside her, the heavy drowsiness of her keen settling over him as a furrow appeared between her brows. "What's wrong?" She looked from his face to Agnes's peaceful one and the furrow deepened.

He lifted Agnes's hand from where it rested beside her hip and rolled it palm up. The skin was clear of marks. He let his keen coil out to test hers; nothing seemed amiss. Her magic was steady and free of Idir's influence.

Movement behind him preceded a groan from Bran. He gently laid Agnes's hand down by her side once more and turned to face the necromancer.

"Did you find Agnes?" Bran asked.

Varlan gave a single nod. "What happened with Savita?"

"I drove her out of the dreamscape, but I am not certain if it was enough to break her hold on Agnes's keen."

"We have a bigger problem now." Varlan glanced at Agnes

before moving his gaze to Nari, who was perched on the chair by Wren's small desk watching them. "The hunt for Savita led us to a door in Agnes's dreamscape, one that had been created by Idir's magic. Agnes went through before we could stop her."

"A door in her dreamscape?" Dara asked. "I felt Bran open some kind of door but not Agnes."

"You felt the barrier and quite possibly the Between as I dragged Savita through," Bran explained.

"It felt like the fabric of nightmares," Dara whispered.

"That sounds about right," Bran said with a shaky chuckle.

"What happened after Agnes went through the door?" Nari asked.

"She just disappeared, and then Savita was crowing about leaping from her trap only to spring her father's. Bran took care of Savita and I eventually found Agnes, but I couldn't wake her and Idir ..." He picked up Agnes's hand once more. Was the skin at the centre of her palm darker than normal? "We need to wake her to find out what happened when she went through that door."

"She should wake at any moment, especially with you fussing about her like a mother hen," Nari said.

Varlan stifled a yawn as Dara's keen stirred heavy around them again. Her pale eyes widened as she looked from Agnes to Nari. She then settled them on Varlan. "I can't hear her dream anymore." There was an edge of fear in her tone that set the hairs on the back of Varlan's neck on end.

"What do you mean you can't hear her dream?" Bran asked.

"Agnes's dreams are always loud. If she's still asleep, I should be able to hear her."

Nari's magic washed over them in a smooth heat. "She's fine, physically at least. Why don't you lot go and get a few hours of actual sleep? I'll keep an eye on her."

"But I want to—"

"Come on, Dara." Bran ushered a reluctant-looking Dara towards the door.

The girl paused at the threshold and studied Agnes, her keen swelling out in a heavy throb. After a moment, she continued after Bran with the door snapping shut behind them.

"You too. That cunning mind of yours doesn't work as well when it's sleep deprived," the healer said as she settled into the chair Dara had vacated.

When Varlan didn't move, her mouth pulled into a frown and her blue eyes flashed in that same way his mother's did when she was about to scold him. "She's fine. I probably just made her dose of sleeping tonic a bit stronger than necessary."

"You never get your formulas wrong."

Her frown deepened. "Go and get some sleep. I don't have to force a tonic down your throat to make you, you know?" She lifted a hand and her keen settled over him like a walm blanket.

His bones began to ache and his thoughts became muddled as his eyelids grew heavy. He pushed back against her keen, and a small smile broke through her frown.

"Your mother always was a stubborn arse as well. Fine. Don't follow my advice, but stop standing there and scowling at her. It isn't going to make her wake any faster."

Varlan moved from the bedside and settled down with his shoulders against the wall. He folded one ankle over the other and his arms across his chest as he rested his head back. Slowly, he let his keen roll over Agnes again, checking for signs of Idir's rot. But he could feel nothing, not even the inquisitive flutter of her own magic. He started to get to his feet.

"She's fine," Nari muttered, and the steady warmth of her healing magic brushed over him, bringing a thick drowsiness once more.

He settled again and closed his eyes. "If anything changes—"

"Grandmother preserve me, go to sleep. I promise I will wake you if *anything* happens." There was a note of humour under Nari's exasperated tone.

Sleep was slow to take him, but when it did it came with a seed of dread and a flicker of red magic souring everything it touched.

CHAPTER NINE

DEANA

Her mouth was bone dry; at odds with the clammy damp that covered her skin. Grit clouded her vision but there was enough light coming in the window to tell her it was midday. Which midday she wasn't certain. It felt like an eon since Rami had first tied her to the bed. Several times he had untied her and taken her outside so she could relieve herself and wash the stickiness of fevered dreams from her cheeks. The first time she had tried to escape, exploiting a momentary lapse in his dogged supervision. He had chased her along the beach; the broiling silence that shrouded him making it impossible for her to use her song. She had collapsed in the shallows, a flash of pearly white scales the last thing she saw before Rami hurled her over his shoulder and dragged her back to her room.

She hadn't attempted to escape again.

Samir had visited her occasionally, trying to coerce her into trusting Astrid. He had insisted that it was only for her own good and that if she would just cooperate, she would see that she and Astrid wanted the same thing. Deana might have found that easy to believe in the beginning, but not now. Regardless of Astrid's insistence that she and Idir were enemies, that she only wanted to stop him and get her revenge for an eon of torment, her goals were not the same as Deana's. Astrid would stop at nothing to enact her vengeance. Not even the destruction of the entire isles would sway her from her course.

A shadow fell over Deana, and Rami's silence brushed along the edge of her song. The sickly glow of his sunken eyes moved to her bound hands, and he tilted his head as though in question.

She gave him a tiny nod.

He reached for the rope, then drew his fingers back and pursed his lips, his brows rising slightly. It was a look that she had come to realise meant, *Don't try anything stupid.*

Even if she had been inclined to attempt another escape, her legs were stiff from disuse. And if she couldn't outrun him when she was at full strength, there was no way she was getting away from him in her current state.

"I'll behave," she said, the huskiness of her voice sounding foreign to her own ears.

He gave one very slow nod, then untied the rope and hauled her to her feet.

The room spun and she fell against him as her empty stomach flipped and a bilious lump rose in her throat. The oppressive pressure of his silence closed over her, and the lump shifted, making her mouth water and her stomach heave. Nothing came up. There wasn't much in her stomach anyway, except a little tea and a clump of heavy bread and fruit. The meagre rations Astrid had deemed 'prisoner food'.

Once the room stopped spinning away from her, she took a step back from him. Rami watched her warily but didn't move to grab her again. He indicated the door and gave a small grunt.

She walked towards it cautiously until she was sure her shaky legs wouldn't betray her. The stairs were another challenge. She leant heavily against the wall and shuffled down each step slowly. Astrid and Samir's voices came from the way of the kitchen, but

Rami steered her towards the closest door that led outside.

The salt-scented breeze coming off the waves was crisp, and it stirred the thin coils of her hair around her face making them tickle and itch. She moved away from Rami to relieve her protesting bladder behind the small bushes not far from the door. When she was done, she returned to Rami who nodded to the bucket of water he had collected. She rinsed her hands in it then splashed her face, letting out a small sigh, then she touched her damp fingers to the tangled mess of her hair and winced. Astrid had brushed it once while Deana lay flat on her stomach under the oppressive weight of Rami's silence, but that had been at least two days ago and the curls had begun to mat together in places.

As Deana attempted to pick some of the bigger snarls from her hair with her fingers, she glanced back towards the fort. Would Astrid allow her to brush it, or would she shear it close to the scalp like she had threatened to?

A grunt from Rami drew her attention to him. He reached out and touched the back of Deana's hand, stilling her fingers as they teased out another knot. With another grunt he dug into the folds of the tattered cloak he wore, regardless of the weather, and pulled out a small object. He made a noise almost like a hum as he stroked his fingers along it before pressing it into her hand.

It was an ivory comb with a run of ten wide tines like a row of long, gleaming teeth. The top edge had been carved to resemble a woman with a long tail somewhere between that of a fish and a dolphin. Her hair was flowing back over her shoulders as though she was swimming against a current.

Rami glanced at the door to the ruined fort then at Deana's hair, before he started towards the edge of the beach and waved her to follow.

She studied his back and then the comb, testing the end of one of the tines against the pad of her thumb. If she was fast enough, she might be able to stab it into the side of his neck. She shook the thought away; she wasn't strong enough to do any real damage and making him mad was not a good idea.

He knelt beneath one of the leaning palms that shaded a particularly pretty section of the beach and pointed to the ground in front of him.

"You want me to sit with you?"

He gave one of those long, slow nods and pointed to the comb before he held out his hand.

Deana's fingers tightened on the comb momentarily, but she handed it to him and sat where he had indicated.

He settled behind her, murmuring something inaudible before his fingers took hold of her hair and she flinched.

He gave a low rumble and waved the comb so she could see it just at the corner of her vision. Once she relaxed again, he began to meticulously pick through the tangles. He wasn't gentle but it seemed to be more from clumsiness than spite, and after a while he started making a soft rumbling sound that reminded her of a song her mother used to sing.

Eventually, the low rumbling hum stopped, and he patted her on the shoulder before moving to sit beside her. He stroked his fingers along the carvings on the comb before he held it out to her.

When she took it from him, he tilted his chin in the direction of the fort and pressed a finger to his lips as he gave one of those slow nods.

"Why—"

Rami shook his head and mimed being quiet again then he pushed her hands and the comb towards her chest.

"Alright." She tucked the comb into her pocket and turned to study the glittering surface of the ocean.

Was this another trick of Astrid's? Another attempt to get Deana on her side? As far as Deana could tell, Rami was Astrid's puppet with very little autonomy of his own—if any. He seemed utterly loyal to her, or maybe it was the iron-tight grip with which she held his magical leash that ensured that loyalty. Either way, the sudden kindness he was showing Deana was unexpected and more than a little unnerving.

She glanced sideways through her lashes at him. His form was ridged, his fists clenched on his knees as he stared at the horizon. He had been human once. An easy fact to forget when faced with his monstrous visage and the world-consuming silence that rolled off him in waves. Was this sudden change in attitude some of that long-lost humanity shining through?

Astrid's song preceded the crisp rasp of her boots on the sand. She stopped in front of Deana, the smile on her lips doing nothing to soften the sharpness of her eyes. That seething anger in her gaze shattered the resemblance to Bran's, leaving only the fathomless dark blue in common.

"Are you in the mood to cooperate today?" she asked in a clipped tone.

"I—"

Rami's silence flooded over her as his fingers caught her arm, the action hidden from Astrid by the slight angle of Deana's body. He had barely moved. His eyes were still trained on the horizon, his face completely expressionless, but his hold tightened a fraction against her skin before he released her.

She turned her attention back to Astrid, who was watching her with her arms folded over her chest.

"Well?" Astrid asked when Deana still didn't answer.

Deana dropped her gaze and then ran her tongue along her lip.

"Back to your—"

"Alright."

"Sorry? I didn't quite catch that."

"Alright, I'll cooperate. What do you want me to do?"

The smile that moved across Astrid's mouth dropped the bottom out of Deana's stomach. "Let's continue our practice from before. Only this time try to avoid half drowning yourself." Astrid gestured to the waves.

Deana got slowly to her feet. The farther she moved away from Rami, the easier it was for her to summon her song. It moved over her, cocooning her in its comforting folds and soothing the fear that had started to dig with numbing claws up the back of her neck.

As she neared the edge of the reaching whitewash, she pushed her song forward and the waves parted leaving a wedge of wet sand in front of her. But the lack of proper sleep and nutrition had depleted her physical reserves and holding the current was difficult. It nearly slipped out of her grip, but she tightened it at the last minute and moved forward, imploring her song to hold back the tidal surge that was building.

Two more steps and a large wave battered against the edge of her magic. It sent a ricochet of force up her arms and down to her toes, shattering her hold and sending cold water splashing up her legs.

"Concentrate," Astrid growled beside her.

Deana bit down on her retort and tried again, but her song was resistant. Instead, she attempted to pull the water towards her. It responded at once, twisting around her in an elegant arc before collapsing back on itself and sending a spray of glittering droplets into the air. She repeated the process, her smile growing as the sun caught the spray in a shining rainbow.

"Stop playing and focus," Astrid reprimanded.

The ocean was nipping at her calves. Its song was joyful today. It coiled around Deana's song, its tempo infectious and making her feel almost foolhardy.

"Deana." Astrid's growl came with a push of her song, the dark seed of shrouded-one magic lurking under the otherwise alluring tune.

The water at their feet gave a turbulent splash as though responding to the quiver of fear that the familiar notes of the shrouded song stirred deep in Deana's core. She swallowed and drew a breath, closing her eyes as she heard Bran's voice across the back of her mind: *'In ... two, three, four ... out ... two—'*

Astrid snapped her fingers in front of Deana's nose, shattering the memory. "Again."

Deana studied the waves once more before flicking a look at Astrid. If Deana lashed out with her magic, would Astrid be at her mercy, or would it just enrage the other woman? She hadn't seen Astrid control the ocean, but she was a shrouded one like Idir and he certainly could, at least to some extent.

"If you would rather go back to your room, that can be arranged."

Deana turned her full focus to the ocean once more. Even if she could catch Astrid off guard, Rami was right there and though he had shown her that strange kindness earlier, she couldn't count on that with Astrid so close.

With another deep breath, she lifted her hand towards the waves and let her song cut through them.

White sand stretched in a sensuous curve ahead of her. It was flanked on one side by a glittering blue ocean and the emerald tapestry of the jungle on the other. This wasn't her dreamscape, or if it was, it wasn't a part she had visited before. Grandmother Ocean was beside her as usual, her eyes hidden beneath a scrap of scarlet cloth. The fist of knotted wood at the top of her staff was partially open, a glowing, emerald-coloured crystal trapped within the web of gnarled fingers. She wore an armoured breastplate made of bleached coral over a crimson shirt, and the skirts swirling around her legs were a mixture of red and wheaten-coloured linen strips.

"Where are we?" Deana asked.

The goddess regarded the landscape around them, the shell

beads and bones adorning her braided locks shifting against each other and making a soft music as she moved. "You know where we are," she finally said, the many layers of her voice sweeping over Deana and leaving a soft swell of echoes across her mind.

"This isn't my dreamscape." Not only did she not recognise it, she felt at her core that she didn't belong here.

A proud smile rolled across the goddess's lips. "Very observant, but you should know that the fabric of dreams and death is liminal. And sometimes when one dreamer brushes up against another, they can find themselves ... entwined." A melancholy seemed to settle over the goddess as she turned her attention to a dark shape farther along the beach. "This landscape has not been visited in an eon. I almost forgot how loud its dreamer could dream."

Deana studied the shadowy figure. It appeared, at least from this distance, to be a man kneeling in the sand. His size and shape almost reminded her of Gendry, but there was something about the set of those broad shoulders that was familiar in other ways. He was too broad to be her brother—

A note of sorrow throbbed through her song at that thought. Kai was dead; he would never dream again. Still, she couldn't quite place the familiarity, so she slowly approached the man.

When she got closer, it became clear that the man was not alone. He was kneeling behind a woman with smooth brown skin and dark almond-shaped eyes. She was singing softly as he pulled a white comb through her ebony locks.

As though sensing Deana's presence, the man looked up. He had warm bronze skin and the shape of his mouth and jaw hinted at Osmarian heritage. But it was his eyes that shocked her. They were a similar warm golden-brown shade to Varlan's and swimming with a deep intelligence, so different from the blank pools of glowing yellow-green magic she was used to.

Was this truly Rami? There was an almost rugged beauty about his features and her mind couldn't completely equate this face with the gaunt one he now wore.

She took another step closer, and the woman stopped singing—her dark eyes widening as blood bloomed across her chest.

The world seemed to tilt out from under Deana's feet and when it righted itself again the scene had shifted. The man, Rami, was now kneeling on bloodstained sand, the comb clutched tight in his fist as another woman stood behind him. Her midnight blue eyes were sharp with rage and her fair hair gleamed in the sunlight. She lifted a wicked golden knife, a gloating smile curving across her mouth. The blade flashed as she opened the man's throat, and his blood splashed the sand—

The rope around Deana's wrists prevented her from sitting up as she jolted awake. It was the dead of night and Rami's oppressive presence was still in the room, but he seemed to be sleeping. As she drew a series of deep breaths to chase the remnants of the dream away, she tested her bound wrists. Had he tied her looser than normal? She glanced in his direction again, but his head was lowered, and she couldn't see the glow of his eyes in the darkness. If he really was asleep, perhaps now was her chance to make an escape. If she could make it to the boat Astrid kept stored on the other side of the fort, then she might be able to flee the island the same way she had fled Lethata.

Carefully, she worked her wrists until she managed to wrench one of her hands free. She chanced another look in Rami's direction; still asleep.

The rush of prickles from the disuse of her fingers didn't stop her from fumbling at the second knot until she loosened it enough to slip its hold too. Her heart pounded in her chest as she slid from the bed, begging her tired legs not to protest. She moved to the window and studied the drop. It wouldn't be a pretty landing; she was doubtful that she could pull it off without breaking bones.

She scanned the room again. There was the length of rope Rami used to tie her to the bed, but it wasn't long enough to reach the ground even if there was something to anchor it to. Rami moved, and she made a mad dive for the bed.

His glowing eyes studied her, and his mouth twitched into what she guessed passed as a smile. He pressed his finger to his lips and moved to the window. Once there, he turned back to face her and then pointed to her and then out the window again.

She shook her head. "I wasn't—"

He held both his hands out, palms towards her, and shook his head. Then he pointed out the window for a third time and gave her a slow nod.

"Are you ... are you helping me escape?"

His eyes widened and he touched his finger to his lips again.

"It's too far," she whispered, edging closer.

He frowned and then crossed to the door, waving for her to follow. He opened it slowly, and Deana winced when the hinges gave a soft groan.

"Why are you helping me? If Astrid finds out ..."

He gently tapped her temple and gave her a long look, the glowing orbs of his eyes flickering almost like candlelight. A deep note of sorrow ran through Deana's song as she held his unnerving gaze. She still couldn't equate the man from the dream with this face, but she sensed that somewhere deep he still lingered. Or perhaps it was simply a tiny part of him that Astrid had failed to corrupt. That realisation sent a quiver through her; there was no way she could know the truth of how Rami had become the creature he now was, but at the centre of her soul she *knew* that Rami's loyalty had not been given freely.

He broke her gaze, leaving a feeling of unsteadiness rolling over her, and then opened the door wider and stepped into the hall.

She followed him down the stairs and out the side door, barely daring to breathe until the star-dotted midnight sky stretched wide above them. He led her to the beach and threw something into the water. A patch of soft teal light appeared on the surface seconds before a head of dark hair broke it. The woman settled her pale silver-green eyes on Deana and then Rami, to whom she gave a single nod.

"Hello, little one," she said as she turned her gaze back to Deana.

"H-Hello," Deana replied.

"Come," the woman said, waving towards the water in front of her. "You do not have long before the damned one wakes and discovers you missing."

"I don't understand." She glanced at Rami, but he was already heading back towards the fort.

He stopped at the edge of the sand and gave her one of those long, slow nods.

"I will take you to Mintura," the woman said.

"Mintura?" Deana turned back to her. "No, I want to return to my friends."

"It is not safe." Something flashed in her pale gaze. "But they will find you when the time is right. And there are answers to questions you haven't yet thought to ask. Answers that you will find in the shrine of the forgotten."

"But—"

"It's now or never, little one. If the damned one finds you here, her wrath will be formidable."

"Why are you helping me?"

"I will answer that question once we reach our destination."

The woman held her hands out as the door to the fort slammed opened, making Deana jump. Astrid let out a yell, and Deana leapt forward, splashing through the shallows until her hands met those of the woman.

Her stomach twisted in a way that reminded her of travelling through the portal with Bran, then a bright teal light blinded her as her body was dragged into the deep.

CHAPTER TEN

BRAN

A crumbling watchtower nestled amid a wall of ragged cliffs marked the coastline of Splade's Watch. This close to the island the air was thick with sound; waves slamming against the foot of the rock face, sending a hiss of spray into the air, and seabirds shrieking and squabbling as they plummeted into the water to chase down a meal.

"Do you think Deana is in there?" Kiki asked, as she and Pippa joined Bran at the side of the ship.

Bran touched his fingertips to the enchanted stone hanging around his neck. Marcus's magic was fainter than it had been even a day ago, the subtle pull that had been leading them to Deana non-existent. "I wish I could say for sure," Bran said as he turned his attention to Kiki.

She had cropped her hair during their stay at Weeper's Cove. Where it had once danced down her back in long chestnut waves like her sister's, it now sat in a shaggy mess about her ears. It suited her. The haunted seriousness that had settled behind her blue gaze did not. She had been tight-lipped about what had happened during her imprisonment on Armada, but Bran could guess, and the thought set a flicker of hot anger burning in the centre of his chest.

"If she's not here, we'll find her," Pippa said, but even her usually bright tone was flat as though she was trying to convince them of a truth she didn't quite believe herself.

Between Deana's disappearance and Agnes's enchanted slumber, the already frayed emotions of the group had started to break. Dara had barely left Agnes's side; she just sat watching her with an owlish stare. She wouldn't move even to eat unless Nari prompted her and then she would return to her vigil immediately once she was done. Varlan was prowling about the ship, the dark mood that dogged his steps making him tense and prone to snap. Only Wes seemed to be able to avoid the full brunt of his wrath. Even Wren and Gendry were at each other's throats. Their normal playful back and forth had become heated and terse. Rufus claimed they had all been cursed, they had stayed too long in the company of the ghosts at Weeper's Cove, and something had attached itself to the ship. Bran wished it was as easy as a curse—a curse could be broken—but what had befallen the ship and her crew was simply a cloud of bitter defeat.

"We're going to edge around the north side of the island," Gendry said as he joined Bran and twins. "We have to be mindful of the reef, but there's a small inlet where we can anchor out of sight of the outpost. Wren thinks it best if only a few of us leave the ship."

"I'll go," Kiki said.

"Now, lass, you've—"

"No, Gen. I'm going. I am not some porcelain trinket that will shatter."

"Kiki," Pippa started, but at a sharp glare from her sister she stopped.

It was strange to see the twins acting so discordant with each other. Before Kiki's capture they had been almost like a single entity.

"Wren and I have already discussed it. Varlan, Bran, Wes and I will be the ones going ashore," Gendry said with a cautious glance in Kiki's direction.

She folded her arms over her chest.

"I don't see why Kiki can't come with us," Bran said, which earned him a warm smile from Kiki and exasperated looks from both Pippa and Gendry. "She knows her own limitations."

"If Kiki is going, I am too," Pippa said, folding her arms to match Kiki's tense stance.

Gendry shook his head, but an amused smile split his beard. "Fine, let's take half the ship, shall we? But you can be the ones to tell Wren."

"Tell me what, my love?" Wren asked as she joined them.

"Kiki and Pippa are coming ashore with us," Bran answered when Gendry didn't.

Wren planted her hands on her hips. Somehow, whenever she did that, she seemed a full foot taller than her stout five feet. Her rust-coloured ringlets were secured under a turquoise scarf that made her dusty blue eyes seem brighter. Her keen crackled over Bran, leaving the hairs on his arms standing on end. "I think that's a good idea," she said after a few moments.

"See, girls, I told you—you what?" Gendry turned his gaze to the captain, and she blinked sweetly at him.

"If anything happens at that outpost, it won't hurt to have more firepower." She grinned and flicked a look at Pippa, who rolled her eyes.

"Really, Wren?"

"It wasn't intentional," Wren chuckled, but she sobered quickly. "More mages in a situation that could turn sour is never a bad idea."

That wasn't exactly true. In fact, Bran could think of a multitude of situations where more mages were the last thing you wanted, but he wasn't going to point that out while Wren seemed to be in the best mood she'd been in for the last few days.

"Well, off with the pair of you to get ready. It won't take us long to find a suitable place to anchor once we clear the reef," Wren said, waving the twins away before she turned her attention to Bran. "Any change?"

He shook his head. "Marcus's magic is still there but the pull is completely gone."

"You don't think ..." Gendry drew a heavy breath as though he couldn't bare finishing the question.

Bran drew the stone out and studied it. Marcus's magic shifted over his fingers like a delicate brush of smoke easily scattered in the breeze. Before, the magic had been strong—an insistent tug behind his navel, pulling him in the direction of Deana. "She's not dead." He was certain of that. If she was, then the enchantment Marcus had placed on the stone would have most likely died along with her. Something else was shielding her. He let his keen roll over the stone once more. Beneath the gentle hiss of Marcus's magic was the deep throb of the protection spell that had originally been placed on it. The enigmatic magic of the Between shifted in ticklish fingers up his spine and he drew his keen into himself. "She is not dead," he repeated. "I am sure of it. But someone definitely doesn't want her found."

"We'll find her," Wren said, touching her fingers lightly to Gendry's arm, "but best put it to the back of your minds for now. You'll both need clear heads when you go ashore. There's no telling what is waiting for you inside the watch."

Gendry nodded then leant across and kissed the top of Wren's head. "We'll be careful, my love."

Kiki seemed full of nervous energy as their small boat drifted away from the Queen and into the shallows at the edge of the island. As they scraped onto the stony beach, she leapt out and splashed to the shore. When she was standing on dry land, her keen stirred and the water that soaked her pants from the thighs down pulled away from the cloth and dropped to the ground in a neat circle around her now completely dry boots.

"Show off," Pippa muttered as she joined her sister.

Kiki simply shrugged.

"Alright," Gendry said as he, Wes, and Varlan joined the twins and Bran after securing the boat. "There is an entry to the caverns not far from here. The main camp was back towards the watchtower on a plateau that overlooks the lagoon. We'll have to navigate the caverns until we find a tunnel branching upwards. It should be marked like this." He knelt and drew a small V-shaped symbol on the ground. "It can be easy to miss if you don't know what you're looking for," he said as he stood once more. "It's best if we move as silently as possible once we're inside the caverns as sound carries farther than you'd think along the tunnels, and we will want to maintain the element of surprise in case Idir *is* the reason for the outpost going dark. Any questions?"

They all shook their heads, and then with a nod Gendry started across the pebble-strewn beach towards the thicket of vegetation from which the sharp cliffs that ringed the island rose.

Once they were inside the tunnels, Bran fell into step beside Gendry with the twins behind them and Wes and Varlan at the back of the group. Bran summoned a mage light, keeping it low to the ground and close to their feet as they walked to avoid the violet glow from alerting anyone farther along the tunnel to their presence. The hairs on the back of his neck prickled as the light bobbed over the smooth floor of the passage, but he wasn't certain if it was the feeling that they were walking into a trap or the soul-scraping sensation of something not entirely human watching them from the shadows.

He had become aware of the spirit almost the moment they stepped out of the watery pool of sunlight that edged into the mouth of the first cavern, and it had been stalking them ever since. It hadn't approached, but it stood out to Bran's keen-sense like a burr in cloth. The weight of its stare was inquisitive rather than malicious, but curiosity could quickly turn to wrath when it came to spirits. Best to be wary and not draw attention to it—not that any of the others would likely be aware of its presence even if he did.

The tunnel they were following turned to the right and then after a few paces they came to a thin branching path that would force them to fall into single file. The main tunnel continued straight, the smooth walls reflecting a wash of purple light back at them as Bran sent his mage light forward to investigate.

"No marker," Gendry said as he crouched and ran his fingers around the mouth of the branching passage. "Can any of you mages feel anything?"

A collection of sensations rushed over Bran as both the twins and Varlan sent their keen-sense out to examine the diverging path. The heavy weight of Wes's warden abilities followed at a more sedate pace; it left a feeling of numbness at the edge of Bran's keen-sense that made him roll his shoulders.

"Nothing that would indicate a hidden marker, if that is what you were asking," Varlan said as he drew his keen back into himself, leaving a stirring of cloying fingers over the back of Bran's neck.

"There is definitely something that way though," Pippa said, indicating the wider tunnel, and Kiki nodded.

"That way it is then," Gendry said and started forward again.

Something shifted in the shadows along the branching passage— a flash of light too quick to make sense of—and then the nagging pressure of something forgotten throbbed across Bran's mind. He rubbed his forehead to try and shift the sensation and started after the others who had drifted ahead.

'Wait,' an ethereal voice cooed from the darkness, and he turned back towards the passage.

He studied the shadows as his keen-sense drifted out. He found the edges of the spirit that had been stalking them but nothing else. With another shake of his head, he started after Gendry once more.

'We know who you are, little foundling.'

He froze and glanced back over his shoulder.

'Yes.' There was a sense of sheer delight in the voice's tone as it hissed through his mind. *'Come find us and we can tell you. Better yet, we can* show *you.'*

A shape shifted in the darkness; one shadow peeling away from the rest and stalking forward. Something landed on Bran's shoulder startling him seconds before a heavy numbness smoothed over his entire body.

"Come on. We're losing the others," Wes said as he turned Bran away from the passage. The warden's bright hazel gaze studied the shadows at the mouth of side tunnel before he met Bran's eye and gave a nod.

"There was something there," Bran's thoughts were thick and sluggish, almost like he had had too much to drink.

"There's been something following us since we entered the tunnels," the warden stated.

Bran cocked an eyebrow at him.

"You don't have to be a necromancer to know when you're being watched."

"This wasn't the same spirit that has been stalking us. It was ... different." He wasn't sure how to describe it, but the voice had felt familiar. He glanced back at the passage,

"It's not a good idea to split the group before we reach the outpost and find out what's going on here."

Wes was right, and Bran knew better than to follow unknown spirits on a simple whim, but they'd said—*Don't be an idiot*, he chided himself. Spirits were known to say anything you wanted to hear in order to get what they desired.

They caught up to the others quickly. Varlan had taken point with Gendry, a pale pink mage light bobbing at their feet as the twins followed cautiously behind them.

Kiki glanced over her shoulder and gave Bran a small smile when they caught up. "Everything alright?" she whispered.

He nodded, and she turned around again to whisper something to Pippa.

They passed several more branching passages as they continued along the main tunnel. Each one was unmarked, and none had the same shifting darkness and echoing ethereal voice as that first one.

Finally, they came to a wider side passage that did bear a small V-shaped mark at about knee height on the opening. Gendry started along the new tunnel, waving for them to follow. Several paces along, the floor became a modest slope upwards.

After a while the tunnel widened again and the darkness around them developed into more of a grey gloom as light filtered in from farther ahead. The light came with a cool breeze that carried the unmistakable scent of decaying flesh.

The smell grew stronger as they rounded a bend and stepped out onto a wide plateau that overlooked the lagoon at the island's centre. The tip of a thin spire of stone stood in the middle of the dark turquoise water, but closer, the ground was covered in dark patches of dried blood and the debris of what appeared to be small huts. Strewn amidst the destruction were bodies, left where they had fallen, some still with weapons sticking out of them and others face down as though they had been slain as they attempted to flee. The source was agitated, leaving an ache at Bran's temples and an uneasy feeling in his stomach. He'd felt this before at Kalhanna where the source was fragile even years after the tragedy that had claimed the lives of nearly every mage and warden there.

As they drew closer to the bodies, Kiki planted her feet and grabbed both her sister's and Wes's arms, pulling them up short. "I don't like this," she said, rolling her shoulders as her keen stirred the air around them.

"It's not a pretty sight, but—"

"It's not the bodies, Gen," Pippa said.

Gendry glanced at Bran, a question in his eyes.

"The source," Bran whispered and then cleared his throat. "It feels ..." He studied the corpses as he searched for the right word.

"Violated," Varlan said.

"Yes, exactly." Bran nodded.

"We'll be careful," Gendry said and moved towards the closest body. As his booted toes drew level with the limp fingers of the partially decayed hand, the source tightened savagely, turning Bran's insides to water as a lump of bile rose in his throat.

"Gendry, look out!" he shouted as the hand lashed out and grabbed Gendry's ankle.

"Shadow's teeth!" Gendry kicked his foot free and backed up.

The body lifted itself from the ground and inspected the knife sticking out of its ribs. It gave it a savage tug, wrenching it free, and then hefted it before turning its dead-eyed stare on them.

"Reanimations?" Wes asked, drawing the sword at his hip.

"I wish," Bran said as his keen built at his core. Standard reanimations he could handle; drive out the spirit possessing the body and they would collapse like puppets without strings. But these undead were another thing entirely. The magic controlling them was intricately woven and stronger than usual necromancy. And depending on the mage who created them, they could be persistent—meaning they could keep reanimating until the body was completely destroyed.

"If they're not reanimations, what are they?" the warden asked.

"Wraiths," Bran replied and let the magic he had allowed to build out.

Threads of purple necromancy shimmered over the closest bodies, causing them to lurch to a halt. The magic burrowed into them, trying to find the animating spirit and drive it out, but there was nothing to find; only the lingering sense of something dark and churning that brought the stench of death and stagnant salt water to his senses.

Swallowing back the gagging lump in his throat, he tried again but the result was the same.

One of the wraiths made a lunge for Bran, and the source around him grew hot as the decaying flesh became shrouded in bright orange flames. The wraith let out a rasping screech and spun away from Bran to charge towards Pippa. It knocked into several of its brethren, setting the ragged clothing hanging from them alight.

As the wraith drew within striking distance of Pippa, Wes lashed out, his sword neatly cleaving the head from the burning body.

Pippa lifted her hands, and the source grew hotter as several more wraiths burst into flames.

A gnarled hand grabbed Bran's arm in a vice-tight grip, and he turned to meet the milky-eyed stare of a wraith as its teeth snapped towards him. He shoved it back and grabbed hold of the knife at his belt. Cold magic danced over him as the blade lengthened. The dark metal shone with a sheen like oil on water and sang through the air as Bran drove it towards the exposed neck of the wraith. The abomination twisted at the last moment and the blade bit into the fetid flesh of its shoulder, eliciting an enraged shriek.

"That's quite enough!" a voice called, and the remaining wraiths immediately collapsed to the ground like discarded toys.

Bran turned towards the voice.

Stalking towards them from the far end of the plateau was a woman with dark skin and bone-white hair. A cold cloud of necromancy rolled forward but there was something oddly familiar about it. All necromancy felt similar, but the keen of each individual mage was nuanced and had its own unique signature, and Bran shouldn't recognise this woman's keen when he had never met her before.

"I know your soul," the woman said as she drew close enough for Bran to note the deep violet shade of her eyes. This close, the glowing purple coral that grew from the skin of her bare shoulders and studded her arms was also apparent. It wasn't like the coral that grew from the shrouded ones, and her keen didn't carry the same taint that theirs did.

"Who are you and why did you attack us?" Varlan asked as he stepped beside Bran, a sword lifted between him and the woman and his keen smoothing across the back of Bran's neck.

"I am Mala, and I didn't attack you—my guards did. They cannot discern the difference between one of the damned king's lackeys and a common trespasser. A simple mistake."

"Mala?" Varlan's eyes narrowed as he studied the woman. "The guardian of lost souls?"

The woman made a small, amused sound. "That was my title once, before the damned king took that which was not his to take, and doomed mortal and god alike."

"Hold up, you're an actual goddess?" Pippa said, taking a step forward so she was level with Bran and Varlan.

"Not exactly a goddess, but that is a concept your mortal mind can understand. I was a handmaiden of Grandmother Ocean. One of many. And as your companion has already stated, I was a guardian of the lost, specifically those lost at sea, and I would gather their souls and guide them to the Isle of the Dead. But that filth, the damned king, stole my power thinking he could use it to claim himself an army with which to pillage the resting place of the Grandmother herself." The vitriol in her tone as she spoke of Idir sent a shiver down Bran's spine. He wasn't sure exactly what she was, but like Vatura, the matron of Weeper's Cove, she wasn't human nor was she any kind of spirit he recognised.

"What do you mean, you know Bran's soul?" Kiki asked as she joined her sister.

Mala's violet gaze shifted between Kiki and Bran, and then a small twitch quirked the corner of her lips. "It is a soul that I had thought lost to the seas of time, one that was promised to me and then stolen away."

"How is that possible?" Bran asked.

Her bone-white brows flicked upwards. "Have your memories been taken?" Her gaze flicked to Varlan and narrowed.

"If they have, it wasn't me," the mind mage said.

"What are you doing here?" Gendry asked, drawing her attention to him.

"My sisters and I were sleeping deep within the tower at the belly of this place. The damned king sought to finish what he had started an eon ago when he trapped us there, but he loosened the bars of the cage enough that I could slip through and drive him back. Now, I wait, guarding my sisters so he cannot claim their powers as he has mine."

"Did you kill the people who lived here?"

She cast a sad glance over the bodies. "Only those who were followers of the damned king. He is responsible for the deaths of the others." Her melancholy shifted and she settled a sharp-eyed gaze on Bran once more. "What do you want here, death bringer?"

Death bringer? That was what Abigail, the matron spirit of the Hartswood grove, called Nea due to her ability to kill by tearing souls from their bodies. But Nea had that power because she was a deathborn. Bran's keen may have been tainted by Nea's and thus taken on some of the traits of hers, but it was not an ability he had been born with or was very skilled in.

"We are looking for a friend of ours," he replied. "We thought Idir ... the damned king, may have brought her here." He pulled the charmed protection stone out of his pocket, and Mala's eyes widened.

"It is true then, that the Granddaughter has been found."

"Granddaughter?" Pippa and Kiki said together.

"The mortal who wields the power of the seas," Mala said as though it was obvious. "If she has joined the damned king's side then all hope is lost."

"She hasn't joined him willingly, but she was taken and this was supposed to help us find her," Bran said, lifting the amulet. The small amount of magic still clinging to it seemed to falter for a moment.

Mala held her hand out. "May I see it?"

Bran placed the amulet on her open palm and the coral studding her skin grew brighter as her keen chilled the air, causing his breath to come out in a small cloud.

"Sejira has found her." A warm smile touched her lips, and she passed the stone back to Bran. "She will keep her safe from the damned."

"Who is Sejira?"

"The guardian of sailors. Follow her glowing fins and she will lead you safely through even the roughest seas, but ignore her warnings, and to the deep she will drag thee." Mala chuckled. "Mortals have such a fascinating way of describing that which they don't truly understand."

"Do you know where Sejira might have taken Deana?"

"Somewhere the damned cannot find her, somewhere that she can gain answers to the questions those of the living have forgotten."

Varlan made a sound, and Bran turned to him. "Mintura. There is a ruined temple to Vask the Forgotten One at the south end."

"Our business is concluded, then. There is nothing for you here." She turned away from them and stated walking back across the plateau. "I hope you find the Granddaughter, but be warned: Vask is not nearly as fond of visitors as I am."

"That's it then? Back to Mintura?" Gendry asked.

Bran examined the stone between his fingers. The magic was

still weak, and giving no indication of the direction they should go. "To Mintura, and hopefully we find her before any other god-kin decide to hide her again."

CHAPTER ELEVEN

#

Agnes was cold. Colder than she could remember having ever been before. The chill brought with it a darkness that pressed in on all sides so she couldn't even see her hand in front of her face. Her memories of how she got to this place were evasive, but flashes like the lingering shards of a dream, showed her a massive door of black stone with a glowing motif of coral and then the sensation of falling before the darkness closed in. Varlan had been there. And Bran too, at the end. He had shouted a warning before she fell.

She hugged her arms around herself to try and rub some warmth back into her body. If it wasn't so dark, she imagined she'd be able to see her breath misting the air. She focused on summoning a mage light. It flickered to life; gold and bronze strands of light twisting around each other with a thin thread of black at its core. But the light only lasted for a few shuddering seconds before the darkness ate it.

When she reached for her magic again to try and summon another light, something nudged at her. A bright prickling sort of sensation that was building at the centre of her chest. It almost felt like the pins and needles that preceded the trance that accompanied her magic, but this was different—hotter and more intense, like layers were peeling away. A snake shedding its skin when it became too tight.

That thought made the sensation intensify to the point that she could barely breathe. She pressed her fingers to her chest and inhaled deeply, forcing the cold air past the prickling lump.

A glow softened some of the darkness in a weak halo of warm golden light that seemed to be coming from within Agnes herself. She drew her fingers away from her chest. The tips were glowing with that same golden light as though she had dipped them in luminescent ink. But the bulk of the light wasn't coming from her fingertips; it was coming from the core of her being, pulsing in time with each beat of her heart.

A single clap sounded somewhere in the darkness, followed by a second, then a third. The slow rhythm continued until a ball of pink light striped with red and black bloomed to life before her. The ball of light drifted higher and higher until a space the size of a small room was illuminated in garish fuchsia light that clashed with the pool of gold radiating from her chest.

A tall, broad-chested man with dark brown skin stepped into the light. His hands were resting together as though he had been the one clapping. Pink coral studded the flesh of his right arm and fanned up the side of his neck and across his cheek. As he stepped closer, his coal-dark gaze settled on Agnes and a shrewd smile smoothed across his lips.

"Hello, Agnes," he said in a deep voice.

She fought the urge to retreat, swallowing down the lump of dread and forcing herself to meet his stare. "Idir?"

"Congratulations are in order; I never imagined you would find this place ... but then you had help. Perhaps I should thank Varlan. Were he not so persistent in his efforts to keep you safe from my daughter's childish attempt at control, then the full extent of your power would still be well beyond my reach."

A tingle stirred at her fingertips, and she clenched her fists to disperse the sensation. She couldn't afford to let her magic take over her senses now.

"Not the talkative type? So different from the sweet, trusting little girl you were when we first met. I'll forgive you for not remembering those days; after all, memories can be *slippery* things."

The prickle grew more insistent, and a thought flickered across the back of her mind. She needed a weapon, something to defend herself. She scanned the space around them, but aside from Idir, herself, and the pale flower petals strewn across the floor there was nothing. "What do you want from me?" she asked at last.

The corner of his mouth twitched, the skin pulling oddly around the coral embedded in his cheek. "I want your power and you are going to give it to me, without a fight. You are beyond the reach of meddling pests here, so be a good girl, and stay still. There will be only a moment of pain before sweet oblivion takes you." He stepped closer, lifting his coral-studded fingers towards her as though he would cup her cheek.

Agnes took a step back. The petals stirring around her feet seemed to gleam oddly in the light, almost like they were edged with polished metal. Her magic was white hot under the skin of her fingers, the world-stealing hiss of the trance a vibrating roar at the back of her mind. Why hadn't it taken over? Normally, the hot-cold prickle was the only warning she got before her magic stole into her body and she lost all autonomy to it. What was different here?

The tangy scent of warm metal filled the air and with that scent the rush of pins and needles grew unbearable.

Idir's smile deepened as he took another step, and then another. Each time he advanced, Agnes retreated until her back slammed against something cold and sleek.

The scaled hide of the colossal serpent.

Her fingers fanned across the ebony scales and the petals twisted in a flurry around her feet, making tinkling sounds like a litany of tiny bells.

Idir's reaching hands caught her shoulders and the cloying pull of his magic washed over her. "Relax, Agnes, it will all be over soon."

"Wait—" Her voice caught in her throat.

Idir drew back slightly but didn't release his grip; the scales beneath her palms warmed.

"This is my dreamscape, right? You have no power over me here!" She tried to fight free of his grip, but he held her pinned as his head tilted back and he let out an indulgent laugh.

"Oh, my dear, if only that were true. The moment you passed through the black door, you entered *my* world, and here, I am king." His magic pressed down hard, stealing into her mind and shredding the last of her resolve to ribbons as glittering fuchsia light exploded across her vision.

She lost all sense of who she was. A starlight-haired woman flashed before her; sweet-scented petals edged with gold and ebony steel brushed over her fingers in the breeze.

'Fight, my child,' a voice echoed across her mind.

"I can't," she whispered.

'You must!'

The voice was gone. Darkness started to close in. She lifted her fingers. The liquid gold at their tips was fading to a deep black.

No. She reached for her magic, but the prickle was growing distant.

"No!" she screamed and shoved back against him with all her might, both physical and magical.

Coral sliced open her palm, but she ignored the hot rush of pain and focused on her desire, her *need* for a weapon. The petals twisted into the air, wrapping themselves around her hand and forming into a sword of pure gold—the centre of the blade etched with strange black runes.

Idir had staggered back as her magic exploded out of her, but he regained his feet and moved towards her again, a look of sheer determination in his cruel eyes.

Agnes lifted the sword and drove the tip forward. The blow glanced off his coral-adorned arm, breaking some of the branching pieces and leaving a thin line of oily ichor on the blade.

Idir let out a roar of pain and rage as he sprang for her, but she twisted away and swung the sword in a wide arc. The blade hissed through empty air, and she teetered a few steps before she could correct her stance.

"You are only delaying the inevitable," Idir growled through his teeth. "Put that sword down before you hurt yourself."

"No—" Dark ropes of kelp erupted from the ground and grabbed her, pulling her off-balance. She lost her grip on the sword and it skittered across the floor, collapsing once more into a pile of gleaming petals.

Idir stalked towards her as she fought against the kelp. "Have you quite finished your experiment with futility?"

Agnes's heart pounded; her fingers groped in the petals, smearing them with blood as she reached for her magic once more. She had controlled it once; she could do it again. She had to.

The heavy sweetness of Idir's magic closed over her and pain shot through her mind.

She closed her eyes. A dark shape stalked across the back of her eyelids, gleaming claws screeching against the floor as it charged—

Idir released her and she opened her eyes. He was getting to his feet a short distance away, his furious gaze trained on the sleek beast of dark metal and glowing magic standing between them. Idir let out a frustrated yell, the garish light of his magic brightening the air around him.

The panther charged. Its claws dug into Idir's back as he turned to flee, then its jaws closed over his neck and clamped down. Idir's kicking legs suddenly stilled as his blood stained the floor.

The glowing eyes of the great cat met Agnes's before it collapsed into a pile of glittering petals.

Agnes sat back against the wall of scales behind her and let out a heavy breath, a sob catching in her throat.

'Now is not the time to fall apart,' the voice from before echoed across her mind. *'You will not be safe until you find your way back to yourself.'*

"How?" Agnes asked as she sat and studied the area around her.

With Idir gone, the ominous glow of his magic had dispersed and she was sitting once more in a small pool of golden light in an unrelenting sea of darkness.

'Follow the light.' There was a note of humour in the voice.

"What light?" Agnes stood and turned in a slow circle. The petals at her feet stirred, tinkling against each other as their metal edges caught the light, but otherwise the glow coming from her was the only light source around. "What light?" Agnes repeated.

The voice remained silent.

Agnes swallowed as a fresh lump of tears threatened. She would never find her way out of this place. She'd never see her father, or Deana, or Wes, or Nari, or ... Varlan again. She collapsed to the floor and pressed her hands into the petals as her despair rolled over her. Why did Idir want her power so badly? It was broken—useless to the one who wielded it.

"He can have it!" she yelled into the darkness. "You hear that, whoever you are? Idir can have my power—every last drop."

'Then you would let yourself be defeated before you have even begun.'

"What's the point in trying to keep it? Idir will just win in the end. It has brought me nothing but grief and pain."

'Oh, my dear child, how wrong you are. But if you would throw it away so easily, then I will take it from you.' There was something in the voice, a tone that almost sounded like a warning.

"Why do you want it?"

'It is mine to give and to take. If you are foolish enough to relinquish it to your enemy, then I will reclaim it.'

Agnes licked her lip. "Why does Idir want it so badly?"

No reply came.

"Typical," Agnes muttered.

A breeze buffeted Agnes, stirring the petals around her into a ticklish cloud.

'The damned one seeks that which was never meant to be his. He needs a key to a lock that cannot be picked. Such a key does not exist —it can only be created.'

A prickle started in Agnes's fingertips at the mention of the key, and she rubbed them together, but the trance was calm, holding back as though it were waiting for her to reach for it.

'Are you ready to stop wallowing in your sorrow?'

Follow the light, the voice had said. Agnes studied the petals around her once more. They seemed to be glowing, some brighter than others. She picked one up and held in front of her. Despite the thin bead of metal that circled its edge, it was soft and pliable. As she studied it, a shimmer of light rolled over its surface.

"Follow the light," she whispered and focused on summoning a mage light. The little orb flickered to life beside her and then abruptly extinguished. How were the petals and Agnes herself glowing when the darkness consumed everything else?

The fingers pinching the petal itched and the trance pushed up against the back of her mind. Could she feed some of the magic that created her mage light into the petals? She focused on the one she held, pushing a little of her magic out through her fingertips and into it. A shimmer of light rolled over it and a sharp pain stabbed through her hand as the petal became a cup-like bloom the size of her palm. The flower let a sweet scent into the air, and she dropped it in shock. It floated gently to the ground and once it was nestled amongst the petals on the floor, it began to glow with a pulsing light. The pulsing became a single beam that rolled through the petals in a wave away from Agnes's feet and extended into the darkness.

"Follow the light," Agnes whispered and took a step forward.

A feeling of warmth rolled over her and she got the sense that whoever owned the mysterious voice was pleased with her. The feeling only grew as she stepped into the middle of the path of light and drew a breath, steeling herself for whatever challenges were waiting in shadows.

CHAPTER TWELVE

VARLAN

The detour to Splade's Watch had proved pointless. Just another thread in the tangled web that seemed to be growing more complex with each passing day. If he didn't sort out which threads were actually important soon then they would likely still be chasing their own tails when Idir eventually figured out how to raise Dumura and fuck the entire isles. Despite his rabid desire to leave the isles in his youth, Varlan had become rather fond of them in recent years, and he wasn't ready to just roll over and let a megalomaniac arsehole destroy them. And quite possibly the world. After all, he doubted Idir's thirst for power would end once he had the isles under his heel. He just wished he could figure out Idir's true motive. Maybe then—

Agnes stirred, her brow furrowing and her fingers tightening on the blanket as she murmured something under her breath. Varlan leant forward in his chair, his mage light following the movement and casting a rosy glow over her cheeks as she stilled again.

He sat back and let out a heavy sigh. None of them had been able to wake her and Dara couldn't access her dreams. She had said she could hear them but when she tried to enter them it was as though Agnes wasn't actually inside her own dreamscape anymore. But that was impossible, wasn't it? Unless Idir's trap had been to drag her somewhere her mind could be more easily manipulated or—no that made even less sense.

Nari was right; the lack of sleep was catching up with him. But Idir's need for Agnes and her particular type of creation magic was another of those threads that he'd been trying to untangle. Idir's obsession with Deana made sense, given her connection to Grandmother Ocean and her ability to control the sea—to devastating effect—but what did he need Agnes for?

She murmured again, and he leant forward, his fingers hovering a hair's width from her brow before he curled them back and let out one of those heavy sighs. He should have stayed instead of wiping her memory and running like a coward. He could tell himself he did it to keep the keystone hidden from Idir, to keep Agnes safe, but it hadn't kept her safe—if anything it had made things more dangerous for her. And now—

"Bright damn it, I'm a fucking idiot."

"You'll get no argument from me," Wes chuckled.

Varlan glanced towards the door where the warden was standing.

"I am under strict orders from Nari to tell you that you must go and eat and then get some sleep," he said as he stepped farther into the cabin. His gaze fell on Agnes and his smile dropped. "No change then?"

Varlan shook his head and pushed himself from the chair as Wes lit the candle on Wren's desk. The warm yellow flame changed Varlan's mage light from a soft rosy pink to a deep coral that reminded him of the insignia from the door in Agnes's dreamscape. With a flick of his hand, he extinguished the orb and headed for the door where he paused and looked back at Wes as he ran his finger down the doorframe. "If—"

"Varlan," Wes warned, his normally gentle tone edged with something akin to cold steel. "She'll be fine. But I promise if there is any change, I'll send for you. Now go and get some rest. Nari isn't the only one who is worried about you." His voice softened once more, and he gave Varlan a small smile as he settled into the chair.

With one last glance at Agnes, Varlan backed out of the captain's cabin and shut the door.

The sea was calm and the night sky above was a deep midnight blue dotted with stars—not a cloud in sight. Gendry, Rufus, and the twins were embroiled in a game of dice. Luca was beside their group, sipping a cup of tea while he watched their antics with mild interest. The knowledge that he had dosed Agnes with mage bane without initially telling her what it was and what it could do to her was still a sore point. But Wes was right that Varlan needed to let it go. Agnes had forgiven the healer. And yet Varlan still wondered if they would be in this predicament if—no. He was just looking for someone to take the blame when the fault lay solidly with Idir and to a lesser extent, Kent. He always knew Kent was an unstable bastard, but whatever plan he was cooking up with that war golem ... He shook his head and turned to scan the deck for Bran. He was not in sight, but Nari was a short distance away braiding Dara's hair. Wren fussed around them, her eyes flicking to the horizon every so often as the wild crackle of her storm magic charged the air around her. That paired with her agitation told Varlan that there was a spate of bad weather on the way. Elijah wasn't about either, so that suggested he was in the hold with Bran.

Varlan headed down the stairs to the hold and sure enough, Bran and Elijah were both there with their heads bent over a map laid out on the makeshift table.

"About time you surfaced," Elijah said without looking up as he traced a line of ink on the map.

"How's Agnes?" Bran asked.

"No change," Varlan replied. "What are you doing?" He dropped his gaze to the map. It appeared to be a rough sketch of Mintura. Elijah was in the process of drawing it, his keen rubbing up against Varlan's with a playful flutter.

"Trying to locate the shrine of Vask. Last any of us heard, it had been swallowed by the jungle," Elijah replied as he frowned at the parchment and dipped his quill in his ink. "Fitting really, for a god of the forgotten."

"It's somewhere around there." Varlan touched his finger to a spot. "At least that is what the mosaic on the floor of the grand pavilion showed. Can't say I have ever set foot in the shrine itself, and those who have can't remember exactly how to find it."

"Do you think it is shrouded by magic like Weeper's Cove?" Bran asked.

"Doubtful. The shrines were all built to be easily accessible to any devotees who wished to pay their respects to the gods and petition for their favour. I imagine it has something to do with Vask himself. Mala seemed to imply that he is at the shrine—I didn't realise that the gods existed so freely outside the Between."

Bran rubbed the back of his neck as he studied the map. "They generally don't. Spirits and other messengers are usually responsible for any reported sightings of deities, especially given that the Sovereigns were imprisoned for an eon. And since Grandmother Ocean has been sleeping for equally as long, I would say that any of her influence is likewise the work of spirits or these *guardians* like Mala." He was still staring at the map, but Varlan got the sense that he wasn't actually seeing it. "I don't think Mala is a goddess. She's definitely some kind of spirit, or something between spirit and human ... like Vatura, so the same could be said of Vask. But without meeting him, I couldn't say for sure." He finally looked up.

"Aha!" Elijah exclaimed, startling them both. "There." His keen gave an ecstatic flutter, and he marked a spot awfully close to the point Varlan had indicated on the map. "That is where we'll find the shrine." He looked from Bran to Varlan. "What did I miss?"

"Just an academic spiel from Bran regarding the nature of gods and spirits."

Elijah blinked at Varlan and then Bran. "My father always said never ask a necromancer for a straight answer—you'll either get a lengthy allegory or a metaphysical lecture," he said with a grin.

Bran laughed. "Yeah, that sounds right."

"I'll go inform Gendry that we know where to start looking. If Wren can keep that approaching storm at bay, we will likely reach Mintura come morning." Elijah blotted the fresh ink then rolled the map and tucked it under his arm as he left.

"We need to talk," Varlan said as Bran moved to follow the cartographer.

Bran stopped and turned. "Well that sounds ominous."

Varlan bit back a laugh at his tone. "You should be getting used to the general air of foreboding by now."

The necromancer's snowy brows arched.

"I've been trying to decode Kai's journal and I think I am close, but then again, I've thought that several times already." He released a sigh. "I also took a look at those books Nea sent back with you."

"And?" Bran leant on the edge of the table, a curious gleam in his eyes.

"And, Idir and I got something very wrong."

Bran's brow furrowed. "What about?"

"The keystone," Varlan said as he moved to the trunk where he stored the keystone and its duplicate. Both stones were wrapped in enchanted cloth that blocked their magic. The cloth made the tips of his fingers numb as though his keen was trying to distance itself from the mage-bane-treated fabric. He unfolded the keystone as he walked back to Bran. The luminous green stone was fractured, the pieces held together by a filigree cage of rose-gold robrillium. Magic twisted over the stone's surface—uncanny magic that left an uneasy feeling in his stomach.

"Can I see that?" Bran held his hand out and Varlan passed him the stone.

The chill of necromancy rolled through the air and the stone seemed to shimmer in response.

"What exactly did you think this stone was?"

"The key to Grandmother Ocean's temple on Dumura. At least that is what Idir thinks it is, and until recently I was inclined to agree with him. I've encountered keystones before and aside from being broken and fused back together, this one seemed no different than any other."

"*Seemed*?" Bran passed the stone back to Varlan and he wrapped it up in the cloth before placing it on the table.

"I think whoever mended it wanted others to believe it was indeed a keystone, but I am not so sure now. Especially after finding this." He unwrapped the second stone, leaving the cloth between his bare skin and the crystalline surface. It was almost identical to the first except it had never been broken and lacked the robrillium cage. Something dark shifted in its luminous depths, and Varlan shivered at the sensation of barbs digging into the edges of his keen-sense.

Bran licked his lip as he regarded the stone. His fingers twitched as though he was fighting the urge to take it and when Varlan held it out, he rocked back a step. "I'd rather not touch that one."

Varlan couldn't blame him. The shifting mass that had awoken when they removed the stone from the shrine of Moalana seemed to be gaining power despite being wrapped in the magic-dampening cloth. He placed it on the table next to the other wrapped stone. It caught the flickering light, making the shifting shadow at its core more evident.

"The keystone doesn't feel like the prison stone though," Bran said.

They had been calling it the prison stone ever since Deana's magic had brought their attention to the soul trapped within.

"No, it doesn't, but it might have once. If it was a prison stone, then whatever was trapped inside may have escaped when it was broken."

Bran's brow furrowed. "That's not really how it works though. With heartstones, once the soul is sequestered in the stone, it can't be removed. Even if the stone were to be broken, it would simply fracture the soul within."

"That's right, but a heartstone is created for the specific purpose of powering a golem so the connection of the soul to the stone has to be stable."

"True." Bran's gaze dropped to the table. "But why hide the stone's original nature and dress it up as something that it is not once it has served its purpose?"

"That's the part I can't figure out."

"And if it isn't the key to Grandmother Ocean's resting place then where is the real keystone?"

"No idea and before you ask, no, Elijah's magic can't find it. When I had him search for the keystone last time, that broken stone is what he found. Unless ..." He let out a bitter laugh and shook his head. "That slimy son of a bitch."

"I'm sorry, which slimy son of a bitch exactly? We know a few."

Varlan let out a huff of a laugh. "Vince."

"Quel'Sapar Vince? Didn't you find this in his vault? Do you think he knows what it is or that he hid the real keystone?"

Vince wasn't smart enough for that, and Varlan doubted the self-proclaimed king of Quel'Sapar knew the true purpose of even half the relics he had sequestered away over the years. For Vince, an item was valuable as long as someone else had an invested interest in it. Still, there was something nagging at the back of his mind. What if Vince had known the true nature of this particular relic? He was keen-less but there were plenty of mages whose services could be bought, and Vince had a way of finding the right mage for any given job. He shook his head again. The complexity involved in such an undertaking wasn't Vince's style, and he certainly had no stake in Idir's campaign to take the isles.

"I don't know if I should be concerned or intrigued about whatever cogs are turning in that mind of yours." Bran's amused tone broke through Varlan's thoughts and when Varlan glanced his way, he was wearing a knowing smile. "We were discussing Vince, then you did that blank stare you do right before you come out with an epiphany or complex plan. You'd fit right in at Hartswood." He added the last with a small laugh.

"I was wondering if Vince switched the stones. He's not capable of altering the stone himself, but he certainly has the resources to make it happen. I doubt he's all that interested in what happens in the isles though. Unless it were to directly affect his foothold at Quel'Sapar and there's little chance of that ... at least for now."

"Could it be both?"

"Both?"

Bran nodded. "What if it was originally a prison stone but then was broken and reforged as a key?" He pushed off the edge of the table, his sapphire eyes bright as he rubbed his hands together. "It would make sense then that the magic embedded in the stone is confusing. And a soul-powered key would be ..." He blinked a few times and a wide grin worked across his features. "It would be a *Nea*."

"What?" Varlan couldn't understand why he was suddenly mentioning Nea. As far as necromancers or really mages in general went, she was an anomaly. But then— "Shadow's teeth! Portals. Why didn't I think of that earlier?"

"You've been a little preoccupied," Bran said.

Varlan frowned. It had been nearly impossible to keep his history with Agnes from the Azure Queen crew members, but Bran had figured it out long before the others. And he was right; Varlan had been acting like a lovesick fool when he really should be focusing on the mission at hand. He let out a heavy sigh.

"Which no one can blame you for," Bran added gently.

"No, you're right. I haven't been thinking straight and my focus has been ... I can't afford to let myself be as distracted as I have been."

Bran cleared his throat. "That's not what I meant."

Varlan held Bran's gaze. It was not a comfortable thing to do. Bran, like many of his kind, had a deep, all-knowing stare that seemed to scrape against the very fabric of your soul. After several heartbeats, he swallowed as he looked away. "Still, I should have realised the portal connection sooner. I can't believe I overlooked that. It makes more sense that the resting place of Grandmother Ocean isn't physically on Dumura but more likely in the Between. You said yourself that the gods rarely walk our realm."

"It would also explain why the keystone is infused with the magic of the Between. Soul magic is the only way to open a bridge across the barrier—one which can be traversed by mortal souls at least—so the spirit that was imprisoned in the stone was likely used as an anchor. But that is an extremely complex and rather dangerous form of necromancy. Akin to the kind of magic the Usurper's followers were trying to use to breech the barrier."

"They succeeded though."

"They certainly gave it a good crack," he laughed. "No pun intended. But it was Nea who did the actual breaking. She's a deathborn and a daughter of shadow. A living bridge between realms and anchor all in one."

"But you can make portals too, can't you?"

Bran rubbed the back of his neck. "Yes, but nothing like what Nea can do and my ability is a result of my keen being contaminated by hers. I wasn't born with it like she was."

"No. But ..." Several pieces were clicking into place. Idir had gone to Beldaren seeking Nea after he learned of the broken barrier and her efforts to mend it. Instead, he had returned with Bran. Bran's keen was familiar enough to Nea's that one could assume his abilities were similar to hers. If Idir had a keystone that could allow him to cross the barrier into the Between, he didn't need a mage who could be the bridge—just one who could use the stone to open the door. And if Bran could be persuaded to open that door in the right location— "Can you open a portal now?"

Bran shrugged and his keen erupted in a burst of cold as an oval of purple light appeared beside them. It was flickering as though unstable and barely big enough for a child to pass through, let alone a full-grown adult.

"That's the largest I can make without losing stability, and I can't hold it for long." He released the magic and the portal snapped shut.

Varlan picked up the wrapped keystone and uncovered it before holding it out to Bran. "What if you use this?"

Bran sucked his lip between his teeth as he eyed the stone but there was a glimmer of curiosity beneath the trepidation, and after a moment he took hold of it.

His keen chilled the air again as he examined the stone in his hand and then the source around them seemed to pull in and pucker before another purple portal burst to life. The edges of this one glowed brightly, a shifting landscape clearly visible on the other side. It was large enough that both Bran and Varlan could pass through comfortably if they so wished.

Varlan stretched his fingers towards the portal; the source grew tight as they slipped through the invisible barrier. The air on the other side was balmy and a gentle breeze blew through the glowing doorway, bringing the scents of pine and fresh-turned earth.

A shadow moved in the depths of the portal, and Bran made a noise before grabbing Varlan's arm and hauling it back. The second the tips of Varlan's fingers were clear of the glittering miasma, Bran's his keen gave a cold pulse and the portal snapped shut.

"I doubt you'd fancy being dragged into the Between by whatever it was that was attracted to the portal," he said as Varlan gave him a questioning look.

"That was the Between on the other side?"

The necromancer nodded. "The physical Between—not the twisted reflection we walk in dreams." He studied the stone still clutched his fingers then held it out to Varlan.

Varlan took it from him and wrapped it in the shielding cloth again. "I'd stake my life on Idir wanting to use this stone to activate a portal to the Between once he raises Dumura."

Bran nodded. "But he'd need a necromancer capable of doing so. It's not a parlour trick that just any mage or run-of-the-mill necromancer would be able to pull off."

"Idir obviously thought you could do it. That's why he brought you to the isles, and you've just proved he was right."

Bran frowned. "I wouldn't—"

"He's a mind mage. All he needs is to get inside your head and give the order."

"Well, Savita tried that already and it didn't work out the way she was hoping."

"Idir's magic might not be as insidiously subtle as his daughter's, but it has centuries of training behind it. It's like comparing a penknife to a war hammer."

"Why didn't he just coerce me himself then?" Bran leant on the table between them.

"It might have been due to timing, or perhaps he thought that Savita had a better chance of *wooing* you to their side without too much need for actual coercion ... Or it could have been the fact that Idir thrives on the planning but prefers someone else get their hands dirty."

"For someone who has spent several centuries planning, he's not the best at actioning those plans. Why not just take Agnes when she was a child and groom her for whatever purpose he needed? Why not do the same with Deana? He seems to have no concerns about killing to get what he wants."

It was a valid question. Idir could have ensured his success if he had stolen both women when they were young girls. The only missing piece would be the necromancer capable of using the keystone to breech the Between. But then he had succeeded in grooming Agnes by altering her keen enough that she was a slave to it. And Deana? He had inserted himself as Chief Soma's advisor even before her parents' death. All her life, he had been there waiting for the opportune moment. He could have encouraged her to develop her keen but instead he chose to emphasise the dangers of it and make her frightened to wield it.

"Why?"

"What was that?" Bran asked.

"Why would Idir stop Deana from connecting with her power? Surely, he would want her to have full control of it. But instead he ensured she was afraid of her own magic and encouraged her to bury it down. Not just him—the guild of singers did too. Kai said they had told her parents that Deana's power was better silenced. Why?"

Bran's eyes widened. "Because when she connects with her power, it opens a direct link to Grandmother Ocean."

"What?"

"Why didn't I realise it? The way the source and the ocean react to her emotions. The enormity of what her magic could achieve with the right focus. The myths surrounding those who are supposedly blessed by Grandmother Ocean. It was there the whole time; all the clues were clear as day and I should have known better."

"If you could stop sounding like the inside of my head that would be good. What didn't you realise? What is she?"

"She's exactly what she said she is. She's *touched* by Grandmother Ocean—the goddess's last attempt to right a world-shattering wrong. Every time she uses her power, it strengthens the connection between her and the goddess. And if Idir is going to exploit her keen to his own ends, then he certainly couldn't allow that connection to grow."

CHAPTER THIRTEEN

DEANA

Cold water fizzed over Deana's legs as she dragged herself from the rolling whitewash onto the damp sand of the tideline. She flopped onto her back and let out a gasping sigh. Fluffy clouds dotted the cerulean sky. A cool breeze stirred the reaching branches that marked the edge of the jungle, making the leaves rasp together as she closed her eyes to fight back the boiling nausea that engulfed her.

A shadow fell over her.

The woman who had brought her here was silhouetted against the sky, her dark hair seemingly dry despite their recent dip in the ocean. "You're still breathing? Good."

That might be true, but the world was spinning and her limbs had been reduced to a squishy numbness that suggested they wouldn't hold her weight even if she had the desire to stand. She lifted a shaking hand and pressed it over her eyes. "Where are we?"

"Mintura."

"Mintura?" She sat up. Her insides rolled and the lump that had started to form somewhere between her abdomen and chest shifted. Saliva flooded her mouth and she twisted sideways to release the contents of her stomach onto the sand.

A cool hand brushed away the hair stuck to the side of her neck while another rubbed gentle circles on her back. "Best if you refrain from any sudden movements for a while. I am told that portal travel can be rather uncomfortable for mortals."

That was an understatement. The portals she had taken with Bran had been unpleasant and made her feel drained and unsteady on her feet, but they had not left her so debilitated. This portal had made her feel as though the ocean itself had chewed her up and then spat her out again.

She wiped the back of her wrist across her mouth and gingerly turned back to face the woman. "Why did you bring me to Mintura?"

"I told you already—there are answers for you at the shrine of the forgotten. Vask has been waiting for you for some time and it is best not to keep him waiting any longer."

Vask? The forgotten god? Why would he be waiting for Deana? And what answers could he possibly have for her?

She studied the pale-green eyes of the woman then let her gaze move over her mother-of-pearl-dusted skin to the luminous tail with its long, delicate fins. Beneath the alluring roll of her song lingered the cold pull of the fathoms. It was something akin to the song of the shrouded ones, but it did not raise the prickling stir of dread at Deana's core or leave the bitter notes of sorrow on the back of her tongue. "Who are you?"

The woman's head tilted as she considered Deana's question. "I have known many names, but to mortals I am Sejira."

The guardian of sailors.

Deana swallowed as another wave of nausea boiled in her stomach. "Why are you helping me?"

"You are mine as much as you are the Grandmother's," Sejira whispered, sadness softening her features. "Long ago, before you were born, I met your mother. Her boat was scuttled in a storm, and she was clinging to a shelf of rock, each wave threatening to take her. The Grandmother spoke to me, implored me to save her. She didn't tell me why this mortal was more special than the thousands of men and women who had ever found themselves in the same predicament. She just wanted me to intervene. So, I did. Like all my brethren, I cannot ignore a direct order from my matriarch." She leant back on her hands and stared at the sky as she continued, "Your mother was clever. She knew that her salvation would come at a price—one she may not be willing to pay. But she had a young boy at home who needed her—"

"Kai," Deana whispered.

"Yes. She feared the storm would leave him an orphan as she did not yet know the fate of her heart mate, so she asked me what boon I would request." The corner of her mouth tucked in.

Deana leant forward. "And what did you say?"

"I could have asked for anything—something insignificant, something material. But instead, when your mother asked me that question that day, my answer was"—she settled a weighted gaze on Deana—"a life for a life. I did not know that it was the babe inside her womb that held the Grandmother's true interest when I made that claim."

"And my mother just promised me to you without any objections?" Deana pushed to her feet, wobbling as her legs shook and threatened to collapse again, and the world spun around her.

"Perhaps if she knew the truth, she might not have. But as I said, your mother was clever, and you were not the first babe she had carried since the birth of your brother. She knew the signs, and I doubt she expected the pregnancy to hold."

A lump formed in Deana's throat that had nothing to do with her nausea. Her quivering knees gave out and she slumped back to the sand. "How could she, even if she doubted—"

"She loved you as fiercely as she loved your brother. Don't ever doubt that. When I came to claim that which I had been promised,

I discovered the gravity of the mistake I had made. I could not claim you; your soul was never your mother's to give. I am certain the Grandmother knew this; she tricked me and in doing so ensured your survival. Because whether I can lay claim to your soul or not, it is mine as much as it is hers. And she knew that because you were mine, I would protect you from the damned when she herself could not."

Deana's head was spinning for a whole new reason. Just how intricate was this web that she was caught in?

"You should go. Vask is waiting. Follow the scarlet beetles. They will lead you to him." Sejira shuffled herself across the damp sand until her lower half was completely submerged in the shallows before she met Deana's gaze one more time. "A last word of warning. Do not give Vask the first thing he asks for, nor the second, and be cautious of the third. The fourth will be safe, but the fifth would be a mistake."

"What do you mean—"

But Sejira had already made a dive for the deeper water, and with a flash of teal-coloured light she was gone.

Deana climbed to her feet and took a few deep breaths to steady herself. Thankfully, the nausea seemed to be passing, but her body was still aching in places she didn't know could ache. She scanned the thick jungle that edged the beach. Sejira had said to follow the scarlet beetles, which sounded simple enough. But first she had to find them, and that was going to be like finding a bean in a basket of pebbles.

It felt like hours later when Deana pushed her way through a dense patch of vines and undergrowth only to stumble out onto the beach once more. She had seen no signs of scarlet-coloured insects, and the jungle was so dense it was easy to get turned around and cover ground that had already been covered.

After the third time going in circles, she had taken a stone and started scoring the trunks of trees to mark her passage. But it hadn't helped. She still ended up back on that same stretch of beach, covered in sweat, and with a burning thirst scratching at the back of her throat.

She collapsed on the sand and let out a frustrated groan. Above her, the fluffy clouds had shifted from crisp white to a brooding grey that promised a storm. It would be night soon and she didn't like the idea of being stuck on the beach in a downpour. Storms at this time of year could be unforgiving, bringing brutal destruction in the form of king tides and wind strong enough to topple even some of the largest trees.

Whilst she had been stumbling through the jungle, she had discovered a small cave. It was barely big enough to fit two people, but the overhang of rock would provide some shelter from the storm. If she found the small stream that led past it again, she could hunker down in the cavern for the night and resume her search for scarlet beetles in the morning.

She pushed to her feet and wandered back into the trees, following the trunks that had score marks until she found the stream. Small fingerlings darted away from her shadow as she bent and scooped some of the clear water into her hand before taking a tentative sip. It tasted fresh enough and the coolness soothed the burn at the back of her throat. She drank her fill and then stood and scanned the trees around her. From memory, she had passed a goosefruit vine. Now if only she could find it again.

She followed the stream for a while until she spied the plump, fist-sized globes with their fuzzy brown coats. After locating one of the riper looking fruits, she picked it and bit into the bitter skin to make it easier to peel and expose the delicate pink flesh. She ate until the hollow feeling in her stomach settled and then she washed the sticky sweetness from her fingers in the stream before picking several more fruits and tucking them into the folds of her shirt.

Keeping the stream to her right, she continued deeper into the forest. It was almost too dark to see by the time she found the cavern. Normally, she would have another hour of light at this time of year. But the storm clouds had grown heavier the longer she walked, and for the last little while she had needed the teal green mage light bobbing along beside her to illuminate the sometimes treacherous tangle of roots and undergrowth. The cavern was up a small outcrop of rock perhaps two times Deana's height. Careful not to crush the fruit hidden in her clothing, she climbed up and crawled into the cave.

It was small enough that her mage light illuminated the entire space, but also deep enough that she could position herself away from the opening to ensure protection from the storm. She removed the fruit from her clothing and settled herself down at the rear of the cavern. Stifling a yawn, she drew her knees to her chest as the trees began to whip outside as the wind picked up. A heaviness had settled in her limbs, but she couldn't sleep. Even if the sounds of the storm didn't keep her awake, the fear that Astrid would find her again surely would.

Morning came with a thin slant of golden light. Deana unfolded her stiff legs and gathered the fruit she had saved for breakfast as she moved to the opening of the cavern. She had managed a few hours of sleep, but the dreams of her parents' death and the churning fathoms rising up to claim her had left her feeling raw, on edge, and like she hadn't really gotten any rest at all.

She sat herself in a patch of warm sunlight at the mouth of the cave and let her legs dangle over the lip as she ate. Crystalline droplets, the remnants of the storm, glittered through the foliage and small birds played in the puddles beside the stream. The stream itself was higher than it had been the day before, the water not quite as clear as flotsam from the storm floated along in small rafts.

Once she had finished her breakfast, she climbed down and washed her hands and face in the cold water. Then she used the comb Rami had given her to pick the tangles from her hair before plaiting it neatly again, then turning her attention to the jungle.

It was going to be impossible to find the beetles and she couldn't spend another day just wandering aimlessly through the undergrowth. She closed her eyes and drew a deep breath, letting her song drift with the breeze as the songs of everything around her washed over her. The shrine had to have a song of its own, one that was different to the organic sounds of the natural world. Her song slipped over a melody that was hard to follow—the beat seemed off, and just as she thought she understood it, it changed again. She latched onto that melody and let her song explore it until she found it pulling her deeper into the trees.

Hesitation rooted her to the spot, but only momentarily. She could do this; she had to do this. She pulled the stone from yesterday out of her pocket and marked the smooth grey trunk of the closest tree. With a grounding breath to chase the last of her reservations away, she started forward and let the strange, hard to grasp song lead her deeper into the jungle.

The day was growing hot, and sweat was starting to run down her spine as the ground sloped downward. The trees thinned slightly to reveal a crumbling ruin tucked in a nest of gnarled roots. A toppled statue lay in pieces at the centre of what appeared to have once been a pavilion much like the one at the shrine of Moalana. She stopped at the edge of the first smooth slab of stone that had most likely been a set of stairs leading up to the pavilion itself. Did this shrine have a trap lying in wait like Moalana's had?

Something skittered past her boots, drawing her attention. A line of small beetles with shiny scarlet carapaces. She wasn't surprised she hadn't found them yesterday; they would have been nearly impossible to spot in the undergrowth.

The beetles scurried towards the fallen statue where they were joined by hundreds—possibly a thousand or more—of their brethren until the statue was no longer visible under the shroud of tiny crimson bodies. Deana rocked back a step as the beetles lifted into the air. They weren't flying, but rather they rose like the swell of a wave and with a flash of red light they dispersed. A man of average build and height was left in their wake. His skin was several shades darker than her own and his hair was cropped so close to his scalp he appeared almost bald. He was dressed in the simple linen pants and shirt the curators of the Mintura seemed to favour. As Deana studied him, she found it hard to keep her focus on his features. He tilted his head as he regarded her in return, and the slippery song she had been following grew louder for a moment. Finally, she was able to keep her gaze on his face. His mouth split into a wide grin that showed a row of neat teeth that were almost too bright a shade of white. But his smile was not as unsettling as the deep scarlet of his irises.

"Well now, this is a most interesting turn of events," he said in a voice that was almost as slippery as his song. The words seemed to shift over her like wisps of smoke before dispersing.

"Are you the guardian known as Vask?"

He let out a silky chuckle. "Yes, yes, of course. Welcome, mortal, you have found me. What is it that you need to forget, or more specifically who is it that needs to forget you?" He opened his arms with a flourish before tucking them back over his chest as his expression turned sly. "Is that a sufficient enough welcome? It feels like an eon since anyone has found me here, though in all reality it could have only been a week. But you are different to the usual mortal that stumbles into my prison demanding aid. You are

something ... *other*, something akin to me and yet vastly different."
He inhaled, almost like a dog scenting the breeze. "It is woven in
your song and layered in your scent, so familiar and yet ... altered
by your mortal limitations." He finally grew quiet, his features
shifting from that sly grin to something almost contemplative.

Deana's head was aching from trying to keep track of what he
had said. The words seemed to enter her mind but then evade
comprehension until they evaporated. "Sejira told me you would
have answers for me," she said when he gave her an expectant
look.

"Did she?" The slyness returned, though it had a sharper, more
predatory edge, and he took a step towards her. "Did she also tell
you that I give nothing for free?"

She swallowed and nodded.

"Perfect, then tell me what your answers are *worth* to you?
Would you give me your name? A simple thing to give that
doesn't cost you anything."

She shook her head.

"Your voice? A lock of your hair? A memory? One rooted in
deep emotion. Or perhaps you would give me your song? Surely it
is more trouble than it is worth."

The words rolled over her, merging until she lost all sense of
them. Sejira had said the safest thing to give him was the fourth
thing he asked for, but which was that? Her name was the first
and he had also asked for a lock of her hair. But what else? A
memory and her song ... her voice.

"Have you weighed the worth of your answers?"

She shook her head again.

"Perhaps you would like more options?"

"No. I just need a moment to think," she snapped as the new
words chased the previous ones away. The headache was growing
sharper, and she rubbed her fingers across her brow. "Can you
repeat my options?"

His eyes narrowed and his expression became sharper. "Why, of course. You already said you wouldn't give me your name. But you can still change your mind about that. Or you could give me a memory, your voice, your *song*, or a lock of your hair."

Was the order different? She clenched her hands, digging her fingernails into her palms to try and focus. She needed her voice and, even though it was responsible for all the pain and tragedy she had endured, the thought of existing without her song was unfathomable. And yet, if she no longer had her song Idir wouldn't be able to use it to raise Dumura and bring destruction to the isles. No, her song was as essential to her as breathing. Surely a lock of her hair could be missed but was it worth enough to her? And was it the fourth thing he had asked for? What was the other request? A memory. That was—

"Time is wasting. Surely it's not that hard a decision to make."

She could part with a memory, something from her childhood that she wouldn't miss but something significant enough to satisfy Vask. But what if that had been the fifth thing he asked for originally? Would it be a grievous mistake to give him a memory? She drew a steadying breath and nodded. "I will give you a memory."

His smile faltered momentarily before snapping into place once more. "A memory. Well then, let's see it." He beckoned her closer.

She climbed the short steps and stopped in front of him.

"Ready?" he asked as he held his hands out beside either side of her face.

She'd seen Varlan use a similar method the time he had entered Agnes's mind and, after taking a moment to summon a memory thick with emotion, she nodded her consent.

The memory became suddenly visceral. The scent of spiced bread, the taste of honey, the infectious beat of music. Images of her past floated before her, leaving a cavernous sensation in their wake until finally the edges started to grow fuzzy and the honey on her tongue turned bitter. Panic swirled in swarming fingers through her core, building until it felt like a thousand insects were crawling under her skin, and when she couldn't bear it any longer, a burst of red light stole the ground from beneath her feet.

CHAPTER FOURTEEN

AGNES

Time had no meaning in the dark landscape that she was wandering. She followed the light beneath her feet until her legs started to protest and fatigue made her thoughts fuzzy. Would it be safe to rest here? What if Idir returned while she was sleeping? She focused on the prickling magic at her core and then crouched and lay her palms against the petals as she concentrated on her need for somewhere safe to rest.

Nothing seemed to happen. Then, the light dimmed as the magic inside her grew hot and the petals stirred as though under the effect of an errant breeze. They twisted into the air, forming a shimmering dome the size of a small tent above her. She sat and tucked her knees to her chest, resting her chin on them as she pressed her back to the wall of the dome. She let her eyes close, hoping that if the heavy sleep that was threatening took her, the dome would stay in place and keep her safe.

A ticklish sensation stirred the hairs on the back of her neck, and she opened her eyes. She was back home in the berth kitchen, the table before her strewn with pieces of metal and strange parts.

"You should get yourself to bed," an achingly familiar voice said from across the room.

Varlan was leaning against the kitchen bench watching her. "I'd take you there myself, but Wes is waiting for me," he said when her eyes met his.

"I thought I locked the door; how did you get in?"

He held a thin lockpick out and then tucked it into his sleeve. "I did try knocking first."

"Oh, you did, did you?"

He let out a low chuckle and pushed away from the bench. "You were preoccupied."

She stood as he approached, moving around the table so it was no longer between them and propping her backside against the edge of it. "And what exactly is so important that it couldn't wait until morning?" She folded her arms as she regarded him.

"Nothing in particular. I was just passing on my way to see Wes and thought I should check on you." He moved closer until the air between them grew heated.

"Right, well, you've checked on me and you probably shouldn't keep Wes waiting, so—" Her words caught in her throat as his hands slid around the curve of her hips.

With one fluid movement, he lifted her onto the tabletop and positioned himself between her knees. "You're the worst kind of distraction, you know?" he said as the fingers of one hand danced in lazy circles up her spine and the other cupped the side of her neck, his thumb lightly tracing the corner of her mouth.

"Oh, really?" She gripped the front of his shirt and tilted her head until their lips were almost touching.

"Yes," he whispered, his breath stirring across her mouth and melting her insides. "The kind of distraction that will get a man killed," he said and then claimed her lips with his own.

Agnes awoke with a sharp gasp. Her lips still felt hot and raw as though the kiss had happened only moments ago, and she pressed her fingers to them. Varlan had taken her memories of that time, destroyed them to hide her involvement from Idir. To protect the location of the keystone. But it had felt more real than any dream.

A sinister laugh echoed around her, and she stared through the shroud of petals still domed over her, searching for the source. Darkness expanded on all sides, but she could feel the oily touch of Idir's stare.

"I had no idea how precious you were to Varlan. Had I known, I could have used that to my advantage. I still can, I suppose. He is a very *useful* mage after all. Did you know his power rivals even mine? Of course you don't. How could you when he all but erased himself from your mind."

He finally emerged from the darkness and touched his coral-studded hand to the wall of her dome. The petals beneath his fingers began to glow with fuchsia light and then turned grey, but the dome held. "We don't have to be enemies, Agnes. I can give you back all the memories Varlan took. All you have to do is submit your powers to me and you will be free."

She shook her head. She was not foolish enough to believe that he would let her live once he had her power. And now that he knew her history with Varlan, he would use that to his advantage. Even though she no longer felt anything for Varlan—no, that wasn't entirely true. Something inside was drawn to him. Some deep-rooted part of her still remembered that connection, those feelings, even if she now found them confusing. And regardless, she couldn't bear the thought of being used as a tool to control him, or anyone for that matter.

"I will never submit," she said.

Idir rolled his eyes and let out a bored-sounding huff. "Yes, of course. Do you know how many souls have told me the same? And how few have actually managed to keep that promise?" He pressed both hands against the wall of her dome and scarlet cracks chased each other across its surface. "Do you honestly think you can win against me? With your pathetic, broken keen and your tattered memories? I've already won, Agnes. I was just trying to give you a sense of autonomy. A moment's reprieve from the pain before the end."

But he hadn't won. She might be trapped in his mind or wherever this was, but while she still had her power, she hadn't been defeated.

Idir slammed his knuckles against the dome this time, and the cracks glowed brighter. Agnes had to do something, anything to get herself out. What she needed more than anything was the door back into her own dreamscape and a way to destroy Idir's attachment once she got there. Her magic prickled under her skin; images flashed across her mind. A great stone tower. A single block that, if dislodged, would bring the entire thing crashing down. She pushed her magic back down as Idir slammed the side of the dome a third time and dead grey petals rained over her.

The dome shuddered, raining more petals, and she focused on Idir. There was something glimmering at the centre of his chest—a piece of coral not like the others. It was metal, a shard of pure gold catching the light. No, it was glowing from within like Agnes was herself. That realisation brought with it a deep certainty. Whatever Idir had taken from her when he broke her keen it was contained in that shard, and she had to get it back.

This time when he pounded against the dome, she dragged the last of the magic holding it together back into herself. The dome collapsed and Idir came barrelling towards her, staggering under the momentum of the force he had summoned to break her shield. Agnes charged to meet him, driving her shoulder into his ribs as she reached for the shard of gold. The coral and metal sliced her fingers, and she smeared blood across his chest as she gritted her teeth and tried to yank the shard free.

The back of Idir's knuckles slammed across her cheek, bringing a scattering of stars to her vision and an ache to her jaw. She gripped the shard with both hands and planted her feet on his thighs as she pulled. He struggled underneath her until he managed to grab a hold of her and threw her off. She slid across the ground, sending up a flurry of glowing petals as the shard slipped from her grasp.

It lay in a circle of black petals between her and Idir, who was probing the hole in the centre of his chest. He let out a snarl as his fingers came away covered in oily ichor then he charged for the shard. Agnes leapt at the same moment, her fingers closing over the warm metal just as Idir's nails raked the back of her hand. She rolled away from him, wiping the shard on her pants before holding it out ready to drive it into her own chest.

"Agnes, stop!" Idir fell to his knees.

"No, I am done listening to you!" The shard burned as it pierced her flesh, and her magic rose in a wild prickle that closed off all her senses. She felt like her body was being turned inside out before the darkness around her dissolved in a violent burst of golden light.

When the light cleared, she found herself on her hands and knees in the pale desert of her own dreamscape. Jagged dark stones rose before her—a pair of ominous doors—the glowing crossed coral motif at their centre duller than it had been before. She rushed towards it, letting her magic swell out on instinct. It burrowed into the cracks between the stone until it found the weakness: the keystone that would bring the rest crumbling down. She pressed her magic into that stone, willing it to break. It shifted, and with a deafening groan the door buckled before collapsing into a heap of dark stones around Agnes. The stones faded from inky black to a deep grey and then they crumbled to dust.

Nausea rolled through Agnes's stomach, accompanied by the all too familiar dead-weight of magical exhaustion. She gingerly got to her feet, only to collapse to the sand once more as the fatigue took her.

CHAPTER FIFTEEN

BRAN

Bran leapt out of the boat and splashed through the shallows. He'd rolled his pants to just above his knees in an effort to keep them dry, but they were saturated to the thighs regardless. Kiki splashed along beside him, her keen rising in a happy, bubbling sensation around her as she reached the beach ahead of him. The water clinging to her clothes pulled away into a ring of suspended droplets and then fell to the ground, leaving her completely dry. She turned her attention to Bran, her keen rushing over his as the moisture wicked away from him and landed in a neat halo around his now dry feet.

"Thanks," he said as he bent to pull his boots on.

The bottom of the boat scraped onto the sand a short distance away and both Varlan and Pippa climbed out. They were followed by Gendry, who stopped to drag the boat as far as he could onto the sand.

"Well?" Gendry asked when he was finished securing the boat.

Bran drew Deana's protection stone out of his pocket and let his keen run over it. The magic clinging to it barely stirred and he shook his head as he slipped it back into his pocket. As his fingertips slid away from the stone, a stomach-turning wash of dread rolled over him. The world closed in for a second as his heart began to pound and cold sweat dampened the back of his neck. He drew the stone out again; an erratic array of red and teal magic was skipping over its surface. The deep rolling sensation of Deana's keen buffeted him and then, all at once, the sensations stopped and the world went still.

"What was that?" Pippa asked in a husky whisper, her face pale as though she had run the same gauntlet of emotions that Bran just had.

"Fear," Varlan said. "More specifically, Deana's fear."

"*Fear*? That felt more like absolute terror," Kiki said, eyeing the stone sitting on Bran's open palm.

"That's still a type of fear," Varlan said dryly. "Why we could all suddenly feel it, I can't tell you. It might have had something to do with the tracking enchantment Marcus put on the stone."

Bran thumbed the hole at the stone's centre. Garret had said once that there were moments that he could feel Nea's emotions through the bracelet Marcus had enchanted to find her. Was this the same thing? Unlikely, given Nea had speculated that it was the connection between their divine blood and not Marcus's enchantment. And Garret had been the only one able to feel Nea's emotions. Everyone seemed to experience Deana's fear. But regardless of why they had, it was a sign that they had to find her fast. "We can debate it later—we have to find her," he said.

"I think I can help with that," Gendry called.

He was standing at the tree line, his fingers pressed against the side of one of the trunks as he examined something on the ground. As they reached him, Varlan crouched to examine the small divots in the sand.

"They could be Deana's, but the storm has destroyed any chance we had of knowing for sure," Varlan said as he stood.

Gendry just grinned at him and cocked an eyebrow. "Storm might have destroyed her footprints, but she's a clever lass."

He lifted his hand away from the trunk to reveal a mark scored into the grey bank.

Several paces into the trees, there was another.

"Do you think they are Deana's? That she left them for us to follow?" Kiki asked as she examine the next scored trunk.

"They are fresh enough to be and we haven't seen signs of anyone else. Whether or not she left them for us to follow, doesn't matter. They should lead us to her all the same," Gendry replied.

"Let's get moving then," Bran marched past Kiki to the next mark.

The scored trunks led them to a small stream, a line of debris marking the rise and fall of the water since the storm. Deana's marks followed the stream farther inland until they stopped at the bottom of a small rise of rock. A dark slice higher up announced the presence of a modest-sized crevice. Had she climbed up there to wait out the storm?

"You don't think she's still inside?" Pippa asked. Her magic was biting the air around him in a warm crackle.

Bran let his keen-sense out and encountered the softest roll of Deana's keen, almost like an echo left in passing. "If she is, something is shielding her magic," he replied, as Kiki started to climb up to the cave.

She disappeared inside and emerged again moments later before climbing down. When she landed on solid ground once more, she brushed her hands on her pants. "She was definitely here," she said as she straightened again.

"Look at this." Pippa bent and grabbed something from the tangle of growth at the base of the wall. She held it out for Bran to take.

It was an ivory comb with a mermaid carved along the top. Ten thick tines emerged from the swirl of sea foam beneath her swimming form. Deana's magic clung to it and though Bran was certain he had never seen the comb before this moment, something about it picked at a place deep inside his mind. He ran his fingertip along the pointed ends of the tines and then handed it back to Pippa, who slipped it into her pocket.

"She probably spent the night here, which means we might not be that far behind her," Varlan said.

Gendry nodded. "Is the stream or this cave on that map Elijah drew?"

Varlan fished out the folded parchment and examined it. "The stream is, and this shelf of rock. It runs farther into the jungle. But the temple should be …" he turned slowly on the spot, "that way." He pointed deeper into the trees; the first trunk was marked in a similar fashion to the ones they had been following.

Bran touched his fingers to it as they passed. The milky sap clinging to the edges of the gash was sticky enough to suggest the mark was relatively recent, perhaps only a few hours old at the most.

As they stomped through the jungle following Deana's marks, the air became thick and humid, making Bran's skin clammy with sweat that stuck his hair to the back of his neck in itchy clumps. The incessant buzzing of insects was an almost deafening hum broken only by the occasional squawking calls of birds.

Gendry and the twins had slowed their pace, dropping back farther and farther, but Varlan was keeping step with Bran. The mind mage was unusually silent, his contemplative frown telling Bran that his thoughts were elsewhere. Bran didn't have to guess what he was ruminating on. Agnes's predicament was a troubling one, even for Bran who didn't have the same intimate attachment to her. He had cursed himself multiple times now for leaving the spirit anchor with Garret and cutting off his easy access to Nea. Nea would know exactly what to do, or at least she'd have a decent theory on how to help Agnes.

He let out a huff and raked his fingers through his hair.

"The temple can't be much further," Varlan said, his steps slowing as he unrolled the map again.

Elijah's magic hadn't included many landmarks on the map. Probably because there weren't many landmarks in the jungle that weren't hidden by the league of grey trunks or the sprawling mess of vines, epiphytes, and shrubs that made the undergrowth.

Varlan stopped moving as he studied the map, and Bran wandered back to him as he lifted his gaze to examine the trees around them. "Where is the next mark?"

"There," Bran said, pointing to a tree several paces away. Just beyond it was another bearing a weeping mark, but beyond that he couldn't tell. He moved to the furthest mark and touched his fingers to it. "There aren't any marks after this one, but no sign of a temple."

Why would Deana stop marking the trunks? He crouched to the ground. There were no signs of a struggle, no lingering fragments of emotion for his magic to craft into a re-enactment. It was as though she had simply decided to stop marking the trunks, but why? The alluring brush of Varlan's keen rubbed over the edge of his keen-sense and he followed it. There was something strange ahead; a twisted patch of the source that was shifting and elusive. It wasn't like the magic of the Between, but it was akin to it. Underneath that elusive magic, barely detectable, was the rolling swell of Deana's keen.

"She's that way," Bran said, and Varlan nodded as he folded the map once more.

They started off again, Bran's legs protesting as he increased his pace.

"Now hang on, you two. There's no sense in—"

Whatever Gendry said next was stolen in a rush of air as the ground slopped savagely and Bran lost his footing. He rolled head-over-tail until he landed in a heap next to Varlan at the foot of a set of broken stone stairs.

Varlan stood slowly and brushed himself off. "I am guessing we found it," he said dryly as he grabbed Bran's hand and hauled him to his feet.

Bran glanced back at Gendry and twins, who were at the top of the slope, gingerly looking for a way down, then he started up the stone steps. The pull of Deana's keen was stronger here, as was the other shifting, hard-to-grasp magic.

When he reached the top step, a ruined pavilion much like the shrine of Moalana came into view. At its centre was a toppled statue, but there was no sign of Deana or anyone else for that matter. Nothing stirred besides a few scarlet-coloured beetles that scurried across the ground in front of Bran's feet.

The air seemed to prickle and his keen rose in response, but the prickling faded almost as quickly as it had started and left his keen as a cold knot at his core and a ticklish sensation between his shoulders. He shared a look with Varlan before stepping towards the statue. The moment his feet left the top stair and he was standing on the broken tiles of the shrine's mosaic floor, the source buckled, sending a surge of magic washing over him.

Varlan cursed and grabbed Bran's arm as though he was going to haul him out of the way—instead, the other mage staggered forward. A sound behind them drew Bran's attention. The twins and Gendry had reached the top of the stairs and collided with an invisible wall that had formed between them and Bran. They pressed against it and Kiki shouted something, but her words were garbled almost like sound through water.

"Six visitors in one day; well, that has to be a new record," an oily voice said. But as the words reached Bran, they started to shift and scatter like a whisper passed through too many lips only to lose its original meaning.

Bran turned to face the man who had spoken. His features were non-descript and hard to focus on, except the scarlet hue of his stare—that was striking and there was something borderline predatory about it. No, not entirely predatory, but certainly unnerving. His dark hair was shaved close, leaving a shadow of thick stubble across his scalp, and his clothes were the simple linen robes like the ones the priests Bran had seen when they first visited Mintura wore. He certainly wasn't human, but, like Mala and Vatura, if he was a spirit, he was not a type that Bran's magic was familiar with. This had to be Vask. That would also explain the difficultly of focusing on his features. It wasn't that they were changing; it was his magic preventing the viewer from committing the details to memory.

"I would invite your friends in but there is nothing for them here. You two, on the other hand—" His gaze flicked from Bran to Varlan, and a smirk twitched the corner of his mouth. "Yes, there is much here that would interest you both, so do you care for a trade? I can give you answers to all your most unfathomable questions, even those you haven't yet thought to ask. How to beat your adversary, how to raise the Isle of Splendour, how to save the girl, or perhaps you would prefer I take that which you cannot purge from your own mind? After all, wasn't life so much simpler when you only had your own wellbeing to consider?" The words slipped over each other, tumbling into a scattered mess that was almost too hard to follow.

Varlan shook his head, though Bran wasn't sure if he was objecting or just trying to clear the dull pressure of the building headache that was left in the wake of Vask's words.

"No? What about you?" Vask turned his attention back to Bran. "What do you seek, *Little Foundling,* hmm? The truth about your origins? Surely such a gift would be worth a considerable sacrifice?"

"We're not here to bargain with you. We are just looking for our friend," Bran said.

Vask's crimson-hued stare moved from Bran to the steps where Gendry and the twins were still trying to get through the barrier. A burst of flame spread across the air as Pippa threw a fireball at it. "You seem to have plenty of friends already. Whatever need could you have for another?"

Bran pressed the heel of his palm to his forehead as the words rattled around inside his mind, eluding capture. It would seem they would get nowhere with the guardian unless they played his game. "Can you give us a moment?"

"Oh, so you do want to trade?" Vask's smile deepened. "And what would your moment be worth to you?"

Bran bit down on his words and flicked a glance at Varlan, who shook his head. "No, forget I—"

Vask leant forward and tented his fingertips, the eagerness shining in his eyes making Bran swallow.

"We're just going to go over here." He moved away from the guardian, and Varlan followed. "Any ideas how to get out of this one?"

Varlan studied Vask before turning back to Bran. "You're the one who's used to dealing with spirits."

"Not the kind they breed here in the isles," Bran muttered under his breath.

"I'm trying to remember what stories I have heard of Vask. His domain is memories or more specifically forgotten memories, but if I know more than that the magic of this place is preventing me from remembering it. We may just have to ask him where to find Deana and pay whatever price he requests."

"She's here somewhere."

"I know, but he's not going to just tell us where or march her out. Not without a trade of"—he blinked and rubbed his temples and his magic thudded heavily against Bran's keen-sense—"equal perceived value. That's it. He won't ask for just one thing. He will give us options and we have to choose which we believe weighs the same as that which we are asking for. There was something else." His keen surged again but he shook his head. "A warning perhaps ... We'll just have to risk it."

Vask cleared his throat. "Life would be a terribly boring endeavour if we didn't take a few risks here and there."

Bran frowned as he considered what Varlan had said, then with a small nod he stepped back in front of the guardian and met his unnerving stare. He couldn't just ask where Deana was—that would make it too easy for Vask to simply tell them without releasing her, and Bran was sure that Deana was somewhere within the shrine. "We know our friend Deana is here. What do you request in exchange for returning her safely to us?"

"What is her safety worth to you? Your eyes? Such a lovely shade of blue I have not seen in an eon. Or perhaps you would trade one of your friends? A friend for a friend seems fair."

Bran drew a breath and tried to stop the words from fading as Vask tapped his chin.

"Neither of those? Then perhaps," his gaze dropped to the indigo-coloured crescent on the inside of Bran's wrist, "a piece of your magic? Just a tiny piece—one you would never miss. Maybe she is worth a single day of your life? Or?" His gaze flicked to Varlan. "Perhaps the thing your companion holds most dear?"

"No." Varlan's voice was tight.

"Are you sure you won't consider it? She is as unique as the one for which you are trading?"

Varlan shook his head.

"Well then, which will it be?"

Bran had been repeating the requests over and over trying to keep a hold of them, but the words were slippery. His eyes? He didn't fancy losing his sight, but would he trade it for Deana's safety? A piece of his keen seemed simple enough, but even the removal of a small piece of his magic could have drastic, irreversible effect. He'd certainly learned that from housing a piece of Nea's keen. Still, it was preferable to losing his sight. Vask had also suggested that he trade the lives of one of his friends for Deana but—

"We haven't got all day. What will it be?" Vask's voice chased through Bran's thoughts, scattering them and leaving the dull throb of a headache behind.

"You suggested I trade my eyes or a piece of my magic, but what else? I know there were more options," Bran said as he tried to stir the memories back up.

"The thing your companion holds most dear, but he has already rejected that idea. However, if you would like to overrule his decision, I will accept it."

Bran shook his head; he couldn't trade Agnes for Deana.

"Still no? Then one of your other friends. You have so many and I so few. I would accept both of the twins if you didn't want to split them."

Bran wouldn't trade anyone else for Deana, but there was one last thing that Vask had not mentioned. One last request that was—

"A day of my life."

Vask's tongue darted along his lips. "A day from *both* of your lives," he said as his gaze flicked to Varlan.

"No, just mine. I'll give you one day, and you will return Deana to us *unharmed.*"

"Very well. Your friend can wait with the others." He flicked his fingers and Varlan staggered backwards as though blown by a strong wind.

"Wait—" he called, but whatever else he said was garbled as he passed through the barrier and stumbled into Gendry.

"Now," Vask said, drawing Bran's gaze back to him, "I'm told dying only hurts for a second." The guardian pressed his fingers to the centre of Bran's forehead.

A cold shiver ran through his body and a tight pain stabbed at his heart as he collapsed onto his hands and knees. Pressure built in his chest as he tried in vain to draw breath and the edges of his vision blurred as a hot-cold panic fizzed through his veins.

"Then again, you should know exactly what it feels like. You've done it before after all."

CHAPTER SIXTEEN

VARLAN

Kiki's fingers dug into the inside of Varlan's wrist as Bran fell to his knees on the other side of the invisible barrier. They couldn't hear what Vask was saying and even if they could, Varlan wasn't sure he wanted to. The guardian's voice was slippery, his words fading into one another making the listener feel like they were trying to solve the most complex of riddles whilst also being too deep in their cups.

"What's happening in there?" Gendry asked, his attention firmly glued on Bran and Vask.

Bran was laying on the ground now, his body unusually still. Vask lifted his gaze and gave Varlan a nod before waving his hand in a quick circle and disappearing in a flash of red light.

The source gave an erratic shudder and Pippa, who had been leaning against the barrier, stumbled forward as it disappeared with an audible pop. She ran to the spot Vask had been standing, but Bran's body had disappeared along with the guardian.

"Did Vask kill him? That was Vask, wasn't it?" Kiki asked as she followed her sister at a sombre pace.

"No, I don't think he's dead. At least, that wasn't the deal that was struck for Deana's safe return to us," Varlan said.

"What deal?"

"The guardians never give their services for free. Bran traded one day of his life for Deana's return to us."

"So Vask has taken him, but where is Deana?" Pippa said. "And why ...?" She seemed to choke on the word.

"Why did it look like Vask was killing him?" Kiki finished her sister's unspoken question.

Varlan pressed his lips together and shook his head.

"One day of his life? Surely, he could have given something else," Gendry said as he moved to examine the toppled statue at the shrine's centre.

"Vask gave us several options, each as unsavoury as the next. As for where Deana is, I would say that Vask will not return her until the full payment has been made."

"Meaning this time tomorrow?" Kiki said.

Varlan nodded. "I suggest we head back to the Queen and let the others know what is going on, then we can return here and wait."

"What if Vask releases Deana before we get back?" Pippa asked.

"He won't." Of that Varlan was certain. In all the tales his mother and the other curators of Mintura had told him, the guardians always twisted the rules of a pact to benefit themselves.

"We can't just leave," Both twins said in unison and shared a shocked look. Ever since Kiki's internment as Kent's prisoner, the twins had been uncharacteristically out of synch with each other.

"I don't recommend staying, but I won't stop you if you want to," Varlan said, and flicked a look at Gendry, who gave a nod.

"Captain's probably not going to be happy with it, but we're coming right back so if you're sure that's what you want to do."

The twins shared another look and then they both nodded.

"We'll stay just in case Vask releases Deana early," Pippa said.

"Alright. If Vask appears again, don't make any deals with him. I'll send Wes back with Gendry. I'm not sure if his suppression can negate the powers of a guardian like Vask, but there's a chance it might come in handy."

Pippa's eyes narrowed as she studied Varlan. "You're not coming back?"

"I—" He didn't like the idea of leaving Agnes without protection, especially as Vask had seemed so interested in her. Then again, she had her father, Wren, Nari, and Luca all there if something happened. "It depends on the state of things on the Queen," he finally said.

"A-ha," Kiki said in a dry tone, and Pippa gave a snort of amusement.

"Star above, girls, leave the poor fool alone," Gendry said with a chuckle and started herding Varlan towards the stairs. "We will try to be back before dark."

"You did what?!" Wren's keen, which had been burring in an angry prickle as they told her what had happened at Vask's shrine, exploded in a shower of bright blue sparks around her.

"Now, my—"

"Don't you dare *my love* me, you great oaf! How could you just leave them there when that god is still lurking in the shadows. What if he comes back and strikes a deal with one of them?"

"The twins are not fools, Wren."

She turned her ire on Varlan as he spoke, but he simply folded his arms over his chest and stared her down.

"Bran is not a fool either and look what happened to him. You can't know for sure that Vask will return either him or Deana. He could have just killed Bran and decided to keep Deana. From what you've told me, that is exactly what it looks like."

"Vask is a slippery bastard, but guardians always honour the terms of their deals. At least, they honour the version that ..." He bit down on the rest of that sentence.

"The version that what?" Wren planted her hands on her hips.

"Nothing. Vask will return them both, and Deana, at least, will be unharmed."

"So, we're at the whims of a—what did you call him? A slippery bastard. And you left two valuable members of my crew— *my family*—within striking distance." She threw her hands in the air and stormed across the deck.

"Wr—"

"If you value your balls still being attached to your body, I suggest you let her simmer down a bit," Gendry said.

"Right," Varlan muttered under his breath. "The twins are more than capable of taking care of themselves though."

"Yes, I know that. And Wren knows it too. But after what happened to Kiki on Armada, she's become a little overprotective." Gendry clapped him on the shoulder then wandered over to Rufus.

Varlan leant against the side rail of the ship and let out a sigh. The door to the captain's quarters was closed, but Wes wasn't in there with Agnes. He was farther down the deck talking with Luca and Elijah. He had said Dara wanted to watch Agnes for a while, so he had let her take over. Nari was reclining in a patch of sun close to the captain's quarters, with a book open on her lap and a collection of small jars containing fragments of shrouded-one coral beside her. Varlan pushed away from the rail and approached the healer.

"There's been no change," she said without looking up as his shadow fell over her.

"I wasn't going to ask about Agnes. I'm curious about what you're doing with that coral."

She placed a finger against the page she had been reading and looked up at him. "Trying to understand the root of the curse. If we can learn that then we can use it."

"Use it to what end? To find a cure?"

"Most shrouded are dead before they turn. They cannot be saved, but they can be liberated from their state of purgatory. For those that are ..." She snapped her fingers a few times, her lips pursed like she was hunting for the right word. "... fortunate," she winced but didn't correct herself, "enough to still be living before the transformation, they might be able to be saved. The coral is like an infestation of fleas. It is a parasite and a rather persistent one. We just need to find the right way to eradicate it without harming the host more than necessary."

A parasite that burrowed into a mage's keen and twisted it, corrupted it— "Is it a form of corruption?"

"Corruption is a disease prevalent in Beldaren and Osmarian mages, but we see very few cases of it here in the isles. So, I don't have enough firsthand experience to answer that. However, given what I have read and what Bran has told me of corruption, I would say they do share *some* similarities. Like corruption, the shrouded curse mutates the person that it infects, twists them into wraith-like abominations, but it is indiscriminate in the choice of its victims. Corruption, however, requires its host soul to possess some form of magic that it can feed off and subvert."

Varlan nodded his understanding.

"Bran mentioned that corruption was akin to a form of possession, however, the afflicted are still independently minded for the most part. Whereas, once the shrouded infection gets established, most victims are absorbed into a kind of ..." she studied his face a moment, "hive mind."

"How long have you studied the curse?"

She bit down on her lip, her gaze dropping to her fingers where they still kept her place on the page. "Since it took my heart mate," she whispered. "Fala thought she could hide it from me in the early stages, thought she could find a cure all on her own and spare me the worry—the heartache of watching her lose herself. Then the guild of singers found out. She'd gone to them for aid, but I still didn't know until Nazali confronted me, asked me why I didn't reveal Fala's affliction to the guild. They were terrified.

Something they thought was a children's story had suddenly appeared in their glittering pavilion. I was still reeling from the news myself. Why hadn't Fala told me, confided in me before going to the guild? Why hadn't I noticed something was wrong?" She glanced at the door to the captain's quarters. "They executed her. They were deafened by their fear and my pleas went unheard. I couldn't save her and I just—something broke inside me that day and it didn't mend again until I met an inquisitive young girl with garishly coloured hair and her doting father, who was equally as heartbroken as me. I don't know if Agnes and Elijah know that they saved me, but they did. When I realised the years I had wasted blaming myself for what had happened to Fala when I could have been looking for a way to prevent it from happening to someone else—" She shook her head. "That's when I started making up for lost time. But you know shrouded ones are particularly hard to find and viable samples of their coral near impossible to obtain."

Varlan leant against the wall and folded his arms. "Did you know Idir was shrouded?"

"Not at first. Certainly not when he came sniffing around Elijah supposedly looking for a map." She studied the door to the captain's quarters again. "If I had known ..." She gave a bitter laugh. "Hindsight is a truly bitter curse."

Varlan let out a huff. "Yeah, hindsight and I are near constant companions these days." He straightened and reached for the door to the cabin.

"I don't know that she'll pull through this unharmed, but she's a fighter," Nari said.

"I know." He gave her a small smile, then entered Wren's quarters.

Dara had her chair pulled right up beside Agnes and her head was laying on her elbows on the bed, the fingers of one hand curled over Agnes's arm. She appeared to be asleep, but the air in the cabin was thick with the drowsy sensation of her keen, and Varlan stifled a yawn.

"Dara, why don't you go and get some fresh—" The moment his fingers touched Dara's shoulder, the room swooped away from him and he landed with a heavy thud in the endless white desert of Agnes's dreamscape.

He shook himself off as he got to his feet and turned in a slow circle, studying the landscape around him. A small white rabbit with mauve-tipped ears and feet was sitting a short distance from him. It cleaned its nose between its front paws then looked straight at him and gave a little jolt, as though shocked to see him. Its eyes were a very familiar shade of pale green.

"Dara?"

The rabbit loped towards him and stood up on its hindlegs and pressed its paws against his shin.

'Varlan? What are you doing in Agnes's dream?' Dara's voice echoed through his mind.

"What am I doing here? What are *you* doing here?"

'Looking for Agnes.' Her tone was sardonic, as though she was stating the obvious.

"You should—"

'I heard her come back; her dreams started singing again. If I can find her, I can help her wake up.'

Varlan let out a breath and his keen-sense built at his core before he sent it out, searching for any sign of Agnes. There was nothing, and then he felt her keen burning bright. But there was something different about it, something he couldn't quite put his finger on. "She's that way," he said to Dara before he started off across the sand.

She hopped along beside him and after a while she picked up pace until she disappeared over the top of a large dune.

Varlan ran to catch up, and the moment he crested the dune he stumbled to a halt. Agnes was lying in a limp sprawl in the centre of an eight-pointed star of dull ash grey sand at the bottom of a crater. Dara had started down the sloped edge of the crater already, causing little avalanches of white sand to race ahead of her. Varlan scanned the landscape with both his mundane senses and his magical ones before he took off, sending a river of sand cascading around him.

He slid to a stop next to Agnes and reached for her but drew his hand back at the last moment. A patch of shirt above her heart was tattered and singed as though it had been burned but the skin showing through the scorched hole appeared unharmed. One hand was open beside her. The black marks from her fingertips were gone, as was the one from the centre of her palm, but in its place was a pale eight-pointed star.

Dara sniffed Agnes's fingers then hopped up onto her chest and stared intently at her face. The dreamscape around them shimmered and images flickered across the pale sky above only to disappear once more as Agnes let out a soft groan.

Her eyelashes fluttered and her fingers twitched then she sat up, dislodging Dara, and covered her mouth as she let out a yawn.

Relief washed through Varlan as her russet gaze found his and a small smile twitched across her lips. "Varlan?"

He fought the urge to fold her against his chest and press his lips to the top of her head. "Are you alright?"

She blinked at him. "I think so. Idir—" She turned her head, her eyes scanning the crater around them as though looking for something. "I destroyed the door," she whispered, then her gaze found Dara and she blinked again. "Where did the rabbit come from?"

"It's Dara."

"Dara? I heard her in my dream." She pressed her fingers to her forehead. "I'm still dreaming, aren't I? You're not really here. You're just a memory, and you'll kiss me and then disappear in a minute."

A chuckle built in the back of his throat. "I can assure you I am really here this time and I promise I won't kiss you." No matter how much he would like to.

She stared at him wide-eyed and swallowed. "You won't?"

"Not unless you want me to, but we do have company." He flicked look at Dara.

"Oh," she rubbed her hand across her forehead again, "everything is all out of order."

"May I?" He lifted a hand towards her temple, and she nodded.

When his fingers brushed her skin, he let his keen smooth over her. Her mind was in chaos, fragments of dream and memory colliding with each other until nothing made sense. He drew a breath and let his magic burrow deeper until it found the source of the tangle. Very gently, he worked at the knot until it came undone with enough force to send him catapulting from her mind.

She doubled over, gripping both sides of her head, and fear seized his throat until she sat up again and tackled him. Her arms squeezed tight around his waist as she pressed her face to the centre of his chest. She was shaking, and he gently folded his arms around her as Dara wriggled into the space between them and settled on Agnes's lap.

After a while, the shudders stopped running through Agnes's body and she pulled back from him, rubbing away the glistening remnants of tears. "I'm sorry. It was just ... This has been a truly terrible dream."

"I understand, and that is why I think," he gave Dara a pointed look and a nod, and she hopped in a tight circle as the dreamscape flickered around them, "it's time to wake up."

CHAPTER SEVENTEEN

DEANA

The heady scent of devotional incense wafted over Deana, bringing with it the realisation that her back was pressed against something cold. A subtle throb like the beat of a heart pulsed beneath her spine. Coloured lights danced across the back of her eyelids and somewhere a small stream was trickling over stones, lending its music to the otherwise still air.

She opened her eyes slowly. The room she was in was lit by a legion of floating candles, their soft light giving everything a golden tint. That many candles should have lent their warmth to the chamber, but the air was cool enough to turn her breath to a plume of white mist. She rubbed her hands against her arms as she stood. The floor beneath her was an intricate mosaic depicting a masked figure standing on an outcrop of rock above a churning ocean, but the waves crashing around the figure were not entirely made of water. They were built from the forms of featureless people, some with their hands stretched towards the figure and others with their backs to turned to him.

Tapestries lined the walls, the images stitched on them slowly changing as the hard-to-grasp melody of Vask's song permeated the air.

Deana turned away from the moving tapestries, searching for the guardian. A large throne of ivory-coloured bones sat in the centre of the far wall facing the tapestries, but it was empty. The stream she could hear was running in a channel around the very edges of the room. It entered through an alcove just to the right of the throne and exited through a twin alcove to the left.

She moved to the left alcove and peered through. There was another chamber on the other side. It appeared similar to the one which she was in but with an ankle-deep red mist pooling across the floor. Voices came from that way, the tone of them prickling the hairs on the back of her neck. She leant farther into the alcove, and something moved on the other side. Then there was the screech of metal against metal and a skeletal form was thrown across the room, its foe chasing after it, sword raised. When it reached the fallen skeleton, it brought the blade down across its neck and the skull went rolling through the red mist with the sound of rattling bone.

Deana bit down on her gasp of shock, but the skeleton with the sword spun to face the alcove. It tilted its head as though it had heard her. The red lights burning in place of its eyes flickered as it crept forward, each step accompanied by a raspy scrape and rattle. Deana moved away from the alcove and turned to press her back against the wall, hoping she was out of sight.

The bones of the skeleton creaked, and she leant forward to chance a glance before darting out of sight again. The skeleton was in the alcove. The red mist pooled around its feet and rolled forward, but it stopped before it entered Deana's chamber as though held back by an invisible barrier.

"I wouldn't wander that way if I were you," an unfamiliar voice said, and Deana's attention snapped to the throne upon which a small monkey was sitting.

She swallowed and flicked a look back towards the other chamber.

"They can't enter this room," the monkey said before yawning widely, showing its gleaming teeth.

Vask's song was the only one Deana could hear. Even her own seemed distant in this place. Was the monkey an aspect of Vask? Or was it something else?

"I am guessing your silence is your poor mortal brain trying to make sense of the predicament in which you find yourself. Usually, the first response I get it is, 'Gods help me, a talking monkey!'"

Deana was having no problem following the words as the monkey spoke, so either making a deal with Vask made her immune to the slippery nature of his voice or the monkey was not an aspect of the guardian.

"Who are you?"

"She speaks!" The monkey gave a sardonic chuckle. "I was beginning to worry that you were broken. Who am I? I am Bohdan, the archivist, or I was once a upon a time when I still wore my human flesh. Now I am the doorkeeper, the first face foolish mortals see when they make the mistake of cutting a deal with Vask. So, what did you trade? A year of servitude? A night of carnal pleasure?"

"I—what? Of course not."

The monkey shrugged. "You'd be surprised how often that happens."

"I traded a memory and in return Vask was going to give me answers to help me save the isles from Idir."

The monkey's white brows hiked up and it hopped off the throne, inhaling deeply as though trying to catch her scent. It rubbed its hands together and a wide, almost human grin pulled across its face. "About time we got some real excitement. It feels like a millennium since someone raised a decent cataclysm." There was far too much delight in the monkey's tone. After a moment though, it sobered and ran its fingers along its chin. "A memory seems a paltry payment for the kind of answers you are seeking."

"It was what Vask asked for. Where is he now?"

The monkey tilted his head. "He left a short while ago. It would seem that he is rather popular today. But he should be returning shortly."

Deana cast another look around the chamber. One of the heavy tapestries was depicting an image of a young girl on her knees sobbing, her face stained with ash. A shadowed form stood before her. He crouched and cupped her chin and a blissful expression crossed her face before the image changed to a younger man leading what looked to be his elderly father up the steps of the shrine.

"Who are the people in the tapestries?"

Bohdan loped to her side, his nose twitching as he studied the tapestry she was watching. "Petitioners. Those who wish to forget or be forgotten, those who want to remember. We don't get as many visitors these days, and certainly none as interesting as you." He looked up at her and his eyes narrowed. "Though the petitioner who followed you today is certainly a strong contender for most interesting."

Deana glanced back at the tapestries just in time to catch sight of a familiar head of stark white hair. She raced forward and pressed her hand against the cloth, halting the image. It wasn't Bran—at least not the Bran she knew. This one was older, his build broader across the shoulders, and he was sporting a white beard that almost rivalled the wildness of Gendry's. The deep blue shade of his eyes was the same though, as were the melancholy notes of his song that swirled out from the tapestry.

"Who is that?"

Bohdan climbed to her shoulder and leant forward to study the man in the tapestry. He lifted a paw towards the fabric as though he would touch it then sat back again. His tail coiled across her shoulder to right his balance as he wobbled. "He is a long-dead fool who was blinded by a thirst for knowledge and ultimately betrayed by the ties of blood and loyalty. By the time he sought to correct his mistakes, it was far too late."

Deana lifted her fingers from the tapestry and the image started moving again. The Bran look-alike was not alone. Behind him was a large man Deana knew well. Though his visage was one she had only seen in a dream, whole and human, untarnished by whatever magic had twisted him into the monster he appeared now.

"Rami," she whispered as she touched the tapestry again. "Why is he here?"

"Like many who want to numb the pain of losing everything—to forget."

Behind the two men was a woman with golden hair and dark blue eyes. The coral that now adorned her skull was missing but she was still recognisable.

"Is there any way to hear what is happening?"

"You're probably not going to like it." Bohdan climbed down her outstretched arm and sunk his teeth into her fingers.

"Ouch!" She snatched her hand away from the tapestry, and his weight dropped from her arm.

"You want to be quick—the image will leave soon." He cleaned the smear of her blood from his face then licked it from the tips of his fingers and let out an almost cat-like purr.

Deana reached forward with her bloodied hand and touched the tapestry. With a flash of teal light and the sound of tearing fabric, she tumbled forward to land on her hands and knees behind Vask.

The world was painted in muted tones as though she was viewing it through a screen of smoke. Vask stood waiting while the three petitioners climbed the steps.

Astrid moved ahead of the other two and dropped into a deep bow before the guardian. "Vask, lord of the forgotten—"

"There is nothing for you here." His tone was oddly sharp, the evasive quality of his voice absent.

"But you—"

The ground beneath Astrid's feet shook and she staggered back a step.

"There is nothing for you here, mortal. Leave now."

Astrid spun around, her dark stare landing on Rami and then switching to the Bran look-alike.

"I told you," Bran-not-Bran said.

Astrid's nostrils flared. "It matters not. There will be another way. Come on. We will find a more willing god."

"You can go, but my business here is not concluded," not-Bran said.

Astrid growled under her breath. "Rami," she barked and snapped her fingers for him to follow.

Rami glanced between Astrid and the other mage then shook his head and took a step towards the Bran look-alike.

"You need to end this madness, Astrid; it will destroy you."

"I know what I am doing, Soren."

"Even the gods won't help you." Soren tilted his chin towards Vask, who was watching them with mild curiosity.

"The gods are fools. They cannot stop what has begun but I can, and you won't stand in my way. Not again." She pulled a golden knife from the sheath at her hip and lunged forward.

A bone-chilling note rose in the air, and she was pulled up short as threads of violet magic roved over her skin.

"Let me go," she hissed through her teeth. "You won't strip me. If you didn't have the stomach to strip Idir after that betrayal in Kutha, then you won't kill your own flesh and blood."

The bone-chilling song grew louder, and Astrid's breath misted the air in front of her as a note of panic entered her eyes.

"Rami ... help me, please," she gasped.

Rami shook his head and moved to Soren's side.

"No!" Astrid yelled. Her song rose, pushing back against Soren's until the air was filled with a discordant cacophony. "I should have

162

killed you when Idir suggested it. He was right; you've lost the heart to do what needs to be done."

A wave of power sent them all staggering back as Astrid's song broke through the hold of Soren's magic.

She recovered first, diving forward with the dagger raised and landing solidly on Rami's chest. The blade flashed in the sunlight, Rami's blood splattering the stairs of the shrine as she opened his throat. Her magic twisted through the air, and she let out a scream towards the sky as green and purple coral sprouted from the exposed skin of her arm.

She turned her focus to the still dazed Soren, darting forward and sinking the blade into his side as she growled words too soft for Deana to hear in his ear.

Rami was mouthing something, his eyes staring blankly skyward, and Vask wandered over to study his twitching body.

"No, he is mine." Astrid spun away from Soren and pointed the dagger towards the god.

"As you say. You might want to finish what you started, lest it all be for naught though."

Astrid sliced the dagger along her own palm and smeared her blood across Rami's face. Her song twisted through the air as she muttered words Deana couldn't understand under her breath. The slit along Rami's throat mended itself and he sat up. His face was gaunt, his eyes two empty dark pools with flickering swirls of acrid green light at their centre.

"What have you done?" Soren had regained his feet, but he was doubled over clutching his ribs. A stain of blood spread across his shirt.

"I chose power." She pointed the dagger towards Soren.

"You chose chaos and in doing so have damned yourself, but I will not let you damn everything else." He lifted his hand, and a portal sprang open beneath Astrid.

Her words were stolen with a wild scream as she dropped out of sight and the portal snapped shut again.

"Rami," Soren whispered as he turned his attention to the ghoulish figure left behind.

Rami tilted his head as though he had heard but his features remained blank.

"I am so sorry. I couldn't save you or Sula," he coughed, and blood bubbled over his chin as he fell to his hands and knees.

Vask edged forward, an eager look shifting over his features. "My, this is an interesting turn of events. Tell me, would you like to make a deal?"

Soren started to shake his head but then nodded.

"So, tell me what it is I can do for you?"

Deana didn't hear what Soren asked for as she was thrust out of the past and back into the chamber where not only Bohdan but Vask were waiting for her. "Tsk, tsk. You traded for answers to your current problems not to peer into the past. Bohdan tells me it was his fault, so I won't insist on further payment, but please do not take advantage of my hospitality again."

"Who was Soren?" Deana asked. His song had called to hers the way Bran's did. In fact, she was certain that both men shared the same song and that was something she had never encountered before. Even if mages shared the same talent, their songs would be similar but not identical.

A strange expression shifted over Vask's face, and his gaze moved away from Deana to something behind her.

She turned and pressed her hand over her mouth.

Bran was laying on the floor at the centre of the chamber, his eyes closed as though in sleep, but his song was completely silent.

She moved to his side and pressed her ear to his chest. Nothing. No beating heart, no subtle rise and fall of breath. His body was stone cold as though he had been dead for hours.

A thick lump blocked her throat and she turned to the guardian. "What did you do?"

"He traded a single day of his life for your *safe* return. I merely took the payment that was offered."

"But he's ..."

"Dead. Yes, that's the point. But don't fret. Death doesn't tend to stick as far as his soul is concerned. It's almost like she doesn't want anything to do with him. Though it could be all that world-altering, unfinished business he has. Now, I believe I promised you answers and given that our time together now has a finite ending, I suggest we get down to business."

She stood and turned away from Bran's body. "Alright. How do I stop Idir?"

The predatory smile flicked at the corners of his mouth again. "You stop Idir by raising Dumura and claiming the wonders found there for yourself."

"Isn't that what Idir wants though? And won't raising Dumura lead to the destruction of the rest of the isles?"

Bohdan climbed up Vask's side and settled on his shoulder. He whispered something in the guardian's ear, and the smile on Vask's face faltered for a moment.

"Destruction does not mean the end; the isles themselves will still exist. But sometimes the bone needs to be re-broken before it can be set right." His voice had taken on that slippery quality again, but where it had been uncomfortable to follow before, now the words slid around her mind like silk—still hard to keep hold of but almost alluring.

"How do I raise Dumura?"

"Now therein lies the question to which I do not have the answer. You are one piece of a very intricate puzzle spanning generations of time and multiple barriers between worlds. I do know you have most, if not all, of the rest of the pieces you require to raise the isle. The question you need to find the answer to is," he moved closer until she had to tilt her head back to meet his crimson stare, "do you have the courage to do what must be done, even if it means accepting the risk of unleashing ultimate chaos on everything you hold dear?" His fingers were like ice as they brushed along her jaw.

Bohdan hopped across the gap between them, his slight weight making her shoulder dip as he settled in place.

"Well?" Vask asked as he released her and strode to his bone throne.

Deana turned away from the guardian, her stare falling on Bran's body. Her heart was pounding, drowning out all other sounds and dulling the shifting notes of Vask's song. She studied the tapestry showing Soren's crumpled form. How much had already been sacrificed to try and stop Idir? How far must she go to see it through? How far *would* she go to avenge her family, to avenge all those who had been destroyed by one man's greed?

"Whatever it takes," she whispered to herself and then lifted her gaze to meet Vask's crimson stare.

His eyebrows lifted in silent question, and her voice abandoned her.

She clenched her fists and gave him a single curt nod. Idir had to be stopped. The kernel of anger that had been growing at her core shifted as a new realisation clawed across her scalp. Whatever was driving her was no longer just a desire to secure a safe future for the isles; it had become a seething craving for vengeance.

CHAPTER EIGHTEEN

AGNES

Agnes's body was a dead weight, the pounding of her heartbeat deafening. She had been in this dream before—the one where her mind seemed to wake before her body. Panic tightened her throat and she struggled against her immobile limbs, silently begging them to respond. The heaviness in her body pushed back, making it feel like she was being held down against the bed. Her breathing quickened and she fought the downward force until she awoke with a sharp gasp.

She tilted her head towards the table beside the far wall, almost expecting Byron to be sitting there watching her. But the table was gone, the light in the room different: a multicoloured spray across the wall as the sunlight passed through stained glass rather than iron bars. She lay back again as the space around her seemed sway in a way that suggested she had had too much to drink, but the subtle lap of water and creak of wood told her she was on a ship. The Azure Queen. That thought stirred a cascade of memories—escaping Kent's prison, losing Deana, slipping into a dream from which she couldn't wake.

An itchy prickle almost like the rushing burning of pins and needles that accompanied her magic stirred along her spine. It was different to the trance though, deeper and from outside her body rather than from within. A warm sluggishness that made her fight the urge to fall back asleep wove through the prickle, and a ticklish impression of fingers roving over the back of her neck joined both sensations.

She sat up slowly. Dara was beside the bed. She appeared to be sleeping with her cheek resting on her arms and a content smile on her lips. Varlan was sprawled on the floor beside the sleeping girl, as though he had fallen asleep on his feet, only to collapse in a heap.

Agnes brushed Dara's hair back from her face, and the girl's nose twitched before she opened one pale green eye. She lifted her head and blinked at Agnes, then let out a whoop and dove forward to hug her.

"I did it!" she exclaimed and leapt to her feet, darting around Varlan, who was rising from the floor, and out the door.

Varlan studied Agnes for a moment, and the sensation of fingers at the back of her neck deepened from a tickle to a gentle roll that was almost soothing.

"How do you feel?" he asked.

"Fine, I think." She rubbed her hand over the back of her neck to try and shift the feeling there, as the door opened and her father rushed in, followed by Nari.

New sensations flooded over her—a bright flutter that set the hairs of her arms on end and a gentle warmth like she was slipping into a hot bath. It was all too much, and she drew back against the wall behind the bed.

"Is everything alright?" Her father swooped closer, brushing her hair back and inspecting her with concern.

The fluttering sensation grew stronger, and she rubbed her arms before sending a panicked look at Nari. "No, something is wrong. I feel—my body doesn't feel *right.*"

Her father blinked at her and then turned his attention to Varlan and then Nari. "An after-effect of the mage bane?"

The warm sensation grew hotter for a moment, and the healer shook her head. "There is nothing amiss. If anything, she is in perfect health for someone who has been through—"

"Don't talk about me like I am not here!" Agnes leapt to her feet, jostling into Varlan as she tried to put some distance between herself and everyone else in the room.

"Agnes, it's alright," Varlan said softly, his eyes locking with hers as though he and Agnes were the only people present. And she wished that was the case. The room felt far too crowded.

"Do you know what's wrong, Varlan?" her father asked.

Varlan's gaze moved to her father and a smile tugged at one corner of his mouth as he gave a nod.

"What's wrong with me?"

"Nothing's *wrong*." He let out a small chuckle as he turned back to her. "It's your keen-sense."

"But I don't have keen-sense. It was broken by—oh. Is this what it feels like all the time?"

"No. I would assume that yours will be particularly sensitive given that it never had a chance to grow alongside your keen. I can't even begin to imagine what that feels like."

Agnes hugged her arms tighter around herself. "Is there any way to turn it off again?"

"Varlan could—"

"No." Varlan cut Nari off with a sharp shake of his head, but his features softened when he turned back to Agnes. "Too many mages have tampered with your keen. I won't risk it."

"It's too much. I can't—" Her breath caught in her chest and her throat tightened again.

"Agnes." Varlan was suddenly directly in front of her, his hands on her shoulders and his eyes searching hers as that rolling feeling moved over her nape and then swooped across the tops of her shoulders. "Breathe."

She glanced at Nari and her father, who were having a whispered argument behind Varlan, but his grip tightened momentarily, and she met his gaze once more as an unnaturally warm calm settled over her.

"Please," she whispered, "please make it stop."

The corner of his mouth ticked. "I don't know that I can and even trying could cause irreparable damage. But I can help you learn how to control it. The main thing is to remain calm and remember to breathe."

She drew a halting breath and then let it out again.

"Good. Now when you feel a new keen, you need to let your keen-sense become familiar with it. Once you've done that, it will be easier to divert your keen-sense away from it."

The sensation at her nape deepened again and she realised it was his keen that she was feeling. She had felt echoes of it before, even when her keen-sense was absent. She focused on that feeling, exploring the edges of it and then delving deeper.

He cleared his throat and rolled his shoulders as his keen brushed against hers, rising in an intimate pulse deep in her core. She licked her lip and dropped her gaze to the floor as she reeled her magic back into herself.

"Sorry," she whispered, her cheeks suddenly hot.

He let out a silky chuckle. "It's alright. I should have warned you—"

The sound of her father clearing his throat pulled her attention away from Varlan. He stepped forward and the bright flutter of his magic plied against the edge of her own, but it didn't quite chase the lingering caress of Varlan's keen away. She pulled her magic towards herself and the sensation of her father's keen faded. It seemed easier to divert her focus from his magic and—she pushed her keen-sense out again until it found the warm edge of Nari's magic. She didn't examine the healer's keen as thoroughly as Varlan's. But unlike Varlan's keen which welcomed her and encouraged her to explore its depths, Nari's was more reserved.

When she finally pulled her keen back into herself, she realised that Varlan was still holding her shoulders, the air between them tight with something as intriguing as it was alarming.

He gave her a nod and let go of her shoulders before taking a step back. Cool air seemed to rush between them, scattering the tension.

"It will get easier, and you usually won't feel a mage's keen unless you are trying to or they are using their magic. But ah," he rubbed his fingers along his jaw, "try not to go too deep. A light touch is all that's needed to familiarise yourself with another mage's magic."

Her father muttered something that ended in a grunt as Nari punched his arm.

A flush moved up her neck and she took a step back, putting more space between her and Varlan. His keen still brushed against hers, unlike her father's and Nari's which she couldn't feel at all now.

"Are you using your magic now, because I can still feel it?"

The look he gave her was inscrutable before he tore his gaze away and settled it on Nari's.

The healer made a small sound in the back of her throat that could have been a laugh. "Some keens *call* to each other, usually if there is some kind of attachment. Like a strong sibling bond for instance, though more often it's—"

"So good to see you awake, lass." Gendry swept into the room and engulfed her in a hug. "It's time," he said as he let her go and then settled his dark gaze on Varlan.

"Time for what?" Agnes asked, happy to change the topic. As curious as she was, she could guess what Nari had been about to say and that was a conversation she wasn't ready to explore.

"Nothing you need to be worried about, lass," Gendry said before his attention moved back to Varlan again. "Are you coming?"

Varlan studied Agnes then gave Gendry a nod. "We'll bring Wes as well."

Gendry raised an eyebrow at him and flicked a look Agnes's way. The sensation of Varlan's keen thickened once more and Gendry gave a shrug before saying, "Can't argue with that," and turned towards the door.

"You should take Luca as well, just in case," Nari said. "I'd go but I am too old to be stomping through the jungle."

"Take Luca where?" Agnes shifted her gaze from Nari to her father before settling it on Varlan.

"We found Deana," Varlan said.

"You found her? When? Why would you need Luca? Do you think she's hurt or ..." She couldn't finish that thought.

"As far as we know, Deana is unharmed," Varlan said, but there was something about the look that slipped over his features that settled a cold dread in her stomach.

"I'm coming with you." She started for the door, almost expecting him to object.

"No, you will stay here so I can keep an eye on you," Nari said.

Agnes turned to face the healer. "Deana is my friend. I want to go and make sure she is alright."

"You've been through an ordeal of your own and until you figure out how to control your reawakened keen-sense, you will be a liability." Nari's tone had that gentle firmness she used when she was trying to get an unruly patient to take their medicine.

"You don't have a problem with it though?" Agnes turned to Varlan.

He rubbed his fingers along his chin and bit his lip as though holding back words.

"Or you, Dad?"

"Actually, I agree with Nari." Of course he did.

Agnes bit down a groan of frustration and spun to face the door again. "Fine, I'll just ask Bran. I am sure he won't have a problem with it."

Varlan made a noise that dropped the bottom out of her stomach.

"What happened?" she asked without turning.

"Deana is being held by Vask, the guardian of the forgotten. To get her back Bran had to trade a day of his life. There's a possibility that ... that we've lost him."

"Lost him?"

"Bargains with gods are tricky things to navigate."

Bran was smart though, especially when dealing with spirits. Surely he wouldn't make a mistake like that. Regardless, the only way they would stop her from coming now was to tie her down. She darted out the door before any of them got the idea.

Gendry was by the rowboat with Luca, Wes, and Rufus. He gave her a wide smile as she approached.

"I'm coming with you," she said before anyone else could say anything.

Luca's brows raised and he looked at something over her shoulder. She glanced back, following the healer's line of sight to Varlan, who was approaching with his hands in his pockets and his thoughtful stare trained on the deck before his feet.

"Agnes, are you sure that's wise? You should be resting after what you've been through," Wes said. A curious numbness rolled over her, almost like when Luca had dosed her with mage bane.

"I'm fine, perfect even. Nari said so herself."

Warmth chased the numbness away. Luca's magic?

"Nari is correct—there is nothing physically amiss despite everything you have been through," the healer said and then nodded to Varlan as he reached them. "You're okay with this?"

"I won't lie, I would rather you stay, especially given that your keen-sense has reawakened and it is going to take you some time to adjust."

Agnes opened her mouth to object, but he held up a hand and she bit down on her words.

"However, if you wish to come, I am not going to stop you."

He wasn't? That was unexpected given how overprotective he had been since they fled Armada.

Wes cleared his throat and gave Varlan a pointed look. The smooth almost seductive pressure of Varlan's keen pressed against her as he and Wes moved themselves a short distance away.

"Well, I have no issue with it," Gendry said. Offering her a hand to help her into the boat, he added, "Come on, lass. We shouldn't waste any more time."

CHAPTER NINETEEN

BRAN

He was in the Between, that much was certain. His body felt strangely weightless, almost like he was nothing more than a cloud of thoughts and magic that could disperse on an errant breeze. The forest around him murmured as though the trees were talking amongst themselves. Otherwise, it was oddly calm. No spirits tugging at the edge of his keen-sense, waiting for his attention as usually was the case when he drifted across the barrier. This was different though. He hadn't summoned the barrier—he had been cast across it the moment his last breath slipped through his lips. This was death then. Regret stirred in his stomach. Regret and something else—mortification. How could he have been so foolish? Rule one of dealing with anything that was otherworldly in nature was never bargain with it. Of course Vask would twist the terms of the deal to suit himself.

He rubbed a hand through his hair and let out a sigh. He'd traded a single day, so did that mean he would awaken in a handful of hours as though nothing had happened? Surely that wouldn't be the case. Those who touched death this intimately, even for a moment, were forever altered by it. Would he become a deathwalker like Declan and Nea? Both had been physically dead, their souls kept safe in a pocket of the Between. Was that where he was now? It would explain the lack of other spirits. But what if he didn't revive? No, surely Nea would have felt the piece of her keen trapped with his either returning to her or being snuffed out entirely. And if she had, then she would come looking for him. He pressed his fingers to the crescent mark on the inside of his wrist. The cold kiss of shadow-tainted necromancy still pooled beneath the surface of his skin.

"When are you going to learn not to make deals with god-kin?" a voice said behind him.

He turned slowly, his keen building at his core ready to defend himself against whatever spirit had drawn close, but his keen immediately died when his gaze locked with his own.

It was like looking in a mirror that added a decade or two's worth of living to his features.

"What was it this time?" the older version of himself asked, as he scratched his fingers through the impressive beard that covered the lower half of his face.

This man couldn't be Bran—it didn't make any sense. A spirit then. A helpful one or one trying to trick him?

"Who are you?" Bran asked finally.

"I could ask you the same but then again, we both know that you should never give your name to anything you encounter here in the Between. Let's just say we share a soul and be done with it."

"Share a soul?"

The man nodded. "Share, are individual incarnations of ... It's all a matter of semantics really. You were me and I will be you. Of course, there are some key differences given the nature of our separate upbringings, but it would appear that we are both still colossal idiots when it comes to dealing with the divine."

Bran rubbed his hand across his forehead. "Did you make a deal with Vask too then?"

The man let out a laugh. "Yes, though he wasn't the only one."

"What kind of deal?"

"I believe I already asked you a version of that question." He folded his arms and tilted his head. The skin just behind his left ear was marked with a small, flower-shaped birthmark. Was he a deathborn like Nea?

"I was trying to get him to release a friend who he had taken."

"She made a deal with him herself then."

"I never said it was a 'she'."

The man gave him a wry smile. "It's always a girl. I couldn't save her either if you're wondering. But if she made a deal with Vask herself, then did she really need saving?"

"Vask had every intention of keeping her."

The older version of himself shrugged. "Were you certain of that?"

Bran bit down on his response. He had been certain Vask wanted to keep Deana, but maybe it was just his guilt at letting her get kidnapped in the first place. And how had she come to end up with Vask? He was certain that shrouded ones, whether they were aligned with Idir or not, had taken her.

"Made a few wrong assumptions, didn't you?"

"I'm guessing you made a few of your own."

That earned him a bark of laughter. "Yeah, I mentioned before that we're colossal idiots. I thought I had it all figured out—make a couple of deals with the right few god-kin and everything would fall into place. Didn't count on a sister with an enchanted dagger and treachery in her heart. I certainly hope she and Idir are happy with their curse though."

"You knew Idir?"

"Of course. He needed a mage in possession of a certain set of skills—in particular one who could open physical doors in the barrier. Even back then we we're in short supply. Got to have that special, necromancer, touched-by-Shadow taint on your soul to pull that sort of thing off." He traced his fingers over the birthmark.

"But I'm not a deathborn."

"You sure about that?" His gaze tracked to the oathmark on Bran's wrist.

"That's a piece of a deathborn's keen, but I am certain I am not a deathborn myself."

The look that crossed the other Bran's face could only be described as smug. "You know, if she'd tried that little trick with any other mage, it would have failed and both she and the brightling would be dead." A shadow chased his mirth away. "Sacrifices for the greater good, or some bullshit like that," he muttered the words softly, but Bran heard them all the same.

"I don't have a birthmark, and until Nea and I created the oathbond, I couldn't do any of the things she can."

The other Bran shrugged. "You're smart enough to know that the true nature of any mage's keen can be hidden or blocked. As for the birthmark?" He waved his hand, and a sharp jolt of cold magic pierced the side of Bran's neck just behind his left ear.

Bran stretched his jaw and pressed his fingers to the spot to disperse the sensation.

"The body you currently inhabit may not bear the mark, but your soul does."

"I was raised by some of the brightest magical minds. Surely someone would have noticed by now. Not to mention, they have intimate experience with deathborn mages. If my soul really is *tainted*, then they would know."

"Vask wasn't the only god-kin I made a deal with, you know? I couldn't just throw my soul forward through time and hope for the best. Idir stole the guardian Lehara's gift of prophecy and even though he can only wield a shadow of the powers he steals, he has access to her gift of foresight, which is why he was always half a dozen steps ahead. I had to make sure my future self would be undetectable to that gift, for as long as possible at least."

"Hang on. You *threw* your soul forward through time?"

"Technically, Nock did the throwing. I just asked him nicely."

"Nock?"

"The guardian of time."

Bran raked his fingers through his hair and turned away from the older version of himself. This conversation was giving him a headache.

"Farideans have such an intricate coterie of gods, or rather god-like beings. In my time, we called them elder spirits. Embodiments of every fathomable aspect of the natural and the metaphysical. Not all are named and not all exist freely between the realms. There is, as you are learning I am sure, a hierarchy."

"So, Nock sent you through time and you became ... me?"

"In a manner of speaking."

"Did my parents know? Is that why they left me outside Hartswood?"

"Parents? You don't have them in the normal sense of a mother who carried and birthed you. Moalana and Nock could be considered your parents, I guess. Which would make you—"

"Divine blooded." Bran whispered as the other version of himself said,

"God-kin."

Bran shook his head. He wasn't human. He wasn't deathborn. What then—no, he was in the Between and he was conversing with a spirit. Spirits were often tricksters by nature. This one was trying to keep him here, keep him distracted.

"You are human in essence. Similar, I suppose, to a deathborn or brightling, though they do require human parents. Your body is human; your soul has become something *more*."

Obviously, this spirit could read his thoughts. He focused on pulling up his mental walls before turning back to face the spirit.

"I assure you that I am not a spirit—well, not a native of the Between spirit. I am not even memory given form. I am a ghost. I was once as flesh and blood as you. I made many mistakes and too late, I tried to rectify them. You are my second chance at redemption and whether you want to believe me or not, Idir must be stopped. He cannot reach the sanctum at the heart of Dumura. He cannot steal the Grandmother's power. You must stop him—whatever the cost." His voice hitched over those last three words. It wasn't exactly sorrow that entered his tone but something akin to it.

"How do I stop him?"

The other Bran opened his mouth and then promptly shut it again before shrugging. "I honestly don't know."

"You don't know? You made deals with multiple gods, permanently altered your soul and then had it thrust forward through time, and you don't have a plan to stop Idir? Why go to all that trouble then?"

The other Bran tapped his index finger against his own temple. "Because Idir knows me too well. You, however, are an almost complete anomaly to him."

"But weren't you just saying that I am you?"

"Yes, but you are also technically not me. We share a soul, but the version that Idir knows—*me*," he placed both hands against his chest, "is dead. Changed irrevocably either by pure genius or abject stupidity, depending on who you ask. And so, yes, you are me, but you are also *you*. You are my essence hammered and honed, but your mind and heart, and most importantly your keen, have been altered by the provenance of your birth and those who nurtured you to adulthood."

Bran rubbed his hands over his face. The headache had become a tight throb behind his eyes and his body felt heavier than it had before, almost like it was sinking into the ground. He glanced at his feet, the movement sending a sharp jolt through his skull. "How does that make me capable of beating Idir if you could not?"

"Because he cannot predict what you will do, even with the edge that Lehara's gift of prophecy gives him. Foresight is a tricky thing. Most events are ever-changing, dependent on the whims of each soul in play. Of course, there are moments that are unavoidable despite the efforts of those involved; the outcome is still nebulous, but the event itself is destined. The raising of Dumura for instance. The island will see the light again, regardless of if Idir is the one to raise it or not. What occurs after the isle has risen will decide which way the pendulum swings and what future the isles will be thrust into."

The words were hard to focus on. The edges furred together as a deep cold swept from Bran's toes to the top of his skull. It wasn't necromancy, but it brought the taste of death to the edge of his tongue as a soft, keening melody burrowed into his thoughts and chased the last of the other Bran's words away.

"What—" He stumbled back as his legs shook, threatening to collapse under him.

"It would seem we are running—"

The world flipped and he expected his back to slam against the ground, but nothing broke his fall. Ghostly hands brushed over his body as it plummeted through space. His vision blurred, reducing the world around him to flashes of colour as the keening became an ear-splitting wail that ended with a numb silence and an unfathomable darkness.

His limbs were stiff and unresponsive; the ground beneath his spine almost unbearably cold. Water was running somewhere close by—the playful trickle of a stream over stones. Something heavy and warm pressed to his chest. A familiar scent reached him, delicate like Osmarian night flowers but edged with the salty tang of a stiff ocean breeze.

The weight on his chest shifted and a whisper of touch ran across his brow and down his cheek.

"Bran?"

He knew that voice.

The touch returned, this time brushing against the hair at the side of his neck and tracing over the patch of skin behind his left ear leaving a ticklish sensation in its wake.

"Why isn't he waking?" The warmth beside him shifted, leaving his side feeling colder than the floor at his back.

Another voice said something in response, but the words slipped over each other and faded before he could make sense of them.

The warmth returned, hands taking either side of his face. "Bran, please wake up." The voice was afraid, and the words brought a rolling sensation over him like he was laying in the bottom of a small boat during a squall.

The warmth recoiled once more as the second voice murmured something, humour evident in the tone despite the indecipherable meaning.

A new sensation. Four points of slight pressure moving up his body as though a cat were walking on him. Weight settled on his chest as the dusty scent of old books and something musty like wet fur invaded his senses. Then a sharp, hot pain shot through his ear.

"Bohdan!"

"You wanted him to wake up." Another new voice. Did it belong to the cat sitting on his chest?

There was a flurry of movement and the weight shifted off him again.

"Bran, if you're in there you need to come back. Please? Please come back."

But he hadn't gone anywhere. He was still there, he was just— cool fingers brushed the back of his neck, and the scent of roses washed over him. A soft, seductively comforting voice whispered across his mind and his body grew heavier still. The voice was telling him to relax, to give in to the sweet numbness and slip away. Oblivion could be his. All he had to do was—*No*. He focused on the dead weight around him. It didn't fit quite right, that was the problem, like a drawer that wouldn't close unless you tilted it just right. He pushed and prodded until he snapped back into place.

He was cold, colder than he could ever remember being before. The ache at his ear was white hot as was the burning pressure in his chest. Why did his chest hurt so much? His throat tightened. He was drowning. No, not drowning—suffocating.

Forcing his body to respond, he sat up with a grating gasp. Cool air rushed into his lungs. It tasted stale, but the relief was instant.

Warmth flooded over him, arms squeezing his sides as a face buried against his chest and a cloud of dark curls tickled his chin. The form that clung so tightly to his was shaking, and he rubbed a hand against her back.

"Hey, it's alright."

She held on for a few moments longer then pulled away from him, her sea-green gaze swimming with tears as she studied his face. "I thought—" Her attention flicked to Vask standing a short distance away then back to Bran once more. "I thought you were dead."

Bran lifted his gaze to the god, who was watching them with a bored expression. "I was dead. Coming back was ..." He didn't want to think about how easy it would have been to just let himself slip into death's embrace. "Are you alright?" He studied her face and then the rest of her. She looked tired and there was a gauntness to her features that hadn't been there before, but otherwise she seemed unharmed.

"I ..." She blinked and one of the tears along her lashes separated from the others and rolled down her cheek. She swallowed and brushed it away. "I am now." She rocked back on her heels, putting more distance between them.

Bran lifted his fingers to the itchy wetness at the side of his neck and pulled them away again to reveal tips stained with blood. He touched his earlobe, finding a small stinging hole. "Where did the cat go?"

"Cat?" An indignant voice sounded as a small monkey appeared on Deana's shoulder.

"Sorry, my mistake. I take it you are responsible for puncturing my ear."

The monkey tilted his chin, and Bran got the impression he was being looked down upon by someone with a strong sense of self-importance. "You're welcome."

"Bohdan," Deana reprimanded softly before standing and turning to Vask. "We can leave now, right?"

"Leave, my dear? Why ever would you want to? You are safe here and now you have company. If you go back out there it will only be a matter of time before Idir finds you and when he does—"

"I know what has to be done."

This Deana was different—more confident or perhaps determined was the better word. Either something had changed or he was still in some twisted pocket of the Between that was trying to trap him. He shook his head and got to his feet, letting his keen-sense test the air around him.

The source stirred in an erratic response to his probing, but it didn't have the vast shifting quality of the Between. It was more grounded, evasive in the same way Vask himself was. Deana's keen was a gently rolling swell against the edge of his senses, but it was unmistakably her.

She glanced his way as his keen-sense retreated from her once more.

"Very well, but know that you could have slipped away into obscurity and avoided the heartache that taking the fight to Idir will grant you. Should you change your mind, you will find my offer of hospitality no longer stands." Vask's voice rolled over

Bran, but it wasn't as hard to follow as it had been before. The god gave an errant wave of his hand, and something tugged behind Bran's navel before his body was thrown through space once more.

CHAPTER TWENTY

#

"You just left Kiki and Pippa out here alone?" Agnes asked as she pushed through the undergrowth.

"They are resourceful girls," Gendry said as he held a branch out of the way for her, "besides, they had their minds set on staying and I didn't fancy having to navigate this thicket with one, or both, of them thrown over my shoulder."

Agnes chuckled at that, but her laughter died as the conversation behind her drifted forward.

"Do you know how she managed it?" Luca asked.

"Not exactly," Varlan replied, but the words were followed by a strained sigh. "I have a handful of theories but none I wish to discuss at this moment." He'd been strangely quiet since they left the Queen, though every so often she would feel the touch of his keen against the back of her neck. It was harder to just brush aside than others, but she didn't mind—the sensation of it was almost comforting.

"We're almost there," Gendry said, drawing her attention back to him as he held out a hand to help her over a messy tangle of roots.

Agnes took the offered hand. Given that he was keen-less,

touching Gendry didn't come with the wave of sensations as her keen reacted to the proximity of other magic. Varlan said it would be different when she got used to her keen-sense, and she hoped he was right. It was easy enough to brush another mage's keen aside and ignore it when she wasn't touching them, but touch seemed to open a direct conduit between her keen and the other mage, amplifying the sensations and making them impossible to ignore.

"She seems to be handling the transition rather well." Luca's voice carried forward again, and Agnes bit down on her growl of frustration as Wes made a noise that wasn't quite agreement.

"You don't think so?" Luca again.

"She's spent her entire life with no keen-sense and to just have it switched back on ... I think only time will tell how it has affected her and she has yet to engage her magic. That could change things," the warden said.

Gendry's hand at her elbow stopped her from turning around and berating them.

"They've all been beside themselves with worry since before we rescued you from Kent."

"That doesn't mean they can just—"

"I think we should focus on the task at hand," Varlan said. Was that tightness in his tone annoyance, or something else?

She looked over her shoulder at him, but his attention was on Wes and Luca, who were farther behind. When he turned back to face her, one corner of his mouth twitched into a familiar smile. It was akin to the look the dream version of him had given her right before they—no. She couldn't let herself think of that. It was too complicated, and if whatever had been between them in past was worth keeping, why had he just wiped her memories and left? Despite the danger Idir presented, surely if it had meant something to him, he would have tried harder to stay. She turned away from him and quickened her pace to catch up with Gendry again.

He glanced sideways at her, a cunning look in his dark eyes. "Sometimes life forces us to make difficult choices and our actions during those times don't always make the most sense."

If she hadn't felt his lack of keen for herself, she would assume he was reading her thoughts.

"Anyway, we've arrived." He thrust out an arm, catching her across the waist before she took a step that would send her rolling down the slope in front of them. The drop that fed into the slope was obscured by the tangled undergrowth, and at the bottom was a clear patch of ground that led to a small, ruined temple.

Two figures were lounging by a toppled statue. They looked up and one of them waved as Gendry started guiding Agnes downward.

When they reached the bottom, Kiki came jogging towards them.

"You're awake!" She engulfed Agnes in a hug.

The sensation of water splashing up the back of Agnes's legs accompanied Kiki's embrace and she tried not to pull away to escape the feeling. She drew a breath and hugged Kiki back as she let her keen-sense explore her magic, being careful not to push too deep.

"Did you find your keen-sense?" Kiki asked as she leant back and studied Agnes's face.

"It would appear so."

Kiki stepped away from Agnes as Pippa joined them and the watery sensation of her keen fled, only to be replaced with a new feeling. This one was warm and crackling, making Agnes's cheeks feel flushed like she had stepped too close to a fire.

Pippa's hug was stiffer and quicker than Kiki's; she held on just long enough for Agnes's keen-sense to rove along the very edge of her magic before pulling away. "It's good to see you awake. I see you brought half the Queen back with you." She looked over Agnes's shoulder to Wes and Luca as they joined Varlan and

Gendry at the bottom of the slope.

"No sign of Bran or Deana?" Gendry asked.

Pippa shook her head, and Kiki said, "No sign of Vask either."

"We should still be on our guard, and I don't think it is wise to spend the night inside the boundary of the shrine," Varlan said.

"Why not? There's shelter inside the temple itself," Kiki said.

"And we can post a guard in case Vask returns. As long as none of us make any deals with him we should be fine," Pippa added.

"How about I help you solve your little quandary?" An oily sensation slid down Agnes's spine as a slippery voice sounded behind her.

Varlan's gaze turned to Agnes and he tensed. A look of fear crossed his features as his attention shifted to something over her shoulder.

The weight of someone's hands landed on Agnes's shoulders and the oily sensation overrode everything else. It was shifting and hard for her newly awakened keen-sense to grasp long enough to make any real sense of.

"Let's get a good look at you, hmm?" the tricky-to-follow voice said, as the fingers on her shoulders tightened and she was spun around to face their owner.

His features were almost as slippery as his voice, and she got the sense that he would be very easy to lose sight of in a crowd. Despite the ambiguousness of his face—or perhaps because of it— her gaze was drawn to his. It was a stare that you could get lost in; a single look that could unfetter your senses and drive your thoughts into oblivion. Deep knowledge and infinite secrets were held in the splashes of dark blood that fractured the brighter crimson backdrop of his irises. And they drew her in as keenly as a snake swaying to mesmerise its prey before it struck.

"Oh my. We are truly at a turning point, aren't we? Tell me, you *precious*—" His gaze flicked to something behind her as he purred the word, a gloating smile gracing his lips before his gaze returned

189

to her and he continued, "—little thing. Would you like your fractured memories back? What would you give to have all those pressing questions of yours answered?"

"Agnes d—" Varlan's words were cut off as Vask lifted his hand and clenched his fist.

Agnes glanced back at the others. Gendry, Kiki, Pippa, Luca, and Wes were by the toppled statue, the air between her and them shimmering like a haze of heat. They appeared to be shouting but she couldn't hear what they were saying. Varlan was much closer. He was doubled over on the ground just behind her, ropes of scarlet-coloured vines holding him in place and covering his mouth.

"What are you doing to him?" She shook the man's hand from her shoulder and reached out to help Varlan. But the moment her fingers touched the vines, the oily sensation of the magic deepened, coating the back of her tongue as the vines tightened, and Varlan let out a pained grunt. She recoiled and spun to face Vask. "Let him go!"

"I won't harm him ... unless that is what you want. But neither can I let him interfere with our business."

"We don't have any *business*. I want you to let him go."

He let out a low, silky laugh. "Be careful, precious. You might not be willing to pay the price of his freedom."

"What do you want?"

A hungry look slid across his features. "That's not how this works, sweet thing. I ask what you want and then we figure out the true worth of your desire."

"I don't want anything from you."

The predatory tone beneath his words reminded her of Idir. She took a step back, careful not to brush against Varlan, who was glaring daggers at Vask from his bound position.

"Are you certain of that?" He closed the distance between them and ran his fingers across her cheek.

She nodded.

"What if I give you a taste of what I can do for you? For free of course." His index finger trailed down the side of her neck and over her chest until it stopped just over her heart.

Her whole body felt aflame, then the ruined shrine around them faded until it was replaced with the kitchen of her berth back on Armada. Varlan sat at the old, scarred table, a steaming mug in front of him and the scent of smoky black tea on the air. He looked up, his warm whiskey-brown gaze meeting hers. Then the world changed again—another memory—an islander with similar features to Deana letting out a rich laugh as he watched Wes and Varlan bickering. Then the kitchen table again, this time scattered with metal parts and her journal open to a diagram of a mechanical cat. She moved to the hearth fire, a cluster of papers that showed diagrams of the hidden compartment in her trunk in her hand. She thrust them into the flames and watched as they cured into ashes. Finally, Varlan and her lying in her bed; he brushed her hair back from her face and kissed her slowly, as though savouring the moment.

"A thousand moments taken from you and I can give them all back. All you have to do is tell me what they are worth to you."

Varlan may have taken her memories but until she had learned the truth, she hadn't realised they were missing. And in the memory Varlan had shown her, his recollection of the events leading up to the memory wipe, he had asked her for her consent to erase them. He hadn't done it without her permission, and it felt as though he was almost wishing she would deny him. Like removing the memories was the last thing he actually wanted to do. But she had agreed to it. Her past self had known what had to be done and she agreed to let him take those months of her life and lock them away, or rather destroy them. He seemed to believe that once they were gone, they would never come back. But now, both Idir and Vask had promised to return the memories. So, were they truly lost?

Seductive fingers brushed the back of her neck.

Agnes. Varlan's voice whispered across her mind. *Don't let him—*

"There will be none of that," Vask said, and the vines holding Varlan tightened again.

He grumbled around the one gagging his mouth, and the touch of his keen disappeared.

"You had your chance and you turned me down."

Agnes studied Varlan before turning back to Vask. "What did you offer him?"

"My, you are full of questions, aren't you? I offered him an escape from the regrets of his past. To forget and be forgotten."

Varlan's keen lightly brushed the back of her neck again. It was so soft a touch she almost thought she imagined it until his voice whispered across her mind.

Do what you must to get outside the boundary of the temple. He is trapped—

Vask's magic slid over her, and Varlan let out another pained grunt.

"Do not test my patience again, lest you want me to force her to watch as I spill your blood over the stones of this temple." The words were clearer than any that had come before, each ringing with ire through Agnes's mind and giving space for the next to follow without consuming it. The oily quality of Vask's keen had also taken on an acrid edge that left a stinging path in its wake.

Something else was nagging at her senses below the weight of Vask's keen; a white-hot prickle at her fingertips and a rushing hiss of sound at the very edge of her hearing. Her magic holding back and waiting for her permission to take over her body rather than just diving in and assuming control. She tentatively reached for it, and it brushed against her mind stirring up a wealth of ideas. A trap could be released with the right tool, even the one that bound this god, and the trap that Agnes herself was in only needed the right words.

"I will make a deal with you," she said.

Varlan struggled against his bonds, his gaze meeting hers with something imploring in its golden-brown depths.

She turned her back on him and gave Vask her full attention.

"You will?" Vask seemed shocked but the look was quickly replaced with mute indifference. "And what is it that you want?"

Vask would make a formidable ally, but be careful. His solitude has twisted him from his original purpose. It wasn't Varlan's voice that entered her mind this time but that of the pale woman who seemed to linger in her dreams.

"Release Varlan and then we can talk."

Vask tilted his head, his lips twitching as though he might object, but then he rolled his eyes and gave a wave of his hand.

Varlan collapsed onto his hands and knees and drew a series of deep breaths before he stood.

"Alright. I have done as you asked now, sweet thing. What price would you pay to have those memories returned?"

"Nothing."

Vask's eyebrows arched.

"I don't want those memories back; I gave them up willingly."

"He can't be trusted, Agnes," Varlan warned, but she shook her head at him.

"You are trapped here. I will give you your freedom and in exchange you will not seek to harm me or my friends—and should we have a need of your aid in the future, you will grant it."

Vask doubled over with a laugh. "You cannot promise that which is not in your power to give, sweet thing," he said once he had sobered again.

"It is in my power to give though. If it wasn't, my magic wouldn't stir at the thought of it."

Vask flicked a look between her and Varlan. His fingers traced a path back and forth across his chin as the oily touch of his magic investigated the edge of Agnes's keen. "I usually take payment before I enact my end of the bargain, but I shall humour you and give you half of your request. I will not harm you or any that you deem an ally. Any future aid will not be given until you deliver on your payment, and such aid will only be given once and will come within the limitations of both my power and my whims. Does this satisfy you?"

Agnes gave him a nod.

"Very well." He waved his hand in a sharp circle and his keen slid over her once more before he disappeared in a cloud of scarlet-coloured beetles.

"What happened?" Wes asked as he ran over. "My suppression had no effect on whatever that was."

"Agnes made a deal with Vask," Varlan said.

"After we all warned you—"

"He agreed not to harm any of us."

"And what did that cost you?" This was from Luca, who sauntered over with Gendry and the twins in tow.

"His freedom. He is a prisoner here; I can free him if I can just create the right key. In exchange for that he has agreed to leave us alone and to grant us one favour in the future should we need it."

They all stared at her, then Wes turned to Varlan.

"To bind a god would take a great feat of magic. To free them again ... is that even possible?"

Varlan studied Agnes and shrugged. "It's not an easy thing to do and for most people it would be impossible—"

"Improbable," the twins said.

"What?" Luca asked them with a frown.

"That's what Bran would say," Kiki replied. "Whenever anyone says something is impossible, he says that given the nature of magic and the source, very few things in this world are actually impossible. Hard, unfathomable, and improbable but not impossible." Her impersonation of Bran's tone was almost spot on.

"That's absolute nonsense. They mean the same thing."

"Not really though," Wes said, and the healer turned his hawkish stare to him.

"Bran got it from Nea," Gendry said. "She says impossible implies the situation is hopeless and completely unachievable. Improbable means succeeding will be ridiculously hard and highly unlikely but there's still hope, especially if you're cunning enough and have access to the right magic or tool."

Magic or tool. Agnes clenched and unclenched her hands as her magic prickled over them. She needed her journal and pen, or somewhere to get the thoughts that were spiralling in a frenzy in the back of her mind out of her head. She reached for her satchel, but she'd rushed off the Queen without a second thought and left it behind.

"We should make camp. We can discuss this once we're settled," Gendry said. "Pip, you're on fire duty," he added with a wide grin.

"Of course I am." Her tone was dry but she gave him a small smile and sauntered off.

That seemed to be the cue for everyone else. Kiki led Gendry away to show him the temple, whatever she said to him lost in the buzz that was slowly consuming Agnes's mind. She rubbed her fingers together as she watched Wes follow Pippa, and Luca pick up his and Wes's packs before heading off after Gendry.

The buzz moved from her mind to her limbs, giving a restlessness to her legs that made her start pacing and shaking her hands to try and dispel the feeling. She had never experienced the trance like this. Normally she would get the warning tingle and rush of sound before she blacked out, only to come back to her body when her magic was spent and its work done.

"You look like you could use this," Varlan said, his voice soothing through the buzz and bringing a moment of stillness. He was holding out her journal and the mahogany pen Gethyn had given her.

Her fingers brushed his as she took the items from him; the resulting tightness at her core had nothing to do with her impatient magic. "You didn't think to bring any ink?"

With a small, silky chuckle he produced a pot of ink from his pocket.

"Thank you."

He was studying her intently, his keen brushing along hers. The sensation of it stilled her mind and tamed her magic, but it set a different kind of tremor at her core—one that she wasn't ready to explore. He cleared his throat and the touch of his magic softened, allowing her own to build again.

"How do you do that?"

"Do what?"

"Your keen made my magic calm."

He ran his fingers along his lip. "Mind magic can influence thoughts and moods, but I wasn't using it just now. And I wouldn't. Not without consent, or good reason."

"But I felt it." Hadn't she? Her magic had calmed the moment Varlan arrived with her journal. The moment her keen had brushed against his.

"Your magic will likely be unstable for a while until you adjust to your newly returned keen-sense, it was probably—"

She shook her head. "No. I mean, yes, my magic feels different. But I felt yours. It rolled over mine and calmed it. Why does it react so strongly to yours but not to anyone else's?"

He let out a shaky laugh. "I am not sure you want the answer to that."

"Don't do that. Don't treat me like my father or Nari would. I deserve to—"

"It's because of our past."

He blurted out as she said.

"—know."

"Yes, you deserve to know. But given that you have no

memories of that time, it would be unfair to put expectations on yourself about how you should feel. I gave you a clean slate, Agnes, to protect you from Idir."

"And that worked so well." Anger was biting at her, scattering the lingering pull of her magic.

He released a heavy sigh and rubbed a hand over his face.

"If you were trying to protect me from Idir, why leave only to come back?"

"Because I couldn't stay away. Wes told me I should, that you were doing fine, but I couldn't ... I tried. Shadow's teeth, Agnes, I tried. But I just wasn't strong enough." There was a raw quality to his voice that stirred something deep in that seemingly empty void of her memories.

"That doesn't explain why your keen affects mine the way it does."

"Sometimes when mages are ... intimate, it creates a bond between them. Here in the isles, they call it heart mates. Songs, keens, that get woven together in some irreversible way and inexplicably draw those souls together. I used to think it was as ridiculous a notion as it was romantic but—"

"That's what both Idir and Savita meant. This bond between our magic—they both said they could use it. That's why you left. You weren't just protecting me or the location of the keystone. You were protecting yourself." A stone landed heavily in her stomach. Everyone said Varlan's sense of self-preservation was his guiding force.

"No." He shook his head. "That was never the case. I left because I love you and once I had wiped those memories, I couldn't bear seeing you look at me like I was just a passing acquaintance. It was selfish, but not for the reasons you are thinking."

I love you. Not loved. She swallowed. Part of her wanted to throw her arms around him and soothe the hurt, but the other was more cautious. It carried a warning that he had tampered with her memories once, and what was to stop him from doing it again. But she had loved him too. She had to have if they had been intimate enough for their keens to have formed a bond. Could she feel that way again? He wasn't asking her to. Regardless of how he obviously felt about her, he had made that clear enough.

"Oh." The word fell heavily from her lips.

"Oh?"

"I just realised ..." She bit down on her lip.

He nodded slowly. "I don't expect you to feel the way you did before and if I could undo the bond between our keens to make things easier for you I would, but that sort of magic is beyond my capabilities. Perhaps Bran might know—"

"It's not just my magic." She swallowed and cast a glance at the others. They seemed busy with organising the small camp. "There's a part of me—lots of parts actually—that remember, even if my mind does not."

"I'm truly sorry, Agnes. If I had known—if I could go back ..." He started to lift his hand, then shook his head and clenched his fingers into a fist. He dropped it again and took a step back, allowing the air between them to cool before he turned and strode away.

Agnes's grip on her journal tightened and she pulled it closer to her chest. The insistent buzz of her magic had completely died down, leaving a gaping hollow in its wake to be filled with questions and doubts and the empty sadness of what-could-have-beens.

CHAPTER TWENTY-ONE

VARLAN

Varlan jabbed a stick into the embers of their small campfire sending a flurry of sparks swirling into the air. The others had long gone to bed, though Varlan wasn't sure how they managed a peaceful slumber with Gendry's not-so-gentle snores echoing off the ruined stones around them. Agnes was curled up not far from Gendry, her fingers twitching as she muttered in her sleep. It was a relief after watching her lie as still as death for days, but he shouldn't be watching her sleep; he should be giving her space and figuring out how he could dampen his feelings. She had said it wasn't just her magic that remembered what had transpired between them. Those words had stirred a brittle hope in him. But it wasn't fair to expect things to return to the way they had been. Given time and space, those instinctual physical reactions should calm down and once Bran came back, they could work on dissolving the ties between Varlan and Agnes's keens. That should make things easier, for her at least.

With a huff, he poked the stick into the edge of the fire and picked up Kai's journal from where it sat beside him. He needed to stop acting like a lovesick teenager and get his head back on straight. Focusing on decoding Kai's cypher would be a good distraction. Leilani had told Bran the journal was important—that Kai had told her if anything happened, she was to get it to Elijah. Why Elijah though? Once he had created the map to find the keystone, his involvement in this whole mess had been complete. And he hadn't had any more luck than Varlan in figuring out the cypher Kai had used. But it wasn't just the journal that Kai had wanted entrusted to Elijah; he had told Leilani to get Deana off Lethata and to the old cartographer as well. That part made a bit more sense at least. Kai had always been concerned about keeping Deana out of Idir's reach. Varlan had assumed it was just an older brother's over-protectiveness until he had learned the truth about the magic she possessed. And now that he had met her and felt that magic for himself—he tapped the journal's spine against the centre of his palm. If his assumption was right, then Kai had figured out how to raise Dumura and that was what he had hidden in the final pages of the journal. But why? Why not just destroy that knowledge? Why leave it, even hidden beneath a seemingly impossible cypher, where Idir might find it? Idir didn't know how to raise the isle. He certainly had assumptions, but as far as Varlan could tell he was just stabbing in the dark. How had Kai figured it out when Idir who had had centuries to had not?

The pale pink orb of his mage light blossomed to life beside him as he opened the journal's cover. The light danced in a rosy hue across the pages as he thumbed through them, staring at the words but not comprehending them. There had to be a missing piece of the puzzle, something he was overlooking or some part still not in a play. The deep rumble of Kai's magic vibrated through him as he got to those pages at the back and something else—a thread of magic that felt almost like the cold bite of necromancy. That colder magic hadn't been there before. If it had, he certainly hadn't noticed and if either Elijah or Bran had, they hadn't mentioned it.

He let the journal fall open on his hand and placed his palm down on top of the pages as he closed his eyes. His keen-sense rolled forward, testing the remnants of Kai's keen that clung to the book and then delving deeper seeking that brush of ice. But he encountered nothing save for the steady shift of Kai's earth magic. Had the necromancy been a trick of his tired mind?

"Can't sleep either?" Kiki asked as she settled on the log beside him.

He opened his eyes and snapped the journal shut. "No. Between Gendry's snoring and the crushing weight of past failures and future dread, sleep is near impossible."

She let out a hallow laugh and took up his abandoned stick, twirling the lit end through the air in a rough figure-of-eight pattern. "Do you want to talk about it?"

"Not particularly," he sighed.

"Maybe talking about it will get it out of your head and you can stop frowning. It would be a tragedy to set too many deep furrows in that pretty face." Her tone was flat like she was trying to joke but her heart wasn't really in it.

He turned to study her. The mage light bobbed with his movement, highlighting how drawn her features had become. The circles beneath her eyes were not as dark as they had been, but she still looked tired, defeated.

"Are you sure you don't want to talk about—" He stopped as a quiver of panic rolled off her.

"*Not particularly,*" she echoed his answer from before.

"I'm sorry, Kiki." He dropped his gaze to the journal in his lap. "Usually I wouldn't suggest it, because memories are important, but I can take them if you want ... or soften the edges of the them so they don't torment you."

She shook her head again. "I need them." Her tone was biting, and she stabbed the stick into the fire savagely before turning a glassy stare his way. "They keep my resolve sharp."

He nodded his understanding. "If you ever change your mind ..."

"Thank you for the offer, but I won't. Not until Byron lies dead at my feet."

"Kiki—"

"You won't talk me out of it; Wes already tried."

"I wasn't going to." He understood the need for vengeance, and in Kiki's case it probably wasn't as much about vengeance as it was about reclaiming her power. It wouldn't change what had happened to her, but it might let her move on from it. "I was going to say you don't have to do it alone."

She held his gaze for a long moment then nodded and turned back to watch the fire. After a while, she rested her head on his shoulder as she dug the lit end of the stick into the ground at their feet. "Don't tell Pip," she whispered.

He gave her knee a squeeze. "I am sure she knows already, but I won't tell a soul unless you ask me to."

They sat in silence. The only sound was the occasional pop or hiss from the dying fire and the scurry of nightlife in the forest that edged the ruined temple.

"Do you think Bran and Deana are going to be alright? That Vask will return them?"

"He will return Deana unharmed; gods tend to honour the terms of their pacts even if they twist them to suit their own desires."

She lifted her head from his shoulder and turned to face him directly. "And Bran?"

They had watched the life drain from Bran, witnessed his lifeless body before Vask had disappeared with it. Magic could circumvent many of the laws of the natural world—even return a soul to a body. But those reanimations were puppets to the whims of their master. Tales spoke of other forms of soul magic that might be exploited to cheat death, but they all came with a heavy price. Death spoiled all she touched in the end, twisted it and left it changed irrevocably. Vask would return Bran to them, but it was highly unlikely that the necromancer would be unchanged by his brush with death.

"I don't know," he said softly.

She frowned but gave him a slow nod. "I suppose none of us are going to emerge from this fight unchanged." The words were soft, barely stirring the air between them, and edged with a deep sorrow that made his magic ache to sooth her.

"No," he replied.

None of them would survive what was to come unchanged but that was the way of life. Even those who led blissfully oblivious, simple lives weren't unaffected by the twisting pull of time. "But that's not necessarily a bad thing."

"Whatever doesn't kill you and all that bullshit."

A small smile tugged at the corner of his mouth. "Something like that."

Morning came and went, and the sun had almost reached its midpoint when the source gave a stomach-churning shudder, and a swirl of red fog thickened the air at the foot of the toppled statue of Vask. With another shudder, the mist parted to reveal Deana and Bran.

"Oh, thank the Bright." Kiki rushed forward and engulfed Bran in a hug.

As she released him and moved aside to throw her arms around Deana, Pippa took her place.

"If you ever pull a stunt like that again, I will boil your insides," she said as she clapped the necromancer on the shoulder then nudged her sister out of the way to give Deana a quick hug. "Good to have you back, Dee."

"Are you both alright?" Agnes asked as she stopped beside Varlan.

Deana nodded. She looked as tired and ragged as the rest of them but seemed otherwise unharmed, at least externally. Bran appeared slightly paler than normal, if that was possible, but likewise he looked fine despite the stain of drying blood that marked his ear and the side of his neck. When his gaze met Varlan's though, there was something almost haunted about it. He seemed to shake the moment away, however, as his gaze landed on Agnes and widened.

"You're awake?" he said, his keen chilling the air.

Agnes rubbed her arms and edged back a step.

Bran flicked a look Varlan's way, one of his snow-white brows flicking upward in silent question.

'We'll discuss it later.'

Bran gave him a nod.

"Go help Luca and Wes break camp." Gendry shooed the twins away and then turned to Bran and clapped him on the shoulder. "Fair warning, Wren is absolutely livid about that stunt you pulled. I suggest you approach her with extreme caution when we get back to the Queen," he grinned. "Not you though, lass. She's been worried sick about you since you disappeared. We all have," he said to Deana, who opened her mouth to respond only to have whatever she said garbled against Gendry's chest as he pulled her into a bear hug.

"How are you really?" Varlan asked Bran.

The necromancer ran his fingers through his hair, making the white waves stand on end. "Fine." The word came with a small, amused grunt and a subtle shake of his head. "Well, mostly fine, aside from the raging headache and bone-deep spiritual crisis."

"I am rather familiar with that feeling," Varlan said.

"Well, you're the idiot who decided letting a god take a day of his life was a good idea. So really you only have yourself to blame for that headache," Gendry said. "What happened to your ear?"

Bran touched the ragged hole in his earlobe. "I got bitten by a monkey."

"*A monkey?*" Gendry's bark of laughter sent a few birds flying.

"Just put a hoop in it and you'll finally start to look like a real pirate."

"We're ready to leave," Wes said as he joined them.

"Good. Let's get out of this Bright forsaken jungle and back to the Queen," Gendry said as he moved off to herd Deana, Agnes, and the twins up the slope away from the temple. Luca and Wes followed but as Bran took a step, Varlan caught his arm.

"We need to talk."

"Can't it wait until we're beyond Vask's territory at least?" Bran cast a glance around the area as though expecting the god to materialise at any second.

Varlan waited for the others to get a little farther ahead and then released Bran's arm. "Did you notice the imprint of necromancy on Kai's journal?" he asked as he started up the slope.

Bran paused, falling back a few steps with a frown. "You're sure it wasn't just my keen lingering after I examined it?"

Varlan shook his head. "It didn't feel like you or any other necromancer I have met. And it was too ingrained with the remnants of Kai's keen to be the result of someone merely handling the journal."

"You're sure it was necromancy?" Bran lengthened his strides to catch up.

"It was only a brief touch, but I am certain."

They walked in silence, but every so often Bran would mutter something under his breath or stop and start to ask a question before shaking his head and moving on again. They were almost to the edge of the beach when he grabbed Varlan's arm, pulling him up short. "I need to see the journal. Do you have it?"

Varlan drew the beaten-up little book out and handed it over.

Bran's necromancy chilled the air as he ran his fingertips over the cover. He opened the book and flipped to the pages at the end, letting his keen burrow into the parchment. Flickers of lilac caressed the book and roved over his skin. The crescent moon tattooed on the inside of his wrist began to glow and expand until the dark moon was surrounded by swirling patterns of indigo ink.

"The others are waiting. What are you—" Varlan shushed Wes as he stomped towards them from the beach.

The warden frowned at him and folded his arms with a distinct, 'Couldn't this have waited?' look on his face.

Varlan let his mind brush against the edge of Wes's. '*Probably*,' he thought when he felt the other man's mind open to him.

Wes rolled his eyes and shook his head.

"You're right," Bran said. "It is necromancy and I think I know its purpose."

"And that is?" Varlan prompted when Bran didn't elaborate.

Bran studied the inside of his wrist with a frown. The swirling lines around the crescent tattoo hadn't faded. He clenched his fist and rolled his hand as though trying to relieve tension in his forearm then blinked at Varlan.

"I'm not certain, but I think there's a piece of Kai's essence woven into the journal. Well, maybe not a piece of him but a lingering impression or ... message perhaps. There are threads of ... *something* tangible there. Almost like the residue left behind after certain events that can be used to trigger re-enactments."

"Could you use the journal to perform a re-enactment then?"

Bran started to shake his head, then flicked a look between Wes and Varlan and said, "Maybe. But if I am wrong then trying could destroy those threads and whatever message Kai left along with them."

Wes cleared his throat loudly. "Then we should get back to the Queen and regroup. Agnes has been in an enchanted sleep full of nightmares and has emerged with an awakened keen-sense that she is still trying to understand. Deana has been through Bright knows what but just looking at her tells me it was something just short of outright torture. And you," his bright hazel gaze narrowed as it landed on the necromancer, "Bran, you *died*. The three of you need to just stop and give yourselves a chance to have a proper rest. We all do. And unless Idir lands in our laps the second we get back to the Queen, everything else can wait," the warden finished with a sharp edge to his tone and a steely glint in his eye.

"Y—"

"And you, Varlan, just need to sit your arse down and let everyone rest. Working out how to outsmart Idir and Kent and Bright knows what other arsehole is waiting in the shadows can wait. Kai's secrets can too."

"I was going to say you're right."

Wes stared at him. "Just like that? No arguments, no duplicity?"

"Just like that," Varlan replied. "I do want to test Bran's theory but there'll be time for that tomorrow."

CHAPTER TWENTY-TWO

DEANA

She sat on the white beach of her dreamscape. The rolling whitewash was cool as it caressed her toes; the spectre of Grandmother Ocean beside her was unusually quiet as though she too were simply enjoying the serenity. The goddess appeared almost youthful in this dream. Her eyes were still hidden beneath a scrap of cloth, but this one was a shade of gold so pale it was almost white. The threads that wrapped some of her long thin braids were all the different colours of a rainbow and her skirts were a mixture of joyful yellows and orange, while the bands of fabric that covered her chest were the same pale gold as her blindfold. Cascading waves were embroidered across both her top and skirt in iridescent threads that seemed to change colour as she moved. The gnarled fingers of wood at the top of her staff were cradling a glowing green stone that caught the light and reflected it in facetted shards of emerald against the sand.

Deana was waiting for the moment the calm of this dream would be invaded by the nightmare of her parents' deaths or the heavy grip of invisible hands dragging her down to drown in the cold dark. The Grandmother had implied in the past that there were lessons to be learned in these dreams, though whatever those lessons might be had completely eluded Deana so far. All the dreams had given her was a heavy desire to see Idir punished for the evils he had committed over the apparent centuries that he had been seeking Grandmother Ocean's power.

"You are troubled," the goddess said at last, her multi-layered voice echoing over itself in a myriad of tones both young and old.

"I am waiting."

"For?"

"For the nightmare to start."

The goddess tilted her head and studied Deana. "Most would seek to avoid bad dreams."

"The sooner it starts the sooner I can face it and then wake up."

"What if it isn't coming? What if you have learned what it was trying to teach you?"

Deana picked up a handful of sand and let it flow out through her fingers. "Have I?"

The goddess's smile was small, the edge of her mouth tucked in the way Varlan's did when those around him finally figured out what he had been alluding to all along. Maybe the thief and the goddess would get along.

"But I don't understand. Vask told me I need to raise Dumura. The dreams didn't tell me that." They hadn't told her anything really.

"Of course they didn't. Dreams are temperamental and often infuriatingly obscure in their lessons." A new voice: one that sounded like a huskier version of Bran's.

The goddess was the only one who ever spoke to Deana in these dreams. Anyone else who appeared seemed completely oblivious to her. She slowly got to her feet and turned to face the man who owned the voice. She'd seen him before, in the tapestry inside Vask's temple. Soren. He looked almost like an older, rougher version of Bran. Though there were enough differences that she could tell they weren't really the same person; but her song told her not to believe her eyes. This man's song and Bran's were identical, even if their bodies were not.

"Grandmother." He bowed to the goddess, and she inclined her head.

"Why are you in my dream?" Deana asked.

A sly smile flickered across his features, and she fought the urge to step back. He might wear a version of Bran's face, but he definitely wasn't Bran. "I'm not entirely sure, to tell the truth. Though I won't complain. It is far prettier here than my usual *haunt*. You're the girl then."

Deana did take a step back at that. "*The girl?*"

"The one worth dying for."

She shook her head.

Soren nodded. "You are. I'm glad to see he managed to save you."

"I didn't need saving."

"From Vask? Yes, you did. You are one of those souls that all the gods want a piece of—a direct conduit to their absent sovereign." He gestured towards the goddess, who seemed to be watching them intently despite the cloth covering her eyes. "Vask would never have given you up freely."

A small part of her suspected he was right, but had Sejira known that when she sent Deana in search of answers to Vask's temple?

"I'm Soren, by the way." He turned to face the ocean. There was a dark flower-shaped birthmark on the skin just below his left ear. Bran had had a similar mark when he woke up in Vask's temple. It was paler than Soren's, but he definitely hadn't had it before his run-in with Vask.

"Deana," she replied automatically. "What's that mark on your neck?"

He touched his fingers to it, a small smile twitching the corners of his mouth. "A reminder of what I am."

"And what is that?"

His deep blue gaze settled on her. It was heavier than Bran's, and she shifted her feet and swallowed.

"A miracle, an anomaly, an abomination—take your pick. I am someone who was never meant to exist. Someone whose birth twisted their keen and made them something too otherworldly to be human and too mundane to be a god."

She frowned.

"My people would call me a deathborn, a child whose gestation and birth has been influenced by the one who would call himself the Master of Shadows."

"Is Bran a deathborn too?"

"Bran is *complicated,* and perhaps that is a question better asked of him." His attention turned back to the horizon once more. "I will say he's doing better than I did."

"He's doing what better?"

"Keeping you safe from Idir. Keeping you … alive." The notes of sorrow that twisted through his song were heavy and bitter and brought the heat of tears to the corners of her eyes.

"You lost someone to Idir?" She knew that pain all too well.

He released a huff that could have been a bitter laugh. "My world, my life, my—"

"Your heart mate?" she whispered.

His brow knitted and he gave her a perplexed look. "Her too, though I didn't realise that was what she was at the time. I couldn't save her or her sister, Sula. Rami's wife." Another bitter laugh. "I couldn't even save Rami in the end. What Astrid did to him is beyond any evil—"

"Astrid killed Sula," Deana said. She didn't know how she knew that, but the knowledge was a bitter weight at the back of her throat.

He nodded. "Rami didn't know the truth. I don't know if he does now or if he's even still inside that monstrosity Astrid made him."

Something human still existed deep within Rami, Deana was sure of that, though Astrid's grip on his magical leash seemed unbreakable. "How did she do it?"

"*How?*" He turned an incredulous gaze her way, but beneath it was a raw curiosity and admiration that reminded her of Bran.

"Yes. She's not a necromancer, but the song she used to change Rami, it was a song of nightmares and death." Song was perhaps too gentle a word. The magic that had changed Rami had been a dirge, wild and raw and all-consuming.

"It was the same power Idir stole from Mala and perverted to create his shrouded ones. He gave Astrid a mere sliver of that power."

"But Rami is not a shrouded one."

"Divine magic was never meant to be wielded by mortal bodies, or minds. Give ten mages a piece of the same god's magic and you will see the rise of ten different atrocities."

Did he think she was an atrocity then? Her song was intricately connected to Grandmother Ocean's magic; she'd felt that connection intimately as the brush of the goddess's breath at the back of her neck in those times she had pulled too much power.

"Power freely given is different to power that has been taken by force or subterfuge," the goddess said gently, and Soren nodded.

"But how can a mage wield a song that is not their own? Use a magic they weren't born to possess? A fire mage can't create rain no matter how much they wish to."

"Can't they? Mages certainly have proficiencies, but there are loopholes and ways to manipulate the source that open doors most people perceive as locked. And that is how Astrid was able to turn Rami into an abomination. I imagine her intent was to make him a wraith and bind him to her service, but her keen perverted Mala's necromancy and then that in turn perverted Rami's warden gift and made him what he is now."

"What type of mage was Astrid originally?"

"A mind mage, though not an overly powerful or stable one. Certainly not like Idir. He promised her a way to unlock her powers, to stabilise them and become a master—become a god. And she jumped at the chance. Then, when he got what he wanted, he cast her aside. But it was too late. I hope she has enjoyed her immortality."

"She said she was seeking a way to end the curse."

He made a sceptical noise. "There is no curse. Grandmother Ocean didn't curse Idir and his followers; Idir cursed them himself. And regardless of whether it is a true curse or not, Astrid's goal is vengeance—nothing more. She will happily live an eternity as a shrouded one if it means watching Idir suffer the consequences of his hubris. You don't need to worry about Astrid. You need to worry about figuring out how to raise Dumura and then fixing everything Idir broke. But if he reaches the resting place of the Grandmother and manages to claim even a speck of her power, then ..." he pressed his closed fists together then flicked his fingers outward as he pulled his hands apart in a movement that reminded her of a large bubble popping, "... the end of the isles as you know them."

Deana glanced at the goddess, but she just returned Deana's look with a knowing smile and the barest of nods as the dream faded around her.

Morning found her leaning on the side rail of the ship, watching the pale fish that she now knew was Sejira dart alongside the boat. Bran's song brushed against hers, and the fish rolled over, showing its dark belly. Then with a flash of fins that could have been a wave, it disappeared.

Bran settled at the rail beside her, and she studied him from the corner of her eye. He still looked pale—not that that was any different to normal really. His white hair and Beldaren colouring made him look like death most of the time. *Fitting for a necromancer.* She stifled a laugh, and he turned his attention to her.

"I should probably give this back to you." He held out the protection charm Kai had given her. An unfamiliar song clung to it, the notes probing against hers and bringing to mind a dog following a scent trail.

When her fingers touched the stone, the song changed to an excited tempo and then grew abruptly silent. "Thank you." She traced her fingers around the edge of the stone and squeezed it against her palm. An instant calm chased the uneasiness she hadn't realised she was harbouring away. "And thank you for what you did at Vask's temple."

He waved her thanks away and turned his gaze back to the horizon, reminding her forcibly of Soren. "It was nothing, really."

"That's not true and you know it. Would you have done the same for Agnes? Or one of the twins? What about Varlan or Gendry?"

His tongue darted along his lip. "Maybe not Varlan. He's too smart to get himself trapped like that. I mean—I'm not saying you're not smart ... Just ..." He pressed his mouth shut and ran a hand through his hair. "Did Vask give you any insight that we can use?"

She nodded. "I need to raise Dumura. Both Vask and Soren are adamant about that."

"Soren?"

"He's—he was Astrid's brother."

Realisation crossed his features. "I know who he is ..." he said softly. A strangely dark look shifted in his eyes, but he turned away from her before she could figure it out. "I'm surprised that you know him. That you've spoken with him."

"He appeared in my dream last night."

Bran's attention snapped back to her. The dark contemplation had traded places with a familiar, unbridled curiosity.

"He seemed as confused about that as I was," she continued.

Bran swallowed and his throat bobbed, drawing her eyes to the soft mark just below his ear.

"Are you ... is he one of your ancestors? Are you a deathborn like him?"

He laughed at that, a tight bitter laugh that bordered on a scoff. "In a manner of speaking, I suppose." He glanced at her out of the corner of his eye and his features softened again. "I'm sorry. It's complicated, and I am not sure I am ready to explore the revelations that meeting him produced."

Soren had mentioned the situation regarding Bran was complicated, but she hadn't expected him to be unwilling to talk about it. Bran was usually so open and almost carefree. Had something so terrible happened while she was gone that it had completely changed him? "We don't have to talk about it."

He gave her a gentle smile. "I probably should talk about it. I've seen firsthand what happens when people bottle everything up until they burst. But no, I am not a deathborn—well, *technically* not, and Soren ..." He drummed his fingers on the side rail. "He's not my ancestor. He is me, or rather he will be me. As I said, it's complicated."

"That explains why your songs are identical."

"They are?"

She nodded.

"But ..." He frowned and rubbed the tattoo on the inside of his wrist.

It looked different to how she remembered it. She was sure it had just been a solid crescent moon before. Now it was surrounded by intricate swirls that almost reminded her of sketched waves or clouds.

"My keen isn't even my own keen anymore. It hasn't been since

I played host to a piece of Nea's magic. That changed it."

Nea's song was similar to Bran's, certainly closer in pitch and rhythm than that of any other necromancer Deana had encountered, but it was still different. And whilst she had picked up on the melancholic notes of Nea's song laced with Bran's, she just assumed it was their familial connection. "Nea's song can't have changed yours. At least not permanently. There is very little that can permanently alter a mage's song. You can pick up traits of other melodies if you spend a lot of time working closely together, but those traits are like dust on a shelf—easily brushed away. Even when heart mates' songs combine, the individual melodies don't change. They twist around each other and weave together until they form a harmony." She rolled her hands around each other then interlocked her fingers. "It might sound like one song but if you listen closely, you can still identify the individual melo—why are staring at me like that?"

His smile had gotten wider the longer she rambled until he was watching her with an acute admiration. "Sorry. I've never had it explained to me so intently before. Beyond the fact that you hear magic rather than feel it, and I couldn't fathom how that actually worked. I still can't, really."

"I can feel it too, but it isn't as easy as hearing it. Have you really never heard magic?" That she couldn't understand.

He shook his head and turned to face Varlan as he approached.

"Hello, Deana, do you mind if I borrow Bran for a bit?"

"No, I don't mind."

Bran flicked a look from Varlan to Deana and then back again. "You want me to examine the journal."

"Wes told me to give it another day, but the longer we—"

"Now is fine. You're right; time is of the essence. But I think Deana should be involved. Kai was her brother, after all, and if it does contain the secret of how to raise the isle then she needs to know."

Varlan turned to Deana. "Of course, I should have—"

"Varlan, do you have a moment?" Gendry called and waved the mind mage over.

With a sigh, he gave Deana an apologetic look. "I'll just see what he wants then meet you both in the hold momentarily." He spun on his heels and marched off across the deck.

"After you," Bran said, gesturing towards the stairs to the hold.

CHAPTER TWENTY-THREE

BRAN

Agnes was in the hold when they arrived, her keen an intense flutter all around her as she stared at the open pages of her journal and muttered rapidly under her breath.

The small chest they had received from Hartswood was on the table beside her, along with several thin pieces of robrillium.

"That's it!" she exclaimed, then snapped the journal shut and started for the door, only to pull herself up short before she slammed into Deana. "Sorry, but it's perfect that you're here. I need some of your blood."

"My blood?" Deana blinked at her.

"Yes, the drops of sea required to reforge the key for the chest: it's not sea water."

"But why Deana's blood?" Bran knew the answer the moment the question left his lips. Deana's connection to Grandmother Ocean, or rather her keen's connection. "Never mind. Are you suggesting that the key requires blood magic to reforge? That's not a path you want to go down."

Blood magic was a topic that mages didn't discuss in polite company, or at all really. Knowledge of the practice in Beldaren had been all but eradicated during Empress Eugenie's reign, so very few mages were aware of it. It was one of those types of magic that started small but quickly spiralled into an addiction to power that came with extreme consequences, the least of which was corruption. It just wasn't worth the risk despite the amount of power it could grant.

"It requires blood, but the blood is just a component; like the robrillium. The magic comes from me, same as it always does."

"Are you absolutely certain that is the case? Blood magic is addictive. One minute you're simply reforging a key, the next you are sacrificing a horde of innocents to level a kingdom."

She folded her arms. "I am sure."

"If my blood is required for the drops of sea then who is the drops of sky?" Deana asked.

"That one is trickier. But given the carvings ..." Agnes moved back to the table and placed her journal down then ran her fingers over the lid of the chest.

Swirling depictions of waves with various sea creatures frolicking through them were carved on the front of the chest. They moved up and over the top where they circled the robrillium keyhole before moving down the back panel of the box. One of the sides bore the image of what looked like a castle with twisting spires that reminded him of conical seashells. The other side showed a massive wave about to consume the same castle. Bran studied the top once more. The waves seemed to convene into shapes at the corners. He tilted his head, trying to figure them out. One looked like the swirl of a perfect circle. The corner diagonally across from it was bare, the waves stopping and leaving a wedge of smooth dark wood. The other two corners bore thin crescent waves that were facing in opposite directions. Moon phases. The patterns in the corners were forming moon phases.

"The moon," Deana whispered.

Agnes nodded excitedly. "So, all we need to find is someone whose magic has the same connection to Grandfather Moon as yours has to Grandmother Ocean."

Bran swallowed as he studied the marks.

"That's impossible. No mage has ever been born who wields his power," Deana said.

"Maybe not in the isles," Bran whispered and cleared his throat. "If Grandmother Ocean has parallels to the Bright Mother, then it would make sense that her consort, Grandfather Moon, has parallels to the Shadow Man."

Agnes's eyes widened as they turned to Bran and dropped to the mark on his wrist. Her keen thrummed against his, leaving a trail of jitters in its wake, and she rolled her shoulders before closing her eyes and taking a deep breath. "I would say it wouldn't work because both Bran and the Shadow Man are not Faridean natives, but my magic seems convinced."

She always talked about her keen as though it were a separate entity to herself. It was a foreign concept for Bran. His magic was an integral part of him—no different to his skin or brain or the blood pumping through his veins.

"Convinced of what?" Varlan asked as he joined them.

"That I can use Bran's blood as the 'drops of sky' required to reforge the key." She patted the top of the chest then slowly looked from one face to the next before settling on Varlan with a confused tilt of her head. "What are you all doing in here anyway?"

Varlan dropped Kai's journal on the table next to Agnes's things. "Extracting Kai's message—wait a minute. Blood? You need *blood* to reforge the key? Agnes, blood magic is extremely unpredictable."

"It's not blood magic," she rolled her eyes, "and Bran already tried to give me that lecture, so spare me. I didn't even realise blood magic was a thing until he mentioned it. The blood is just a piece of the puzzle. It's no different to a plate of metal or a rivet of robrillium."

Varlan turned to Bran.

"It's her magic. She understands how it works better than anyone else." Bran shrugged and picked up Kai's journal. Now that Varlan had brought the subtle threads of necromancy clinging to it to his attention, he wasn't sure why he hadn't noticed them before. It wasn't normal necromancy either. It was tainted with the shifting magic of the Between itself in a way that suggested whoever it belonged to either wasn't entirely human or wasn't human at all.

He opened the journal and flipped through until he reached the pages where the gibberish started then placed his palm against the parchment. His keen built in a cold twist at his core then the mark on his wrist began to itch as it ignited in a soft lilac glow. Whatever essence of Nea's magic left attached to the mark was drowned out by the surge of his own power. Something clicked into place inside him, like a block that had been slightly skewed at the foot of a tower. The words on the page glowed in an array of shades of purple, then twisted and shifted before reforming themselves into coherent sentences. A ripple ran through the source and the barrier between worlds pressed against his back. He reached for it. A dense forest of pines appeared before him; their dark branches woven together to form an impenetrable wall. He lifted his hand and touched his magic to the branches. They creaked and groaned and then sprang apart to make a doorway. A man was standing on the other side. He was tall and broad and something about the shape of his eyes and line of his mouth reminded Bran of Deana.

"Kai?"

The man took a step forward as though he would cross the barrier, but he stopped short and frowned as he pressed his hand against the air in front of him.

Bran lifted his own hand. There was a slight resistance as though the barrier was stopping Kai from coming through, but it still remained permeable. If anything other than Kai wanted to slip through, it could. Bran moved forward. The shifting fingers of the Between plied his hair and tugged at his clothes until he was standing in the fractured landscape of the intangible Between: the version of the realm that souls walked in dreams; the broken topsy-turvy reflection of the real world where spirits waited to breach their way into the mortal realm. It was vastly different to the ever-changing landscape of the physical Between but no less dangerous.

"Bran, isn't it?" Kai's voice was deep but somehow almost musical. Perhaps that was the effect of lingering so long in this pocket between realms.

"Yes, that's me."

Kai gave him a thorough once over then nodded, though Bran got the sense he was coming to some internal conclusion rather than nodding for Bran's benefit.

"Tell Varlan the answer can be found beneath the—" He grunted and lifted a hand to his throat. "Damned curse." He shook his head. "Most of it is in the book, but the missing piece—the most important piece—it's hidden ..." He twisted his mouth as though looking for the right words. "*Where the singers touched the sky,*" he finished with a sardonic grin. "Varlan should be able to figure that out." He frowned and let out a remorseful sigh. "And tell Deana I'm sorry. I know what is being asked of her seems impossible, but she *can* do this. She's braver than she realises and ... and I'm proud of her."

"I will."

"And give her this from me."

Bran tensed as Kai reached forward and pulled him into a hug. When Kai released him, he cleared his throat. "Anything else?"

"Just don't let Idir win," Kai said with a grin.

Bran returned the smile. "We have no intentions of that." He stepped back through the barrier and inclined his head to Kai before lifting his hand and willing the branches of the pines to weave back together.

As the hedge faded and the ship's hold came into focus once more, he leant heavily against the edge of the table.

"What happened?" Varlan asked. He was standing between Agnes and Deana. All three of them were watching him with various looks of concerned curiosity.

"I spoke to Kai."

"You did?" Deana's voice trembled.

Bran nodded. "He said to tell Varlan that the answers are in the book and that the missing piece is hidden where the singers touched the sky. He said you'd be able to make sense of that."

Deana toyed with the protection stone, which she had once more secured around her neck. "Is that all he said?"

"No, he wanted me to tell you that he's proud of you and regardless of how impossible it seems, you can do it. You're braver than you know. All true, of course."

A soft flush lit her cheeks, and she cleared her throat. "Thank you."

"He also wanted me to give you this—" He moved around the table and pulled her into a hug, expecting her to stiffen and pull away. But she roped her arms around his waist and squeezed before he let her go.

"He didn't have one of those for me, did he?" Varlan asked, his tone lighter than Bran had heard it in weeks.

"No. But if you want one ..."

"Maybe later," he laughed.

"This is ..." Agnes's magic prickled through the air. She had picked up Kai's journal and was flipping back and forth through the newly revealed pages. "These are instructions and schematics to construct a ..." She blinked and focused on a passage of text before dropping the journal onto the table and pressing the heels of her palms to her forehead as her magic thrummed violently.

"Agnes?" Varlan's momentary mirth was replaced with deep concern as he shifted towards her.

"I'm alright," she ground out through her teeth, before releasing a breath as her keen settled again.

"Was it your magic trying to take over? You still haven't—"

"I'm fine, Varlan," she snapped.

Bran shared a look with Deana, then picked up the journal and examined the page Agnes had been looking at. "That can't be right?" He flicked back a few pages and scanned the text.

"What is it?" Deana asked softly.

"It's instructions on how to build a—"

"Portal." Agnes said, at the same time he did.

"A portal?" Varlan's eyebrows cantered towards his hairline, and he took the journal from Bran. He flipped rapidly back and forth through the pages and muttered under his breath as he read different sections before he snapped the book shut and tapped the spine against his palm. "What was the other thing Kai said?"

"The missing piece is hidden where the singers touched the sky. There seemed to be something preventing him from telling me the location outright, but he said you'd be able to figure it out."

"Where the singers touch the sky," Varlan repeated.

"Touched," Bran corrected.

"That doesn't make any sense. There aren't any locations—"

"'Wenfred and the singers of woe'," Deana said softly.

"Who?" Varlan asked.

"It's a song, a very old and unpopular song given that it tells a tale full of sorrow and death. Wenfred went on a quest to find the place where the singers touched the sky."

"Why would Kai think I would know it?"

"Perhaps he thought you had heard it before. He would often hum the chorus when he was thinking. You know—" She hummed a slow-building melody, and recognition lit in Varlan's gaze but also Agnes's.

"I know that song. Why do I know that song?"

"Kai," Varlan said flatly. "I have heard it. The tune at least. He was always bloody humming."

"No, not the tune. I know the words," Agnes said.

Varlan's keen stirred, and her shoulders tensed.

"Music, like scent, can be a powerful trigger for memory. But if Kai was the one who taught you that song, you would have lost your memory of it along with all your others when I took them."

"Is it possible they could be returning?" Agnes asked.

Varlan shook his head.

"But both Vask and Idir offered to return them. If they could then they can't be completely gone."

"Empty promises to entrap you," Varlan said bitterly.

"Perhaps not completely empty," Bran said, and Varlan turned an incredulous look his way. "Nea encountered a seemingly endless field of memories in the Between. They were her memories and Garret's, but that would suggest that memories can't be completely destroyed. They had to go somewhere when you took them."

"So, we could find them in the Between? If … if I wanted to." There was an edge to Agnes's tone like she wasn't sure if she really desired the truth.

"Maybe. But we would most likely have to physically go there, and we have way too much on our plates at the moment to add another extremely complicated, ridiculously dangerous, and possible fool's errand into the mix."

"Bran is right. We need to focus on the mess we are already in. This song, 'Wenfred and the singers of woe', does it mention where the singers touched the sky?"

Both Agnes and Deana shook their heads, though Agnes seemed to be singing part of the song under her breath as she did so. "Not specifically," she said after a moment.

"There must be clues in the words. Can one of you write them down for me?"

Agnes picked up her pen and journal and turned to a blank page then started writing.

"I'm going to have a more thorough read of this," Varlan said as he waved Kai's journal, "and then see if Wes has an opinion on it."

"You said the journal would tell us how to raise the island, not build a portal," Bran said.

"I believe I said I *thought* Kai had figured out how to raise the island and then made the logical conclusion that that is what he had hidden in the journal. I wasn't *certain*. Either way, Kai's findings are connected to Dumura." He flicked a look at Agnes, who was discussing the lyrics she was writing down with Deana, then stepped closer Bran. "If Idir needs to build a portal on the island then his tampering with Agnes's keen makes a lot more sense," he whispered so quietly Bran almost had to read his lips to catch it.

"Portals," Bran started then leant forward and lowered his voice more, "were usually constructed from stone. Agnes's affinity is metal. Surely an earth mage would make more sense."

"If that was the case, he wouldn't have killed Kai. Idir is not the type to waste anything he considers a *valuable resource*," Varlan whispered bitterly and then cast another glance at the two women before he grabbed Bran's arm and tugged him towards the door.

Once they were outside, Varlan released his grip and took a step back. "The structure could be made from anything. The trick with a portal would be—"

"Weaving the necessary magics together and setting their purpose. Something only a creationist can do effectively."

"Exactly. And Idir needing a Shadow-blooded mage makes a whole lot more sense now. Agnes can create the portal and you can activate it. A permanent, stable portal anchored in both this world and the Between makes more sense than coaxing you to make a portal whenever he wishes it. With a permanent portal, he could—"

"It does make sense, but portals were never completely stable. That's why the technology was abandoned."

Varlan studied something over Bran's shoulder, though it was one of those looks that suggested he was lost deep in his own thoughts. He tapped a finger against his lower lip then his attention moved back to the hold door. "What if ..." He finally met Bran's eye again. "What if a specific soul was used as an anchor for the portal? The type of soul that can already bridge this world to the Between."

That wasn't how portals worked. Then again, typically, portals had been constructed to travel within the mortal realm itself—not to cross the barrier into the Between. However, if Idir wanted to find Grandmother Ocean's resting place and claim her power as his own, he would need to travel physically to the Between. That's why he needed a mage like Bran to get him there. But then getting back would be a problem. A permanent portal, on the other hand, could solve that problem of returning, provided the portal could be stabilised. But it only had to be stable long enough to complete one return trip to and from the Between. After that, it didn't matter. But anchoring a portal with a soul? "That's not ... I mean, it's not impossible. But it would be extremely difficult, and technically it would make the portal a golem." He blinked at Varlan, who was nodding.

"Everything is starting to make a twisted kind of sense, isn't it?" There was humour in his tone, though it was the bitterly ironic kind.

CHAPTER TWENTY-FOUR

AGNES

"Weeper's Cove is the safest place for us," Gendry insisted.

He, Varlan, Bran, and Wes had been bickering about their next course of action for a while. The twins were watching the argument unfold with bored expressions like they had seen it all before and Wren was frowning, her mouth a tight line like she was biting her tongue. The air around the captain crackled with the static of her magic, the sensation of it making Agnes's teeth ache and her hair prickle as though lice were crawling through it. She raked her fingers over her scalp and pulled her keen-sense back towards herself.

It was hard to focus with so many mages in the room. The warm throb of Pippa's fire magic clashed against the breath-frosting cold of Bran's necromancy. Deana's keen was deep and rolling like waves crashing upon a shore—so different to the bubbling coolness of Kiki's. Then there was the numb void of Wes that reminded her of the sensation in her fingertips from handling robrillium for too long. And, of course, consistent and intimately familiar, the alluring pull of Varlan's mind magic lingering beneath everything else and calling to her own keen in a way that was both confusing and comforting.

She lightly chewed her lip as she studied him. He was examining the map that was spread on the table between him and the other three men. The corner of his mouth tucked in like he was biting or sucking on the inside of his cheek; that was something he seemed to do often when lost in thought. He picked up the piece of parchment that was lying beside his fingers. It was a page torn from her journal. The one she had written the words to the song on. He scanned the words and checked the map then his gaze flicked to Deana before it found Agnes's and the corner of his mouth ticked into the briefest of lopsided smiles.

"The place where the singers touched the sky could be referring to at least three locations," he said, cutting over whatever Wes had been saying. "The Guild of Singers Pavilion on Lethata," he tapped the map, "Splade's watch," he moved his finger across the map, "or," a look in Gendry's direction this time, "Weeper's Cove."

"That's an awful lot of ocean to cover," Wren said, her keen burring against Agnes's as she stepped up to the table.

Agnes pulled her keen-sense in tighter and drew a breath. How did other mages manage to ignore all the sensations around them? Could they keep their keen-sense tucked away and only bring it out when they needed it? Maybe she just required more practice. She pushed her keen-sense towards the numbness of Wes, and he glanced her way. The numbness shifted, becoming a heavy blanket that folded over her and cut off every other sensation; even the constant thrum of her own magic seemed to be stilled.

"Lethata is the most likely place that Idir is hiding, and we can't hope to set foot in the Pavilion without arousing the suspicion of the guild of singers. Especially since they are likely to believe I, and quite possibly Deana, are responsible for Nazali's death," Bran said.

"We could try Weeper's Cove first," Gendry said.

"Splade's Watch is closer though. It would make more sense to check it on the way to the cove," Wes argued.

"Do we even need to locate whatever it is Kai wanted us to find? Especially if Idir can use it to build a portal. Shouldn't we be trying to do the exact opposite of what Idir wants?" Pippa asked as she moved to stand beside Wren.

"Vask was clear that in order to put a permanent stop to Idir, we will need to raise Dumura," Deana said. All eyes turned to her, and she seemed to shrink in her seat as she swallowed. "Not just raise it but raise it and find a way to wake Grandmother Ocean. If Varlan and Bran are right, and she is not in her temple on the island but rather in the Between, then we will need a way to get safely to her in order to wake her. That may mean building the portal ourselves." She cleared her throat. "Kai's journal seems to imply that will be the case."

They all fell silent once more but the air in the room remained charged with a tension that had nothing to do with anyone's magic.

"Let's go to Splade's Watch then," Gendry said, breaking through the moment. "I doubt we'll find anything more than Mala's undead and a bunch of dusty ghosts there, but if we can cross it off our list on the way to Weeper's Cove we might as well."

Everyone murmured their agreeance and then started making for the stairs out of the hold.

Agnes caught Deana's arm as she moved to follow the twins. "Do you mind if I get that blood now?"

Deana shook her head.

"Bran, can I borrow you for a moment?" Agnes asked as Bran ducked to follow Wes up the stairs.

"Are you absolutely sure about this?" Varlan asked, startling her. He was leaning against the table, his golden-brown gaze settled on her with an inscrutable expression. Ever since the altercation at Vask's temple, he had seemed withdrawn and stiff as though trying to keep his distance.

"Yes," she simply replied as she gathered her things and placed them on the edge of the table.

Varlan's mouth twisted but he said nothing more as he gathered the map up and then rolled it neatly and tucked it away.

Bran and Deana shared a look then Bran said, "Ready when you are, Agnes."

She set a bowl on the middle of the table then placed a thin finger-length piece of robrillium inside. Next, she lifted a small vial Nari had given her. Several shards of pale pink and orange coral rattled within.

"Is that shrouded-one coral?" Deana's voice was tight, her eyes wide.

"The shards of broken voices." Agnes nodded. "I couldn't figure that part out until I heard Dara mention that shrouded ones have fractured songs. *Broken voices.*" She licked her lips. Before her keen-sense returned, she had felt nothing from the various specimens in Nari's collection. But now the magic rolling off the coral made her feel queasy. There was definitely something wrong with it, a lingering perversion as though it had been poisoned.

"Agnes, I—"

"I know it's dangerous, but I know what I am doing," she said, cutting Varlan's objection short.

He folded his arms and pressed his lips together as he shot a look at Bran, who shrugged.

Agnes uncorked the vial and tipped the shards of coral into the bowl then she picked up an awl and tested the tip before holding her hand out to Deana.

Deana let out a breath and laid her hand palm up against Agnes's.

"Sorry about this," Agnes said as she pressed the tip of the awl against the pad of Deana's index finger.

Deana hissed through her teeth as the awl pierced her skin and blood welled. Agnes carefully tipped Deana's finger over the bowl and counted out three drops of her blood. She repeated the process with Bran then laid the awl down and closed her eyes.

Relearning how to use her magic now she had functioning keen-sense was proving a challenge. Before, her magic had always been there ready to swoop in and take complete control. But now it lingered just at the edge of her senses, waiting for her to reach for it and summon it forward. It still washed over her in a haze of pins and needles and a hiss of white noise, but she no longer lost all autonomy to it. She centred her focus on her desire to construct the key and coaxed the waiting magic forward. It responded like a released spring, bounding forth and sending a rush of hot-cold prickles up her spine. The sensation culminated in her fingertips as the deafening buzz of the trance reduced the room around her to a pinpoint of light that illuminated the components within the bowl. The magic gave an unruly surge, and she nearly lost her grip on it. Heat burned across her brow and her temples throbbed as blood pounded in her ears. She tightened her grip on the magic and pushed it forward, willing it to infuse the items in the bowl and transform them. The glow surrounding the components became so bright she had to shield her eyes.

All at once, her magic retreated—snapping free of her grasp and leaving her unsteady on her feet. The room spun around her, and a pair of strong hands caught her as she teetered back a step. An achingly familiar scent of smoky tea and Osmarian spice rolled over her and she opened her eyes and pulled away.

It was Varlan who had caught her. He was studying her face with a strangely guarded expression. Agnes tore her gaze away from his, only to encounter Deana's concerned stare.

"Sorry. My magic functions differently now. It's taking some getting used to." Her head was still swimming, and the bone-aching fatigue of magical exhaustion made her hands tremble. She clenched her fists to hide the shaking.

"It worked, I think," Bran said as he pulled the key from the bowl and offered it to Agnes.

It was small and delicate. The rose-gold shaft was topped with a swirling wave that resembled a crescent moon, and the teeth of the key were formed from the coral which had been reshaped and welded together with veins of robrillium.

"But will it open the chest?" Deana asked.

"There's only one way to find out." Varlan lifted the chest onto the table. There was something off about his tone, but he gave her a small smile as he indicated she test the key.

Agnes tilted the key towards the lock but then pulled it back. "Should we get the others?"

Bran shook his head. "And spend the next three hours arguing over whether to open it or not?"

"Fair point." Agnes gave a tired chuckle and slipped the key into the lock.

It was a perfect fit, but the moment it clicked open the key grew too hot to hold and Agnes released it with a hiss of pain.

"That can't be good," Bran said, drawing Agnes's attention away from her stinging fingertips to the key once more.

The scent of heated metal filled the hold as the lock began to glow red hot and the key melted.

"No." There was nothing she could do to fix the lock now. She rested her hands on the top of the chest and immediately lifted them again. The wood was as hot as the key had been. The world around her seemed to hold its breath then release it in a heavy shudder that rattled her already exhausted bones and made the swimming in her skull turn to a deep throbbing ache that sent spots dancing across her vision with each pulse.

Swirls of golden magic poured from the destroyed keyhole and roved over the ebony sides of the chest, leaving trails of smoking wood in their wake. Then all at once the shuddering stopped, and with a loud click the lid of the chest popped open.

Footsteps pounded down the stairs into the hold as about half the ship's crew came rushing into the space, all wearing various looks of concern.

"What in Bright's name are you lot doing in here?" Wren asked, her magic a wild crackle around her.

"Opening that." Bran indicated the chest.

"Is that the chest from Hartswood?" Gendry asked, pushing past Wes and the twins. "The one that contains several items that could kill us and only one that will be helpful?"

Bran nodded.

Agnes staggered backwards. The assault of so many different keens in the small space when she was already fighting off the exhaustion of using her magic was completely overwhelming.

Deana caught her and said something that was lost in the garble of sound that was stealing through Agnes's mind. A wash of numbness rolled from her toes to the top of her skull as Varlan and Wes both appeared in front of her. They moved, and Luca's sharp features took their place as she was jostled from Deana's hold into someone else's.

Luca said something but she only caught several words: exhaustion, mother's balm, and sleep.

No, she didn't want to go to sleep. Last time she had felt like this and gone to sleep, she had found herself in Idir's trap.

"No sleep," she managed to say, though her voice sounded far away and foreign.

"It's alright," someone whispered back, or yelled; it was so hard to tell with the throbbing inside her skull.

Something was pressed against her lips; a soft, slightly minty scent stirring her memory. Mother's balm. The liquid was cool as it slid across her tongue. It tasted as minty as it smelled but also sweet. Her magic stirred, bolstered by something in the tonic, and the pounding in her skull settled to a hollow throb.

She became aware of the hard floor and tangle of legs beneath her, then of the shoulder that was supporting the back of her head and the solid arms keeping her upright as the rejuvenating liquid slid down her wickedly parched throat.

"She'll be fine," Luca said, his voice fuzzing in and out of focus.

The chest pressed against her back vibrated as an inaudible voice rumbled out a question.

Luca said something in response then Wes shifted into focus.

"Come on. Let's get you to bed," he said as one arm slipped beneath her knees and the other behind her back.

"I don't want to," she muttered as he lifted her, and she rested her cheek to his chest. He smelled different to Varlan—something akin to sun-warmed citrus and was that clove?

"Healer's orders, I'm afraid," he said, though she felt the words against her ear rather than heard them.

Wes rolled her carefully into her bunk and moved out of focus again as sleep clawed heavily up her body and smoothed across her mind in a way that was impossible to fight.

CHAPTER TWENTY-FIVE

VARLAN

The source tightened then shuddered. Agnes's attention was on the chest, but Varlan's focus was on her. The tired tilt at the corners of her mouth and the dark circles that had smudged their way beneath her eyes told him that using her magic to create the key had taken a far greater toll than it should have.

The chest clicked open, startling him from his thoughts as a rumble of feet pounded into the hold.

Wren appeared at the foot of the stairs first. "What in Bright's name are you lot doing in here?" she asked, the static buzz of her keen prickling uncomfortably against Varlan's own.

"Opening that." Bran said.

Wes and the twins were directly behind Wren, but Gendry nudged them out of the way as he asked, "Is that the chest from Hartswood? The one that contains several items that could kill us and only one that will be helpful?"

Bran nodded.

"Varlan," Deana warned, drawing his attention to Agnes, who was swaying on her feet. Her keen was an erratic flutter around her, spiking savagely and then stilling once more with the hallmarks of magical exhaustion.

Varlan moved to catch her as she fell backwards, but he wasn't quick enough. Deana was, though, her knees sagging as she took Agnes's full weight.

"Get Luca or Nari," she said, her voice straining as she started to lower Agnes to the floor.

"Is it exhaustion?" Wes asked as he reached Agnes and Deana at the same time Varlan did, his suppression rolling out and cutting off the flutter of Agnes's keen.

"Everyone out," Luca said as he joined them.

"I've got her, Deana." Varlan carefully lifted Agnes from Deana's grasp and then sat, pulling her into his lap and resting her head back against his shoulder so Luca could examine her.

"It appears to be magical exhaustion," Luca said as his magic swelled in a warm throb around Varlan. "Wes, I need some mother's balm and the sleeping tonic. We need to stabilise her keen and then let her sleep it off."

Agnes twitched and rolled her head as she whispered something under her breath that sounded like a 'no'.

"No sleep," she finally gasped out in a voice quivering with barely contained panic.

"It's alright," Varlan whispered and let his keen brush over the edges of her fear, softening them to try and calm her down.

Wes returned with Luca's medical kit and removed two vials, checking the labels carefully before handing them to the healer.

Luca mixed the contents of the two vials into a third empty one and then gave it a good shake before bringing the edge of it to Agnes's lips. Tilting her head back gently, he tipped the contents into her mouth. She didn't fight him. Instead she swallowed the tonic and let out a shaky sigh.

The effect on her keen was almost instant, stabilising the erratic flutter into a weak thrum. A hollow echo of its usual quality but reassuring none the less. She shifted as though trying to sit up but then seemed to grow limp and heavy once more.

"She'll be fine," Luca said.

"Do you think it's just exhaustion? I believe this is the first time she has fully engaged her magic since getting her keen-sense back."

Luca nodded. "It was definitely exhaustion. We knew that there could be problems with her magic stabilising with her reawakened keen-sense. She's used to her magic functioning a certain way and —"

"Now's not the time," Wes said as he crouched in front of Varlan and gave Agnes a small smile. "Come on. Let's get you to bed." He lifted her from Varlan's grasp and turned towards one of the bunks that lined the sides of the hold.

"I don't want to," she muttered sleepily.

"Healer's orders, I'm afraid," Wes said with a gentle laugh as he deposited her in bed.

Luca packed away his medical kit and started for the door. "Aside from a splitting headache, she'll be fine when she wakes," he said before disappearing up the stairs.

Varlan moved to the table and studied the chest. In all the excitement, they hadn't even looked inside. Three glowing heartstones were nestled in the plush velvet that padded the interior of the chest. One red, one blue, and one a strange pearlescent white.

"Get Bran," he said to Wes, who had come over to have a look himself.

"Are you sure now—"

"Yes, right now."

Wes flicked a look at Agnes's sleeping form then hurried from the hold.

He returned a moment later with both Bran and Deana.

"Those are heartstones," the necromancer stated as he peered into the chest.

Deana was leaning over the chest, her magic washing around

her and then dragging back again as she studied the stones. "Are you sure that is what they are?"

"Absolutely," Bran said as Varlan nodded.

"Wasn't there supposed to be a weapon we could use against Idir in the box?" Wes asked.

"Well, a heartstone would count as a weapon once it was used to power a golem," the necromancer replied.

"But which stone do we choose?" Deana asked. Her hand hovered over the stones and then she curled her fingers back and touched them to the protection charm hanging against her chest.

Varlan let his keen roll over each stone. The red one whispered with magic that brought the taste of ash to his tongue and made him tug at his collar as his temperature rose and a murderous intent slid through his mind. The blue was more subtle: a soft kiss of cold shadows at the back of his neck and the weight of a well-balanced sword in his hand. He felt nothing at first from the white, but then the scent of salt breeze laced with the heady aromas of night-blooming flowers and devotional incense twisted around him. The scent came with a cold, dense pressure and the sensation of being dragged into deep water. He withdrew his keen-sense and tried to shake the feeling away.

"Any ideas?" Bran asked. His cold keen stirred around the chest and then receded once more.

"Not the red one," Deana answered, and Wes nodded in agreement.

"Agreed, I am not even sure the soul within that one was ever human," Bran said. "Opinions on the blue?"

Deana pressed her lips together and frowned as her keen swelled forward to inspect the stones once more.

"I sensed nothing inherently bad about it," Wes said, "but there was something almost deceptive about the magic it contains."

Bran nodded. "The white?"

"It's empty, isn't it?" Wes asked.

"No." Varlan and Bran said together.

"There is definitely something there, but I am not sure we want to tamper with whatever it is," Varlan added.

"I actually think the white is the right one," Deana said softly.

"You do?" Bran asked as he turned to face her.

She nodded. "It is connected to Grandmother Ocean somehow. Of the three, it is the one my song is the most comfortable with."

Varlan let his keen-sense investigate the blue stone once more. Wes was right about its magic being deceptive. It was certainly shrouding some aspect of its nature, but not necessarily a bad aspect ... No, he got the sense the duplicity was more about hiding a vulnerability than anything truly malicious.

When his keen-sense touched the white, an image of an old woman with ashen pigment smeared over her dark skin and a tattered blindfold covering her eyes flashed in his mind. His fingers twitched instinctively towards the stone. "I think Deana is right about the white stone being the one," he said as he turned to Bran.

The necromancer nodded. "The red wants blood and doesn't care whose it gets, the blue puts on a front of strength but will abandon the fight or even change sides depending on the perceived odds of the situation, and the white"—his magic chilled the air—"the white wants freedom as much as it wants vengeance. But ultimately it wants the equilibrium to be restored."

"So, we agree it should be the white?" Varlan asked, and the other three nodded.

Taking a deep breath, he reached for the stone and paused at the last second to meet each set of eyes in turn. They all nodded again, and he flicked a look at Agnes as he released the breath and touched the stone. Magic surged up his arm, making his teeth ache as a choir of voices burrowed through his mind. The woman with the blindfold flashed through his thoughts again, her smile wide and satisfied, then the world grew quiet once more. The chest snapped shut and disappeared with a puff of black smoke and an off-kilter shudder through the source.

"I guess that was the correct choice," Bran said.

"Wes, get me another piece of the mage-bane-treated cloth; I think we should keep this shrouded until we figure out how to use it."

The warden nodded then hurried off.

"What now?" Bran asked.

"Now we rest until we reach Splade's Watch, then depending on what we find there we can start piecing the rest of this mess together."

By nightfall they had reached Splade's Watch and were anchored in the small bay they had used the last time they visited the island. Over the last hour or so, the gentle breeze had turned into a biting gale that sent salt spray slamming against the side of the ship. Nearly everyone had turned in for the night, aside from Rufus who was on watch and Gendry who was keeping the boatswain company. They were further along the ship, hunkered behind a collection of crates and playing a game of liar's dice.

Varlan had turned down their offer to join in favour of a quiet patch of shadows in which to sort through the turbulence of his thoughts. A lot had happened in the last few days, and he hadn't really had a chance to sit and work through it all. Pieces were clicking rapidly into place, but he needed to make sure they were the right pieces and they weren't just digging themselves into a deeper furrow. Or worse, playing right into Idir's hands.

He shut his eyes and leant his head against the crate behind him. They had instructions from Kai about how to build a portal, a portal they would likely need to construct once they figured out how to raise Dumura. But Agnes's magic would be needed to construct the body of the portal and she hadn't even been able to form the key without exhausting herself. Why had her keen reacted like that though? Was it her reactivated keen-sense interfering with her magic or something else? Did actively wielding her magic rather than just being a channel for it take a bigger toll on her body? If making the key exhausted her reserves to the point that Luca had to give her a dose of mother's balm to stabilise her again, then creating the structure for the portal would kill her. He bit the inside of his cheek. That wasn't an option. They would just have to make do with the temporary portals Bran could create. He'd already proven he could use the keystone to boost his magic to make the portals big and stable enough to pass through. Though he'd insisted they wouldn't be as precise in pinpointing the area of the Between they needed to travel to, and despite being stable they would be extremely temporary, given the amount of source needed to channel to maintain them. But they couldn't risk Agnes's life when there was another way.

The numb warmth of Wes's suppression reached him before he felt the warden settle down beside him.

"Agnes woke up," he said. "Nari is in there fussing over her, but she's fine."

"What about next time?"

"We'll figure it out." He held up a bottle and tilted it towards Varlan. "It may just be an imbalance that will sort itself out in time. Idir fractured her keen, causing parts of it to mature at different rates, so either her keen-sense will need to evolve or she will need to learn how to channel her magic in a different way."

Varlan took a sip of the liquid in the bottle. Osmarian rum, judging by the spiciness. "Both will take time we don't have."

Wes took the bottle back from him. "Only because you're too stubborn to actually help her."

"Her mind was in tatters after what Savita and Idir did to her. The risk—"

"I'm not talking about using your magic. At least, I'm not talking about tampering with her mind—come on, Varlan, you're smarter than that."

"So people keep telling me." He released an amused grunt and took the bottle when Wes offered it again. "Intelligence is not the same as common sense. If I had realised what we were actually up against with Idir sooner, if I hadn't wiped her memories or Kai's, if I hadn't let Kai leave ..."

"Hindsight is a bitch," Wes muttered, "but dwelling on how you should have done things differently won't help us now. And it could have turned out a hundred times worse. Do you want my honest opinion, or do you want me to blow hot air up your arse?"

"The usual." He took a larger sip from the bottle this time, grimacing as it warmed a path to his stomach.

"I think you're scared. You told yourself it would be easy, that in time you'd get over her because she was just another girl, right? Too late you realised just how deep in trouble you were, but you didn't care and still don't. You've made peace with the depth, and you'll happily drown. It's been, what, three years? Four? And you haven't so much as looked sideways at another woman. You want to keep her safe because you love her, but you're also trying to keep yourself safe because you're terrified of what loving her means. So, every time things start to feel like they did before you get all up inside your own head and push her away again." He accepted the bottle from Varlan once more.

"I'm not scared about my feelings for Agnes. I'm concerned about what will happen to her if she redevelops feelings for me."

Wes made a noise of derision and swallowed another swig of the rum. "Maybe you should let her decide what risks she wants to take. And aside from you taking her memories, which she consented to, everything else that happened to her was Idir's doing ... or Kent's." He tapped his fingers against the side of the bottle. "Did you think that maybe if you just let go and stopped trying to control every minute detail that things might still work out how they are meant to?"

"I—"

Wes cut him off with a stern look. "The Varlan from five or six years ago would have tucked tail and run the moment he realised just how messy this whole situation was. And I would have followed, no questions, but you didn't cut your losses and run this time. Maybe because this is bigger than stealing some random antique for some bored noble who has every intention of double-crossing you, but I don't think that is the case. You never cared about the fate of the isles but then something changed, and it wasn't a change for the worse. The old Varlan would never have been able to figure this mess out, so why are you still trying to use his way of thinking? His way of controlling all the pieces on the board and planning seven moves ahead? The new Varlan has something the old Varlan could never even imagine adding into the calculation."

"If you say love, I will toss you over the side of the ship."

Wes snorted and handed him the bottle. "I was going to say altruism."

"I was never truly selfish."

Both of Wes's eyebrows arched. "You were opportunistic and valued your own self-preservation above all else."

"Not true. I always considered your wellbeing as much as my own."

"Alright, I will give you that. But you have to admit the old Varlan would never have worried about the fate of the isles and all in them."

"I will concede that point," he said with a laugh.

CHAPTER TWENTY-SIX

BRAN

Eight of them disembarked the ship to explore Splade's Watch. Varlan and Gendry were at the front of the group, Varlan's pink mage light bobbing along beside them and sending shadows reaching across the walls of the tunnel. Pippa and Deana were right behind them, followed by Wes and Kiki, leaving Bran and Agnes at the very back of the group. Agnes had been quiet since they left the Queen, a deep frown creasing her forehead and her keen a tense bubble around her.

The toll creating the key had taken on Agnes was troubling. She hadn't channelled enough of the source to result in exhaustion, but it was definitely exhaustion that she had suffered from. Bran had exhausted his keen to the point she had before. That moment of crushing fatigue rolling over you while your connection to the source spluttered was agonising. He let his keen-sense examine her keen now. It seemed stable for the most part, though it still felt tattered and almost hollow in places; the lingering after-effects of what Savita had put it through when she used her mind magic to force Agnes to construct Kent's war golem. The persistent wounds to her keen had been slowly healing themselves before she had gotten her keen-sense back from Idir, and they shouldn't have stopped healing just because her keen-sense had returned. Was using her wounded keen responsible for the exhaustion? That made the most sense. But Agnes's whole situation was complicated, and it could be something more sinister at play.

"Can you stop that?" Agnes asked, breaking through his thoughts.

Bran glanced at her. "Stop what?"

"Brushing your keen against mine. The cold is making my teeth ache."

He supressed a smile. "Sorry, I was just—"

"I'm fine. There's no need for everyone to keep checking on me."

"I wasn't checking on you. I was trying to work out why using your magic has become so draining. With your keen-sense functioning again, albeit in a hypersensitive state, your magic should be more stable than ever. I think the problem now is most likely the holes left behind by Savita. If we could figure out how to close them then that should stabilise everything and significantly lower the risk of exhaustion."

"Varlan said tampering with my keen could worsen the damage." She folded her arms and frowned at the mind mage's back.

"He's not wrong. It does require an extremely delicate hand and if it goes wrong then, yes, it could worsen the damage or even take away your magic entirely. For most mages that would be a fate worse than death."

She plied one of her plaits through her fingers, twisting it around before releasing it and repeating the process. Her keen folded inwards with each pass of her hands until it was nothing more than a soft fizz at the edge of his keen-sense. "Varlan won't risk it," she whispered and then shot a sharp look Bran's way. "He said you might be able to dissolve the connection between our keens."

"Connection between your keens?"

She nodded. "There is something that connects my keen to his.

He said it can happen when mages are ..." her cheeks darkened, "*intimate*."

Bran stopped walking. Was she referring to physical intimacy or something deeper? He'd never heard of, or experienced, any kind of bond being formed by physical intimacy, but if she was talking about the deeper connection between two people then maybe that made more sense. Or was she referring to a soul bond like the one between Nea and Garret? But that required the implementation of several archaic and prohibited magical practices, and there would be obvious markers not just on Agnes and Varlan's keens but their bodies as well. He touched his fingers to the oathmark on the inside of his wrist.

"He likened it to what Farideans call heart mates," Agnes prompted softly.

That made more sense. Deana had mentioned that mages' keens could weave together and form a bond, but it wasn't a concept that existed much outside of old stories in Beldaren. Farideans, however, seemed to give the concept a lot of weight and if he was honest, he'd certainly seen evidence of it happening between mages back home.

"Either I broke you or ..."

"Sorry." He shook his head. "I don't know if that kind of connection can be removed. Despite their seemingly volatile and delicate nature at times, keens can be extremely stubborn when they want to be. But even if this bond could be removed, are you sure that you would want that?"

"I honestly don't know, but Varlan seems to want it."

"Are you certain?" There was plenty of evidence to the contrary, unless, of course, Varlan was simply presenting it as an option because he thought it was in Agnes's best interests. That was ridiculous but also completely in character.

"He said so himself ... Well, not in so many words."

"Agnes ..." He searched the tunnel ahead. The glow from

Varlan's mage light had softened until they were standing in a patch of murky shadows. With a flick of his fingers, he summoned his own light. The soft lilac orb illuminated the air around them and sent the shadows scurrying. He gestured to the tunnel and started moving again. "Agnes, what do *you* want?"

"Me?"

"Yes. If you want my opinion, then Varlan suggested getting the connection dissolved for one of maybe three reasons. One, he thinks that with your memories gone you deserve to have a completely fresh start, even if that means living your life without him in it. Two, he thinks your feelings may have changed now that your memories are gone and he doesn't want you to feel obligated by the lingering connection between your keens. Three, he thinks that by putting distance between you he can protect you from some perceived disaster that is linked inexplicably to the intimacy between you." He counted each point off on his fingers then rolled his eyes. "Or four, some ridiculously convoluted combination of all three. This is Varlan we are talking about, after all."

She laughed at that.

"So, don't worry about what Varlan *says* he wants. Worry about what you *actually* want."

"And if I don't know what I want?"

Bran shrugged. "Then don't worry about it. You've been through enough over the past few months. Quite frankly, I would just ignore it and focus on recovery and survival. Chances are Idir is going to come out of the woodwork any day now and we'll be too busy trying to prevent the catastrophic destruction of the isles to worry about much else."

She gave a decisive nod. "Alright. So back to my messed up keen —how do we fix that?"

"We start small. Get you to use your magic to create something easy so we can see if it was just your magic or if it was the act of creating the key *specifically* that caused the exhaustion. If it is something to do with your magic itself then we may need to get Dara to send you … and possibly Varlan, back into your dreamscape to see if you can fix the damage from within." He nodded to himself. "That would be the safest course of action, I believe."

"Why Varlan? What about someone else like Nari or Wes?" Her tone was reserved like she already knew the answer.

"Nari's magic is limited to healing injuries of the bones and flesh; she can certainly assist with the physical symptoms, but she can't heal the mental or spiritual wounds which are most likely the true root of the problem. Wes could block your magic, even permanently if he does it from inside your dreamscape, but he can't mend it."

"What about you?"

"Is there a reason you don't want Varlan to do it?" He studied her face while he waited for her answer.

Her brows furrowed and she scanned the tunnel ahead as though looking for the mind mage in question. "No, I just— everyone always suggests him."

Bran laughed. "Because he's a *mind mage* and he is the best equipped to deal with the damage done by another mind mage. Also, your dreamscape is a bridge between your *mind* and your soul. It is the part of you that touches the Between. I can certainly assist from a spiritual point of view, but my skills are better suited to dealing with the dead. As you are still alive, it would be a much easier process for a mind mage rather than a necromancer."

"And you think Varlan would agree to it? To go back into my dreamscape and tamper with my keen?"

It was a valid question. Varlan and Garret had an awful lot in common when it came to protecting their loved ones. Though, Varlan's moods were too mercurial for him to pull off the warden's more stoic tendencies, but despite that they were certainly well matched when it came to brooding. "He's overprotective almost to the point of smothering, but he ultimately wants what is best for you and will see reason. But we might not need to *tamper* with your keen at all. It could have been the act of creating key itself. We'll only know once you try to use your magic again."

She nodded slowly and her keen gave a little flutter against his. "We should probably catch up to the others."

They continued along the tunnel in silence and now that Bran's focus wasn't on Agnes, he could feel the creeping sensation of the spirit from last time following them. As before, he sensed nothing malicious from it, just a mild curiosity. It followed them until they passed one of the side passages then it disappeared as though that curiosity had been satisfied.

The lilac glow of Bran's mage light found the rosy edge of Varlan's as they reached the main branch that led up to the plateau. Gendry and the others were waiting for them, the girls sitting with their backs against the wall and Varlan pacing in front of them, his shoulders tense.

"Told you," Wes said as Agnes and Bran reached them.

Varlan rolled his eyes and flipped a coin through the air.

Wes caught it and tucked it into his pocket with a satisfied smile. "You're getting too easy to beat."

"We thought it best to wait in case those wraiths are still present on the plateau," Gendry said.

Bran let his keen-sense wander farther along the passage towards what had been the main camp of Splade's Watch. He found the cold edge of Mala's necromancy and the dark churning power lying in wait to animate the bodies of the former residents of the Watch. "They're definitely still there, though whether they will recognise us and remain dormant or reanimate and attack this time I couldn't tell you."

"Only one way to find out I guess." Gendry started along the tunnel.

"Hold up, Gen," Wes said, and Gendry turned back to face the group. "Shouldn't we figure out how we're going to search the Watch? We don't even know exactly what it is we are looking for."

"Agnes's magic will know," Pippa said as she stood and held her hand out to pull Deana to her feet.

"Yes, but are we just going to turn over every stone until we find it or realise it isn't here?"

"If it is here, it will most likely be in the tower," Varlan said.

"The tower that is beneath at least a hundred feet of water?" Wes folded his arms.

"That's why Deana is here," Varlan gave Deana a smile.

Deana nodded.

"Couldn't we just ask Mala and save the trouble of displacing the lagoon to get to the tower?" Kiki asked.

"We can try." After his run-in with Vask, Bran wasn't sure he was ready to deal with another god-kin just yet. "But there is no guarantee she will be forthcoming with the information."

"Hold on. Didn't she say that her sisters were sleeping down there? She's not going to want us to go poking around the tower if it might endanger them," Pippa said.

"There is also the possibility that I won't be able to get us safely down to the tower," Deana said. "Moving that much water and holding it back long enough for everyone to search might be well beyond my abilities." She twisted her fingers together and frowned at her feet.

"I agree with Kiki," Agnes said. "We should just be honest with Mala. She helped you last time, right?"

"Yes. After her guard zombies attacked us," Gendry quipped. "Could be worth a shot though. I certainly wouldn't like to get on her bad side by charging in and doing something that she may interpret as a threat to her family."

"It can't hurt to see if she's in a helpful mood. Just don't bargain with her or promise her anything," Bran said.

With a nod, Gendry spun around and continued along the passage. Pippa jogged to catch up to him then Agnes, Deana, Kiki, and Wes followed, leaving Bran once more at the back of the group this time with Varlan for company.

"Is everything alright? Did something happen?" Varlan asked once they had started moving.

"Agnes just had a few questions about her keen."

Varlan let out a heavy breath and nodded.

"She also asked me if I could remove the connection between your keen and hers." He studied the mind mage out of the corner of his eye.

Varlan's brows flicked upwards but then dropped into a contemplative frown. "She did?"

Bran made a small sound of assent. "She said it was something you wanted. That you seemed to think it wouldn't rectify itself given time."

"It's been three years, and it hasn't faded."

"Did you think there might be a reason for that?"

Varlan rubbed his fingers along his lower lip. "Not one that makes any kind of logical sense outside of a children's story."

Bran laughed. "And you still want me to try and dissolve that attachment?"

"It is in Agnes's best interest that you do."

"Are you sure about that?"

"It is unfair—"

"I knew it!" Bran laughed again. "Shadow's teeth, Varlan, pull your head out of your arse."

"I'm sorry?" Varlan's eyes narrowed and his mouth shifted into a tight line.

"You haven't even thought to ask Agnes what she actually wants or how she feels. You are just assuming that given her mind no longer holds the memories of your time together her feelings will never return. Did you stop and consider that maybe those feelings weren't changed when her memories were taken? They were untethered from reason and buried, but not destroyed."

For a moment, Bran wasn't sure that the mind mage wasn't going to punch him but then Varlan released an amused sound of his own. "It's complicated."

"That's life for you. Look, if you want me to see if this connection can be dissolved, I will. But there is nothing to stop it from forming again and is it really something we need to be worrying about when we still need to figure out how to raise an island, build a portal, save a goddess from a megalomaniac arsehole, and somehow survive all of the above and not do catastrophic damage to the natural order of things in the process?"

"Well, when you put it that way—"

A shudder ran through the source, leaving the oily sensation of reanimation magic in its wake.

"The wraiths." Bran and Varlan said at the same time and then took off towards the mouth of the cave.

They skidded to a stop behind the others, who were staring down a group of shambling undead. The wraiths weren't attacking yet though. They were congregating around Mala, who was appraising the small group from the Queen.

Her violet gaze shifted to meet Bran's and the smallest of smiles ticked at the corners of her mouth. "I see you found the Granddaughter," she said, tilting her head towards Deana, "but why have you brought her here?"

"We seek a way to construct a portal and think it might be in the tower," Bran said.

The goddess shook her head. "There is nothing down there but drowned knowledge and the testament of mortal folly."

"We won't disturb your sisters."

"If you raise the tower, the damned one will come for them—I cannot allow that."

"We have no intentions of raising the tower, just displacing the water while we search it," Gendry said, and the goddess turned her gaze to him; her wraiths all mimicked the movement, heads tilting as though their clouded eyes were studying him.

"She is not ready for such a feat. Not on her own." Her attention moved to Deana and then back to Bran. "And I doubt you will find what you are looking for down there, so why risk disturbing my kin, or worse—leaving them vulnerable to the damned one?"

"What if we didn't expose the tower?" Deana asked.

"Unless Sejira gave you the ability to sprout a set of gills, I don't think you'll be able to explore the tower in its current state," the goddess answered.

"I think I can create a bubble, only big enough for one or two of us. But it will take a lot of focus and magic, so I won't be able to—"

"What if your magic fails while you are down there?" Pippa asked.

Deana shook her head. "It might be our only chance," she eyed the goddess, who was watching her with a hawkish stare.

"I will allow you to attempt this but do not disturb my sisters or you will wish Vask had kept you as his pet." She disappeared in a cloud of violet mist, leaving a shimmering ring of silver sand where she had been standing.

"This plan is too dangerous," Pippa said.

"We have to try at least. If it's too much strain on my magic, then we'll turn back."

"Who should go?" Kiki asked.

"I should," Agnes said, and Varlan shifted beside Bran but didn't say anything. "Kiki was right before; my magic will recognise anything it can use to construct the portal. It will be faster."

"I'll go too," Bran said. "That is if you think you can create a bubble big enough to house all three of us."

Deana's keen rolled over him then receded and she nodded. "I can try at least."

"Good. If your keen starts to fail, I might be able to lend you some of mine, or worst case, I can attempt to portal the three of us out of there." Bran hoped he didn't have to rely on trying to make a portal, but if it would save them from drowning then he'd risk it.

"Alright," Deana said and headed to the path that seemed to wind down the side of the plateau to a small beach at the edge of the lagoon.

"Are you absolutely sure about this?" Bran asked her as she slipped her boots off and moved to the edge of the water.

"No," her sea foam gaze held a shimmer of fear and she swallowed, "but I can't let my doubts stop me anymore. Ready when you are." She gave the others a small smile and then waded into the lagoon as the heavy wash of her keen rolled through the source.

CHAPTER TWENTY-SEVEN
DEANA

Deana bit off the gasp that rose when the cold water of the lagoon enveloped her thighs. Her song surged around her as she focused on shaping the water. She dragged a wave up over her head before folding it down and pulling the sides together to form a seamless bubble around herself. The water fought back, quivering and threatening to collapse, but she drew a long, slow breath and then another, centring her mind and allowing her song to twist with that of the lagoon.

The lagoon's song was different to that of the ocean which fed it. Quieter and more contemplative, it was disturbed only occasionally by the raucous clash of waves breaching the wall of rock and reef that cut it off from the rest of the ocean until the high tide.

Another breath in and the song of the tower nestled at the heart of the lagoon reached her. It was the quiet melancholy of discarded dreams. Closer, she could hear the shifting song of Bran. It had once frightened her but now was the familiar touch of cool fingers plying through her hair and the clandestine whispers of deep knowledge. Agnes's song was brighter, its playful rhythm supplying a beat that made her toes twitch with the desire to dance. She turned to face them both, their forms blurred silhouettes on the outside of her bubble. This was the tricky part—maintaining the bubble while she expanded it enough to house all three of them.

She held her hands out to the side and pushed her song against that of the lagoon. Slowly, the walls of her bubble shifted and widened, then a seam of teal light appeared in one side before the water parted like a curtain.

Agnes stepped through the opening first, her eyes wide as she examined the sphere of water above them.

When Bran stepped inside, it became clear Deana would need to expand the bubble farther. Digging her toes into the sand, she pushed her hands out harder, her arms shaking under the strain as her magic attempted to manipulate the song of the lagoon. The water splashed and threatened to collapse, then, with a shudder that rocked through her song, the sides of the bubble sprang wider and stabilised.

"I don't know how long I can hold this, so we have to hurry," she said as she took a step towards the deeper water.

Bran and Agnes kept pace with her and soon the world grew dimmer as the water of the lagoon closed over the sphere.

Those first few steps once they were completely submerged stirred a tight tangle in her stomach. Green-toned light filtered down in thin flickering shafts that glittered against the surface of the bubble. Fish darted away from them, some finding courage and coming back to inspect the strange orb that had invaded their drowned landscape. A shadow passed over them as a large, grey-dappled ray cruised lazily across the top of the sphere.

They ventured deeper until the sandy floor beneath their feet sloped sharply downwards. Here the water around them was a deep blue and though the exterior of the bubble was glowing with the gentle teal colour of Deana's magic, it did little to illuminate the underwater world much farther than several paces beyond where they were standing.

"The tower shouldn't be much further. How are you holding up?" Bran asked, his voice echoing strangely off the water around them.

"I'm alright for now, but we should try to be as quick as possible." She was surprised how easy it was to control her magic. Once the bubble had stabilised, it took barely any effort to keep her song twisting around its boundary and holding it together.

"Agnes, what about you?" Bran asked.

"I'm great. This is beyond fascinating; did you see the sea dragons back when we passed through the fan weeds?" There was an excited edged to her voice that fluttered through her song, increasing the tempo momentarily.

Bran laughed softly. "I did see them." His song swept over Deana and a small orb of violet light appeared just outside the edge of their bubble. The violet glow reflected over them, mixing with the light from Deana's magic and making the sphere shimmer like a translucent slice of mother-of-pearl. "Shall we continue?" He indicated the slope ahead of them, his light dipping low to illuminate a path forward.

Deana nodded and started moving again, carefully picking her way around the rocks that were strewn across the sand. A flash of white out of the corner of her eye made her pause as her throat thickened with the memory of near-drowning. But it was just Sejira in her fish form. She swam in easy circles around them as they continued down towards the shadowy bulk that could only be the ruined tower.

By the time they reached the foot of the tower, the weight of the water around her was threatening to buckle her knees. Here the stones littering the sand were denser, making it harder to pick a clear path to the section of wall that appeared it could allow them entry. A soft glow was emanating from the jagged opening. When they reached it and stepped through into the cavernous space beyond, Agnes let out a gasp and grabbed Deana's arm.

A glistening dome of rainbow magic took up most of the area before them. Six bodies were laid out within the boundary of the dome, their arms crossed over their chests as though in death, but their songs twisted through the air around them, the combined melody leaching raw magic into the world and forming their waterproof cage. Or was tomb a more apt description?

"We should proceed with caution," Bran whispered, his song swelling out as he examined the dome.

Shadows moved around the far side of the sleeping goddesses; their inky forms appeared almost human but then their song reached Deana. It was the tainted melody of the shrouded ones. Icy fingers that had nothing to do with Bran's magic scurried up her spine and a white-hot pressure seized her chest. The bubble faltered, cold water dousing them before she managed to stabilise it again. Her hold was trembling, threatening to collapse again at any moment, but Bran laid his hand lightly on her shoulder.

Cold magic swept from the tips of his fingers down her arm and across her chest to settle behind her navel. It was almost heavy but also soothing, like a cool cloth pressed to a feverish brow. His song enveloped hers, lending it strength, and her song greedily consumed everything his had to give, twisting and changing, developing a new harmony. It was frightening and invigorating all at once. The sphere around them stabilised then expanded once more.

The three shrouded ones came right up to the edge of the sphere, fanning their webbed fingers out across its glowing surface. They wore monstrous faces of death-pallid skin pulled tight over bone, their seaweed-strewn hair floating in dark halos around them. The coral that studded the skin of their cheeks and arms was highlighted with shades of soft lilac and turquoise-toned luminescence. There was something haunting about the looks with which they regarded Deana, but when their eyes found Bran, they pulled away from the sphere and retreated beyond the far edge of the dome once more. There they burrowed into the shadows like oversized eels, the bio luminescence of their coral the only indication of their presence.

"They won't harm us," Bran said, his voice slightly strained. "I don't think they belong to Idir; their magic feels different."

"I don't think I want to stay around and find out their true intentions though," Agnes said.

Deana nodded, not trusting herself to speak.

The channel between her song and Bran's was still open, and when she glanced his way, he slowly lifted his hand, drawing most of his magic back into himself but leaving a small cooling throb at her core. Her song latched onto those lingering notes of melancholy and death and refused to release them again, but she could worry about that later. Right now, she needed to focus on maintaining the bubble of air around them. Whatever Bran had done, it had made that significantly easier; it had strengthened her magic, chasing away the fatigue that had been starting to eat at her and bolstering her song with a vigour that she had never experienced before.

"Do you see anything that speaks to your magic, Agnes?" Bran asked as he studied the murky shapes beyond the edges of the bubble.

"Not yet." Her song grew louder for a moment and a ball of gold and bronze light appeared outside the circle. The mage light moved through the water, illuminating the ruined furniture around them and then dancing across a dark void that looked like it had once been stairs.

The pale form of Sejira swam in lazy circles at the edge of that dark void, and Deana swallowed. "I think we need to go that way."

They moved across the room, careful to give the slumbering goddesses and their shrouded guard dogs a wide berth. When they reached the stairwell, Agnes's light highlighted the extent of the damage done to it. If there had been a floor beneath the one they were currently on, the access had been completely cut off by sand and the glossy black obsidian of cooled lava flow. With up the only way open to them, that is where they went. As they followed the treacherous spiral to the floor above, the walls of Deana's bubble flexed and rippled, smoothly reforming around the edges of each obstacle. Each time the sphere adjusted, the seed of Bran's song would spiral through her own, keeping the magic steady.

The stairs eventually led to another cavernous room. The debris suggested it may have been some kind of library. Floor-to-ceiling shelves lined the walls, their contents long eroded by the ebb and flow of the tides. Shapes that could have once been tables and chairs were scattered across the floor, and in the middle of them lay a large dark shape. The sides of its broad head were adorned with a fringe of burgundy gills that fluttered in the water around it. Deana had never seen a creature like it before. Its massive body was almost lizard-like, covered in a pebbled black skin rather than scales. There were flashes of vivid pink at its throat and along its sides. It appeared to be dead but there was something about its stillness that sent a warning note through her song.

Agnes's fingers closed around her wrist, the rhythmic drumming of her song rattling around Deana's mind before it calmed again.

"What is it?" Bran asked in a whisper.

Deana glanced down; Agnes's fingers were wrapped around his wrist as tightly as they were wrapped around her own.

"I don't know," Agnes whispered back, "but we should avoid waking that creature at all costs."

Bran nodded. "Do you sense anything else here?"

Agnes started to shake her head then stopped with a frown. Her song picked up tempo as it drifted around them. "There is *something*, but it is very faint and I am not sure if it's in this room or—" She turned her attention to the opening on the other side of the room. "Can you pull the walls of the bubble in closer before we attempt to cross to the other stairwell, Deana?"

Deana tightened her song around the edges of their sphere and drew them inward. The bubble contracted easily but the movement stirred little clouds of sand that drifted in eddies towards the creature.

They all seemed to hold their breath as the sand settled and the creature remained inanimate. When they started forward again, the movement once more stirred the sand. This time it washed forward in a larger cloud, settling over the fluttering gills. The floor beneath them shuddered and a series of hot-pink runes lit up over the creature's body before it lifted its head to regard them with one of its luminous aqua-coloured eyes.

"What do we do?" Deana asked as the creature swayed its head like a snake waiting to strike.

"There!" Agnes's song picked up tempo as she pointed at something that had been obscured by the bulk of the creature.

It was a small contraption that looked like it had been carved from obsidian.

When Agnes took a step towards the object, the creature tilted its head then opened its wide maw to show multiple rows of tiny glistening teeth before snapping its jaw shut again and sending forth a current that buffeted the sides of Deana's bubble.

"I'll get it," Bran said. The melancholy notes of his song deepened, and a small disc of purple light appeared below the object. Another disc of purple opened above Bran's hand, and he caught the object as it fell through.

The moment Bran's fingers closed around the device, the creature surged forward. Its mouth smashed through the top of the bubble, and they all dodged out of the way.

The sphere shuddered as Bran was thrown clean through its wall. The creature charged towards him and he swam away from it, diving behind an overturned table.

"What do we do?" Agnes's voice was tight with panic, her song drumming so loudly against Deana's own that she could barely think.

The creature charged for Bran again, and Deana sent her magic spiralling. It churned the water between Bran and the creature into a frenzy of bubbles. The creature dodged backwards, its tail slamming into the wall of Deana's bubble and sending a shockwave through her song.

She lost her grip on her magic and water smashed against her from all sides, sending her flying head-over-tail and making her lungs burn as she was forced to hold her breath. She lost sight of Agnes and Bran as the thrashing creature and twisting currents stirred the sand into a cloud.

Something closed tight around her wrist, and she saw Sejira's face seconds before a flash of teal-coloured light sent her hurtling through the fabric of the world.

She stumbled into the shallows, still unsteady from travelling through Sejira's portal, before falling to her hands and knees as she turned to search frantically for Bran and Agnes. They were nowhere in sight. That meant they were still down there in the sunken tower. A wave splashed over her and then another as panic tore up her spine and weakened her knees, making it impossible to stand.

"What happened?" Varlan gripped her shoulders, his song soothing over hers. "Where are Agnes and Bran?"

"I have to go back. They're still down there." She shrugged his hand off her shoulder and forced herself to her feet, and her focus narrowed in on the spire of the ruined tower. Her song built, drowning out all other sounds, and she thrust her hands forward, parting them as she implored the water to answer her command.

Waves churned around her legs and then opened in a seam towards the tower. But the weight of the water was too great, and it snapped free of her hold, sending a jolt through her song that nearly gave her whiplash. Spots danced across her vision and the copper taste of blood coated her tongue.

She ignored the pain and the warning notes that were trilling across her mind and spoiled her magic for another attempt.

Discordant notes rocked through the song of the world, followed by a tearing sound that silenced everything else.

She spun towards the beach where the sound emanated from. A glowing doorway of purple magic glittered in the sunlight. Bran's song poured from that doorway seconds before it sprang open, sending a rush of water across the beach. Two bodies rolled through the torrent and Varlan started running towards them.

With an ear-splitting screech and a thud that shook the fabric of the world, the creature from the tower launched through the portal before it flickered and snapped shut.

Gendry and the others dove out of the way of the creature as its momentum sent it barrelling across the sand and slamming into the path that led up to the plateau.

Bran and Agnes got gingerly to their feet amid the debris that had spewed from Bran's portal, and despite looking half drowned they appeared otherwise unharmed.

The creature turned in a slow circle and let out a world-consuming bellow as it charged. Agnes dove out of the way, pushing Varlan back as he reached them. But Bran stood his ground, the air around him crackling with violet light as his song increased in volume until the melancholy notes became the icy wail of darkness and death.

The creature pulled up short, its body shrouded in the purple glow of necromancy as Bran gritted his teeth and clenched his fists towards it. He yanked his arms back as though pulling the magic back into himself and the creature thrashed, letting out another of those ear-splitting screeches.

"Shadow's teeth," Bran exclaimed and sent a single glance Deana's way moments before he silenced his song.

He just stood there as the creature charged, and Deana pressed her hand over her mouth to try and hold back her scream as he disappeared into its cavernous maw.

Gendry let out a roar and charged forward as both Pippa and Kiki's songs twisted around Deana's.

The creature turned in a clumsy circle and then dug its feet into the sand as though preparing for another charge, but its form shuddered and thrashed, and the glowing pink markings along its sides turned violet. Bran's song twisted through the air once more, and the runes turned black before the creature gave a convulsing shudder then exploded, sending chunks of oily black flesh flying in all directions.

When the world calmed once more, Bran was standing on the scorched sand with a green stone that was nearly identical to both the keystone and the prison stone clutched in his hand. "Well, let's hope that's the last time I ever have to do something like that." He gave her a shaky smile and let out an almost delirious laugh.

Everyone else was just starting at him with mouths agape, but Deana shook the shock away and splashed through the shallows. She charged across the beach and, despite the viscera that covered him from head to toe, threw her arms around his neck, making him stagger back a step. "I thought you'd drowned and then that thing—how are you still standing?"

"Apparently, death doesn't want me." The humour in his voice was strained and he gave a sharp intake of breath that made her release him. "I'm alright," he said lightly, patting his side with the hand not holding the stone. "Just a few bruises and maybe a cracked rib."

"What in Bright's name was that thing?" Gendry asked.

"Whatever it was, it was guarding the tower," Agnes said. Her voice was almost inaudible after the assault of so many songs.

"Did you at least find anything useful for your trouble?" Wes asked.

"Useful? I'm not sure, but definitely something that my magic is interested in," Agnes replied, holding up the small black device the creature had been laying on. It looked almost like a sextant.

"Right, well, we can discuss that back on the ship. Bran, make sure you have a good rinse off before you see Wren. I doubt I need to tell you the tizz she'll get in if she hears you served yourself up as a willing meal for the leviathan's runty cousin," Gendry said and then marched towards the path leading back to the plateau before looking back over his shoulder in exasperation. "Well, come on, you lot. Stop standing there gaping like a school of stunned fish and move your arses."

CHAPTER TWENTY-EIGHT

AGNES

"Alright, I'm ready," Agnes said.

And she was ready, wasn't she? She flicked a glance at Varlan, who was standing beside Bran with his arms folded and an unreadable look on his face. His eyebrows rose slightly in silent question as though he could sense her hesitancy. He probably could, stupid Bright damned mind mage that he was.

A smile quirked one corner of his mouth. She both liked and hated that smile. It was small enough that most people might not notice it or pass it off as a simple tick, but it was a real smile—not just one put on as a barrier to hide his true intentions. It also ignited that confusing sensation deep at her core that remembered they had been more than just friendly acquaintances.

"You'll be fine," Bran said and pushed a rod of copper across the table towards her. "And if you're not, Wes will suppress your keen before things get out of control."

Agnes flicked a look towards Wes, and he gave her an encouraging smile, the warm numbness that seemed to surround him most of the time rubbing against the edge of her keen-sense.

She turned her attention to the objects on the table and picked up the rod of copper Bran had nudged her way. They had decided that recreating something she had successfully created in the past would serve them best, and Agnes had decided to make a light like those she designed to light the interior of Armada. It was something she knew her magic could handle, and given that it had been her first working creation before her keen had fully matured, it should be simple enough to achieve without taxing her now.

Running her fingers along the length of the piece of copper, she closed her eyes and called her magic forward. It was easier than last time, but the buzzing pressure of a headache formed behind her eyes. She drew a deep breath and then released it as the tingle started in the tips of her fingers and intensified into the hot-cold prickle of pins and needles.

The trance pressed against the back of her mind with a world-consuming hiss that intensified the ache behind her eyes. Her magic was there and ready to work—all she had to do was embrace it. She opened her eyes once more and met Varlan's gaze; concern was swimming just below the surface, but he gave her a tiny nod.

With a nod of her own, she dropped her guard and let her magic sweep forward. It surged along her arms and a metallic taste coated the back of her tongue then the world turned white.

She pivoted in a slow circle. The pale woman in the glittering golden gown was standing behind her. There was a concerned furrow between her brows, but it smoothed away as she gave Agnes a doting smile. Beside her sat the black metal panther, its head dipped low as its glowing eyes studied her.

"I am pleased you did not let Idir win," the woman said as she laid her fingers on the panther's shoulders, "but I fear your fight is not yet over."

A stiff breeze buffeted Agnes, sending her plaits flying and driving the pale metal-edged petals that littered the ground into a stinging flurry.

The trance hissed and fizzed around her, and the woman and panther disappeared as the white walls of the world became blinding. She clenched her hands as the prickle in her fingertips grew unbearable before a soothing numbness smothered over everything and she found herself leaning heavily against the table in the Queen's hold. The world swam in and out of focus as the cold sweat of exhaustion slicked the back of her neck and brought a lump of bile up her throat.

"I told you this wasn't a good idea," Varlan growled at Bran.

"It was worth a try. You can't keep—"

"Was it? Because—"

"Hey!" Wes's tone was edged in cold steel, his normally easy-going demeanour replaced with a commanding sharpness.

Both Varlan and Bran turned to face him.

"This is not helping. Bran, what did you say our other option was?" Wes asked, his tone still tense but less cold.

"If Agnes is okay with it," Bran studied her face for a moment, "then we can get Dara to send both Agnes and Varlan into her dreamscape and they should be able to find and fix the issue from there."

Varlan looked like he was about to say something, but Wes lifted a finger in his direction and then turned his attention to Agnes. "Is that what you want?"

She drew a breath, waiting for the wave of nausea to pass then straightened and twisted one of her plaits around her fingers. Honestly, she wasn't sure. Last time they had entered her dreamscape, they had managed to spring the trap Idir set in her keen. What if they caused more damage?

They were all staring at her expectantly. She gave the plait a firm tug and then released it. "I don't know ... Can I talk to Varlan in private for a moment?"

While Bran and Wes made for the door, Agnes busied herself by rearranging the small pieces of metal that littered the table. Her fingers shook with fatigue as she ran them through the small bowl of robrillium shards. The numbing aura of the metal was almost soothing, and she was still running her fingers through the shards when Varlan cleared his throat and her attention snapped to him.

"What do you think I should do?"

Several emotions chased each other across his features before they relaxed into that infuriatingly hard to read stare. "I think Bran is right about going into your dreamscape, but last time ..." He shook his head and picked up the piece of copper she had dropped, turning it over in his hands and then tapping it against the middle of his palm.

"But if we don't try, then what?"

He tossed the copper back onto the table and rubbed his hands over his face. "I don't know. Every option I can think of has risks, some of them more grievous than others, but none of them acceptable."

"Do you think Wes should accompany me into the dreamscape instead?"

"Wes?" His eyebrows twitched upwards then a deep frown settled across his features. "You mean to attempt to permanently block your magic? Agnes, that's a—"

"Fate worse than death. I know. But I'm living that reality now. I can't use my magic without fear that it will kill me. I am tired of all the looks, the pity, the fear, the walking on eggshells, the being talked about like I am some kind of experiment gone wrong." She pressed her face into her hands in an effort to stop the tears that were building.

"Agnes ..." His tone was as whisper-soft as the touch of his keen at the back of her neck. "Everyone is just—"

"Trying to help. I know that too. I'm just scared. This ..." Her voice cracked as she gestured to herself then the table between them. "This is worse than losing all autonomy to my magic. If you can't figure out how to fix my keen from inside my dreamscape, then I want you to take my keen-sense away again."

"Agnes—"

"Please. Getting my keen-sense back from Idir ruined everything. If giving it up means things go back to the way they were then I am fine with that. I've lived my entire life without it anyway and I managed okay."

He studied the items on the table like he was trying hard not to meet her gaze, but eventually he looked up and gave her a nod. "I don't think it will fix this issue with your keen, but if that is what you want—and there's no other option—then I will remove your keen-sense." He lifted a hand to stop her as she went to speak. "If I can. And if I am certain that it won't cause further damage."

"Thank you." She moved around the table and hugged him.

He stroked a hand over her head, the other smoothing across the middle of her back before he pressed her gently against his chest and returned the hug. "You might want to hold that thanks until after we've emerged from your dreamscape," he whispered, his breath stirring her hair.

She pulled away from him again, trying not to focus on the nagging sense of forgotten memories that his scent brought boiling to the surface.

Agnes got a strong sense of déjà vu as she settled herself on the edge of Wren and Gendry's bed in the captain's quarters. Nari was carefully measuring out sleeping tonic into two cups while Bran and Varlan discussed something in hushed whispers by the door. The bed moved beside her as Dara sat and touched the back of her hand. Dara's magic made Agnes's eyes heavy, and she bit down on a yawn, lifting her hand to cover her mouth when she failed to stop it completely.

"Alright, everyone get in position," Nari said, shooing Dara into the chair beside the bed and waving Varlan over.

He settled on the floor with his back resting against the bed and his hands folded neatly in his lap. He gave Nari a smile when she handed him one of the cups containing the sleeping tonic.

Bran leant on the wall by the door, his magic a cool pool around him.

"Ready, Agnes?" Nari asked, holding out the second cup.

Agnes's fingers shook as she took the cup. Last time she had taken this sleeping tonic, she had spent at least two weeks in an enchanted sleep, navigating through nightmares until she managed to wrest her keen-sense back from Idir.

"It will be alright." Nari gave her shoulder a little squeeze.

Agnes nodded, not trusting herself to speak, then swallowed the liquid in the cup. It was bittersweet and sent a warmth spreading through her body that made her head swim. She passed the cup to Nari then lay back and closed her eyes.

Dara's magic rolled over her as the girl placed her hand on her brow, the cool tips of her fingers the last sensation Agnes felt as she was swept into oblivion.

She landed heavily on the white dunes of her dreamscape. Wind stirred the sand into ripples and snatched at her hair and clothes. A small white rabbit was sitting at her feet. It cleaned its mauve-tipped ears and then twitched its nose as Varlan materialised in front of Agnes.

The seductive touch of his keen plied over her as he slowly inspected the landscape around them. "Can you feel anything amiss?" he asked when he turned back to face her.

She focused on her keen-sense and sent it outwards, past the familiar touch of Varlan's magic and the drowsiness of Dara's. Nothing seemed wrong. She pushed it further until she brushed up against a sensation that was dense and cloying and definitely out of place. "There is something there." She pointed to the horizon, another jolt of déjà vu running through her.

Varlan flicked a look at Dara and then started off in the direction Agnes had pointed.

The further they wandered across the sand, the more the sensation of wrongness deepened until they came to a bronze fountain. Opalescent water bubbled over the fountain's sides as if it was fed by an underground spring. Lush plants with crimson leaves and small white flowers grew from the damp sand. A gentle breeze shifted through them, making their leaves rustle and whisper and causing the light to reflect off the thin metal edges of the petals.

Agnes let her keen-sense examine the fountain, and the sense of coming home settled at her core. There was something else though, lingering beneath the surface. The cloying sensation she had felt before. It was almost like Varlan's magic but heavier and it left a thick sickly-sweet taste on her tongue. She edged closer to the fountain; a dark pink fish with black stripes was swimming in graceful circles through the water. As her keen-sense touched the fish, Savita's dark stare flashed across her mind and her back slammed into Varlan as she retreated from the edge of the fountain.

"What's wrong?" His keen smoothed over her nape then drifted away from her towards the fountain.

"I think I felt Savita."

"Are you sure?" There was an edge to his voice. "She shouldn't still have influence on you; Bran got rid of her."

"Did he though?" Savita's silky voice echoed around them and the water pouring out of the fountain turned dark as a shadow rose from the pool and formed into Idir's daughter. She gave Agnes a warm smile and then licked her lip as her coal-dark gaze moved to Varlan. "Oh, it has been fun watching you scurry about in a panic through her eyes, and I did warn you what would happen if she attempted to use her magic." Her self-indulgent laugh had a simpering edge that roused a ball of heat between Agnes's shoulders.

"Get out," Agnes growled.

Savita tilted her head, her infuriating smile still firmly in place.

"Oh, my dear, sweet, Agnes, don't you realise you are mine? I own your magic and it is only a matter of time before I own your mind as well."

"I said get out!" She planted her feet and pulled on her magic.

The sand behind her and Varlan rose in a tidal wave that shadowed the dreamscape. She thrust her magic forward with the intent to drive Savita from the dreamscape. The wave smashed down, burying the fountain and Savita along with it. Agnes was knocked off her feet. She rolled across the ground, the sand grating against her skin and leaving stinging welts in its wake. When she regained her footing, she spun around to search for Savita again.

The mind mage was staggering about. Blood oozed from her temple and her clothes were tattered and torn, revealing a collection of weeping scraps and cuts. Varlan was a short distance away with Dara peeking out of the neck of his shirt, her wide-eyed stare seeming to match his.

Petals were strewn across the wet sand where the fountain had been, their dark metal edges glinting in the light. Agnes focused on those metal edges, willing her magic to latch on to them and shape them.

"You can't drive me out—all you'll do is destroy your own dreamscape," Savita said, but there was something about her tone. A note of uncertainty?

"You don't *belong* here." With each word, Agnes sent a pulse through her magic; the petals twisted around her and then fanned out, hovering in the air between her and Savita like a cloud of tiny daggers.

The cloying fog of Savita's magic pressed over her and one by one the petals started to fall, then the weight of Varlan's hands settled on her shoulders. The seductively familiar touch of his magic smoothed along the edges of her keen-sense before it twisted around her, bolstering her own magic. The falling petals rose to join their brethren once more, bronze and pink light rippling across their surfaces.

"No!" Savita stamped her foot and the sweet taste on Agnes's tongue turned sour.

"Sorry, sweetheart," Varlan said, and her mouth slipped into a thin line. "You no longer have any power here."

His magic pulsed against Agnes's, and she let her own fly. The cloud of petals converged on Savita the way the tidal wave of sand had. Each petal tore across her skin, leaving trails of inky smoke in their wake until, with an enraged scream, she disappeared in a cloud of black sand.

The ground rumbled and the fountain reformed, the bubbling trickle becoming a torrenting river that tore across her dreamscape and left a path of lush foliage and bright metal-edged flowers in its wake.

Varlan spun her around. "Well done!" His grin was infectious, and he pulled her tight against his chest, causing Dara, who was still hiding his shirt, to squirm free.

She hit the ground beside them with a soft plop and gave him what could only be described as a look of pure disgruntled fury. Well, if a rabbit could look furious. When he released Agnes, she staggered back a step.

Turbulent emotions were charging about under her skin and buzzing through her head. Memories that wouldn't stay quiet despite their lack of substance. Feelings that she knew were real whether she knew why she had them or not. Her thoughts singled in on one moment that she could remember, or rather a reflection of a moment given to her by Idir. What if that was the answer? Varlan was convinced those memories were gone, but Bran said that memories could never truly be erased.

"Everything alright?" Varlan asked, a small furrow forming between his brows as he studied her face.

She gave him one decisive nod then grabbed the front of his shirt and pulled his mouth down to meet hers.

CHAPTER TWENTY-NINE

VARLAN

Varlan froze as Agnes's form pressed against his own. His mind went blissfully quiet the moment her lips touched his. The shock wore off quickly though as she pulled away from him again with a little furrow of confusion between her brows. She maintained a loose grip on the front of his shirt a beat or two longer before gently smoothing the fabric out then taking a step back.

Her freckles almost disappeared as her cheeks darkened and she cleared her throat. "I'm sorry. I probably should have asked first," she murmured.

He shook his head. His thoughts had ground to a near complete stop and the connection between his tongue and brain seemed to have been severed. "It's alright," he managed to say after a moment. It was more than alright, but a part of him was unsure why she had kissed him—not that he didn't want her to, but if it was—

"I just thought that maybe it would unlock my memories." She played with one of her plaits and turned her attention to the fountain.

He resisted the urge to tell her it was impossible to retrieve those memories and instead asked, "Did it help?"

She frowned. "Not the way I was hoping. The memories didn't come back, but ..." She drew a deep breath and then met his gaze. The little starbursts of copper that ringed her pupils seemed to sparkle with determined purpose. "But it made me realise that these things I've been feeling, the echo of emotions, of our connection, they are real. And they are *mine*, and I don't want them to go away."

Her keen brushed against his; it was steady and stable, the wounds left by Savita completely gone.

"You're sure?"

She let out an exasperated breath and rolled her eyes. "For Bright's sake, Varlan. Yes, I am sure. I know I loved you before you took my memories. There have been enough moments rife with fragmented emotions and otherwise unexplainable familiarity to tell me that. And deep at my core, I know I still do love you, even though I can't remember exactly why."

"You do?" Inwardly, he groaned. It would be really nice if his tongue could catch up to his brain again.

"As weird as it is to not be able to remember the particulars ... Yes, I believe I do, and Bran is right. Our—"

"I really don't want to talk about Bran and his theories at the moment." He laughed and then cleared his throat before he closed the gap between them. "If you're alright with it," he took a gentle hold of her chin and traced his thumb along the edge of her lower lip as he tilted her face towards his, "I'm going to kiss you ... properly this time."

He waited, lips hovering just out of reach of hers until she gave him the most subtle of nods, then he closed the distance and claimed her lips with his own.

One of her hands bunched in the front of his shirt as she pulled herself up to meet him; the other slid over the front of his shoulder and then across to cup the side of his neck, her fingers plying through the hair just above his nape. She made that little sound in the back of her throat, the one he had thought he would never hear again, and he tugged her closer, lightly nipping her lower lip just to hear her repeat it. Smiling against her mouth, he started to pull back and let her up for air. But she tugged him to her again and deepened the kiss, her tongue exploring his until something butted against the sides of their legs.

Agnes pulled away, and Varlan followed her gaze to the disgruntled looking rabbit at their feet. '*You can smooch later. It's time to go back,*' Dara's voice echoed across his mind. '*The others are waiting.*'

"Sorry, Dara. Yes, of course we can go back now," Varlan said, releasing Agnes and taking a step away but not before pressing one more tender kiss to her lips.

Dara hopped in a small circle and the dreamscape shimmered around them before fading to black.

He woke up with his back against the side of Wren and Gendry's bed in the captain's quarters.

"Well?" Bran crouched in front of him, his sapphire gaze flicking from Varlan's face to the bed over his shoulder.

"It was Savita." Varlan nudged the necromancer out of the way as he got to his feet.

"Savita? But I got rid of her."

"Not all of her, apparently. She was hiding deep in the centre of Agnes's dreamscape, but she's gone now. Agnes drove her out all on her own." He couldn't contain his proud smile. Agnes had taken control of her magic in a way he never thought she would be able to. Not through any real fault of her own—it was just the way her keen had developed without keen-sense. But now that her keen was whole, he was not surprised why Idir had tampered with it.

"Well not all on my own. You did lend me some of your keen," Agnes said as she sat up and gave him a small smile.

Bran's attention shifted to her. "And you think it worked?"

Agnes shrugged. "There's only one way to find out." She slid from the bed, her fingers lightly brushing the back of Varlan's hand as she moved past him on her way to the door.

Varlan and Bran shared a look then started after her.

"Oh sure. Thank you, Dara, for your help," Dara quipped from the chair beside the bed.

"Thank you, Dara," Varlan said as he reached the door and shot her a smile.

She dipped her head and then got to feet to follow him onto the deck.

As Varlan stepped out of the captain's quarters, he caught sight of Agnes with Wes close on her heels ducking down the stairs to the hold. He gave Dara a pat on the shoulder and a nod then joined Bran as he reached the stairs.

"You really think you fixed the issue?" Bran asked.

"Agnes is right. There's only one way to know for sure."

Bran studied his face for a heartbeat. "And you're okay with letting her try again?"

"Of course."

One of Bran's snowy brows arced but he said nothing as he skipped down the steps into the hold.

Not only were Agnes and Wes at the table, which was still strewn with Agnes's things, but Deana was there too. She had the black sextant they had found in the sunken tower cradled gently in her hands.

"So, I had a theory, or rather my magic did, about this sextant and this." Agnes indicated the device before she unwrapped the cloth from the keystone. She laid the stone gently on the table as her keen fluttered around her. "See the divots along the edge?" she took the sextant from Deana and pointed to several places along the frame, "and this empty setting here?" She passed the sextant back to Deana then picked up a small hammer.

Her magic built around her, the flutter becoming an almost invigorating buzz as it rubbed against the edge of Varlan's keen-sense. The hammer began to glow with the soft bronze and gold light of her magic then she slammed it down on the keystone. Nothing happened at first but then the glow of Agnes's magic shifted from the hammer to the robrillium that held the fragments together. It glowed white-hot for a moment then disintegrated into a pile of rose-gold-coloured dust. The pieces of vibrant green stone finally released from their binding fell apart. Agnes took the sextant back from Deana and her magic built again, twisting around her in threads of gold and bronze and forming swirls across the air that looked like arcane equations. She pressed the heel of one palm against her forehead and squeezed her eyes shut as she leant her hip heavily against the table.

Varlan's stomach tightened into a knot, and he shot a glance at Wes as the numbness of the warden's keen-sense brushed against him. Bran lifted a hand to both of them, his mouth a grim line and his attention firmly on Agnes. How long could they let her go when it appeared she was still struggling to control her keen?

"Dee," Agnes said after a moment, "I need some of your magic."

Deana's keen swelled out, washing over Varlan and leaving him with the sensation that he was on a rocking boat. Flickers of teal that mimicked the rolling swell of painted waves wove through the threads of Agnes's magic. The fragments of green stone glowed in shades of emerald, gold, and turquoise, and then lifted into the air to hover around the sextant as Agnes held it out. Her magic gave a white-hot flutter then a blinding flash sent spots dancing across Varlan's vision.

When the spots cleared, Agnes and Deana were both leaning heavily against the table and breathing hard as though trying to catch their breath.

"Did it work?" Bran asked as he edged towards the table.

"I think so ..." Agnes picked up the sextant. The shards of keystone had been inlaid into the black metal; the crucible at the centre was still empty. Strange magic shifted over the whole device in flickers of emerald and turquoise.

"What do you think goes in the centre there?" Wes asked.

"Maybe one of the other green stones," Deana said. She was eyeing the device with a mixture of curiosity and trepidation, her keen lapping gently against the edges of Varlan's keen-sense.

Agnes retrieved both the wrapped prison stone and the heartstone Bran had extracted from the creature guarding the sextant. She held the heartstone first, her magic an inquisitive flutter. After a few moments, she shook her head before her attention snapped to the box of broken parts that had been her mechanical cat. There was a familiar glint in her eye and her fingers twitched before she clenched them into a tight fist and placed the stone down.

"I am fairly certain that one is just a dormant heartstone," she said.

"Dormant? The creature I pulled it out of was certainly active enough," Bran said and picked up the stone himself, his magic stirring in cold fingers up Varlan's spine. "You're right though. Whatever soul was supposed to be contained in this is long gone. Which is highly unusual." He turned the stone over in his hands, examining it from all angles before placing it down again and frowning at it.

Agnes was still staring at the box of cat parts, her fingers twirling the end of one of her braids. "Is it possible to transfer a soul from one heartstone to another?"

Bran started to shake his head then tilted it to the side, one brow arcing as he rubbed his fingers across the other. "I've never heard of anyone doing so, but in theory it shouldn't be all that hard. You're not creating a new heartstone, just transferring the power source from one to another, and given the soul in question is no longer tethered to an actual body ...." He nodded to himself. "It should be simple enough. Why do you—"

"Right, before we get ourselves well off track," Wes said, flicking an exasperated look from Bran to Agnes, "what about the prison stone?"

Agnes shook her head. "I'd have to touch it to be sure and I don't think I really want to."

Varlan couldn't blame her. There was something not right about the soul that resided within that stone. It was something dark and seething that craved vengeance, and even Bran had said that he wasn't sure whatever it was had ever been human.

Bran picked up the stone and freed it from its wrapping. The seething, dark mass inside twisted, making the light reflecting through the emerald surface appear like flickering green flames. His necromancy coiled in a chill around him, and as Agnes edged closer, her fingers reaching for the stone only to hover just short of it, her keen intensified again from a gentle flutter to a heated buzz.

With a small nod and a huff of resignation, she took hold of the stone and placed it into the empty socket on the sextant. Her magic flashed in a bronze glow then she lifted the completed sextant. Light reflected through the device, sending a kaleidoscope of green patterns over the wall. Agnes made an adjustment to the position of the sextant and the patterns changed. Another adjustment and they shifted into something that resembled a map.

"That's Lethata ... and Mintura," Deana said, edging towards the wall and pointing the two larger islands out.

"It's the whole isles," Varlan said, joining her to examine the shapes that depicted Splade's Watch, before the volcano had sunken its middle, and Weeper's Cove.

Agnes made another adjustment and a large 'X' appeared halfway between Lethata and Weeper's Cove.

"Dumura." Varlan and Deana said at the same time then shared a look.

Varlan's attention was stolen when Agnes's magic fizzed savagely against his and the sextant clattered onto the tabletop as she dropped it. She lifted her hands to shield her eyes, and Varlan did the same as beams of bright green light shot out of the crystal from all angles and a crackling sound filled air.

With an ear-ringing pop, the crystal exploded and peppered them all with tiny shards. Varlan lowered his hands slowly. Dark emerald-coloured mist was swirling from the shattered crystal and solidifying into a humanoid shape in the space between Wes and Bran.

"It's about bloody time," a sharp voice said as the mist cleared.

A man was now standing where the mist had been. His skin was a shade or two darker than Deana's, but his eyes were the same pale sea foam as hers. Waves were tattooed over his bare arms and chest. The wheaten-coloured linen pants that were slung low on his hips were tattered at the knees, leaving the lower half of his legs bare. His head was shaved at the sides and the jet-black lengths left in the centre were secured in a long braid that hung forward over one shoulder.

His pale gaze swept over Varlan then Agnes before landing on Deana, and his lip curled into an almost greedy smile. "Well now, this is just perfect."

"Who are you?" Deana's voice shook and her keen splashed against Varlan.

"Of course, where are my manners?" He dipped into a bow. "Reeve, high chief of the Shadow Isles and half-brother to that treacherous snake Idir."

CHAPTER THIRTY

BRAN

"Shadow Isles?" Bran asked, breaking the silence.

Reeve's pale gaze turned to him. "*You.*" The word was half-snarl, and Bran darted backwards as Reeve lunged in his direction.

Wes slammed into the much larger Reeve, pushing him against the wall and pinning him there with a surprising strength, the numbness of his suppression thickening the air around them both.

"I believe you may have me confused with someone else," Bran said calmly. "Let him go, Wes," he added, but not before he had placed the table between himself and the hostile chief.

"I'd not forget a soul stink like yours." Reeve brushed himself off but didn't make another move to attack Bran.

"I imagine you wouldn't but, despite the familiarity of my ... *soul stink,* I can assure you that I am not who you think I am."

"You smell like him, look like him, talk like him ..." His eyes narrowed. "But I will humour you because there's nothing in this realm or the next that would have ever enticed *him* to extract me from the prison he put me in."

"Soren entrapped you?"

The corner of Reeve's mouth twitched and something dark flashed behind his gaze. Bran wasn't certain he was human, but he also wasn't a god like Vask. There was something familiar about his bearing, and the fact he referred to Bran's magic as soul stink niggled at Bran's memories. He had also referred to himself as chief of the Shadow Isles, which was not a name Bran had ever heard for a place in the mortal realm, but it certainly could have been a place in the physical Between.

"You're from the Between, aren't you? Are you a Brightlander then? I doubt you're Nundle."

Reeve's eyes narrowed. "I told you already I am from the Shadow Isles. Well, I was, an eon ago, before my bastard half-brother stole me from my homeland and had his pet spirit mage force me into a stone then cast me into the bowels of obscurity."

"Idir is your half-brother? But he is human—mostly human, I guess, if you ignore the cursed part of his soul."

"He was mostly human back then too; our father was not discriminate with which mortals he chose to rut with. A fault that saw the creation of several abominations and ultimately led to his premature demise."

"Mortals? Was your father a god?"

Reeve shook his head. "He certainly would have liked to think so, but no. He was only what your kind would call a demi-god. He possessed just enough divine blood to give him the power and invulnerability to make him and his offspring a danger to the true gods."

Deana made a small sound, and Reeve's attention switched to her. His eyes darkened with an unmistakable hunger.

Bran took a step in her direction, putting himself between them. Wes had also edged around until Reeve would have to move past him if he wanted to get to either Deana or Agnes. Though the chief didn't seem interested in Agnes or Varlan at the moment.

"You have the Grandmother's scent," Reeve said to Deana, though he didn't make any move towards her.

"I share part of her song."

"Why do you associate with Idir's filth?" His lip curled as he jutted his chin towards Bran. "Surely you know what will happen if Idir breaches the Grandmother's resting place and steals even a fragment of her power?"

"We are trying to stop Idir." She stepped past Bran, folding her arms across her midsection as she stared the large chief down. "Bran is not Soren, and he is not *Idir's filth*. None of us are. We are victims of Idir's plotting, just like you." Her keen trembled against Bran's. "So, instead of threatening us, why don't you tell us why Idir had Soren put you inside that stone and what this has to do with Dumura." She lifted the sextant off the table and held it out.

Reeve's eyes widened, and he reached for the device, but Deana held it back from his grasp.

"Your intention is to stop Idir? Kill him?" Reeve's gaze slid over each face before settling on Bran's once more.

"If he can be killed."

He studied Bran, then nodded slowly. "You can kill him, or at least you can separate the divine aspect of his soul so I can kill him. Soren could have too, but he let Idir charm him—"

"Soren turned against Idir in the end."

"If that is true then his change of heart came far too late."

Bran nodded. He couldn't argue with that, but he wasn't Soren—despite sharing the ancient necromancer's soul. And having not lived a life in Soren's shoes, he couldn't say if he would have done things differently. It would seem that Soren had made a lot of questionable and rather dark choices before changing sides though. He drew a breath then held his hand out to Reeve. "I believe we have gotten off on the wrong foot. I'm Bran, and this is Deana, Agnes, Wes, and Varlan."

Reeve's gaze flicked to the crescent moon on the inside of Bran's wrist and a smile crept across his lips before he took hold of Bran's hand and shook it. When he released Bran's hand, his gaze moved back to Deana and the sextant. "If you give that to me then

I can show you how it's connected to the place your kind call Dumura."

Deana's free hand touched the protection stone and she cast a meaningful look in Varlan's direction.

The soft, seductive touch of Varlan's keen thumbed across Bran's nape before the mind mage gave Deana a small nod.

If Reeve sensed the scrutiny of Varlan's magic, he didn't show it. Though Bran was sure he would have felt it; he was definitely a mage of some kind himself. His keen had the same shifting quality of the Between, and it was highly likely—given he had labelled himself a high chief—that his magic was multi-disciplined.

Deana gingerly held the sextant out, and Reeve took it just as carefully. The device looked small in his large hands as he ran the tips of his fingers, almost reverently, over the shards of emerald stone along its frame.

"We must go outside," he said at last.

Wes moved to the door and opened it before standing back and indicating the large chief go first.

Gendry, Wren, and the twins immediately surrounded Reeve once they all emerged onto the deck. Wren's keen crackled, charging the air with static, and Gendry's fingers sat loosely on his hip, close enough to pull the knife he wore on his belt from its sheath if he felt the need.

"Where'd he come from?" Gendry asked.

"Out of the prison stone," Agnes replied.

"The one you were all scared of touching? Nope. I'm not even going to try and understand the mechanics of that, but can he be trusted?"

"Yes, that stone. I don't think even I understand it fully, and I have an intimate understanding of the type of magic required for such a feat." Bran shrugged. "And whether he can be trusted or not remains to be seen."

Gendry's posture relaxed. "That's good enough for me," he

turned his dark gaze on Reeve, "but I'm watching you. Try anything and your guts will paint the deck faster than you can blink."

"Gendry," Wren warned.

Reeve didn't seem affected by the threat. Instead he walked calmly between Gendry and Pippa to the front of the ship. His shifting keen twisted through the air around him and a beam of bright green light shot out of the sextant.

"Follow the light and it will lead you to Dumura."

"And then what? The island is at the bottom of the ocean," Pippa said.

One of Reeve's brows lifted, though his mouth remained an inscrutable line before he turned a pointed look in Deana's direction. "We go down, set the key into the lock, and then sit back and wait for the magic to do the rest."

"What about the portal? We have no idea how to create that and we don't even know that we have all the necessary parts," Agnes said.

"Everything you need is waiting on the island. But the moment it sees the sun, Idir will know and his army will come for you. You need to be prepared to fight him. If he reaches the Grandmother before you wake her, he will succeed in destroying this part of your world and its counterpart in mine."

The bright afternoon had slowly given way to the lilac tones of twilight and once they had set a course following the beam of emerald light away from Splade's Watch, things had been relatively quiet. A dark band of brooding clouds was building along the horizon, their inky expanse flashing occasionally with distant lightning. Though Wren didn't seem concerned at the moment, and given her sensitivity to storms that was comforting.

Reeve was sitting at the bow, his eyes closed and hands clasped into fists on his knees. The sextant was on the deck in front of him, the green glow casting ghostly shadows across the planes of his face. The twins, Luca, and Wes were playing a rather rowdy game of liar's dice with Rufus and Gendry, their shouts getting louder with each consecutive round.

Agnes was perched amidst a small stack of crates near the door to the hold. She sketched in her journal, a bronze and gold-striped mage light dancing about her as she murmured under her breath. Her keen was a gentle flutter against the very edge of Bran's keen-sense.

Nari and Varlan sat near Agnes, a bottle of Gendry's favourite spiced rum between them as they conversed softly. Nari let out the occasional laugh and after a while, Elijah, who had been keeping Wren company at the wheel, joined them.

Bran let out a long breath as he studied the silver-lipped waves lapping against the side of ship. He had been trying to keep his mind busy, to avoid having to think about the revelations that Soren had presented him. But now that they had a moment's respite, his thoughts kept spiralling back and demanding that he process the information about his provenance.

In the past, he would have gone running to Nea for her insight and in this particular situation it would be invaluable. Once she got over the initial shock of the revelation of course. Very little caught Nea completely off guard, and imagining the look on her face when he told her the answer to the question of where he had come from—a question that had plagued everyone at Hartswood for two decades—brought a wide grin to his lips.

Deana's keen rolled against the edge of his keen-sense before she cleared her throat and leant on the rail beside him. "Do you think we can trust Reeve?" Her voice was a soft whisper and she glanced towards the bow.

Bran followed the line of her gaze to the man in question. His back was still straight, his strange magic a shifting pool around him as he stared at some point on the distant horizon.

"I don't know for certain, but at the moment our goals seem to align with his." He shrugged.

"His song is so strange."

He nodded. Reeve's keen was shifting and evasive. Just when your keen-sense thought it had figured out the true nature of his magic, it changed. "He's not of our world. He's a native of the Between and a rather important one if he is to be believed." Bran did believe him based on his keen alone. Many of the residents of the physical Between were tribal in nature and lived under rather straightforward hierarchies based on the quality of an individual's magic.

Deana's gaze dropped to the waves, and she released a long breath.

"Did you really want to ask me for my opinion about Reeve, or was there something else?"

Her attention flicked briefly to him and then back to the waves. "Is Kai like Reeve now? A native of the Between?"

Bran shook his head, but she wasn't looking at him. "No. At least, not in the same way. Kai's spirit is lingering ... trapped—"

She gave a sharp intake of breath, and he winced.

"What do you mean he's trapped? Can he not join the ancestors?"

"Some souls linger because they have unfinished business. I would say Kai had some pretty big unfinished business given the role he has played in the events we are now living. But I got the sense that he is not lingering by choice. He mentioned a curse ..."

"Idir's curse?" She turned to face him, her fingers brushing the side of his hand as she changed her grip on the rail.

"Perhaps."

"Soren said that Idir was not cursed by Grandmother Ocean, but it was a curse of his own making."

"Curses can often be of our own making, and Soren *would* know the nature of Idir's curse." He shook his head. "Has he visited your dreams again?"

"No," she frowned, "and I would rather he didn't. As friendly as he seems, there is something about him ... a sorrow, a darkness ... something that makes me feel uneasy, but I can't quite put my finger on it."

Bran kneaded the knot at the back of his neck. "Do I—"

"You and Soren are not the same person," she said. "Despite what he said about you sharing a soul, and despite the identical melodies of your songs." She held his gaze for a few moments, something contemplative swimming in the depths of her sea foam eyes before she turned away. Her fingers fidgeted with the edge of her protection stone. "You used to make me uneasy, but not really in the same way he does. Your song ..." Her keen rolled against his then pulled away again. "... the way it seemed to call to mine ... It's deep and melancholic like the fathoms themselves. It terrified me ... but not anymore."

"Not anymore?"

Her cheeks coloured and she rocked back a step, shaking her head. "No. Now it just makes me feel safe. Like Kai's used to."

She thought of him as a brother then. He was surprised by the hollow disappointment that thought settled in his stomach. He knew she had grown important to him, but until that moment he hadn't realised that that importance had become something more intimate than their building friendship. Or maybe he had, and he hadn't been ready to truly admit it.

"You're calm and steady like Kai was. Easy to talk to, and you just accept me as I am." She brushed a lock of hair behind her ear and then cast a glance over the others, who were still scattered across the deck. "Everyone here does. They all just welcomed me into their fold, without judgment or expectations, and that's something I'd never felt before, outside of my family and Indira."

She grew quiet and turned to lean on the rail once more, her gaze tracking along the horizon as a small smile touched her lips. "Kai would have liked you. Do you think he was happy despite being trapped?"

"I would say so. Our encounter was only brief, but I didn't get the feeling he was a tormented soul."

"Do you think he'll be able to move on if we stop Idir?"

It was hard to say. He might have moved on once his message was delivered, but Bran got the impression that whatever was keeping his spirit trapped was more persistent. Stopping Idir would likely allow him to move on, unless the curse he mentioned wasn't explicably tied to Idir's fate.

"You don't have to humour me," Deana prompted.

Bran leant his elbows on the rail and rubbed his thumb over the oathmark. "I'm honestly not sure. He may have only been lingering long enough to deliver his message, but if not, which I believe is more likely the case, then stopping Idir might free him. If he wants to go."

"If he wants to go?" She toyed with the protection stone, her keen lapping briskly against Bran's.

"He might want to stay and keep an eye on you."

"Oh. That's a nice thought, but I—wait, do you hear that?" She pushed back from the rail, her keen rolling heavily over his.

He couldn't hear what she could, but he could feel the seething taint of shrouded magic. The ship shuddered, tossing him off balance as he turned to warn the others. Everyone was on their feet already, the mages spooling their magic and the keen-less drawing their weapons.

They all watched the water, waiting for the owner of the tainted magic to reveal themselves. Then something landed on the deck with a heavy thud. A dark, hulking shape that looked like a clump of brown seaweed. It shifted and straightened into the form of a tall man. His face was a gaunt mask of humanity. Skin which may have once been a similar warm brown to Deana's was now murky with the pall of death. The sunken pockets where his eyes had been were lit with orbs of soft light a sickly shade somewhere between yellow and green. A thick cloud of numbness hovered in the air around him—some perverted form of a warden's suppression perhaps.

"Rami?" Deana's tone was tight with fear.

The man's attention shifted to Deana and he shook his head, his mouth pulling into a frown.

Bran edged forward, putting himself between Deana and Rami.

Rami's sickly gaze moved to Bran, and he froze. His mouth opened like he was trying to speak, but only a strange rasp came out.

"What's taking so long?" a woman's voice asked from behind Rami.

When he didn't respond, the voice's owner stepped around him. She was tall and slim with long golden hair on one side of her head. A crown-like growth of green and purple coral adorned the other side of her skull. There was something naggingly familiar about the rest of her features, especially her eyes.

"Thought you could escape before I was done with you, did you?" she asked Deana in a tone that was mockingly saccharine.

"Astrid," Deana simply said.

"Come easily and I won't hurt any of your friends."

Deana shook her head.

"No?"

"You might want to do a head-count before you start throwing threats around," Kiki said as she and Pippa moved over to flank Deana and Bran.

Astrid didn't seem bothered. She merely tilted her head to the side and smiled sweetly as she said, "Rami," and snapped her fingers.

He moved forward, the oppressive bubble around him

expanding until it rolled heavily over Bran, Deana, and the twins. It was far heavier than any warden suppression Bran had felt before and it didn't just cut off his connection to the source, but it seemed to steal all sound from the world as well.

Deana grabbed Bran's wrist, her fingers digging tightly into his skin as her other hand clutched the protection stone; her wide-eyed gaze was locked on Astrid, who looked completely bored.

After a few moments of letting the crew members panic in silence, Astrid touched Rami's shoulder and the sound returned to the world as his power retreated. Unlike a normal warden's suppression, Rami's power left a lingering numbness and it took Bran several tries to reconnect with the source.

"Now, Deana and I have unfinished business and I would rather this didn't turn into a fight. We do all have the same goal after all."

"And what goal is that?" Varlan asked.

"To stop Idir."

"I'm not going with you," Deana said.

Astrid frowned and made a tutting noise. "Don't be foolish. You *need* me."

"No, I don't."

Astrid's nostrils flared and she took several steps towards Deana. Bran put himself between them and Astrid stopped short, her dark blue eyes widening.

"Soren?" she whispered. "That's not possible—I killed you."

"So I've heard, but I'm not Soren. It's an easy mistake to make. Apparently the resemblance is truly remarkable."

Astrid seemed to shrink in on herself and then threw a glance towards Rami. After a moment though she turned back to Bran and squared her shoulders. "It is in Deana's best interest to come with me. I can teach her—"

"She said no," Reeve stepped forward.

"*You!*" Astrid retreated to stand with Rami, her gaze flicking from Bran to Reeve and then to Deana. "He will betray you; they both will," she warned then climbed over the side rail of the ship and dove into the ocean.

"Rami!" she called.

Rami dug into the folds of his tattered cloak and pulled something out. He stomped across the deck and shoved it into Bran's hands then gave Deana a slow nod before turning and marching to the side of the ship where Astrid had disappeared. He turned once more and gave both Bran and Deana another slow nod then leapt from the deck.

Bran looked down at the object in his hands. It was a key carved from some kind of bone. Inlays of gold twisted over its surface and a small, faceted round of dark amethyst was set into the top. The sight of the key ignited a deep sense of familiarity at his core, but he had never seen it before. Had it belonged to Soren? He tucked it into his pocket as he turned to the others, who were all fussing over Deana.

Reeve caught Bran's eye. His gaze briefly dropped to the pocket in which Bran had stashed the key, but he said nothing before returning to the bow of the ship and settling down with the sextant once more.

Bran studied his back. Something about the man had truly frightened Astrid. Until he had made his presence known, she had been confident that she could capture Deana, despite being severely outnumbered. But as soon as she had seen Reeve, she had tucked tail and fled. Why? Whatever the reason, Bran was sure Reeve would not be forthcoming with the answers.

CHAPTER THIRTY-ONE

DEANA

"Are you alright?" Pippa and Kiki asked as soon as Rami had disappeared over the side of the ship.

"Yes." It wasn't the complete truth. Seeing Astrid on the deck of the Queen had brought a sick feeling to her stomach, and the fear of finding herself in that small, dark room again was lingering in clawing fingers between her shoulders. She drew a slow breath and released it.

"I've never felt suppression like that," Wes said as he and Varlan joined the twins.

"Or heard of a mage who could wield silence as a weapon," Varlan added.

"Astrid did that to him," Deana said softly. "She murdered him and then—" She flicked a look at Reeve as he stalked towards the bow and then moved her attention to Bran, who was watching him. "I don't know what she did exactly, but Soren said it had something to do with the power Idir gave her—power he had taken from Mala."

"He's some kind of sophisticated wraith," Bran said, his gaze still trained on Reeve and his brows tented with something that wasn't his usual curiosity. "I would say when he was living he was a warden, but whatever Astrid did to him perverted his power. I've never actually heard of mages or wardens being turned into wraiths and retaining their powers in any kind of fashion. Except —no, she doesn't really count." He rubbed a hand over the back of his neck.

"Do you really think she wants to stop Idir too?" Kiki asked.

"She wants revenge, and she doesn't care how she gets it," Deana answered. She rubbed her thumb over the hole in the middle of the protection charm, its familiar song plying through her own. Were she and Astrid really that different?

"Why did she give up so easily though?" Pippa asked. "She saw our new *friend* and just ran away with her tail between her legs. It was weird, right?"

Deana's attention wandered to Reeve where he sat at the bow, the sextant in front of him sending its beam of emerald light out in the direction of Dumura. "Soren is the one responsible for trapping Reeve in the prison stone, so there is a good chance Astrid would have known him. Astrid was Soren's sister," she added in response to the blank looks everyone except Bran were giving her.

"That explains her reaction to Bran," Kiki said. "I imagine that seeing the brother you thought you'd killed several centuries ago alive and kicking is quite the shock."

"Alright, you lot, enough chit-chat. I'm going to use the Queen's enchantment to put some distance between us and this particular stretch of ocean," Wren said as she stepped up to the wheel once more.

"Here, lass." Gendry appeared at Deana's side with a length of rope. He looped it around her waist and tied a neat knot then moved back to the row of anchor points and gave the other end a sharp tug to ensure it was secure. He then did the same with the lines that Bran, Varlan, and the twins were all tying around their own waists.

"Lifelines, just in case the transition is rough," Rufus offered in explanation as he ducked past her to secure his and Wes's lines.

"All lines secure, my love," Gendry called and then moved to join Deana. "I would recommend taking a seat and grabbing hold of something solid. There's a reason we don't use the transportation enchantment all that often." He sat beside her and gripped one of the wooden loops that were secured at various places beneath the rail.

Deana had assumed the loops were just tie points for securing cargo, but now that she saw more of the crew taking up place as Gendry had done, she wondered if their intended purpose was something else. She sat next to Gendry and grabbed the loop beside her head. It wasn't the most comfortable position but as the ship started to shudder violently beneath her, all thoughts of discomfort were replaced with trepidation. A surging song tore through the air and the water beneath the ship began to hiss and boil, then the world was consumed by a blinding teal glow.

The deck felt like it dropped out from beneath her. Her hands shook and became slick on the loop, making her tighten her grip until her knuckles started to ache. She was overcome with the feeling of being suspended in midair; her stomach hovered somewhere around her chest for the count of several heartbeats before it plummeted to her toes, and the ship stabilised once more with a heavy jolt that sent a thick mist of icy salt water over her.

Her eyes were still squeezed shut when a heavy hand touched her shoulder, and she nearly jolted clean out of her skin.

"Easy, lass, it's over now."

She opened her eyes. Gendry was bent in front of her, a reassuring look in his eyes. She unlaced her stiff fingers from the loop then took hold of his offered hand.

He pulled her to her feet and the world spun around her, raising a thick lump in her throat and flooding her mouth with water. Her stomach heaved and she sagged against the rail of the ship, only just managing to get herself in position over the side before she lost the contents of her stomach.

Gendry pulled her hair away from her cheeks, securing it with one hand at her nape while he rubbed circles on her back with the other. "It never gets any better," he said softly.

Deana had thought she was getting used to portal travel, but this had been something else entirely. It was similar to the surging quality of Sejira's magic but interwoven with the expanding, contracting sensation of travelling through one of Nea's portals.

When there was nothing left in her stomach, she gingerly pushed herself away from the rail and straightened. The world spun around her again and she closed her eyes as she drew a deep breath. Gendry offered her a clean cloth and a water skin, and she took both gratefully. After washing her mouth out, she took a small sip then dampened the rag and wiped her face. The touch of the cool cloth chased the last dregs of nausea away, but she still didn't trust her shaking legs to carry her very far.

"Where are we?" she asked as she let her gaze wander along the white beach that flanked the right side of the ship.

"I don't think it has a name anymore, but we've been here before. It's where ..." Gendry scratched his fingers through his beard and gave her a sheepish sort of look. "It's where we stopped after our escape from Armada."

"Oh." Deana drew another steadying breath and then released it slowly. Last time they had stopped at this small island, Astrid had kidnapped her.

"We're not going to let it happen again, lass." Gendry placed a hand on her shoulder.

"I know." She gave him a small smile.

"Sorry about the transition, though admittedly that was one of the smoother ones," Wren said as she joined them. After taking a moment to study Deana's face, her gaze shifted to Gendry. "Headcount, my love."

He moved away to check on the others, and Wren gave Deana's arm a little squeeze. "Based on the maps and common myths about Dumura, we are probably a day's sail at the most from the point where the island used to exist. I would suggest that we make camp on the beach and take a day or two ensure we are ready. If Reeve is correct, we will be facing down Idir once we move for Dumura."

Deana's stomach did a little flip that she wasn't sure was connected to the lingering malaise of trans-dimensional travel, but she nodded.

Wren gave her arm another squeeze then turned to Gendry as he returned.

"All crew accounted for. Some dealing with the transition far better than others."

"Thank you, my love. We're going to make camp on the beach and—"

"Are you sure that's wise?" Gendry flicked a pointed look at Deana.

Wren's hands found her hips and she frowned at him. "Everyone needs a chance to stretch their legs and have a proper rest. Astrid will not sneak up on us again now that we are aware of her."

"Very well. I will organise the crew."

Deana and Agnes were sitting at the edge of the golden light from the crew's campfire, their backs lit with the soft teal glow of one of Deana's mage lights. Every so often one of the others would shoot a look their way and then scan the darkness beyond them. Deana couldn't blame them for being on edge. She was as worried as they were that Astrid might find them again, but she hadn't wanted to sit closer to the heat of the fire or the noise of the camp. Since the transition, as Wren called it, the surging notes of the transportation magic still lingered within her song and though they were fading with each passing hour, they left her feeling feverish and jittery. The others had wanted her to stay closer to the light of the fire but had finally relented when Agnes offered to stay with her, and Deana had promised to keep her mage light lit to provide further visibility beyond the edge of the firelight once the sun had fully set.

"Wren has implored me to ask if you are both sure you want to stay out here," Wes said as he delivered two bowls of stew that Gendry had thrown together with their meagre supplies.

"Just for a little longer," Deana said as she took the bowl and spoon he offered her.

Wes let out a sigh and then sat beside her.

"What are you doing?"

"Wren thought you might say that and she told me if you did, that I was to stay with you until you were both ready to come back in."

"Are you sure it's Wren who's worried?" Agnes asked, sending a pointed glance towards Varlan.

"Well, no. After feeling what Rami can do, *everyone* is a little concerned. And rightly so. I've never felt another warden like that."

"I don't think Rami would hurt me." Rami might be Astrid's puppet, but there had been moments when he seemed to rebel against her control. He might not be able to throw off her hold entirely, but Deana sensed that deep down his conscious would win in the end.

"How can you be certain? Bran said he's a wraith. Aren't they just puppets of their creators like those undead at Splade's Watch?" Agnes asked.

Wes made a noise, and they both turned his way. "He's nothing like the wraiths at Splade's Watch. Even Bran has no idea what he is, and he has been musing about it—at great length—since we made camp. Bloody necromancers." He muttered the last two words under his breath.

They continued their meal in silence, with Wes watching the shadows beyond the pool of Deana's mage light. Occasionally, the dull throb of his power would brush against Deana's song, silencing it momentarily. There were similarities between Wes and Rami's power, like there were with all silencers—wardens as they were known outside of the isles. But Wes's power only silenced the songs of magic; Rami's stole all sound from the world. At first, Deana had thought it an aura that pervaded the very air around him, but it seemed that he could control it.

She pulled the ivory comb out of her pocket and ran her thumb over the teeth. Soren had said he wasn't sure Rami was still inside the monstrous husk that Astrid's stolen magic had made him, but Deana was certain he was. She had noticed the fragile sorrow in his ghostly eyes, the cautious gentleness when he had brushed her hair, and the twist in the corner of his mouth when Astrid had delivered an order that he didn't agree with. He never rebelled openly, but Deana wondered how far Astrid needed to push him before he did.

"Dee?"

She blinked up at Agnes, who was now standing in front of her.

"They are ready to discuss raising the island." Agnes offered her a hand.

"Where did Wes go?" Deana asked as she let Agnes pull her to her feet.

"I'm here." He stepped out of the darkness behind them. "I was just making sure there was nothing lurking out in the shadows. I am fairly certain there is nothing out there besides the island's ghosts. Shall we?" He indicated they go ahead of him.

When they reached the camp, Gendry took Agnes and Deana's bowls and gave them a rinse before plonking them on the stack to be properly cleaned later. They settled down on the logs around the fire, Deana squeezing in between Pippa and Kiki, and Agnes and Wes sitting next to Luca. Deana did a quick headcount. Nari, Dara, and Rufus were missing, but Rufus had stayed back on the ship and Nari and Dara often sat out of these discussions.

"By my calculations, we have about a day's worth of sailing before we reach Dumura's location. But I want us prepared for what we'll encounter when we get there," Wren said, drawing everyone's attention to her. "Reeve?" She gave him a pointed look then moved back to stand with Gendry.

"I have already explained this. When we reach Dumura, Deana and I will go down to the sea floor and place the key in the lock—"

"What key exactly?" Gendry asked.

Reeve held up the sextant in answer. "Key, blood, command, and then—" He mimed the island rising with his hands.

"Blood?" Bran asked, his tone tight. "No one said anything about blood."

Reeve stared at him blankly. "The Grandmother's blood is required to activate the magic."

"Deana's blood you mean." Bran folded his arms and levelled his sharp stare on Reeve.

"Yes. As she is the current Granddaughter, her blood carries the Grandmother's essence. The blood must be given willingly; I will not take it by force. But the rest of you must be prepared because the moment we begin the process of raising the isle, Idir will feel it. And he will come."

"But Idir can't reach Grandmother Ocean until a working portal has been constructed, right?" Agnes asked.

"That will not stop him from trying. Exposing the island will place all the pieces necessary for his success within reach."

"So why raise it? Why not just leave it where it is and go after Idir?" Pippa asked.

"The island must be raised to reset the balance that Idir upset. Idir cannot be stopped until the Grandmother is awoken and the powers Idir took from her children are returned."

"So, we need to raise an island from the bottom of the ocean, build a portal while trying to defend said island from Idir, and then race him across the wilds of an insanely dangerous magical realm to find the sleeping goddess and somehow wake her before he does?" Pippa asked.

Reeve nodded.

"Then what?" Kiki asked.

"Then we kill Idir and reset the balance."

"And what will happen to the shrouded ones?" Deana asked.

"Once Idir meets his demise, they will be free of their curse."

"And everything I need to construct a portal is on Dumura?"

Reeve turned his pale stare to Agnes and nodded.

"You do know that my magic works with metal? If I am to construct the portal, I will need some kind of metal and most types don't do too well with prolonged exposure to salt water."

A look of mild annoyance crossed Reeve's features, and he held up the sextant again. "The mundane metals of your realm perhaps, but Shadow steel is not of your world; neither is the metal you call robrillium. You will find both where the original portal used to stand."

"Original portal?" Bran asked.

"Yes, the one that Idir had Soren corrupt. The same one that I destroyed, earning me an interment inside a hunk of enchanted rock."

"Are you all ready to do this?" Wren asked, but her gaze fell on Deana and then Agnes.

Agnes glanced Varlan's way. The seductive notes of Varlan's song stirred, and then Agnes turned back to Wren and nodded. "As ready as I can be."

"Deana?" Wren met her gaze. "You have final say, as you are the one who will be most in danger."

She thumbed the hole in the centre of her protection stone and nodded as Agnes had. "I am ready."

"So be it. Get some rest, the lot of you. We sail at dawn."

By the time the Queen arrived at the supposed location of Dumura, Deana's stomach was a knotted mess. Reeve's sextant had been humming for several hours, its song weaving through Deana's own and making it impossible to focus. The sextant wanted one thing and the closer it got to the seat of its purpose, the louder it became—until it had her pacing the deck earning worried looks from everyone except Reeve.

"It's time," Reeve said, stepping into her path as she turned to make another pass down the deck.

She didn't trust herself to speak so just gave him a nod then moved to the side of the ship.

"Hang on." Bran caught her arm as she turned her focus to the waves.

"It's alright. I'm ready."

Judging by the way his mouth tucked in at the corner and the concerned look that made the azure fragments in his midnight-blue gaze shine, the lie obviously didn't fool him.

"We should not delay," Reeve said, and Bran shot him a loaded look before focusing on Deana once more.

"You don't have to do this if you don't want to. We can find another away."

She drew a slow breath and then released it, counting to four before she repeated the process again, and a small smile twitched at the corners of Bran's mouth.

"I can do it. I have to."

"None of us *have* to do anything, but I won't argue that point with you. Still ..." He gave her arm a squeeze, his song moving over her and burrowing between the melodies of her own, bolstering it and making it loud enough to drown out the song of the sextant.

"What did you do?"

"I just lent you a little bit of my magic, like I did at Splade's Watch. I won't be down there to help if you get into trouble this time ... so ..." He rubbed the back of his neck. "Just be careful."

"I can feel Sejira down there and she won't let anything happen to me, but I will be as careful as I can." She gave his hand a squeeze then dove over the side of the ship.

This part of the ocean was cold enough to stop her breath, but she focused on treading water while she waited for Reeve to join her. For someone of such large stature, he barely made a splash when he entered the water. As his head breached the surface again, Deana swam closer and called her song. She folded the water around them, creating a bubble. But unlike the one she had crafted at Splade's Watch, this one was harder to move.

When she was confident that the bubble was steady, she focused on the currents around her and let a small part of her song break away to control them. After a couple of tries, the bubble moved out of the shadow of the Queen and then started to descend.

Down and down they went until no light seemed to penetrate the water around them. Bioluminescent jelly fish bumped against the sides of the bubble and other sea creatures scurried away from their approach. The pressure against the sides of the bubble increased, and a slick sweat dribbled down Deana's cheeks and spine as she was forced to slow their decent and reel the part of her song controlling the currents back into herself.

"We're almost there," Reeve said.

"I can't keep us moving and maintain the sphere." Talking was a strain and she closed her eyes as the coolness of Bran's borrowed magic smoothed through her song and steadied it.

"You are the Granddaughter; the ocean is yours to command without limits." His tone wasn't sharp but stiff and matter-of-fact, as though he were telling her something she should already know.

A fissure of annoyance darted up her spine and she opened her eyes again. "I am still only human."

He moved closer to her and lifted a hand towards her.

She pulled back as far as she could and eyed the hand with trepidation.

"The spirit mage lent you some of his power, yes?"

She nodded.

"An honourable gesture, but his magic is inadequate for the task at hand. Let me help you."

She swallowed and moved closer again.

"Close your eyes and relax."

Relax? Just like that? With the ocean around her threatening to break through the last of her resolve and crush them both? If they were lucky, the pressure would kill them before they drowned. Pushing those thoughts down, she closed her eyes and focused on her breathing. Bran's voice echoed through her mind each time she paused to count, *'In ... two ... three ... four ... Out ... two ... three ... four ...'*

Reeve's hands were cool against her feverish cheeks. His shifting song roped through hers, but it didn't burrow between the notes the way Bran's had done. The longer Reeve's song twisted over hers, the more she spotted the similarities to her own. His magic didn't come from Grandmother Ocean—and it certainly couldn't control the deep the way hers could—but his song had an affinity for the sea that she had never felt in another mage before.

She opened her eyes to find him watching her with a look that she'd never been on the receiving end of before. His thumbs moved delicately over her cheeks, leaving an almost ticklish feeling in their wake. His pale gaze moved to her lips, and she shook her head as she took a step back.

The bubble quivered around them, and she thrust her hands out, tightening the threads of her song to stabilise it again. "Thank you," she said in a tone that was hollow even to her own ears then she cleared her throat.

Reeve was studying her with a strange expression, but he seemed to shake it off after a moment and said, "It is not much further now."

Her focus returned to the waters around them, and she teased a small thread of her song away from the bubble again. Reeve's song twisted along with that thread of power; it was a strange sensation. The piece of Bran's magic had become seamlessly interwoven with hers, and she wielded it as easily as her own. But Reeve's remained heavy and separate, and even though it did strengthen her song, it took her a few tries to control the magic without effort.

Sejira's pale fish form appeared outside the bubble. She swam in a slow spiral around them as they continued their decent. Then, when Deana couldn't hold the magic any longer, their feet found the sand of the sea floor.

Large ghostly crabs scurried away from the edges of the bubble and a blue glowing eel retreated into a cavernous tangle of rock to their left.

Reeve pulled out the sextant. The crystals along its frame glowed a bright emerald green, casting harsh shadows across his face. Steam was rising from the ground beneath their feet, the hissing song of volcanic vents drowning out the swirling harmony of the tides. Another song permeated the swirl and hiss—a song as familiar as Deana's own—the enigmatic melody of Grandmother Ocean.

Sejira swam back into view. She flicked her fins and darted away before coming back and repeating the movement again.

"That way," Deana said, and she started across the sea floor, following the pale glow that was Sejira.

Slowly, the sand gave way to a set of stone steps leading up to a small pocket of air encasing a pillar of age-pocked stone. As they climbed the stairs, the wall of Deana's bubble met the edge of the other and the song of Grandmother Ocean washed over her. Panic skittered up her spine as she momentarily lost her hold on her own bubble, but instead of bursting it seemed to merge with the one around the pillar, expanding wider to encompass both Deana and Reeve and the area directly around the column. Once Deana's song settled again and she regained her hold on the now much larger bubble, Reeve stepped forward and set the sextant into the groove at the top of the plinth then gave it a twist. It locked into place with a sharp click that seemed awfully loud as it echoed off the water around them.

"All it needs now is your blood and your command." He held out a small knife. It had an ivory handle carved to resemble a swimming mermaid; she recognised it as one of Gendry's.

Gingerly, she took the knife and pressed the tip to the pad of her index finger. She winced as it broke the skin and a bead of blood ran down the blade.

"No, you will need more than a drop." Reeve held his hand out. "Give me your hand."

She released a long breath and looked for Sejira. The pale fish was hovering in the water beside the bubble, and she dipped lower as though nodding. Deana laid her hand on Reeve's.

He traced his fingertips along the centre of her palm. "The blade."

When she passed the blade to him, he took it and touched the tip lightly against the top right corner of her palm.

"Do not look at the blade—look at me," he instructed in a soft, strangely calming tone.

The moment her gaze levelled on his, white pain sliced across her palm.

He tucked the blade away and lifted her hand over the sextant, squeezing it to force her blood to flow freely.

She forgot how to breathe—the pain in her hand was nothing

compared to the dirge that ran through her song.

"Give it your command." Reeve still held her hand tight, her blood splashing over the sextant and turning the emerald stones a crisp turquoise.

Deana tried to rein in her song, to focus on anything but the wailing cacophony that was sending agonising jolts through her skull. The bubble shook around them, threatening to pop, but the notes of Reeve's magic held it together. Flashes of sound snapped across her mind so fast it was hard to pick one song from another, until a soft melancholy harmony caught her attention. It wasn't her song, but it was safe and steady and calming—and she latched onto it, letting its soothing coolness permeate her entire being. The soft, whispering melody of death magic grew stronger, bolstering her flagging strength and renewing her focus. She drew a burning breath and then released it and turned her song towards the sextant. Teal-coloured light poured down the plinth and across the ocean floor.

The world shuddered around them. A bristling, tearing sound akin to portal magic choked out everything else, and Reeve dropped his grip on her hand as a beam of that same teal light shot skyward.

The water around them sprang apart as the ground continued to shudder, then with a jolting shake that knocked Deana to her hands and knees, the island started to rise into the sun.

CHAPTER THIRTY-TWO

#

"Bright damn it!" Ink blotted the page, smudging the sketch she had been completing and staining the side of her hand. She placed her pen and journal aside and dabbed at her skin with a cloth.

"Here." Kiki held her hand out, her cool keen smoothing against Agnes's and bringing to mind the sensation of dipping her toes into a cold stream.

Agnes held her hand out, and Kiki traced her fingers along the stain. Water flowed over Agnes's skin, following the path of Kiki's touch. Once most of the ink had washed away, Kiki released her.

"That's a useful little trick," Agnes said as she dried her hand on the side of her pants.

"It can be," Kiki said. She picked up Agnes's journal. "I can't do anything about this, I am afraid. Is that a panther?" She tilted her head as she studied Agnes's sketches.

"It is." She took the journal when Kiki offered it and examined the diagram. "It's a new design for my mechanical cat. Just a dream, really. I don't know where I would find enough of the right metal to make it work." She blotted the stain until it was dry and then closed the book. "They've been down there too long."

Kiki settled beside her and patted her knee. "There's not much we can do but wait. Gendry keeps telling Bran not to birth those kittens he's carrying on the deck, but I can't blame him for being worried. I don't like the way Reeve kept looking at Dee."

"Like he owned her?"

"Exactly." Kiki tucked her knees up to her chest and rested her chin on them.

"Varlan said he sensed nothing bad in Reeve's thoughts and—"

"Nothing bad in the thoughts Reeve let him see."

Kiki had a point about that. Varlan's magic wasn't completely infallible, and Reeve's keen was one of the strangest Agnes had encountered so far. It was twisting and full of secrets—dark secrets if the lingering feeling of unease was anything to go by. Bran had said it was the magic of the Between. Agnes had felt the Between's touch when she crossed through Bran's portal at Splade's Watch. And while Reeve's keen was similar to that magic, there was something more unsettling about it.

"One of you needs to distract me," Pippa said as she dropped down to sit next to Kiki. "Varlan seems to be teaching Bran the art of brooding, Dara is talking to her ghosts, and everyone else is too on edge to be around."

"You'd have better luck with Dara," Kiki said.

"There has to be something we can talk about that will take our minds off the fact that Deana could be drow—"

"I kissed Varlan," Agnes said in a rush.

Both twins turned stunned stares to her.

"When?" Pippa asked.

"Pay up," Kiki said at the same time.

Pippa begrudgingly pulled a coin out of her pocket and dropped it into Kiki's open palm.

"I'm not sure it technically counts; it was just once, and it happened while we were in my dreamscape."

"Happened in a dream doesn't count—give me that coin back." Pippa made a grab for the coin.

Kiki moved her hand out of reach. "It definitely counts. She didn't say in a dream. She said in her dreamscape—hey, Dara," she called.

Dara wandered over and frowned at the struggling twins. "Yes?"

"If you were to transport someone into someone else's dreamscape and they kissed, does that count as a real kiss or a dream kiss?"

Dara looked from one twin to the other and then Agnes. "I would say it counts as real and if you are asking, yes, Agnes kissed Varlan and then he kissed her."

Kiki gave Pippa a smug grin then pocketed the coin. "Thanks, Dara." She turned her gaze back to Agnes and batted her eyelashes. "So?"

"So?" Agnes echoed.

"You can't just announce something like that and not elaborate," Pippa said.

Agnes hadn't thought about that. She had just said it on an impulse to stop Pippa from mentioning the one thing that had been plaguing her since Deana and Reeve disappeared beneath the waves. She remembered that rush of terror when the bubble had burst under Splade's Watch, the burning in her lungs as she ran out of air, and then the tormenting sensations of traveling through the portal. To think Deana might be down there—

"I don't know ... It was just a kiss." A ridiculously good kiss that made her knees go weak and stomach flutter just thinking about it.

Dara made a small sound and sat in front of them. "It looked pretty intense from where I was standing."

The twins grinned widely, and Pippa moved around to sit next to Dara.

"I'm not going to go into details. Things are still complicated, and we haven't even discussed it since we emerged from the dreamscape."

"Why not? If you're waiting for the right moment," Pippa rolled her eyes, "you'll be waiting a while. With how dangerous this endeavour of saving the isles is proving to be, we might all be dead before you get the chance."

Dara nodded sagely.

"I take it you have given Deana and Bran the same lecture then?" Kiki said.

"Of course not. It's far too much fun watching them trip over themselves. Besides, Wes and I have a bet going on when one of them will figure it out. So I am not going to sabotage my chances of winning." Pippa grinned.

"I don't think either of you will win that one," Dara said, her head tilted as though she was listening to something. "There are too many knots in their destinies to know for sure."

Agnes fought back the shiver at the eerie tone that had taken over Dara's voice.

Pippa and Kiki shared a look. "Dara!" They both reprimanded.

"We were trying to avoid focusing on the doom and gloom," Pippa added.

"But you just told Agnes we could all die tomorrow."

"I meant it in a seize the moment way, but you had to bring your prophetic ghosts into it." Pippa's tone had the playful barb of sibling stirring. It wasn't something Agnes had ever been on the receiving end of, having no siblings herself.

Dara rolled her eyes. "You know I can't help it; they just whisper in my ear whether I want them too or not."

"But you don't have to relay the message," Kiki said with a grin.

"That's also something I ..." Her head angled to the side again, and a blank look stole across her features.

Agnes rolled her shoulders as the air around her seemed to tighten with a buzz not unlike the magic of the trance. "What's going on?"

The Queen rocked as the ocean became turbulent. A beam of teal-coloured light erupted from the waves in front of the ship and shot skyward. The world seemed to shudder then hold its breath, and Agnes covered her ears expecting a massive clap of thunder.

No thunder came but the ocean in front of the Queen parted, revealing a dark chasm. With another shudder and an agonising grating sound, the sunken island began to rise from the deep.

It seemed to take hours for the island to finish its ascent, but Agnes couldn't really be sure. Her entire world had been reduced to a ratcheting tightness. Bran had said it was the source resisting the rise of the island. He'd added that last time he had felt the source in this state, the barrier between realms had torn.

Once the island stopped rising, the pressure released in an instant, sending a whiplashing shockwave out in all directions, and if Agnes hadn't been holding tight to the rail of the ship she would have collapsed onto the deck. Keeping her white-knuckled grip on the rail, she waited for the shockwaves to recede then turned her attention to the island that stood in what until now had been open ocean as far as the eye could see.

It wasn't the largest of islands, but it rivalled the size of Weeper's Cove. The previously drowned landscape was a barren waste of pale stone and dying sea creatures, who had been marooned during the island's ascent.

"Where's Deana?" Dara asked as she leant against the rail beside Agnes.

"There." Kiki pointed to a smudge in the distance that looked like a small hill with a pillar on top of it. There were two dark shapes moving at the base of the pillar.

"Gendry, Bran, Varlan, Wes, and Luca are going ashore," Wren said as she joined them.

"We'll go too," Pippa said and started across the deck to where Rufus was preparing one of the long boats.

"Not you, Dara." Wren grabbed the girl's shoulder as she moved to follow the twins. "They need you to go too, Agnes."

"I know. I'm on my way," Agnes said. The moment the world had calmed again, she had begun to feel the pull of something calling to her keen-sense—most likely the metal Reeve had said belonged to the destroyed portal.

"Be careful," Wren said, her eyes scanning the cloud-free horizon. "There's a storm coming."

"I'll try," Agnes said then moved to grab her satchel before joining the others at the long boat. Rufus held out a hand to help her on board and she settled onto one of the seats between Varlan and Bran.

"No sign of Idir yet," Bran said as Gendry and Wes worked the pulley ropes, and the boat began to lower towards the waves.

"With any luck, he's far enough away that we'll have a day or two's head start on him," Varlan said.

Agnes studied the horizon as Wren had done; there was nothing but an endless blanket of blue, but her stomach tightened. She could sense something out there that her magic knew intimately. "Something is coming," she whispered.

Varlan's keen thumbed across her nape, and Bran's chilled the air. They both turned to stare at the horizon before sharing a look over the top of her head.

"It is probably Idir. Still too far away to tell for sure though," Bran said.

With Gendry and Wes sharing the rowing, their boat closed the distance between the Queen and the risen island quickly.

As the boat scraped onto the newly exposed beach, the twins wasted no time in disembarking and hurrying across the waterlogged landscape towards the place they had last seen Deana and Reeve.

The moment Agnes's feet touched land, however, her magic swelled in a hot-cold wave of pins and needles and the hissing buzz of the impending trance. She doubled forward, resting her hands on her knees and trying to catch her breath as a myriad of ideas flashed across her mind. Just beneath the surface of sand and silt was an abundance of metal that made her fingers twitch and her magic sing. Metal she was born to command.

"Agnes?" Varlan's hand splayed gently across her back and he crouched beside her, his whiskey-coloured eyes swimming with concern. How had she never noticed the little facets of gold trapped within them before?

"I'm alright. It's just there is so much metal here. I think it's the same metal as the sextant—shadow steel—it's calling to my magic, but I think I can ignore it." She straightened and focused on pulling her keen-sense into her core and holding it there. She could still feel the pull of the metal, but it wasn't as intense. "The sooner we find this portal though, the better."

"Agreed," Bran said and then started off after the twins, who now had a substantial head start.

Agnes and Varlan followed him, with Gendry, Wes, and Luca bringing up the rear.

It didn't take them long to reach the sloping ground that led to a set of stairs, and at the foot of those stairs was Deana. She looked shaky on her feet, and as they drew closer the bleeding slice across her palm came into view.

"Luca," Bran said as he jogged past the twins and caught Deana's arm as she staggered.

"I'm okay," she said. "Just a little tired."

"Let me see." Luca reached them and took hold of her injured hand. He clicked his tongue as he examined it then shot a venomous look at Reeve. "Do you know how hard it is to heal hand wounds like this? Next time it would be better to just open a wrist."

When Reeve didn't respond, Luca shook his head and his keen warmed the air as a pale green glow roved over Deana's palm.

She winced and let out a gasp.

"Gently, Luca," Bran reprimanded.

"I'm being as gentle as possible. If Reeve hadn't sliced so deep—"

"Luca," Varlan warned.

While Luca was tending to Deana's wound, Agnes wandered up the stairs. They led to a small plateau. The pillar they had seen was set into the top, but just beyond it was a large oval-shaped recess full of sea water and one rather large white crab. Agnes's magic fought against her hold. This had been the location of the portal. She moved around the edge of the recess and then crossed to the other side of the plateau.

There were no stairs leading down on this side; just a slope of fractured stone littered with chunks of dark metal that gleamed with a sheen like oil on water where the light touched them. It was the same metal as the sextant—the same again that edged the pale flowers of her dreamscape. Shadow steel, Reeve had called it. A metal born of pure magic that originated not in this realm but in the Between. At the sight of all that gleaming metal, she nearly lost her fight against her magic. The trance hadn't completely taken over her since she had finished Kent's war golem, but the violent buzz beneath her skin that threatened to override all her senses was terrifyingly familiar. She swallowed and took several steps away from the slope.

"There is no time to delay," Reeve said.

Agnes nearly leapt out of her skin. When had he gotten so close to her? She retreated a step and drew a calming breath. "I just need a moment." She fumbled with the fastening on her satchel.

"Take all the time you need," Varlan said as he approached. There was a stiffness to his shoulders as he turned to Reeve, his usual languid grace replaced with that air of cunning authority he put on when he was dealing with the likes of Kent and Idir.

"Every second we dawdle gives Idir a chance to catch us."

Varlan stepped between Agnes and Reeve. He seemed taller

than normal, and she imagined he was staring down his nose at the chief.

Reeve didn't seem bothered though. He merely folded his arms across his tattooed chest and returned the mind mage's stare.

"It's alright, Varlan. I am ready." She laid her fingers on his arm and gave a tiny squeeze of reassurance.

Varlan's brows lifted in silent question as he turned to face her.

"I'm sure. And Reeve is right; we need to act quickly."

"If your magic—"

"I'll be careful." She lifted her hand again lest he notice that her fingers were still shaking despite her insistence that she was ready. *It's not fear*, she told herself. Not fear—just the effort of holding her magic back when it wanted release.

If Varlan was privy to her thoughts, he didn't show it. He just pressed a gentle kiss to the top of her head then took a step back. "What do you need?" he asked.

"I'm not sure yet ... Is Deana okay?"

He nodded. "She's with Luca and the twins. Gendry and Wes are keeping watch for Idir."

"Where's Bran?"

"I'm here." The necromancer joined them. His keen was an icy cloud around him, and it seemed to grow colder when he settled his gaze on Reeve.

"Alright. We need either Deana or Kiki to get rid of the water in this pool." She turned to face the oval-shaped recess.

Reeve's strange keen thickened in the air around them then the water began to run over the lip of the pool and down the slope, until nothing was left except the large pale crab. It scuttled away from them, its bright orange underbelly visible now the water was gone.

Agnes stepped down into the empty recess. Robrillium runes had been inlaid in the stone. They shone like they had been freshly polished despite having spent several centuries on the ocean floor.

She couldn't make sense of them, but her keen knew their purpose. A dull ache was building behind her eyes from holding her magic back. With a deep inhale, she pushed it down once more and then gathered it neatly in her hold before she slowly released the breath again. Once she was sure she had full control, she let her magic feed out bit by bit, holding the all-pervading buzz back as long as she could before she let it claim her.

She opened her eyes to an expanse of pure white. The woman in gold was standing beside her, a gentle breeze stirring her spun-starlight hair and rolling the petals that were strewn across the ground against each other, causing them to make a soft tinkling sound.

"Am I in my dreamscape or is this the trance?"

"Both and neither," the woman answered. "This is your canvas—the source of your power. Of course, you are not familiar with it, given the nature of your relationship with your magic until very recently." Her voice was soft and soothing. The kind of voice Agnes's father used when he used to tell her bedtime stories.

"How does my magic work here?"

The woman fixed her with an exasperated look. "I thought you had already figured that out when you confronted Idir. All you need to do is think of what you need and then command your magic to deliver."

"I am sure it is more complicated than that."

"Perhaps it is, but perhaps you are just stalling because you are afraid of exploring your true potential. I should warn you, Idir draws ever nearer, and he is not alone. If you do not build the portal now, through your own volition, he will take the choice from you."

"So, you're saying I have no choice regardless. Either I figure out how to build the portal right now or Idir will force me to build it anyway?" She didn't like the sound of that. When Savita had used her mind magic to force Agnes's keen to work, it had sent her spiralling into a magical exhaustion that had almost killed her. That was not a place she wanted to return to.

The woman shrugged. "The choice is simply whether *you* remain in control or not."

"How long do we have?"

"It is hard to say, but I would advise you to act now. Time moves differently in these pockets between realms." She disappeared in a cloud of golden petals that fluttered to the ground where they mixed with the pale metal-edged ones at Agnes's feet.

"Right, so I just need to think of the portal. But what did it look like?" she said to herself. Kai's journal had called it an arch. A great dark arch etched with runes.

She closed her eyes and conjured the image in her mind. The petals twisted around her, their metal edges surprisingly soft as they brushed over her skin. The image solidified and the ground beneath her feet started to quake. She opened her eyes. The white void was gone, replaced with a darkening sky far above her and cold hard stone beneath her back. Someone was cradling her head in their lap, and she stretched her neck, tilting her head back until she saw it was Varlan.

Liquid metal was twisting through the air around them, almost like splodges of iridescent ink. Bronze and gold magic twisted in ribbons of light over each splodge, waiting for her silent command.

She sat up slowly. "How long was I out?" It was hard to tell how much time had passed, but the darkening sky was one part twilight and one part brooding storm clouds drifting across from the horizon.

"Long enough to make me start to worry," Varlan said softly.

Agnes got to her feet and focused on the threads of magic holding the liquid metal suspended. There was something missing. She scanned the scene around her until her gaze found Bran, and a quiver of knowing stirred at her core. "I need your magic."

Bran moved over and held his hand up in front of her. She pressed her palm flat against his, and aching cold swept from her fingertips up her arm to pool across the centre of her chest. The tips of her fingers glowed violet, and she pushed the magic back out of herself and twisted it around the threads of her own.

Bran's palm grew icy against hers and the tattoo on the inside of his wrist began to glow. The way he controlled his magic was different than how she controlled hers. It wasn't a separate entity that he was harnessing but rather an innate part of himself. She closed her eyes and focused on the way he was ordering and then tying the threads of his magic around hers. A great expanse of interwoven threads of every colour imaginable flashed momentarily across her mind as he secured the last knot and anchored their realm to the Between. He met her gaze and gave her a nod.

"What was that?" she whispered.

He gave her a knowing smile. "The source."

Agnes knew all magic came from the source, but she had never imagined it to be so pretty. With all those glittering threads just out of reach, why were mages restricted to— *Focus, Agnes,* she chided herself and gathered her control once more before sending the final command along the threads of her magic.

The molten metal swirling around them glowed bronze and then coppery gold and then darkened to black once more. It shifted over their heads and formed into a towering arch that caught the first flash of lightning from the approaching storm. One last push of magic and the liquid became solid, fusing into place and fizzing with power.

A wave of exhaustion rolled over Agnes, making her teeth ache, and she slumped against Bran.

"Agnes?" he asked and flicked a look at someone over her head.

"I just need a nap," she muttered as Varlan slung his arm around her waist and guided her over to sit with Deana.

His keen rolled across her shoulders, giving her magic a precise inspection, and he nodded. "You'll be fine."

She stifled a yawn. "Did it work?"

"Better than you could have imagined."

Was that pride in his tone? She could figure that out later. Right now, Deana's shoulder was particularly comfy and she couldn't keep her eyes open any longer.

CHAPTER THIRTY-THREE

BRAN

Agnes had done it. She'd—they'd combined their keens and created a portal. The magic leaching from it thrummed in the air around the arch, charging Bran's hair with static. That magic had the enigmatic signature of the Between and it pulled at Bran's keen as though calling him home. He'd never seen a portal quite like this one. Most of the portals back in Beldaren were long dead. Those that hadn't been destroyed out of fear held nothing more than faded echoes of the magic that had once charged them. And very few of them were made to actually cross the barrier into the physical Between. Only one in Bran's knowledge had ever served that purpose, and he wasn't certain if it was the portal's original function or the influence of Nea's magic that had allowed it to open that particular conduit.

Reeve touched his fingers to the arch and let out a satisfied grunt. "Now you need to activate it before Idir reaches us." There was something in his gaze that turned Bran's stomach. That same wanton desire that Bran had noticed him studying Deana with.

Bran cast his gaze over their small party. Agnes appeared to be dozing on Deana's shoulder. Deana was examining the pale scar across her palm, the dark circles under her eyes as troubling as the thin quality of her keen. The twins and Luca were standing a short distance away from Deana and Agnes, their eyes trained on the darkened horizon as a peal of thunder shook the world.

"He's right," Varlan said as he joined them.

"I know, but we still need to proceed with caution. Travelling through the portal is going to be dangerous. When Nea and Garret travelled to the physical Between, they landed in a trap that stole their memories," Bran said.

"It is a risk worth taking." Reeve's gaze darkened. "Unless of course you are stalling until your master reaches us."

"I am not Soren," Bran said tightly. He flicked another look at Agnes and Deana then turned to Varlan. "Tell Gendry to signal Wren to move the Queen."

Varlan nodded and hurried away.

Bran shifted his attention back to the portal and placed his hand against the line of robrillium runes that twisted over its surface. His keen pulled back from the metal, leaving a numbing sensation beneath his skin, but he ignored it and sent a silent command through his magic. The portal quivered in response, the air in the centre of the arch shimmering with ready power.

The source bristled and the Queen disappeared from view in a teal-coloured flash. They had agreed that Wren would take it and the remaining crew back to Weeper's Cove once those on Dumura had activated the portal. Wren had not been happy with the plan of course, but in the end, she had seen reason.

Turning his focus to the portal once more, he frowned. It should have opened but still it shimmered, waiting for something else, some kind of—key. He studied the sextant set into the plinth in front of the portal. The previously green fragments of keystone were glowing a soft turquoise and thrumming with the rolling signature of Deana's keen. The air around the sextant was tight as though the source was stirring in anticipation. Bran moved to the plinth and placed his hands on it. His keen stirred eagerly at his fingertips, and he let it roll forward in a cold wash. The stones shifted from turquoise to violet. Bran's magic melded with Deana's as a line of violet light shot from the sextant to the middle of the portal. A thread of turquoise twisted around that beam of purple, moving slowly in the direction of the portal.

"We need to hurry," Wes said.

"The ward mage is correct," Reeve said, his pale gaze trained on the ocean where a school of dark shapes was approaching the island. "Open the portal now."

"I'm trying, but the magic needs time. If we rush it there's no telling what it will do," Bran said. He lifted his hands from the plinth but didn't sever the connection of his magic to the portal, despite the dull throb that was starting at his temples.

"We need to cross through the portal now," Reeve said.

"And leave our backs open to Idir?" Wes inquired.

"Idir will use the distraction of a fight to slip past us and through the portal. Staying and facing his forces is a death sentence."

"That's the sanest thing you've said since you emerged from that stone, especially now the Queen and our only other means of escape is gone," Gendry said. "How long do you need?" he asked Bran.

"I don't know. It should have opened as soon as I sent the command, but it's like the magic needs time to wake up. It has been dormant for a long time, so that would make some sense."

The twins joined them at the foot of the portal followed by Deana, who was supporting a tired-looking Agnes.

Varlan looped his arm around Agnes's waist and tucked her neatly against his side.

"Are we going—" Deana's question was cut off by a bone-shaking clap of thunder that rocked the world as lightning struck the water just to the left of where the Queen had been. Sparks showered the air and the first of the dark shapes emerged from the shallows.

Deana's keen swelled over Bran and crashed down the slope to the beach. When it reached the ocean, a wall of water erupted around the island. She wasn't fast enough to stop Idir or the several shrouded ones closest to the shore that managed to dive forward right before the wall closed. The dark shapes of more of Idir's shrouded pressed against the wall, but they couldn't pass through. Idir and the handful of shrouded that had managed to make it past were now stalking up the beach towards them.

"It would seem you've picked up a few new tricks, Deana. Your parents would have been proud," Idir called in a mocking tone.

Bran pulled Nea's dagger from the sheath at his belt. With a silent command and a touch of his magic, the blade lengthened and the hilt reshaped itself until he was holding a well-balanced longsword. The dark metal gleamed with the same oil-on-water sheen as the portal behind him.

"We cannot win this fight," Reeve said as he eyed the blade almost reverently. "Not yet anyway."

"Bran, get that portal open," Gendry said. "Luca take Agnes. No offense, but Varlan is better in fight."

"No offence taken—that's a sound call." Luca shouldered the burden of Agnes and stepped towards the portal arch.

"Go with Luca," Gendry said to the twins.

"But, Gen—"

"Now, Pip. Reeve is right. This is not a fight we can win, and Wren will skin me alive if I let anything happen to you girls."

"What about Deana?" Kiki asked.

Deana's keen was a surging squall around her, her eyes flashing from their normal soft teal to a deep navy blue.

"She'll be right behind you," Bran said and placed his free hand on the plinth again.

The portal shuddered in response to his urgent command but still did not open.

"Don't let him get the key," Reeve said as Idir bore down on them.

Everyone scattered as Idir charged for Bran. One side of his face was vibrant with life, his coal-dark eye glittering with malice. The other side was pallid flesh pulled and puckered around the orange and pink coral that studded his skin. His lips curved into a sneer and a sword of coral materialised in his hand as he lashed out at Bran.

Bran met the strike, his shadow blade grating down the hardened coral with a screech.

Deana's keen faltered and the shroud of water dropped for a second before she regained control. It was enough time to allow a few more of Idir's shrouded ones to crawl onto the beach.

"You can't beat me," Idir said as he made another lunge.

Bran dodged and then advanced, making a jab for Idir's exposed side. The blow landed, snagging through Idir's shirt and leaving a line of black-tinted blood in its wake. Idir let out a roar and charged, forcing Bran to dance backwards until his spine slammed against the pillar. Pain sliced through his shoulder, and he looked down at the sword of coral sticking out of his skin. It was pulsing with a dull red-orange glow, a wrongness seeping from it and sliding through Bran's keen like poison.

Idir's smile became wickedly triumphant.

Bran grasped for the sextant behind him. The second his fingers closed around it, he sent another urgent command through his keen. The source bristled and with an echoing tear the portal sprang open, casting a violet glow against the growing night.

"Go," he yelled, forcing his knee up between Idir and himself and then shoving the much larger man back.

Idir staggered and the coral embedded in Bran's skin broke off, causing a jolt of white-hot pain that blinded him momentarily.

Sextant held firmly in one hand, Bran drove his sword forward through Idir's wide-open defence. The blow sliced a thick line across Idir's stomach and he dropped to his knees, his hands holding the wound together.

"I can't be killed by mortal means," Idir panted as he lost his grip momentarily and part of his insides slid through his fingers.

"I know, but that should slow you down." Bran turned and started for the portal.

Gendry and Varlan were dispatching the last of the shrouded who had made it through Deana's wall of water.

"Go," he told them and then rushed to Deana. "We have to leave." He touched her arm, and her keen flooded over him. It was wavering. She was dangerously close to the point of exhaustion. "Deana, you need to stop drawing power."

She turned to him, her eyes not flashing now but a solid fathomless navy. "They must be stopped," she said in a voice that was not her own.

"I know, but we can't stop them now. We need to run."

She tilted her head and then nodded slowly. "You know what you must do, little foundling." She flicked a pointed look to the portal, then Deana's keen abruptly cut off and she slumped against him.

The wall of water dropped and shrouded swarmed the beach.

Bran slid his blade back into its sheath and scooped Deana into his arms, ignoring the tearing pain in his shoulder. He ran for the portal, sliding through on Gendry's heels.

The passage was faster than normal and when he staggered through the other side he looked immediately for Agnes.

"Destroy the portal!"

"What?!"

"Now, Agnes. There's no time to argue."

She shot a panicked look at Varlan, who in turn settled his calculating stare on Bran and after a moment nodded. "Do it."

Agnes's keen rose in a bright flurry and ribbons of bronze and gold twisted their way around the portal. A dark hand reached through the glowing surface as the black metal arch turned to liquid and the portal collapsed in on itself. The hand dropped to the ground, fingers still twitching as dark blood oozed from the amputated wrist.

"Well, now what?" Pippa asked.

Bran turned slowly. Deana was growing heavier by the moment and the pain slicing though his shoulder wasn't nearly as troubling as the sense of wrongness that was working its way through his keen.

"Luca!" Wes said as he rushed forward and took Deana from Bran.

"Oh, that's not good." Luca was eyeing Bran's shoulder with apprehension. "Wait, don't—"

But Bran had already pulled the shard of coral from his shoulder. The relief was instant as the seething wrongness halted its advance through his keen, but then a warm numbness rolled through him as his blood started to flow freely from the wound.

Well, that's not good, he mused as the ground thudded against his knees.

Luca stepped forward and his keen boiled through Bran's blood. The wound itched and burned as the skin started to knit itself back together. After a while, Luca pulled his hand away from Bran's shoulder, leaving a pale jagged scar where the coral blade had been. "For someone who seems so intelligent, you can be an absolute fool at times," Luca said as he inspected the scar.

Bran still felt dizzy and though the magical poison had stilled its progress, it lingered like a burr stuck in the fabric of his keen. Discomfort aside, he could worry about that later. Right now, they were trapped in the wilds of the physical Between with no way home. The liquid metal of the portal had seeped into the ground and disappeared. It didn't matter though; they could figure out a way to get home once they found the resting place of Grandmother Ocean. The goddess herself might even be able to help them once they woke her.

"We need to be careful, and we need to find somewhere to rest."

He cast a look at Deana's limp form tucked against Wes's chest. "Reeve?"

The chief was studying the pale beach that extended in front of them, the mint green waves lapping gently against the shore. He turned and pointed at the tangled jungle behind where the portal had stood. "There used to be a cave not far from here. It should be a safe place to rest if we can find it. Interesting choice to destroy the portal."

"Grandmother Ocean told me to." Bran shrugged. The fresh scar tissue in his shoulder pulled slightly with the movement.

Reeve led them into the jungle and up a slope. Gendry took over carrying Deana and Wes helped Varlan support Agnes. Both women needed a good sleep and Bran needed a chance to sit down and try to figure out what the seed of poison in his keen was and how he could get rid of it. His scar itched and he rubbed his fingers against it, trying not to scratch the still tender skin.

Night was falling when they stumbled into the cave. They followed the passage a short way and then it opened out into a very familiar-looking cavern. A faded tapestry was hung on one wall, a stream looping around the perimeter of the room past a throne on which sat a small, brown and white monkey.

"Bohdan?" Deana said sleepily.

"Does that mean Vask is here too?" Bran asked, and immediately everyone except Reeve tensed.

"No, he cannot leave the mortal boundaries of his shrine," Bohdan said as he tented his front paws in a very human-like gesture. "I am not bound by such restrictions, which is why Vask sent me here to wait for you. He needs to make sure his assets are protected after all."

"His assets, both Deana and I, have served the terms of our deal."

"Deana has yes, but your debt I am afraid is eternal. Did Soren leave that little bit out?"

Bran swallowed as he studied the monkey.

"What's he talking about?" Varlan asked.

"Soren made a deal with Vask, but he also made one with Nock and Moalana. He had his soul changed and then sent forward in time in an effort to beat Idir."

Bohdan's head tilted to one side. "Oh, he certainly was scant on the details. But then he always was a wily snake who liked to twist the truth to suit his own means. Extremely god-like behaviour for someone born of mortal flesh," the monkey mused. "He is the one who encouraged Idir to seek out a way to claim the Grandmother's power. His apparent change of heart may be the reason for Idir's curse, but then Idir was always going to double-cross him in the end anyway. So who can say for sure?" He shrugged. "Regardless, Soren's greed for knowledge was the catalyst that started it all, and like Idir you've all played right into his hands."

TO BE CONTINUED ...

THANK YOU FOR READING

A MELODY OF DEATH

I hope you are enjoying the *Isles of Bright and Shadow* trilogy so far. I would love it if you left me a review either at your favourite online store or on any online reader platform such as Goodreads or Storygraph.

Follow the link below for news about upcoming releases and future projects:

GLOSSARY

Bind-shackles: Bands of robrillium that prevent a mage from using their keen by blocking their connection to the source. Each pair is struck with its own key. If this key is lost, that pair can only be unlocked by a warden's keen.

Brightling: Extremely rare keen-folk who have the ability to absorb and use the keen of others or turn a mage's own keen against them, even though they seem to have no keen of their own.

Brightfish: A type of fish found primarily in the Faridean Isles, they moult at the beginning of their mating season and the colour of their new scales is said to be prophetic in nature.

Corruption: A type of possession / magical disease that primarily affects mages. The afflicted become increasingly violent as they slowly lose control of their minds and their keen. There have been no cases of corruption since the defeat of the Usurper.

Creationist: A type of mage who doesn't manipulate an element but can alter a certain type of matter. Elijah is a creationist whose talent is related to ink and parchment, specifically the realm of cartography, and Agnes' affinity is metal.

Dream-singer: A Faridean mage who has the ability to control the dreams of others. They are extremely rare, and Dara is the only known dream-singer currently in existence.

Heart mate: The Faridean term for soul mates.

Heartstone: A magical crystal in which a necromancer can trap a soul to be used to animate a golem.

Keen: The soul essence of an individual or the 'flavour' of their magic. Interchangeable with the word magic, however, *keen* generally refers to the feeling of the life force of an individual and how that part of them interacts with the source as a whole. Magic is more so the direct effect they have on the world through channelling the source.

Keen-folk: A general term that covers all types of magic-users, not just mages and wardens, but seers and other gifted.

Keen-less: Those without magic.

Keen-sense: The ability to sense magic. Something all keen-folk innately have but also something that certain keen-less can possess (though this is rare).

Keen-touched: Sometimes interchangeable with keen-folk but generally used to refer to those keen-folk who are not mages or wardens. Seers and those gifted with 'low-magic' i.e. savants and prodigies who cannot control the source but have uncanny abilities regardless.

Keystone: A special stone used to unlock magical locks or open trans-dimensional portals.

Lock-stone: A trans-dimensional construct that can be used as an anchor for magic. The lock-stone outside Hartswood solidifies the wards around the estate and protects it.

Mage: Keen-folk who have complete control of the source in one element E.g. weather (storm mages), fire, earth, water, healing, mind, death and the spirit world (necromancers) etc. There are certain nuances among the generic types of mages. For example: Sophia is a water mage, but she is particularly skilled with frost and ice magic. Declan is a storm mage who has an affinity for lightning, something not all weather mages are comfortable with.

Mind-singer: The Faridean term for a mind mage.

Oathing: A kind of soul marriage between two mages. The bond dissolves after death. Often used for shorter-term pacts between individuals.

Oathbond: (sometimes called an oath ward) Refers to the connection created by an oathing.

Oathmark: The physical representation of the Oathbond often appears like a kind of tattoo.

Reanimation: Undead given 'life' by a necromancer. They are created by forcing a spirit, whether once human or not, into a corpse. They are generally mindless puppets controlled by the necromancer who resurrected them.

Robrillium: The enchanted metal used to create bind-shackles. It ranges in colour from light-pinkish gold through to a deep rose gold.

Silencer: The Faridean term for warden.

Singer: Because Faridean mages most often experience magic as sound they refer to their mages as singers.

Shadow-kin: What the Farideans call those who possess the blood of the Shadow.

Shadow-touched: Those that have been somehow touched or tainted by the Shadow. They could be divine-blooded or cursed. Those who are possessed or corrupted are sometimes also referred to as Shadow-touched.

Shrouded ones: Undead merfolk-like creatures who are said to be the handmaidens of Grandmother Ocean. They are rumoured to be able to infect people through the magical coral that adorns their skin.

Song: Instead of calling the magic / life force of their mages keen, Faridean mages refer to it as the song of the mage. In some cases, song seems to be another term for what Beldaren and Osmarian mages will call the source, though Faridean mages do still refer to the source.

Source ship: A rare magical ship. There were only a dozen ships ever created though many of them have been lost over time.

Soul-singer: The Faridean term for necromancer or spirit mage.

Spirit anchor: A relic that contains a small piece of a mage's keen.

Spirit-glass: Enchanted mirrors, usually made of obsidian or black glass, through which necromancers use to communicate. They can become corrupted and slowly steal the life force of those using them; functioning ones are rare as a result of this.

The barrier: The veil between realms as seen by necromancers. It can appear in a range of different ways depending on the individual interacting with it. E.g. Nea's barrier is a hedge of pale-pink and grey roses, and Nonna's is a bramble of blackberries.

The Between: A magical spirit realm that the souls of the dead are believed to pass through on their way to the grove of the ancestors.

The Source: The fabric of the universe from where keen-touched get their powers.

Warden: Keen-folk who can suppress the keen or connection to the source in other keen-folk. Theorised to be a type of mage even though they don't channel the source. Originally called ward mages.

ABOUT THE AUTHOR

C. E. Page writes emotionally rich, character driven tales of magic and adventure, primarily in the adult epic fantasy genre. Her stories feature demigods and other divinely assisted misfits who would prefer it if megalomaniac fools would stop trying to destroy the known realms in their search for power.

She lives on the east coast of Australia with her partner Evan, their two children, and one of the world's quirkiest dogs.

An avid reader and gamer, she loves devouring a good story in whatever form it takes.

You can find out more about her and her upcoming works at: www.cepageauthor.com

Or by subscribing to *The Epic Ramble* newsletter: http://cepageauthor.substack.com

ALSO BY C. E. PAGE

SOVEREIGNS OF BRIGHT AND SHADOW

Nea has spent the three years since the purge at Kalhanna on the run. Convinced that if she keeps running then the dark fate that awaits her will spare those she loves—But fate has other ideas.

Corruption is a disease with no cure that ends with a rapid descent into madness and violence. And until now it only targeted mages. But an infected warden has shown up challenging everything Margot thought she knew. To understand this recent development, she needs someone who knows possession ... She needs Nea and lucky for Margot, her warden friend Garret has been ordered to track the rogue necromancer down.

From the moment Garret finds Nea he is dragged into a deadly game of dark secrets and brutal machinations. A game that spans not only centuries, but the barrier between the known realms. After a revelation that will change the lives of mages and wardens forever, he must learn to trust not only himself but the enigmatic necromancer whose fate has become irrevocably tied to his own.

Can they find a cure before it's too late, or will they be swept away by powers beyond any of their control?

THE STORY BEGINS IN
DEATHBORN